THE CLERIC'S VAULT

ERNEST DEMPSEY

**Get Ernest Dempsey's Best Selling Novel,
two introductory novellas,
PLUS, special VIP Pricing on new releases!**
Become a VIP reader and get all the great stuff by
visiting ernestdempsey.net or
Check out more details at the end of the book.

What readers are saying about Ernest Dempsey.

"I love the pace. You start reading and you keep telling yourself you will stop but you have to read one more page."

"The action is great and I like how I learn about stuff that I never knew before."

"I loved The Secret of the Stones and told Ernest Dempsey to hurry up and write the next one!"

"Finally, a writer who doesn't get bogged down in too much description and character development. Just give me a fun story to read. Dempsey does that perfectly."

"I love Sean Wyatt and his crew. I hope Ernest Dempsey gives each character their own book."

"I liked The Secret of the Stones so much, I read it twice. I can't wait for the next one."

For my sweet Megan.

Prologue
Cuenca, Ecuador
1982

"Padre, donde esta la chiave?"

The young priest rushed his words in Spanish, standing over a bed of plain white linens. An awkward look of desperation covered his face. He'd been trying to comfort the older man, who lay there dying, with words from standard prayers and parts of scripture. His efforts though, were clearly halfhearted, a way of going through the motions.

The question about the location of the key betrayed why he was really there.

A pale half-moon seeped through the few clouds that dotted the night sky and cast an eerie glow into the small dormitory. The air was cool and somewhat soothing.

Carlos Crespi was racked with fits of coughing that shook his rickety, metal bed. The old man was sure the end was near but uncertain of the moment. He clutched the bed sheets with a firm grip, fighting away the creeping pain that seemed to grow incrementally with every passing moment.

His bald forehead was wrinkled from the struggle with death, his bushy gray eyebrows furrowed in a combination of frustration and agony. The once jovial, dark eyes squinted against the pain.

The young apprentice watched with a stoic face as he continued repeating the prescribed lines, reaffirming that the padre would be assured eternal life in heaven.

The dying man knew the words were simply a formality to rub him into give up his secret.

Father Carlos was no fool. He knew the real reason why this eager young man had been sent to his aide six months prior. His constant and pressing questions about the vault gave that motive away far too easily. He had taken the young priest to the vault only one time. When he had turned on the single light in the storage room, the man's eyes had betrayed his real intent.

The collection.

For years the Vatican had tried to peel away the secrets of Padre Crespi's mysterious vault. Somehow, they'd always come up empty. Revered by the locals, the old man had given them nearly his entire life in service. And in return, they watched out for him and the antiquities they had gifted him. Whenever outsiders would ask the people where he had gotten such wondrous relics, they simply replied, "the forest." Now, though, on death's door, the old priest would surely have to pass on his treasures to someone. After all, he couldn't take them with him.

Another fit of coughs racked him and the bed shook violently. The young priest reached down to brace the crude, metal frame that squeaked loudly with each movement. When the coughing ceased, he could hear a rattle in Father Carlos' chest. It wouldn't be long now. And he needed an answer.

"Padre, I beg of you, where is the key to your vault? It must be preserved in the name of the church, for the glory of God." The heightened desperation filled the man's voice. He was afraid what would happen if Crespi did not bestow the key to him.

Two other monks stood by the door, pesky witnesses that would prevent him from simply breaking into the vault and taking what he believed rightly belonged to the Vatican.

The sentence seemed to snap Crespi out of unconsciousness and his eyes opened slowly, to narrow slits. He lay very still and turned his head towards the young man, gazing at him with a curious look. "The glory of God?" he asked.

The young priest nodded. "Si, father. For the Church and God."
Father Carlos laughed, careful not to arouse another round of coughs. Then he smiled a gentle smile that the entire city knew so well. "I'll give you my key," he hesitated. "But you must carry this message to the church."

"Of course," the young priest said and smiled at the old man. "Whatever you ask."

The coughs returned violently and a thin red line eased its way out of the corner of Crespi's mouth. His eyes went wide momentarily then he laid his head back down on the pillow.

"Father, tell me your message," the apprentice urged.

Crespi looked at him again and slid a frail hand inside the tattered brown garment he wore. A second later, he produced a simple key. The long piece of brass had an odd design on the end, what appeared to be a spider inside a circle. As the assistant reached for the key, Father Carlos grabbed him with his other hand and with surprising strength and pulled him close.

"The treasures of the kingdom are for the righteous," he paused, raising the strength to finish his message. "The lights shall guide them as beacons in the darkness. Only the righteous shall eat of the tree of life."

A sickly rattle came from deep within the padre's chest. He released his grip and eased back into the bed, unconscious.

The young priest looked down at the man and placed his hand under Crespi's nostrils.

Still breathing but not for long. What did the message mean? He didn't care. He had the key and access to all of the fabled wealth that the old man had been hoarding for years. It had been given willingly and the two Ecuadorian monks would bear witness.

He would certainly make sure the Vatican received most of the wares. *Would anyone notice if a few pieces went missing?* The young man doubted it.

Satisfied that the sick padre was unaware, he slipped out of the room and into a dark hallway lit with a few candles along the walls. The black iron candle holders were covered in wax that could have been from a decade before.

Another nurse was waiting outside and glanced questioningly at the young priest. He simply shook his head and walked by quickly.

He made his way through the labyrinth of halls and portals until he found himself in a courtyard in the center of the monastery grounds. Directly in front of him was a large, wooden door. He'd seen the enormous door many times and had asked Father Carlos to show him what was within but the older man had refused every time, save for once. The only time he'd been allowed to see the vast treasure was for mere minutes. Now he had it all to himself.

He rushed over to the door and slid the key into a large, silver-looking lock. A quick look around confirmed no one was watching. He'd suspected as much at this hour of the evening. The few monks that helped run the modest compound had retired for the night hours ago, except for the two in the room with Crespi.

With a quick twist of the wrist, the inner workings of the lock were undone. He tugged on the old, metal handle, swinging the large door out slowly.

The inside of the room was dark with no windows to provide any sort of illumination. Fortunately, he'd prepared for that contingency. His hand removed a small flashlight from within his robes and he switched it on, ready to take in the majesty of the vast treasure of Father Carlos Crespi. Instead, he was greeted by a vacuous chamber of empty wooden shelves, cobwebs, and dust.

The vault was empty. *Impossible. Where was the gold, all the ancient relics?* The young man ran his hands along the empty shelves and searched the entire room for several minutes. He found nothing.

Suddenly, bells began to ring from the top of the chapel on the other side of the courtyard. The dinging sound echoed through the sleepy city as dark clouds moved across the face of the moon once again. Carlos Crespi was dead.

Chapter 1
Las Vegas, Nevada
Present

"I'm all in."

Sean Wyatt stared across at his opponent. His icy gray eyes were calm, almost matter-of-fact in their appearance. He pushed all of his chips across the rounded line on the green felt of the World Poker Tour table.

He was a terrible bluffer. A fact he'd recounted many times throughout his life in work and with women. Fortunately, at the moment he knew he had the best hand.

The other man had bet twice, once on the flop and once on the turn. Now, the young adversary looked uncertain. He'd seemed a little nervous since the moment he'd sat down at the table.

It was day two of the $1000 dollar buy-in event at The Kings of Vegas Poker Tournament and clearly the kid was rattled. He looked about 25 or 26. Unlike some of the cockier, younger players Wyatt had come across in recent times, the young man across from him seemed a little greener and far less sure of himself.

The young man's dark, curly hair was disheveled. Beads of sweat formed on his head above a long, sloping nose. His greenish eyes looked panicked behind the black wire-framed glasses he wore. The sound of chips clicking throughout the room echoed loudly, slightly dramatizing the moment further.

Wyatt made a quick note of how the kid's hands shook terribly when he had a big hand. At the moment, Wyatt imagined a Richter scale was going crazy somewhere.

Sean knew that meant the guy probably had a big pocket pair lower than Wyatt's two black aces that lay face down on the table.

They'd made it into the money hours earlier and everyone in the Rio was elated to have gotten their $1000 back, plus about that much more in prize money. Sean always laughed at people who only cared about making it into the payout. *Where was the fun in that?* The thrill was trying to make the final table and winning the whole thing.

Sean had needed some R&R for the week. Since he knew Tommy would be busy for a while trying to decipher their recent discovery, he figured a little time off wouldn't be a problem.

He'd asked Allison to come out to Vegas with him, but she had been ordered back to Washington and reassigned, or so she'd said. Sean wasn't surprised that she'd been sent back into the field so quickly. That was one of the reasons he'd left the agency after such a short term. Another mission always waited.

Part of him had wanted to see where things with her might go but there were a whole list of problems with trying to date someone who worked for Axis. Living through it for several years had showed him that. So, he did what he always did and traveled alone. He didn't mind, except for the lack of conversation. Sometimes that was a good thing.

He'd caught an early morning flight out of Atlanta two days earlier and thanks to the assistance of an old friend, a suite at The Venetian had opened up miraculously the day of his arrival. It was nice to have friends.

"I call," the younger player said. The young opponent's voice snapped Sean's attention back to the poker table. The kid flipped over a pair of queens. Pretty much what he figured.

Sean turned over his pair of aces and saw agony wash over the other player's face almost instantly. The young man knew he only had two cards in the deck of 52 that could save him.

The dealer discarded the top card and turned over the fifth and final card on the table, the queen of clubs, giving the younger player three of a kind. The young man yelled out a cheer of ecstatic relief and raised his fists in triumph. A combination of groans and jubilation erupted from the crowd. The other players at the table said nothing but were clearly stunned at the outcome. Sean just smiled cynically as he watched the dealer rake all of his chips over to his opponent.

Wyatt stood and reached out a hand to the man who had just eliminated him from the tournament. The guy calmed himself down enough to accept the gentlemanly gesture and clasped Sean's hand clumsily.

"Nice hand, kid." Sean said.

"Thanks. Wow. I'm sorry man. That sucks."

Sean laughed. "In poker, never say you're sorry." Then Sean winked at him, "besides, these kinds of things come around eventually."

The younger player smiled, understanding what he meant and went back to his seat, exhilarated.

Sean headed over to the cashier to pick up his winnings and, a few minutes later, made for the door. Along the way a few people consoled him on the bad beat he'd just received. One particular Canadian professional had stopped him on his way out.

"You are way too good not to have won one of these things," was all the man had said. *Maybe,* Sean thought but he knew he didn't really need the money. The young gun who'd just taken his chips probably had a lifetime's worth of student loans to pay off. So he was okay with the loss. He stepped outside into the young night. Warm desert air greeted him, instantly causing his mind to forget the cool air-conditioned comfort from where he'd just come. Nine o'clock at night in late fall, and it still felt like late spring back home.

On the horizon, just over the mountains that surrounded the basin in which the city rested, a pale remnant of sunset gave its last gasp against the coming of dark. Wyatt had visited Las Vegas on several occasions and every single time he'd been fascinated by the weather. The city was always sunny and extremely hot in the summers. He remembered strolling down the strip one day in June thinking he'd accidentally walked into a huge oven. The fall wasn't so bad, days were in the low to mid 80s and the evenings cooled off considerably.

Back home in the south, people complained it was too hot in the summer time. And while the humidity certainly made it seem warmer than it was, at least there was a cooling breeze that soothed the senses somewhat. Out in the Nevada desert, the wind only seemed to make it worse like someone was turning on a heating fan.

Sean started to make his way to a cab, dancing through the mass of people coming and going to the Rio. There was no shortage of taxis lined up outside the casino and Sean hailed the closest one. A few minutes later he was in the back seat, en route to his hotel

The ride back to The Venetian was only five to ten minutes, although it seemed like the cab driver took the "scenic route." On the Las Vegas Boulevard, otherwise known as "the strip", pedestrians crowded the busy sidewalks. Some were sober, others considerably less so, taking full advantage of the city's lack of laws concerning walking around with enormous amounts of visible alcohol.

Some people carried vessels that were shaped like plastic guitars with straws sticking out of them. Others just carried giant cups filled with booze of various kinds. Sean wondered how good those drinks could possibly be, made from cheap liquor and watered down with mixers. They must have done the trick, though. Revelers laughed and stumbled around the city with huge smiles on their faces.

A colorful array of lights and digital signs beamed down the main strip with enormous monstrosities rising above them into the desert night sky. Paris, Cosmopolitan, Caesar's Palace, Aria, Wynn, Mandalay Bay, Bellagio, and MGM Grand had all taken their places as some of the more upscale locations. Some of the less fancy casinos stood out like an eyesore, badly in need of renovation to keep up with the esthetic appeal of the newer venues.

The taxi pulled up to the entrance of Venetian's main lobby and Sean's mind returned to his present location. He loved The Venetian and it's neighbor, The Palazzo. He paid the taxi driver and left an extra five on top as a tip.

The uniformed doorman greeted him with a smile beneath his thick, graying mustache and Sean nodded a thank you as he passed by. The familiar scent that filled The Venetian wafted out of the door and embraced him upon entry. He couldn't place the scent precisely, but it seemed like a mélange of jasmine, vanilla, and spice.

Inside the hotel lobby, he was greeted by a dismantling array for the senses. A circular room opened up to a dramatic domed ceiling, in the center of which was a round skylight. Elaborate frescoes of angels, gods, and saints surrounded the clear opening. Columns of white marble accented the walls and corners, crowned with golden footings and crests. On a cream-colored and brown marble floor in the center of the room, stood a golden spherical fountain. The shiny, metal strips that made up the globe were braced by angelic, armless creatures like a figurehead on the front of an old ship.

He turned left and headed down a vaulted hallway of similar appearance that led to the casino and the elevators just beyond. High above him other frescoes of various Italian origins both mythical and religious adorned the arched ceiling. He'd marveled at the artwork. The detail of each relief and the colors that were incorporated made the scenery inside the building nothing short of spectacular.

The day before he had taken a stroll around the mall area within the complex that connected to The Palazzo. He was amazed at the job the builders had done with the ornate canals that mimicked the ones in Venice, complete with gondolas and singing gondoliers. The layout was designed to make one feel like they were actually in Venice right down to the smaller version of San Marco Square.

Shops lined the walkways surrounding the canals, providing any visitor with a breathtaking array of old-world style and modern convenience. There was even an artificial partly cloudy sky painted on the ceiling to make it feel like patrons were outdoors.

How much money went into this place? He couldn't help but wonder as he entered the elevator to the tune of Phantom of the Opera. The musical's Las Vegas home happened to be The Venetian at that time. He'd heard good things about the show and was considering taking it in at some point.

Sean looked both ways as he exited on the tenth floor. Old habits died hard. Even though he'd not been a government Agent for a few years now, some things were ingrained in him.

The last few months he'd found himself relaxing a little more, getting back to "normal" life. That is, until a few weeks ago. The episode with Tommy's kidnapping had brought everything back. He thought about the gun hidden in his room. Never could be too careful, especially considering recent events.

The hallway opened into a circular roundabout that led to rooms, suites, and a bridge to the Venezia Tower where an additional pool and more restaurants were located. Swimming pools and restaurants were something that The Venetian certainly didn't lack. He recalled thinking the hotel must have had more eateries than a moderately sized city and the pools were a nice luxury to escape the heat; in the summer they were a necessity.

As he neared the door he pulled his card key out then slid it into the reader. The suite was one of the nicer rooms he'd stayed in during his travels. And he'd travelled a lot. Its view overlooked the main two pools below but beyond the city, dark brown mountains protruded into the night sky. Tonight though, the room was completely dark. Housekeeping must have closed the drapes and automated roman blinds.

After throwing his key and wallet on a dresser, he flicked on a light. The dark form in the corner of the room near the window caught the peripheral of his eye. So did the shape of the gun.

Chapter 2
Nevada Desert just outside Las Vegas

Alexander Lindsey's old eyes stared out the luxury helicopter's window at the dark, jagged mountains below. He'd always loved flying. Helicopters had been of a particular interest, though flight in general had always been fascinating to him. The quick rise and fall, the many different directions one could take, and sheer speed were all very exhilarating. It had never made him nervous like some unfortunate souls. Of course, his ancestors seemed to have always been a little more reckless than others. They'd had to be careful in so many other aspects of their lives that thrill seeking had become a way to balance things out.

The moonlit mountains below sped by as the Agusta A-109 cruised smoothly through the evening air; it's silver exterior reflecting bending images of earth's solitary satellite.

He loved the turbine-powered conveyance. It was far more convenient than a private jet-smaller, more maneuverable, and easy to hide if needed. He had used the elegant vehicle for a wide variety of purposes, some of which were more sinister than others.

The desert had been a place of solace for a long time for his family. After being tormented back east and in the mid-west during the 1800s, they'd managed to find a sanctuary in the American Southwest.

Safety. Security. Things that were taken for granted now that he had become extremely wealthy and powerful. And the vermin across from him could have wrecked everything.

"I did everything you ever told me to do, Alex!" His victim begged from the other side of the cabin, interrupting his thoughts.

The squat, chubby man struggled with no avail against his bonds, hands tied behind his back with rope. Heavy chains encircled his body and legs. Veins were raised just beneath the skin of his temples, his face red from straining. A few droplets of perspiration dripped down his fleshy forehead.

Two other men, Lindsey's personal bodyguards, were the only other passengers in the cabin.

"You can't do this! You need me!"

The desperate pleas were unfounded and irrational. There were plenty of other options available. After all, Alexander Lindsey had operatives in nearly every branch of the government. Getting a new spy would not be a problem.

Lindsey gazed unsympathetically at the plump man. For the last two years he had proved useful. An inside guy at the Justice Department was a nice thing to have. He'd pretty much known whenever he was being watched and been able to deftly sidestep many potential problems. However, Gary wasn't the only one working for the Order and his prisoner's usefulness, it seemed, had run its course.

"What exactly did you tell them, Gary?" Lindsey asked, peering into the man's soul. "And stop wriggling around. You should face your end like a man not a squirming little baby."

Gary Holstrum looked down at the gray seat for a moment then back up. "I only told them a few things. I swear. It was stuff that isn't even important. It wouldn't implicate you in anything. I had to give 'em something!"

"It's important to me, Gary. What you have done has put everything I've worked for at great risk."

"No," he shook his head. "I would never do anything that would put you in danger, Alex. I've worked for you for two years now. You know me."

Lindsey sat silently for a moment, as if contemplating the man's words. He *had* served him well. But too much was at stake now.

Events of the prior weeks had been most productive. The first golden chamber had been found with the accompanying clue. Now, Tommy Schultz was working with a professor at Georgia Tech to unravel the location of the second chamber. Nearly everything had gone according to plan, except for a few little wrinkles. However, those problems would be dealt with soon enough.

The older man cast a quick glance at one of his bodyguards and gave a nod. Acknowledging the unspoken order, the huge man stepped over to the door nearest the prisoner and pulled up the latch that slid the mechanism open. Dry desert air rushed into the cabin along with a significant increase in noise. A moment later, the helicopter crested a small ridge and suddenly, a vast body of dark liquid spread out below them. Lake Mead.

The bodyguard grabbed Gary and forced him to the edge of the door, his face sticking out over the expanse of the lake. He screamed, tears streaming down his pudgy, red face. "No! Please! Don't do this, Alex!" His voice pushed over the sound of the wind and the turbines outside.

"What did you tell them?!" Lindsey raged.

"I only told them that you were interested in finding some lost treasure. I told them it was stupid, that you were just some crazy old rich guy who liked to hunt for ancient artifacts. I swear that's all!"

Alex nodded. "I see. So they know nothing of The Order or exactly what we are trying to accomplish?"

Holstrum shook his head sincerely. "They know nothing. Honest. They wouldn't believe it even if I told them."

Maybe he was telling the truth. Perhaps he wasn't. But someone in the Justice Department had become curious. That never happened unless there were loose lips somewhere.

"Ok, Gary. I believe you."

Lindsey nodded at the bodyguard who loosened his grip, slightly.

Relief flooded the captive's face. "Thank you. Oh, thank you Alex. You're doing the right thing. You won't be disappointed."

A look of disgust came across the older man's face and his eyes narrowed. "I told you never to call me Alex." For a brief moment, Holstrum's face seemed confused. Lindsey nodded again. Suddenly, the bodyguard tensed and shoved the bound man out of the open door. His scream faded quickly as he fell hundreds of feet towards the black depths of the lake below.

Lindsey peered down to see the portly body produce a white splash in the dark liquid then disappear into the abyss. A moment later there was no sign anything had even happened.

Created by the construction of The Hoover Dam, Lake Mead's depth could be as much as 590 feet at its deepest point. Finding the body would be nearly impossible. It was doubtful anyone would think to look there anyway. Helicopter flights in the area from Las Vegas to the Grand Canyon and back happened all the time so their little jaunt wouldn't even raise an eyebrow.

Alexander stared out across the expanse of the lake that led up to craggy, dark mountains in the distance as the bodyguard slid the door shut and locked the latch again before returning to his seat on the other side of the cabin. Out the opposite window, the lights Las Vegas glittered in the distance. An eyesore, but a convenient one. It was only a short ride from his mountain complex into town to get anything they needed. With so many tourists, it was easy to become one of them. No one remembered anyone. Which was what he wanted, to not be noticed.

His thoughts lingered on the last few words his insolent spy had uttered. In his younger days, Lindsey would have never considered calling an elder by their first name. The new generations, it seemed, did not believe in courtesy. The times of calling people

"Mister" or "Miss" had long since passed. Although, soon, he believed, the world would come to know him by a different title. He smiled at the thought. *The Prophet.*

Chapter 3
Atlanta, GA

Tommy Schultz felt exhilarated. He shook hands with various patrons, donors, and local elites as they all paraded by him and exited building. Normally he hated wearing a black tuxedo and bowtie, but that night he didn't mind. His dark, thick hair was styled neatly. Black rimmed glasses sat atop his pointed nose in front of blue eyes. His skin was more tanned than normal due to the sun exposure he'd experienced while working on the chamber project in central Georgia.

It was a proud event for him. His artifact recovery agency, known as IAA (International Archaeology Agency), had recovered the single most significant archaeological find in United States history.

The golden chamber they found near Augusta, GA was estimated to be worth over $500 million dollars. Of course, the government only gave the IAA a small fraction of that, but the reward had been substantial enough to put the agency's holdings to over $200 million. Not too shabby for a bunch of researchers.

He'd also orchestrated a deal to bring some of the artifacts to the Georgia Historical Center for an exhibit, along with some other items including a long, ocean-going canoe that had been uncovered on Weeden Island. The ancient boat's discovery was significant because it showed that the natives were capable of sea travel and trade thousands of years ago, playing right into the idea that perhaps they'd even navigated the Atlantic at some point.

There was a feeling of regret, too. His friend, Frank Borringer, had been murdered because of his obsession with finding the golden chambers of Akhanan. Another man, a state parks worker had also been killed in the wake of the race to find the first room of gold.

He counted himself lucky in many ways. The men that had kidnapped him could have killed him at any point. The things that had kept him alive were his wits and luck. He hoped neither of those would run out anytime soon. Like it had for his parents.

His parents had been intense savers and scrupulous investors. They had been wealthy, discreetly so, very few ever knowing the fortune they'd amassed in secret.

Though their salaries barely topped six figures combined, they were able to scrape together millions. Tommy had inherited everything when their plane went down in South America twelve years before.

He squinted away the pain, trying to imagine how proud they would be to see tonight's exhibit. There were only a few regrets in his life. With his parents, he just wished he could talk to them again one more time.

After a few minutes, the glass and steel expo hall had nearly emptied and he stood alone surrounded by red draperies and enormous pictures of some of the artifacts from the chamber discovery. The lights of Atlanta's skyscrapers and hotels poured in through the clear glass ceiling. A look at his watch told him it was getting very late.

He scooped up his iPad and water bottle off of a nearby chair and started to leave the room when he noticed a familiar figure standing silently in the corner near the door. The man was young, in his mid to late twenties. Tall, strong, with short dark hair and eyes to match; Tommy figured Will Hastings was popular with the ladies but as a police detective he doubted the poor guy had much time for anything social. There was something about him though, that seemed a bit off. Tommy couldn't put his finger on it. He figured it was probably just his imagination. Maybe it was ambition. It was tough to sense those things. He was a historian not a psychologist.

He stepped towards the policeman and extended his hand. "How you been, Detective Hastings?"

Will allowed a momentary smile as he gripped the archaeologist's hand, but it faded quickly. Tommy noticed the change of demeanor. This wasn't going to be a happy visit. "It's about your friend, Dr. Nichols."

Tommy's face instantly expressed concern.

Terrance Nichols was a mathematics professor at the Georgia Institute of Technology, more affectionately known as Georgia Tech. Schultz had received a call from the professor a few days after his discovery of the golden chamber. Nichols had developed a code-breaking software that could decipher nearly any code on earth. The software would make understanding ancient lost languages much easier. The man was so excited he'd gone off in a rant of technical mumbo jumbo that Tommy would never understand. All he cared about was whether or not the program worked.

After arriving back in Atlanta, he'd copied the odd assemblage of letters and symbols on the back of the stone disk he'd found in the chamber and delivered it to Nichols. The code on the first stone was deciphered by Professor Borringer. The inscriptions were a combination of ancient languages that had been unused for centuries. This new stone threw a monkey wrench into everything. The odd letters and symbols were completely foreign to Tommy. Never in his life had he encountered anything like them. Fortunately, Nichols had presented a solution that could potentially help them move quickly towards finding the location of the next chamber.

Tommy's thoughts quickly returned to the matter at hand. He could tell Detective Hastings didn't want to deliver whatever news he had. "What about Professor Nichols, Will?"

Will hesitated for a moment before answering. "He's been murdered."

Chapter 4
Las Vegas, Nevada

Sean was angry with himself, though he couldn't show it. Maybe he *was* getting sloppy. He stared at the shadowy figure in the corner of the room.

"Getting the drop on the great Sean Wyatt is a tricky thing to do." The voice was feminine and familiar.

The lithe silhouette stepped from the shadows near the large window, revealing a woman in her upper forties. Her brown hair was cut neatly just below the ears framing a lean, defined face. The brown eyes looked serious as they peered at him. She wore a gray, form-fitting dress-suit that looked like it was made strictly for business. Though, it did accentuate the right spots.

Sean let out a deep sigh. "Hello, Emily." He emptied the contents of his front pockets onto the dresser while she lowered the gun and returned it to a concealed place within her suit's jacket.

"Nice to see you again, Sean." She smiled, seeming to relax for a moment.

"You're lucky I didn't shoot you," he said with a casual warning.

"And you're lucky I let you quit the agency," she replied coolly.

"Would you like something to drink?"

"I already took the liberty." She picked up a half-full rocks glass from the coffee table and helped herself to a seat on the plush, pale-green fabric of the sofa. "You want one?"

Of course she had.

He shook his head. "Thanks, though."

"Suit yourself," she quipped and raised the glass in a mock toast. "Although, after that bad beat you just took, I'd have one."

He snorted a short laugh. She had a point. "You saw that, huh?"

She nodded with a raised eyebrow.

Sean had worked with Emily Starks at Axis for a four years. She'd actually trained him when he had arrived at the agency fresh out of college. The woman was persistent and calculating, two big reasons why she was now the director of Axis. When their former boss, Grant Rawson, resigned to take a position in the White House, Starks was by far the best replacement. She knew what she could get away with, like the glass of whiskey in her hand. Emily didn't always play by the rules, which occasionally got her a meeting with someone in the Justice Department. But more often than not, her gut instincts had proven correct and more than a few times she had saved lives.

Sean plopped down in a desk chair near the window and stretched his hands over his head, leaving them there for a moment. "So, to what do I owe the pleasure of your company at this hour...in Las Vegas...on my vacation?" He asked, cynically.

Emily took another sip of the brown liquid and contemplatively rolled the ice around in the glass. "We need your help, Sean."

Sean's face never flinched. He figured she needed him for something. It wasn't often the head of one of the better government agencies in the Justice Department came around just for drinks and chit-chat. "I assume by *we* you mean *you* need my help."

She smiled and took another swallow. "This is pretty good whiskey." She glanced at the glass for a second. "That's partially right, yeah." She looked up from the glass.

The few moments of pleasantries were apparently over. He was curious to see where she was going with the talk. She fingered the rim of the cup for a moment then set it back on the table. "Have you ever heard of the Hermetic Order of the Golden Dawn?"

Sean shook his head. "Only in passing. Isn't it a dormant secret society or something like that? They fell off the map in the early 1900s for the most part." He paused a moment in thought, looking at the ceiling. "Seems like I read something about them being interested in magic."

"The original members of Golden Dawn were very much into magic," she confirmed his memory. "They had an enormous impact on Wicca and other groups that developed occult-type systems."

"So, we can blame the Goth trend on them?"

She ignored his joke. "They were originally formed by three former freemasons. The three men were also members of another, more secretive group called The Rosicrucians.

"Sounds like they were busy guys. I don't even have time to give blood."

"The founders were Wescott, Mathers, and Woodman," she went on. "Woodman was at the top of several different secret societies, one of which was the Order of the Red Cross of Constantine. He had been a doctor in his early life. Not much is known of him because he died shortly after Golden Dawn was established."

Sean tried not to seem bored. "I'm assuming all of this ties into you needing my help."

Emily cast him an irritated glance.

"I'm sorry. Go on," he insisted.

"Wescott and Woodman were both physicians: Wescott a coroner and Woodman a licensed surgeon. Both had Latin mottos. Woodman's: Magna est Veritas et Praelavebit-"

"Great is the truth and it shall prevail," Sean chimed.

"Show off." She continued, "Wescott's was similar: have courage to know."

Sean rubbed his eyes and looked over at the clock. It was way too late to be getting a history lesson.

"So, what was the third guy's?"

"He didn't have one. Mathers was different than the other two. As I said before, Woodman and Wescott were both doctors. They were both members of several different organizations. Mathers was a clerk and was introduced to the freemasons by a friend.

"While Wescott and Woodman seemed occupied with discovering truth, Mathers seemed more interested in what the various secret organizations could do for him. The other two died before he did, and when he left the Order in 1903 it was reportedly because of many debts."For the last hundred years, the Golden Dawn was thought to be dormant, like you said. Now, it seems, they have resurfaced."

"Meaning what?"

She reached down and grabbed another draught of the brown liquid before continuing. "The Order of the Golden Dawn was an unnecessary addition to an already saturated period of secret societies. Most of the members were part of the Rosicrucian sect, as well as the freemasons. These guys didn't put this group together because they were bored."

"What are you trying to say, Em?"

"I'm saying that they were looking for something."

Sean raised his hands, exasperated. "Which was?"

"We believe they were looking for the golden chambers, specifically the fourth chamber."

"What's so special about the last chamber?"

She leaned forward. "Apparently, they believe that within the fourth chamber there is something powerful, something that can give the order extraordinary control over the tides of human events."

Sean stood up. "How many of those drinks did you have before I came in here?"

Emily rolled her eyes. "Look, Sean. What we know is that this group was inactive for a long time after having a precarious beginning and abrupt end. But it seems now they have a new leader and he will stop at nothing to find the fourth chamber."

He was standing at the window looking out at the lights of the boulevard below. "And who is that, this 'new leader'?"

"Have you ever heard of Alexander Lindsey?"

"Might ring a bell. Eccentric rich guy. Seems a lot like Howard Hughes. Stays out of public mostly." He shrugged. "What about him?"

"We think he is the one behind what happened to you and Tommy a few weeks ago."

Sean's head spun. "Look, Em. I'm retired from government work now. My job is with IAA." He could tell she understood. But there was something she wasn't telling him. "Who's the *we* you referred to earlier?" he asked. "And why are they interested in me?"

Suddenly, the conversation was interrupted by a sound coming from the entrance. Someone was trying to open the door.

"Looks like they aren't the only people interested in you," she raised an eyebrow.

"Friends of yours?" He hoped.

She shook her head slowly.

Chapter 5
Las Vegas, Nevada

The Agusta's engine hummed above as the helicopter sped through the night, headed towards the mountains to the north of Las Vegas. The city blinked busily in the darkness of the desert through one of the cabin windows. Alexander peered through the window, lost in thought. Soon he would be back in his bed, safe in the mountain compound he'd had built decades ago. It was nice to have money. It could buy you fame or solitude. He preferred the latter, especially considering his mission.

He knew where his great grandfather had failed, he would succeed.

The cell phone in his left jacket pocket rang silently, interrupting his moment. He glanced at the number on the screen and then answered the call. "I trust everything is going according to plan?"

The voice on the other line was young but confident. "Not exactly. We've had a complication with the code interpretation. I'm on my way to fix the problem right now."

Another issue. The "complications" that occurred a few weeks ago had turned into a full-blown fiasco. What was supposed to be a quiet operation had become a media frenzy. The public was fascinated by the treasure hunt, intrigue, and murder. At least nothing pointed his direction. Attention was not something Lindsey wanted. Not yet. Now every treasure hunter on the planet was trying to figure out where the next chamber was.

"What happened?" he asked abruptly.

"I believe that the others may have made a move to try and locate the information." There was a slight pause. "Whoever they sent made a mess of everything."

Lindsey's blood boiled and his eyes narrowed, filling with rage. "Those fools. I told them not to interfere. But they just can't leave well enough alone."

Their organization was built around three controlling members, a triumvirate of sorts. They made executive decisions concerning the Order that most lower level members never even knew about. It had always been that way, since the very beginning.

He realized he'd been silent for a moment when his man spoke again. "Not to worry, sir. I will handle it. I trust you will take care of things with the other two."

He thought for a brief second about how to approach things with the others. For the most part, the other two were obedient and submissive. They always agreed to whatever he decided was best for the Order. It was nice to have puppets. Lindsey knew they were jealous of his power and loathed the fact that he had almost autonomous control over the organization. But under his leadership what had been a broken and forgotten group had risen from the ashes of obscurity and amassed money in the billions along with a tremendous amount of behind-the-scenes clout in political arenas. While conspiracy theorists talk about the Bildeburg Group and the Freemasons, The Order of the Golden Dawn were pulling more and more strings by the year.

"Make sure you take care of things quickly there." He paused momentarily, considering something else. "What about the Las Vegas issue?"

"Our men are moving in now, sir. That problem will be eliminated within the hour."

"Good." Soon, his operatives would have the location of the next chamber. And then, only a few short steps away from....His thoughts trailed away into a plethora of grand possibilities.

Up ahead, he could see the pale lights of his mountain compound. A mansion cut into the rock itself, the facility had cost millions. But it provided him with a hidden fortress where he could escape watchful eyes. Even satellites would have a difficult time spotting the 15,000 square-foot palace. So natural was its appearance with the surroundings. For a long time he'd stayed concealed in the shadows. Soon, he thought, the time for laying in wait would come to an end.

Chapter 6
Atlanta, GA

Professor Terrance Nichols never had a chance.

Dark crimson oozed down the hole in the front corner of his drooped head, a splattering of it decorated the thin carpet on the other side.

His body still sat in his desk chair in front of a computer monitor. The screen was on, casting an eerie glow in the dark laboratory. Tommy surveyed the scene in shock.

Crime scene investigators were all over the place working busily to gather any fragments of evidence they could. Others were taking pictures with their digital cameras trying to piece together the event. Police tape lined the doors and walls of the laboratory.

"Looks like it happened this morning," Will said standing slightly behind Tommy. "We're doing everything we can to find out who did this and why."

Tommy could only muster a slight nod.

"Tommy. We need your help here. You were friends with Nichols. Do you have any idea why anyone would do something like this?"

Inside, Tommy wondered. Surely it wasn't happening again. Professor Borringer had been murdered because Tommy had gotten him involved. What had originally been a simple favor of translating some ancient text had gotten Borringer murdered. Was Nichols the second?

Will broke his thoughts. "Tommy, had you been working with Dr. Nichols on anything lately?"

Tommy snapped back to the moment and nodded. "Yeah," he began sullenly. "I brought him a copy of the stone disc we found a few weeks ago. There was a code on the back of it, a sequence of letters and symbols unlike anything I've ever seen before. Terrance told me he had some software that he believed could decipher the meaning of the sequence."

"Is there anyone else that knows that you were working on this with him?"

"No." Tommy shook his head. "Sean knows, but he is in Las Vegas."

"He's the only other one? McElroy doesn't know?"

Joe McElroy had been instrumental in the discovery of the first chamber. His knowledge of ancient Native American history was staggering and had actually surprised Tommy at first. He'd been shot during the events leading up to the discovery and was taking a little time off to recover. Tommy was going to offer McElroy a job with IAA as soon as he felt better. They could use a person with his level of learning. But Joe wasn't aware that Tommy had been in contact with Dr. Nichols.

"No. He doesn't know. He's been taking it easy the last few weeks. Pretty sure his wife won't let him leave the house either."

Will chuckled slightly at the thought.

Tommy's face was filled with regret. He somehow felt responsible for the death of his friend. Then it changed to curiosity. "Do you know what was on the computer?" ill shook his head. "Not yet. We have been trying to get the scene swept and make sure there is nothing we missed. You think whatever they were looking for might be on the hard drive?"

A group of men in sterile-looking outfits gently removed the body from the chair and placed it in an ordinary coroner's bag. Tommy watched as the men carefully zipped the cocoon closed.

"Probably. Have you already done what you need to do to the area?" He looked at Will blankly.

"You want to take a look, don't you?" Will seemed apprehensive.

"It's my fault Terrance is dead. I need to know what he died for."

Chapter 7
Las Vegas, Nevada

Emily cast Wyatt a worried glance. "Whoever that is, isn't with me" she hissed. The fumbling noise at the door continued.

Sean stepped close to her and whispered in her ear, "Take off your clothes."

"Excuse me?" She looked incredulous.

"Trust me. Just do it. Hurry up." Sean said and undid the buttons on her blouse with a quick yank.

"You better know what you're doing," she said angrily under her breath.

"Lay down on the couch there," he pointed to the sofa. "And try to look sexy."

She shot him a sarcastic stare, while she hurriedly finished undressing down to her black bra and underwear, a move that only took her a few seconds with the outfit she wore. Then she laid down on the couch, propping her head up on her hand in an effort to look casual yet alluring.

Sean had slipped over to the dresser and removed his gun from the drawer and taken up a position in the corner near the bed. He would be out of the intruders' sight until they moved beyond the wall that separated the bedroom from the foyer and bathroom. Whoever was entering the room would first see a half-naked woman before they would catch a glimpse of his hiding place. He hoped that moment of distraction would give him the advantage.

The sound of the door opening echoed through the room. Sean held his breath. He couldn't see Emily from his crouching position but imagined she was struggling to stay calm. She'd been a great agent but sometimes fieldwork wasn't her forte.

For a moment, there was no sign of the intruder. They were probably checking the bathroom first. Then, Emily's voice interrupted the tense silence. "Come in," she said seductively.

The man stepped into view wearing a tight, long-sleeved black shirt and matching pants. He looked like he was in his mid-thirties.

In his hand he carried a Glock with a sound suppressor attached, which he lowered slightly at the sight of the nearly-naked middle-aged woman on the sofa.

Sean squeezed the trigger twice, sending two rounds into the left side of the man's chest. The intruder gasped as he fell against the wall and crumpled on the floor. Suddenly, a muffled popping of shots came from behind the corner creating spider webs of cracked glass through the large window at the other side of the room and sending Emily diving to the floor in-between the coffee table and the couch. There were more than one of them.

James Collack was sipping a cup of coffee he'd purchased downstairs at The Coffee Bean when he heard the distant pop of shots being fired. Something had gone wrong. Both of his men had been sent into the room with silenced weapons. The sound of normal gunfire meant that the idiots had somehow alerted Wyatt to their presence.

He stood from his seat in the Venezia Tower Bridge and straightened his black suit and tie.

"Do you hear that?" The female voice came through his earpiece.

"Yeah, I hear it." He paused. "Which is why we planned for this."

From his position, Sean couldn't tell what Emily was doing. She was pinned down on the other side of the room behind the sofa. Fortunately, she had a little extra cover because the living room portion of the suite was sunken in, about three steps lower than the bed area.

The silent pops ceased for a moment.

Sean wasn't sure if he should move in to attack or wait for the assailant to come around the corner.

Before he could decide, three loud retorts pierced through the silence from Emily's position.

He was glad she still had her gun.

Sean used the new swath of cover fire to take a chance and go on the offensive. He hoped that her shots had momentarily thrown the intruder off guard. Deftly, he lurched over to the corner and looked down at Emily. With his hand he motioned for her to fire another shot in the vicinity where she'd been aiming. She accommodated by popping one more round into a painting that hung opposite of the bathroom door. As soon as she had, Sean turned the corner and unleashed two shots of his own at the man crouching by the bathroom door. The invader never had a chance. Emily's shots had done exactly what Wyatt had hoped. He didn't even get his weapon raised before bullets pierced the center of his chest and lower neck.

The body slumped to the floor, shocked eyes staring wide at the ceiling as the last few moments of life slipped away. Sean reached down and found an earpiece on the dead man. He pulled it up to his own ear in time to hear the instructions, "cover the elevators and the end of the hall." He turned his attention to Emily who was already getting her clothes back on. "We have to go."

She passed him an understanding glance and slipped on her shoes. Her blouse remained only half buttoned and now her hair was tousled. As she reached the railing of the three steps leading to the bed area, she turned around for a moment.

"Hurry," Sean said.

She reached down and grabbed the glass and finished off the last of the cold drink.

"No sense in wasting good whiskey," she said nervously.

He just shook his head.

"Ok, what's the plan?"

"I just heard on the second guy's radio that they are covering the end of the hall and the elevators. I say we go for the elevators."

"But you just said there will be men there." She looked dubious.

"There's only two ways to go from this room. Towards the elevators provides more options of exit. And we're going to have a fight either way we go."

He had a point.

She gave a quick nod.

Sean stepped to the door quickly and eased it open, taking a quick glance at the immediate setting in front of his room. Then, leading with his gun, he aimed first down the hall to the right towards the elevators and then to the left. Closed doors lined the vast, empty hallway.

"Clear both ways. I'll cover you," he said. "Go."

She ducked underneath him as he continued looking both directions and darted across the hall to a doorway about two rooms down. He did the same and wedged in a portal across the hall from her. A muffled shot came from the other end of the hall, tearing into the wall next to Sean. Seconds later, a barrage of more rounds were sent their way.

Emily tucked into the doorway as far as possible. Fortunately, they'd chosen a spot where the walls jutted out slightly, perhaps for load bearing. But that little extra construction provided them safe refuge for the moment.

Sean peeked around the corner and sent a volley of three shots back down the hall, sending the four men at the other end, reeling behind the corner. He looked back towards the elevators. Nothing yet.

She saw him flick his head to move and obeyed while he fired two more shots. Sean gave a quick glance back to make sure Emily had made it to the roundabout where the elevators met four dispersing hallways. She kept her gun trained into the large area and motioned for him to continue.

Why weren't the men at the end shooting? He didn't have time to ponder and took off, letting one more shot loose into the vacant hallway behind him as he sprinted into the intersecting hall.

Sean quickly slid a new magazine into his gun.

"You always carry extra ammo on vacation?" she said sarcastically.

He ignored the cynicism and pointed straight ahead beyond a circular, vinyl couch.

"Tower bridge," he ordered. Just as he did, an elevator dinged. "I don't think that's our ride," he said.

Angela Weaver stood against the wall calmly holding her Glock with both hands. The new box-style sound suppressor looked bulky but was actually quite light.

She'd ordered her four men to flush Wyatt out of his hotel room and down the hall towards Venezia Tower. *If they got lucky and made the kill? Bonus.* She hadn't expected that, though. Not from these mercenaries. She'd also not expected the woman who accompanied Wyatt. The face seemed familiar, but she couldn't' place it. Of course, in the confusion, one of the four men had taken a bullet to the leg and was writhing in agony. Blood trickled from his thigh.

Professional killers? Barely.

"Can you walk?" she asked, coldly.

The man shook his head while he clutched the wound. "I don't think so."

She lowered her weapon and squeezed the trigger, sending a bullet into the man's head. The body went limp as the other three looked on in shock. "Don't get shot," she said plainly. "I don't pay you to get hit."

The others nodded grimly.

The elevator doors began to open as Sean and Emily jolted across the room and two men in similar attire to the ones from before stepped out with weapons raised. Slightly surprised to see their targets so soon, they only got off a few wild shots as Sean and Emily fired first, pounding them with several rounds. One man dropped to the floor while the other slinked back into the elevator.

The doors closed quickly, something that had irritated Sean on a few occasions during his stay. This time, though, he was grateful as it bought them a few extra moments to clear the circular room and get into the tower bridge. He scooped up the fallen enemy's handgun and kept moving.

As they turned a corner and entered the skyway at a full sprint, it was then he realized why the attack thus far had been somewhat half-assed. At the other end of the corridor stood a tall, young-looking man in a black suit and tie with four other men dressed in the matching long-sleeved shirts and black pants, all holding guns aimed in their direction. Three of the men were standing, two others crouched down on one knee, poised to fire. They were being herded to a place with no escape.

Chapter 8
Atlanta, GA

Tommy carefully plugged in the narrow computer tower and connected it to a monitor. They'd taken the brain of the unit to a separate office from where the crime scene investigators were still working. He wasn't even sure what he was looking for but he knew that whoever had killed Terrance was looking for the same thing.

Tommy clicked the mouse on a few different files hoping to find something, anything that might be related to what Nichols had been working on. He went into the recent files that Nichols had been working on but noticed nothing unusual there. Thinking back to a few weeks ago, he remembered Sean telling him how they had found something at Borringer's house. The old man had hidden it on a shelf, in plain sight. He typed in a search for files with the word *decipher* in them. Nothing came up. Then he tried typing in *code breaker*. Again, nothing.

Minutes went by as he kept hammering away at the keyboard trying to find any clue as to where the files could be. Finally, he leaned back and let out a huge sigh of frustration. "I have no idea what he had or where he put it," Tommy said with resignation.

Will ran his hand through his hair. *He was pretty sure Tommy Schultz and his friends still had no clue he was working for the Order. But he still had to be careful.* In the background, a few other CSI workers were busy finishing up, packing cameras, tools, and other technical devices.

He racked his brain to come up with an answer, but these types of things weren't Will's strong point. He hated riddles. The more straightforward things were the better.

Then Tommy had a thought. He sat forward again and clicked on the search bar, this time entering his own name. T-O-M-M-Y. The screen blinked for a second and then one file appeared in the left hand corner. It read, "Tommy's project."

Will scooted in closer. "You got something?"

"Looks like it," Tommy answered, annoyed that he'd been concerned with some complex combination of words when the answer was actually very simple.

He clicked on the file. A dialogue box opened. The words inside it were not what they'd wanted to see. *Password required.*

Chapter 9
Las Vegas, Nevada

Sean was angry at himself for being so stupid. He should have seen what they were doing. Should have seen it from a mile away. Maybe he had gotten rusty.

A young man in a suit stood at the end of the corridor with a smug look on his face. Something about him seemed familiar but Sean couldn't place it.

"Your luck has run out, Mr. Wyatt," the suit yelled down the glass hallway. "Throw down your weapons. There's no way out of here."

Sean's eyes darted around, trying to find an escape route but there was none. The tower bridge was encased in glass and steel, ten floors above the ground. A jump would be suicide, if he could even get the glass to shatter.

"Who are you?" he shouted back.

The man didn't answer at first. He apparently wasn't into conversations. Instead, he raised his weapon. "Last chance, Wyatt!"

Suddenly, the suppressed sound of a small, automatic weapon could be heard off to the right of the enemy position. A bullet tore into the suit's left shoulder and sent him reeling back, taking his aim away from Wyatt and Starks. A barrage of bullets sliced through the other four men as they all turned, too late to react. The first three were sent flying backwards with round after round riddling their bodies. The fourth dove out of the way but had launched himself directly at Wyatt. Sean snapped out of his trance and finished him with a single shot to the head and he fell face down on the thin carpet. "Go!" he yelled at Emily. She didn't wait to hear it twice and took off towards the pile of bodies.

Angela and her remaining men heard the chaos around the corner. They'd taken up a position at the entrance to the tower bridge and waited to see if their quarry would try to backtrack. She'd heard the exchange between James and Wyatt. *Idiot. Why hadn't he just shot them there?* Now there was someone on the other side with what sounded like an automatic weapon.

She shoved one of the men aside and stepped to the corner to take a peek at what was happening. As she leaned her head around the edge of the wall a shot rang out and erupted the wall right in front of her face. Her reaction was quick and she ducked back out of sight immediately. *That was too close.*

Sean had barely missed the target's head, but he'd sent a message.

While Emily ran forward towards the Venezia Tower, he'd covered the rear in case any of the men waiting behind them decided to get brave and move up. To his surprise, it looked like a woman had taken the quick look around the corner.

All of the enemies lay motionless. Suit and tie was gone but Sean realized there was no time to look for him.

Standing twenty feet away down the hall on the right was a woman in a pair of khaki shorts and a black v-neck tank top. She was holding a HK-5 sub-machine gun with a silencer equipped on the end. Over top of her shirt hung a thin, black leather coat that stopped just above her knees. Sean stared at her for a moment. Her black hair was down to her chin in the front and a little shorter in the back with tanned skin that spoke of years spent in the sun, probably on a beach. Deep, brown eyes stared back at him, sizing him up. When she spoke, her lips seemed to move in slow motion. "We should probably leave," she said in a distinct, Spanish accent.

Emily was less mesmerized by the strange woman's beauty and more by her impeccable timing. "I agree."

Just as she spoke, a shot popped from the other end of the corridor. She tucked in behind the corner of the bridge wall. The Spaniard loaded a fresh magazine into her HK-5 and cocked the mechanism.

"What happened to the guy in the suit?" Sean asked.

"I shot him but he got away," the mysterious woman answered. "Follow me."

Sean gave one quick look at Emily and nodded.

The woman took off, leading them down a long, lavish hall of the Venezia Tower. Huge windows to the left opened into a pool area filled with wrought iron fences, gazebos, and vine rails. Above, on the domed ceiling, were more ornate frescoes done in the Venetian

52

style with more cherubim, warriors, and bare-chested women. *Seemed to be a common theme.* Along the walls, gas powered sconces burned flickering flames constantly. Their savior stopped and cut into an alcove where a concierge desk was unoccupied. Sean and Emily followed.

"What are we doing?" Emily asked, confused.

The chiseled, feminine face turned. Her dark eyes peered at Starks. "Making sure they don't follow us."

With that, the woman peeked around the corner at the five men charging recklessly towards their position.

She pulled up her weapon and trained a laser site on one of the sconces close to where the men were running. She waited a moment then squeezed the trigger.

The candle erupted sending a jet of flame across the room. One of the attackers was caught by the burst, his upper body disappearing in the fire. He emerged on the other side and tried to douse the flames by rolling on the floor but the damage was done. The rest of the men stayed back, not seeing a way around the fire that continued to pour from the wall at shoulder level. All they could do was listen to their comrade screaming in agonizing pain. The Spaniard looked satisfied and glanced back at the other two. "Let's go."

A sharp, burning pain radiated from James's shoulder. He'd turned just as a woman had started firing on his position. The bullet had ripped through a part of his shoulder's skin but fortunately was not a direct hit. Amid the chaos, he'd retreated around a corner behind the restaurant, trying to take up a better position until his partner's unit moved in to assist. He hoped they would arrive soon.

He listened as her group pursued the targets down the large corridor. Just as he decided it was safe to join them in the chase, a bright orange flame reflected down the hallway walls accompanied by a flash of heat. Ducking back for a second, he then peeked around the corner to see the wall of flame engulfing one of Angela's men and sending her and the others falling backwards. Sprinklers on the ceiling overhead began to shower the area with water. Perhaps he would need to head off their quarry by taking a different route.

Angela had jumped back as the bright flames roared across the hall. She lifted one arm to protect her face from the sudden surge of heat. As she turned her head away, she thought she noticed something near the corner at the end of the hall but had to dismiss whatever it was. Sprinklers had come on soon after the explosion. She could hear sirens in the distance which meant they were running out of time. One thing she liked about the casino-hotels was that all of their surveillance efforts were concentrated on the gaming floors. Very little attention was paid to the hallways or adjoining corridors so at least they wouldn't be identifiable.

Through the flames, she could make out the outline of the man that had been burned and knew she couldn't risk leaving him there to possibly survive. So, Angela raised her weapon and fired two rounds through the inferno planting a bullet into the man's chest just as he rolled onto his side. The wailing faded away sharply. She turned to the remaining men and pointed around the corner to the rear. "That way."

CHAPTER 10
Nevada Desert

Alexander Lindsey began to open the passenger door to the helicopter before it had completely touched down. He was outraged that his subordinates would undermine his intricate plans. He would need to put them both in their places so that such an occurrence would never happen again.

Rosicrucians had been extremely secretive in the middle ages. If the sacred bond of trust was broken, a terrible fate awaited the offender. When the Order of the Golden Dawn was founded, they adopted many of the sacred rites and rituals of the Rosicrucians, including their laws and punishments. Throughout their history there had been few challenges to authority.

In the early days of the Order, some celebrities were permitted to join. Temples were opened in various parts of England, Scotland, and France. Just like any empire, they'd overextended themselves. It was difficult for the three primary adepts to maintain control of all the different temple followers. Some of the underlings had wanted to know more than they were permitted by their sacred documents, The Cipher Manuscripts, allowed.

Lindsey strode across the stone landing platform and through a recessed entrance on the side of the mansion that led to a large wooden door. He swung the heavy thing open and stormed inside to a dark hallway. The air inside was much cooler and damp than the desert outside. One of his bodyguards hurried to keep up and closed the door behind him while the Agusta's engine began to wind down on the helipad. "I want you to call the others and have them here within the hour" Alexander said to the bodyguard. "They have some explaining to do."

"Yes sir," the man nodded and veered off down a separate hallway.

A few steps later, Alexander turned into a much larger, vaulted corridor. It was lit with electrical wall sconces and the illumination revealed cherry-wood paneling that matched the floor. He slowed down his pace slightly, walking by old paintings along the way. The portraits seemed to be arranged in a sort of chronological order, from oldest to newest. He'd had all of the paintings brought over from Europe. It had taken quite a bit of work to find them all. But, with some diligence, he'd recovered the pictures of every Imperator of the Order since its inception.

The Imperators were the unquestioned leaders of the society. Although the two other adepts were of nearly equal authority, the Imperator made command decisions whenever the need arose. Their Cipher Manuscripts, however, never called for anything like what his two adepts had done, a fact he was going to remind them of shortly.

After making his way beyond the portraits, he turned into a room furnished with a lavish, oak desk, and a stone fireplace in the center of the outer wall. His feet carried him, almost unconsciously, over to the bar he'd had installed when the home was built. The study was his favorite place to forget everything in the outside world. It was also his favorite place to drink, usually alone. Although, from time to time, he would allow himself the less discreet pleasures the world possessed. He was the Prophet, not the Saint.

His bodyguard entered the vast chamber as he finished pouring himself a glass of scotch. He loved the drink. Single malt, eighteen year. Not like the crap they served at most restaurants.

"Would you like some ice, sir?" the guard asked.

He waved his hand signaling that he didn't. Instead he asked, "Are they on their way?"

The strong, young man nodded, his expression never changing. "They should arrive within the hour, sir."

"Good," Lindsey said with a sneer. His eyes narrowed at the thought of putting his associates in their place.

Chapter 11
Atlanta, GA

"Password?" Tommy wondered out loud. "I have no idea what that could be." He leaned back again and thought for a thirty seconds. Where was this all going? The last several weeks had been insane. People had been killed. And even though the discovery of the chamber had been an amazing one, part of him wished he'd never seen that stone. Then he had an idea. He leaned forward and typed in the word *Akhanan* into the dialogue box and hit enter. The computer screen flicked and switched to a program that Tommy had never seen. It was Nichols' culminating work, a masterpiece of programming genius that could, apparently unscramble almost any ciphered message conceivable, even ancient dialects. At the top of the page that appeared, it simply said *Tommy's Project*.

Will leaned in closer to see what the rest of the computer had to reveal.

The translation was worked out in a short amount of time, considering the obscurity and randomness of the symbols. I'm not sure what the translation means. I'll leave that to you. I hope this helps.

Terrance

In desert mountains above the meadows' sand, the sunlight points the way. The lions watch the gate to the spider's lair. Though the distance is great, take guidance from the eagle's wings to the river between the great mountains in the southern land. Leaves of three unlock the door.

"Apparently, Dr. Nichols had solved the language problem before he was murdered," Tommy said in a reverent tone.

"What does it mean?" Will asked, curiously.

Tommy thought for a moment. *The lions watch the gate.* There were a lot of things he knew and understood about history but for this one nothing came to mind. "I'm gonna have to call Mac. He's the expert on this sort of thing. But I'll have to wait until the morning. He'll be asleep by now."

Will nodded, understanding. "Just give me a shout when you talk to him."

"Sure thing." Then he added, "Will?"

The two men had stood to leave the room. It was mostly quiet now. The hours of work done by a slew of detectives and investigators had come to an end, and the crime scene was now vacant through the windows beyond the small office, save for the humming computers.

"Yeah?"

"Thanks for letting me know...you know, about this. Terrance was a friend."

Will understood. "Trust me, Tommy, I'm going to make whoever did this pay dearly."

There was an odd sort of determination in the cop's voice, almost sinister. Tommy passed it off and led the way out the door of the lab.

Chapter 12
Las Vegas, Nevada

The mystery woman led the way down the long corridor, past the pool area outside and to a smaller hallway, ending at some stairs and elevators. Normally, Sean would suggest taking the stairs but the lifts in the Venetian were so fast he figured speed was worth the slight risk of running into more trouble. They rounded a turn that opened up into an elevator room and Sean pressed the downward arrow button. It only took a few seconds before one of the six doors signaled with a ding that it had arrived. The three rushed in and the strange woman hit the button that would take them to the level where they could access the parking garage.

Two older women in fanny packs and visors looked at the three of them with wide-eyed terror.

"Fake guns," he waved the piece casually. "We're with one of those reality-experience groups," Sean said to the ladies with a smile as they stared at the weapons. "You know, we make you feel like you're actually having the experience of being with a bunch of special agents."

One of the ladies turned to the other. "Ooooh. I told you we needed to do one of those things, Beverly." She turned back to Sean, "Which company are y'all with?" The woman's deep, southern accent was unmistakable.

He raised an eyebrow. Before he could answer, the elevator mercifully reached their destination.

Saved by the bell.

The door opened and the three of them exited quickly into the hallway, careful to conceal their weapons.

Fortunately, the foreigner had the coat she could use to hide her larger gun. Probably how she got into the hotel without being noticed. Well, that and any security personnel were probably not checking her out for weapons. "This way," she said hurriedly. They walked quickly past a few closed newsstands and coffee shops and through a pair of glass double doors. Once into the parking garage, they stopped, each one looking around to make sure the coast was clear. "My car is at the other end," the woman declared.

Carefully, they started walking quickly towards the other side of the level. "Who are you?" Emily asked. "And why are you helping us?"

The woman turned her head and shot Emily a searing glance. "The second question will have to wait for now. My name is Adriana Villa."

About eighty feet away, a door began to open up on the side of the huge area. The barrel of a gun emerged followed by a few of the men from before. Adriana and the others dropped to the floor behind a row of cars just as a muffled pop echoed off the concrete walls and floor.

"We've found them in the parking garage," Angela said into her radio. Her team had discovered an alternate route to the parking level through a separate series of hallways and elevators. "Where are you?" she asked.

James answered in a quiet voice through the earpiece, "I'm right behind them."

At the other end, Sean attempted to aim his gun through the maze of tires and bumpers but he couldn't get a clear shot. "How much further to your car?" he asked Adriana as a window shatter nearby.

"It's the black Audi SUV at the end," Adriana replied and pointed towards a vehicle that sat another hundred feet away.

"Ok. Just stay low and they shouldn't be able to get off a clear shot." He hoped that was the case since he couldn't get a clean angle either.

They began creeping along, staying low to the ground. Sean watched the feet behind the rows of cars as they split up and moved around to flank their position. Then he heard the door behind them creaking. Someone was behind them.

James eased open the heavy service door to the garage and was instantly furious at how loud the action had been. Surely the creaking had given away his position. Still, if Weaver and her remaining men did their job it wouldn't matter. They could squeeze their quarry into a tight space and then execute them. He shifted his weight, crouching low as he led with the long silencer barrel through the slight opening in the doorway before peeking around the edge.

Sean noticed the black box of the sound suppressor easing into view. They would be sitting ducks if they stayed put. Emily and Adriana saw what he was looking at and read his mind. They needed to get out of the aisle. Moving as one, they darted out of the thoroughfare and into the next row of cars just clear of the line of sight from the opening door. The three all stayed low, watching as the newcomer moved quickly to the first set of cars in the row where they were hiding. All they could see was feet in between the tires. The villains were going to try to hem them in.

The sound of a car engine revved from the end of the room where Adriana's vehicle waited. It was accompanied by the deep thumping from a sub-woofer. Sean watched as a silver Cadillac Escalade rounded the turn into the parking area headed directly for the men and woman who were trying to flank their position. The driver was apparently unaware of what was happening. As the odd scene of hitmen dressed in black, armed with guns appeared in front of the driver, he stopped the large SUV. Sean couldn't see inside because of the windows were tinted far darker than most state laws permitted. For a long, awkward moment, everything in the building was frozen in a stalemate. The hit squad was still crouched down, facing the oversized Cadillac. Then, one of the back windows began to roll down and Sean could see a familiar black object in the driver's hand.

The silence erupted into a volley of shots as guns on both sides of the rear seat opened fire on the crouching assailants who returned rounds of their own at the silver SUV. The sudden shooting sent the pursuers diving for cover. Sean glanced at the other two as if questioning whether they knew what was going on.

Both women shook their heads confused. "Get us out of here then," he said to Villa. He didn't have to say it twice.

Adriana bolted towards her car, using the fray behind the other row of vehicles as a moment of distraction. The parking lights of the car beeped, signaling that she had unlocked the black Audi. Emily and Sean ran after her and all three reached her ride in mere seconds.

James watched the chaos unfold. Two of Angela's men had already been downed. She and the others were pinned back, only able to sneak a few shots from behind a few cars. The diversion had given Wyatt enough time to escape.

But who was in the Escalade? Did Wyatt have someone helping him? Surely not. He was in Vegas on vacation. Bullets ricocheted off the concrete and steel around him. He had to help Weaver. Sean Wyatt and his two accomplices would have to wait.

James jumped out of his position and darted towards the Escalade from the side, pounding the driver's window and door with rounds from his Glock. Before the man in the back could react another two bullets were sent into the dark interior. The dark hand holding the gun lurched backwards violently as bullets found their target. James assumed one of his shots had found their mark and emptied the rest of his magazine into the silhouette of the driver and the remaining man in the back seat.

65

Adriana revved the engine, backing her Q7 out quickly then wheeling the car around the row. The tires squealed as they peeled around the drive and down into the exit tunnel.

"Who were those people chasing us?" Sean asked, panting for breath from the passenger's seat in the back. He looked at Emily who was also breathing heavily in the front.

Adriana whipped the car out of the parking garage and past the valet area outside of the Venetian. "I'm guessing the Order of the Golden Dawn."

James continued firing on the Escalade until his Glock began to click, signaling that it was empty. Angela and the few men left from her team stopped firing as well. No more shots came from the bullet riddled SUV. Just to be safe, James ducked low as he approached the vehicle and reloaded a fresh magazine into his gun.

He stepped close to the rear door first, weapon trained on the open window. Inside the back were two dead African-American men. In the front, a larger black man sat in the driver's seat. Bullet holes dotted the windshield. Some of the rounds that pierced the glass had also found the driver. He was alive, but barely. James could hear his labored breathing turning into a gurgle. The man's lungs were filling with blood, a particularly strenuous way to die from his experience with it. He'd killed many adversaries that suffered the same way. Every time it appeared like the person was going through hell just before they got there.

At least, that's where James assumed they'd gone.

Weaver moved closer to the SUV, gun trained on the lone survivor. James opened the driver's door. The huge beast of a man held one hand to a chest wound as blood seeped through his fingers. "Who are you?" James asked raising his gun to the man's head.

A look of disdain crossed the dark skinned face. The hand holding his chest clenched, extending only one finger in defiance. With the other, he tried to raise his gun one last time. James squeezed the trigger. The suppressed barrel popped sending a new splash of blood and various red fragments all over the passenger's side of the front of the SUV. The body slumped over sideways.

Angela and the rest of her men stood close by. "Who were those guys?"

"Nobody." He eyed the excessive jewelry on the man's fingers and neck. "Too much bling for these guys to be pros."

She eased her weapon into a holster concealed by her jacket. "Who were the other two with Wyatt?"

He looked in the direction the black Audi had gone. "I'm fairly certain the woman in the gray dress was Emily Starks."

"Axis? What was she doing here?" Weaver looked concerned.

"Maybe they were having a secret rendezvous. They *did* work together for a few years at the agency." Even he didn't agree with his assessment, though.

"What about the other woman?" she asked.

"I have no idea. But whoever she is just complicated things." He touched the small gash in his shoulder. "That means there's another player involved."

"You don't think she's Axis, too?"

James looked down at his left shoulder. Blood still oozed slowly from the bullet's damage. "No. I think she's something else entirely."

Chapter 13
Washington, D.C.

A black iPhone vibrated angrily on top of the dark, wooden nightstand. After ten seconds of ringing, a tanned, masculine hand reached out and grabbed the device, lifting it so his eyes could make out the caller's ID. He wondered who had the gall to interrupt his sleep at this hour of the morning.

Eric Jennings had been somewhere between a sandy beach and the 18th hole in his dreams. Now the call he was receiving interrupted that.

In the soft glow of the phone's face he noticed the slender feminine body lying next to him. *Money may not be able to buy happiness but it can sure buy a lot of other stuff.*

He answered the call gruffly, "This better be good."

The voice on the other end paused. "It's not, sir."

"What do you mean?" he sat up in the bed and looked back over at the sleeping escort. The phone call hadn't awakened her.

"Wyatt had help," there was another moment of silence. "He got away."

Jennings was not a man to be taken lightly. He'd ascended in the Justice Department by being ruthless and direct. He'd always been careful not to piss off the wrong people but cunning enough to know when to cut throats. Surely, his agent on the other line knew this.

His eyes were tired. For someone in his mid-fifties he seemed to carry the burdens of man thirty years older. "Then go get him," he answered, annoyed.

"We aren't certain where they went, sir."

Jennings rubbed his eyes. "Who was with him?"

"Agent Starks was one of them. We didn't recognize the other woman. We'll have to run a check once we get connected to the system. Shouldn't take too long."

Jennings thought for a moment. *So Emily was there. Why? What was Axis up to? Perhaps he had a leak.* That was something he'd have to attend to later. Although, it could have been a coincidence.

"What should we do sir?" The voice on the other end of the line asked.

"I already said, go get him. Wyatt can become a thorn very quickly. We cannot risk letting him find out what we're up to."

"Understood, sir."

Jennings thought for a moment. His conversation had finally aroused the young woman next to him, but she had only stretched for a few seconds and then gone back to sleep. "Don't make me regret putting you on this assignment, James. You and Angela are my best agents. I have made you privy to things that only a precious few know about. If you fail me, you know what the consequences are."

There was silence. Then, "Of course sir. We won't fail you or the Prophet."

With that, Eric hit the end button on the display and set the phone back down on the little table. He looked back over at the silhouette of the naked woman underneath a thin sheet, accented by the streetlights of Washington D.C. coming through his second-story window. She'd been vigorous early, a real pleasure to bring home. He wondered if she would be at this hour of the evening as he reached over and slipped his arm around her waist. Besides, he needed something to take his mind of the problem that had arisen in the desert.

Chapter 14
Las Vegas, Nevada

Adriana whipped the Audi SUV out onto Las Vegas Boulevard and pressed hard on the gas. They sped down the strip passing the Palazzo, Wynn and Encore as well as the last few major Casinos in the area. The car's unique strip of LED headlights did little to change the brightly lit streets of the Boulevard. "Ok girls, someone needs to tell me exactly what is going on and right now would probably be the best time to do it." Sean said as he leaned forward from the back seat.

What had been a fun vacation with some gambling and maybe a few shows had turned into a bloodbath inside his favorite hotel.

Some of the less famous spots in the city blurred by as their driver tried to make sure she hit every green light possible.

Finally, their luck ran out and she slammed on the brakes at a red light.

She looked around in all the mirrors to make sure they weren't being followed before speaking. "You friend is right. They are with the group that calls themselves The Order of the Golden Dawn."

Emily cast him a quick glance as if to say, "I told you so."

The light turned green and Adriana continued talking, satisfied that they were safe for the moment. "Ms. Starks, what you think you know about this organization is irrelevant to what they are capable of and the extent of their reach." She gave a look out of the corner of her eye as a warning.

"How do you know what I know about them?" Starks replied.

"I don't," Adriana responded. "But I know how your government works and your agencies usually never know the whole story."

She ignored the slighted glance from Starks. "I have been following their movements and actions for some time. They have been extremely active over the last year, as Ms. Starks made you aware of earlier, Senor Wyatt. However, no one in the intelligence community seems to know why they have all of the sudden started moving pieces on the chessboard of the world again. I do."

"And just why is that?" Emily interrupted.

"They have been looking for the Golden Chambers of Akhanan," Adriana gave Sean a quick look.

"Yeah, that much we know. But we beat them to the first one, and I don't think they are going to come anywhere close to the next one. We took care of that little problem." Sean spoke with a little swagger in his voice.

"Did you?" she asked. "I would say from the events of the evening so far that you are incorrect in that assessment." She made another quick turn and merged on to a highway leading out of town.

"Where are we going?" Emily looked suspicious.

Adriana looked straight ahead into the darkness outside the city. "Somewhere safe."

Inside the vehicle became silent as she drove. For fifteen minutes no one said anything. The lights of the city began fading further and further away until the town was just a bright spot in the middle of the desert. The black Q7 cruised through the rising twists and turns of the mountains easily, living up to it's sports-car lineage. As the jagged mountain crested, the asphalt vanished into dirt and gravel. Villa made a quick right turn onto another dusty roadway and slowed down slightly. Up ahead, sitting next to a large rock formation was a sandstone building. Its wood appointments and craftsman design were uncommon for the area, more suited for somewhere like the northwest or maybe in the southern United States. Dim lights emanated from within and a large, metallic garage door began opening on the underside of the house as they wheeled around a slight downgrade turn that led into the port.

"Nice place," Sean broke the long silence.

Villa barely gave him a look out of the corner of her eye. "Gracias." Her Spanish accent was alluring. She spoke with a confidence that was extremely attractive. It didn't hurt that she was gorgeous, too.

She brought the car to a halt and switched off the engine and opened her door. Something in the corner of the garage caught Sean's eye as he exited the vehicle. It was red, smooth, and tough looking. No fairing, single swing arm, big front and back tires. It called to him from across the room. "Ducati Streetfighter?" he asked, impressed.

"Si, Senor Wyatt," she answered with a smile. "I love to ride. When Ducati came out with this one, I bought it immediately."

Sean thought about his small fleet of motorcycles back home. Each one had a unique sound, rhythm, and feel. He'd ridden them all extensively and loved each one like they were his children. She interrupted his thoughts as if reading his mind. "I understand you have quite a collection of bikes yourself, Mr. Wyatt."

He grinned slightly. "It's nothing major. Just some I've worked on and restored over the years. I've never ridden a Streetfighter, though. What's it like?"

Her smile was slightly wicked as she raised an eyebrow. "Like strapping a grenade to your chest."

Chapter 15
Nevada Desert

Alexander paced slowly around the small, circular wooden table.

The other two men, Albert Mornay and Jonathan Carrol, sat nervously in their chairs, uncertain why they'd been called at this time of night but both thought they knew the answer.

"Gentlemen, I'm sorry to have 'roused you from your slumber this evening, but it seems we have a problem," Lindsey began, not expecting the other two to start the conversation. They were both weak men, easily controlled. Well, until this last little outburst.

Mornay's family had been involved with Golden Dawn since the 1920s. He'd basically been grandfathered into the order. The man had never done a day of hard labor in his life. Tall, slender, with a beak for a nose and a high forehead, he was the realized image of Ichabod Crane.

Carrol was different. He'd been a low-level suck up in some company for a long time until he finally got promoted to the level of partner. Though he'd worked hard for the Order, he had given away his best years. Now in his mid-fifties, the man looked like he was pushing seventy. A real "yes" man, Jonathan Carrol took crap from everyone who gave it out so long as it helped move him up the ladder.

Both men had their usefulness. They had money and some influence in certain circles. More important than that, they could be manipulated however Alexander saw fit. He'd known that Carrol and Mornay resented the fact. They knew their position, and neither was willing to do anything to jeopardize the possibility of becoming top dog at some point in the future.

Lindsey had taken the reins ten years ago from his predecessor. He'd served the old man well, learning everything he could about the Order. It was his benefactor that had seen the ambition in Alexander's eyes. That understanding had led him to reveal the secret of the lost golden chambers of Ahkannan. It was a secret that only a few people knew.

"So why *did* you call us, Alexander?" Mornay asked. His thin eyes blinked in irritation. He'd always been the more annoying of the two. Unfortunately, he would be the next in line to be Imperator of the Order. The man was rash and foolish. It had probably been his idea to go after the scientist in Atlanta.

Lindsey eyed both men with fierce scrutiny. *Knowing Carrol, he'd probably just nodded and said nothing rather than put up a fight.*

"Why?" Lindsey answered boldly. "Because there is a dead Georgia Tech professor in Atlanta right now because of your foolishness."

Carrol perked up slightly, a look of concern washed across his face. He'd become clearly less comfortable.

Mornay tried to play it a little cooler. "So?" he asked as he leaned back in his chair, feigning a lack of concern.

Alexander stopped pacing and placed both hands down on the table, peering into the man's soul with cold and calculating eyes. He'd had enough of

Mornay's snide disrespect over the years. Mornay's family line had brought him into this little world but Lindsey could take him out. In the moment there was nothing he could do according to the laws set forth by the founders of the Order. But the day would come. "Your idiotic attempt to steal the translation of the second stone has potentially brought our operation to light. Do you realize that?" He was on the verge of rage. His face became red and a vein on the side of his neck bulged slightly.

Mornay cowered only a little. "What about all the stuff that happened a few weeks ago, Alex? The police, the feds, everyone is watching us now. It's only a matter of time until they start asking questions." He raised a finger in Lindsey's direction. "You have put us in more danger than anything we've ever done."

"Don't you ever raise your finger at me, Albert! How dare you question my authority!" His voice boomed through the conference room like thunder in the night. "Unlike with the little 'play' you two made, I conversed with both of you before moving forward. You didn't even ask me for permission. It is strictly forbidden to use an asset without the agreement of the Imperator." Frustration and anger poured out of him.

"Guys, let's just take it down a notch," Carrol finally entered the conversation. He looked uncomfortable with the confrontation that was taking place.

Lindsey wasn't surprised at Carrol's reaction. *He didn't have the stomach for what sometimes needed to be done.*

"You were unavailable," he continued. "We had an asset nearby, and we felt like we could make the move with little risk."

That was certainly out of character for Carrol, Lindsey thought. *More than likely, it had been Mornay's idea and the worm didn't have the spine to say no. Either way, they were wrong for doing it.* "The events from a few weeks ago were unfortunate but were necessary," Alexander began. "They got us the result we needed which was finding the first stone."

"It does us no good if it stays in the hands of those morons from IAA," Mornay injected.

Lindsey stood straight. "Will has control of the situation, Albert," his tone chastising Mornay as if he were a small child who had broken a window.

"We didn't feel like that is the case," Albert replied indignantly.

"You acted without consulting me first. That is strictly against our code." Lindsey was right and Mornay knew it. They'd taken a huge gamble.

Carrol looked increasingly less comfortable. "We just wanted to speed things up. That's all. You weren't around so we made a decision and went with it."

"And now we have a mess to clean up in Atlanta," Lindsey looked disgusted.

"What are you going to do?"

Alexander looked at Carrol. "Our agent is taking care of it now." He paused, thinking for a moment.

"See to it that neither of you do anything like this again. You know what is fully within my rights, if necessary. An act that endangers the order is an act of treason."

The room was smothered by an ominous silence. They knew he was justified. And the laws of the Order were very clear. If the acting Imperator ever believed anyone in the organization had committed treason he could have the accused put before the council and executed. It was a simple monarchic system when it came to that charge. Even the adepts were vulnerable.

An adept's execution had only occurred once in the century since the Golden Dawn had achieved prominence. In 1946, the post-war world was a place of uncertainty. Though World War II had been an enormous atrocity, more than a few shrewd businessmen had made their fortunes off of it. Aramus Dawson was one such character. He'd profited millions of dollars making vital parts for the weapons that the US Air Force took into battle. While many made money on the planes, Dawson made his on the guns that took down other planes. At the age of 45 he was still one of the youngest adepts to ever ascend to the chair. Unfortunately for Aramus, his greed and ambition were such that they caused him to hoard some of the money he was supposed to contribute to the Order. Every man, down to the most insignificant initiate, had to pay their tithe to the organization. Ten percent of all gains, just like in a church, went to the group. It was how they maintained an operational bankroll and how they were able to function in secrecy and yet extend a powerful arm into places other groups could not. Dawson's Imperator had warned him not to hold back funds from the Order. If necessary, accounts could be called into question. If the accused could not or would not produce any evidence against their supposed wrongdoing, they could face punishment at the discretion of the Imperator. When Dawson's bank accounts were requested he refused, boldly challenging the right of the Order to ask for such personal information.

Unfortunately for Aramus, the order controlled many of the banks in the United States and a few in Europe. It only took a short time before documentation began coming to light that showed the greedy adept's treason. He'd kept tens of millions of dollars from the order, only paying a fraction of the tithe he was required to give. If the numbers had been just slightly off, that was excusable, a technicality that could be overlooked. But such an enormous amount had to be accounted for. Aramus defiantly stood his ground, claiming he had earned that money and deserved to keep it. He'd evidently forgotten how the order had helped him fund some of his investments in the first place. In front of a conclave of 12 peers, the other adept, and the Imperator, he stood trial for treason. His judgment was swift and unanimous. Death.

The means could be decided solely by the Imperator himself. They had a room in their secret gathering place that could be used for just such an occasion. In the center of the large, semi-circular room, an enormous brass bull rested over a fire pit. On the side of the metal sculpture was a door. They had adopted the "brazen bull" from ancient Greece where it had been a rare form of execution during a particularly sinister reign of power.

The victim was placed inside the metal beast and the door close. A fire was then lit underneath, effectively roasting the victim. The most effective and disturbing means of torture was to keep the fire burning low. Hot coals could keep the person inside alive for extended periods of time, cooking them even slower than a higher flame. Internal pipes were fastened to the victim's face and exited the mouth of the bull so that the screams of those inside would be amplified and contorted for any observers. As soon as his sentence was pronounced, Aramus Dawson realized the gravity of what he'd done. He then began to beg and plead with the conclave to give him another chance, promising to give them double what he owed.

The group was unimpressed. Once he was dead, they would take control of *all* of his assets, a fact the Imperator made sure he knew just before the brass door was sealed.

Mornay and Carrol cast each other a quick, uncertain glance. There was just such a device on the premises. They'd both seen it in passing while on a tour of the compound.

"We won't make any decisions without consulting you again," Carrol said sheepishly.

Mornay said nothing; his silence revealing that he understood the gravity of the situation.

"Good." Lindsey turned around and walked towards the door.

"Alex," Mornay spoke up.

He turned and looked back at the snooty character.

"Any word from our mole in the Justice Department?"

Alexander stood thoughtful for a moment, considering the man he'd had thrown from the helicopter earlier that evening. When he spoke, it carried a cryptic tone. "I don't think we'll be using him anymore."

Chapter 15
Atlanta, Georgia

Tommy and Will had what they needed, though Tommy's friend had had to die for it. Both men tiredly strolled out of the lab and towards the exit of the building and simultaneously noticed some kind of movement at the end of the corridor. The other detectives had already left the premises leaving only two policemen to guard the crime scene, both of whom were nowhere in sight.

"Did you see that?" Tommy spoke just barely above a whisper.

Will nodded and pulled his gun out of its holster. A flash and short pop burst from the dark shadows where they'd seen the motion, pinging a bullet off the wall nearest them. Both men ducked into the alcove of the opposite doorway to take cover.

"Didn't the police check this whole building for suspects?" Schultz wondered out loud.

"Yeah. They did." Will turned around then edge and squeezed off two quick rounds. Two more shots replied from the other end, one shattering a door window behind them. "Whoever killed the professor must have come back for what they were looking for."

Tommy looked skeptical. "To a fresh crime scene?"

"I've seen dumber things done by criminals. It's the only thing that makes sense here. I guess he figured we'd be less likely to suspect such a move."

"True. Or maybe the guy never left the building."

"We're going to have to change plans, Tommy. My guess is they figure you have what they're looking for." He looked at Schultz with a serious eye.

Tommy knew what that meant. They were willing to kill whoever got in their way to get what they wanted. "What's the move then?"

Will thought quickly. "My car is out back. I'll lay down a little covering fire while you go. I'll meet you out there."

"I can't let you do that." Tommy shook his head.

"It wasn't a question." He gave a sly grin. "Now go."

The young cop swung around the corner again on one knee letting off a series of shots in the direction of their attacker. Simultaneously, Tommy took off towards the door closest to their end. He could hear Will's weapon laying down a steady barrage of hot metal as he barged through the door and out into the Atlanta night. He kept running until he saw what he believed to be Will's silver Dodge Charger. Though it was unmarked, he recognized the similarities between that and other more obvious police units.

More muffled shots rang out inside the building. Tommy wasn't sure what to do. He wished he could help the young officer but he was unarmed. What if Will was shot? Then the assailant would surely come out the way he had exited a moment ago. He noticed a fairly large rock near the front of the car in the landscaping bed and grabbed it quickly then stepped around the back of the car and ducked behind the trunk.

A few more shots popped then suddenly the door flew open. Will sprinted from the building as fast as he could. He unlocked the doors with his remote key while slowing to a halt.

Tommy stood up, rock still in hand. "Whew. I'm glad it was you."

"I think I may have got him." Will noticed the stone and raised an eyebrow. "What were you gonna do with that?"

The rock dropped to the ground and Tommy held up his hands to the side. "Not a clue."

"Get in the car. We better get out of here." Will jumped in the front seat and gunned the engine.

Tommy slid into the passenger's side and looked back up at the building as the detective jerked the car backwards. "Here we go again."

Chapter 16
Washington, DC

There was a crisp feel in the air that always seemed to come with late autumn. Eric Jennings took a deep breath of the fresh early air as he strolled along the downtown sidewalk.

It had been an uneventful morning thus far. He'd sat through a few meetings and listened to various reports.

Some of the other agencies had been inquiring about some funding that seemed to be missing from his budget, a fact he promised he would look into. At the same time, Jennings had warned them to monitor their own agencies. *What he did with his money was not their concern. How dare they.*

Fortunately, the careless agent with the loose lips had been discovered before too much damage could be done. Jennings had questioned using Gary Holstrum from the beginning. He was ambitious and eager yet lacked discipline, something that had been apparent. It seemed, however, the young, pudgy agent had been a little too mouthy about a few things. Thus the ongoing questions arising from the other bureaus. A bump in the road easily fixed.

Agent Holstrum had been unwittingly lured to Las Vegas, told he was being sent to a tech conference going on at the Palazzo. Like pretty much any young go-getter, he didn't need to be asked twice about an all-expenses paid trip to Las Vegas. He'd arrived a few days before, more than likely excited about four days of gambling, drinking, and debauchery in "Sin City." What he'd not expected was to be pulled out of his penthouse suite in the middle of the night by two men dressed as bell-hops. Their tranquilizers worked quickly. Jennings had suggested them personally when the plan had been orchestrated. After the unconscious Holstrum had been delivered to The Prophet, Jennings didn't need to know anything else. Lindsey would handle it how he deemed fit. Though, if Jennings had to guess, he'd say the man had probably suffered until the moment of his last breath.

The phone in his left jacket pocket startled him, ringing loudly. He checked the screen then answered. "I trust you enjoyed the package I sent you?" he said into the device.

"Yes, Eric. It won't be giving us anymore trouble." The voice paused. "Is everything going according to plan?"

Jennings thought for a moment. Lindsey was no fool. By this time, news of the shootout had been posted all over the news and there was too much carnage to cover up. The press had been fed a story about one man acting alone, firing on federal authorities. The gullible and always hungry press seemed to love it and ran the story, almost without question. Even without all the media attention, Jennings knew Lindsey was probably fully aware of what had happened before anyone else. "We hit a snag," Jennings said, carefully.

"A snag?" the voice asked.

"We lost several assets. My two points are handling it." He wondered where Collack and Weaver were at the moment. They'd not reported in yet.

"Yes. I'm aware of the incident in Las Vegas. It's quite the mess," he sounded irritated "I hope I haven't misplaced my trust in you, Eric." The line held an unspoken threat.

Jennings understood the statement. Failure was not an option. "It will be handled, sir. I assure you."

"See to it that these little messes do not become common place. We are near the end of the race. It must be finished. Make sure Wyatt is taken care of."

"It won't happen again."

The line was momentarily silent.

Then Jennings added, "There was an unanticipated interruption, sir."

"Interruption?"

"Two women appeared. One was with Wyatt in his room when our men moved in. We think it was Emily Starks. The other one is an unknown. Apparently she took out several of our agents."

"Unknown? Did anyone get a good look at her?"

"We are checking security cameras now but she could have been disguised. It may be difficult to get an ID."

"Do you have their location?" Lindsey was sounding more and more annoyed.

"Not yet. We should by noon."

Alexander's voice was pensive. "Don't take them out yet. I want to know what they're up to and who this

mystery woman is. They may be of use to us after all.
Then when the time is right...." He trailed off.

"Yes sir." The line went dead. Jennings checked the
screen and saw that Lindsey had hung up.

Chapter 17
Nevada

Sean awoke and shook his head. He was lying in a room with walls made of solid wood planks. The bed was soft, softer than most he'd slept in. He leaned over to a nightstand and checked his phone to see what time it was then swung around the edge of the bed and walked over to the window overlooking the jagged mountains to the north. A quick inspection of the small guest closet revealed a plush, white robe that extended down to his knees. There was a slight chill in the air so he decided to help himself and slipped into the cozy garment.

The interior of the mountain top chalet was much larger than the exterior belied. It was a narrow building, probably thirty to forty feet wide. Counting the garage there were three floors, two of them housed the living quarters of the home. The layout was unique. He'd learned as much by way of a quick tour from their host the previous night. A great room opened up into the kitchen and dining room with hardly any dividing walls whatsoever. On the first floor a master bedroom and an office area took up some of the space along with a porch that opened up on the side of the house and wrapped around to the front, overlooking the basin and the far-off city below. In the living room, enormous windows displayed the breathtaking desert view. Upstairs on the second floor were two guest rooms, another master bedroom and bathroom and an outdoor patio that faced the other direction into the mountains and beyond to the north. The furnishings were simple but modern, an eclectic mix of black leathers, dark frames, and brightly colored draperies, photos, and artwork.

Sean walked slowly into the living room as the sun was peeking over the mountains to the east. The smell of fresh coffee lingered in the air. His host sat comfortably in a deep leather sofa near the window in a terry cloth robe identical to the one he was sporting. She held a large coffee cup in her hand.

"I see you made yourself at home," she said sarcastically, her Spanish accent seemed extra thick in the morning.

He looked down at the robe and spread out his arms as if showing it off. "I figured you wouldn't mind." He ran both hands down the sides of it, feeling the supple texture again then added, "This thing is really soft."

"They are better than the ones that were given to you at the hotel, yes?" A smile told him she appreciated the compliment.

"Definitely," he returned the grin.

"Would you like some coffee? I have it brought in from one of my family's estates in Guatemala."

"You have a coffee farm in Guatemala? Didn't look like a coffee farmer the way you handled yourself last night."

She stood up and eased past him, leaving a fresh scent of perfume dancing around his nostrils.

"I'm not a coffee farmer, Senor Wyatt," she replied while she set down her own cup and filled another identical one nearby from a steaming, steel pot. "Cream and sugar?"

He nodded and smiled. "I'll take mine how you take yours, por favor."

The Spanish caught her off guard slightly and she cast him a playful glance out of the corner of her eye. "Well, I take mine with milk and a little sugar. Will that be ok?"

"Sounds perfect."

She mixed the concoction and handed it to him, which he accepted graciously then proceeded to follow her back to the sitting area. They sat down across from each other, he in a matching one-seater.

"Is your friend still sleeping?"

"Probably," he said as he took a long sip of the aromatic coffee.

There was a moment of awkward silence. He lowered the cup from his mouth and made a gesture with it. "This is really good."

"Gracias," she nodded to him.

"So," Sean changed the subject, "you obviously know about me. But I know absolutely nothing about you? What's your story?"

She laughed slightly at the question. "There isn't much to know."

He took another big sip of the creamy, brown liquid. "Mentirosa."

The Spanish word surprised her and a snort escaped her nose in mid-sip causing her to nearly spill her coffee. "I am not a liar, Mr. Wyatt."

"Please, call me Sean."

"Very well, Sean," she said in a sarcastic tone. "I was born in a small town about thirty minutes outside of Madrid. My father was involved in many different business ventures. His affairs led him to be out of town much of the time. Eventually, my mother became very ill. When she died, my father was crushed. We grew very close for the months after her death." She paused and took a deep breath. The pain was still very close to her heart. "My father is a tremendous inspiration for me. He always treated me like his princess. When I went a way to University, he would call every week to talk to me and ask how I was doing." There was a slight tone of regret in her voice.

"So you left home to go to school?"

She nodded. "As much as I loved my father, I had to leave. Business was starting to take him away again and the pain was too much to bear without mother around."

Sean understood. He felt lucky he'd been able to keep his family around as long as he had.

"I feel like because he spent so much of his life working to give his family a better future, he missed out on so many things that the world has to offer."

Wyatt felt like saying something but he held back. Instead, he tried to lighten the mood. "If your other adventures were anything like what happened last night I'd say it's probably best that you leave him at home," Sean grinned wide.

"Perhaps," she laughed a little. She changed subjects. "After I graduated from University, I started working a little here and there with some small scale antique collectors from Europe and Asia. At first I just did it because I needed the work. Then one day I was checking my bank account and I saw something very strange."

"Lot of money missing?"

She shook her head. "The opposite. Someone had made an enormous deposit into my account. I felt certain there had been a mistake, but I was assured that the balance was correct. I can only assume my father must have put the money there. But he never said why. "So I used that money to do what I loved. I traveled the world, searching for antiquities on my own. I became what you American's would call a treasure hunter. But I don't do it for the money. I do it because I love history. Nothing beats that feeling you get when you find something that hasn't been seen or touched for hundreds or thousands of years. It is like nothing else."

"What do you do with the artifacts when you find them?" he asked, curious.

"I keep them in my collection," she answered pointedly.

"You don't feel like they should go to a museum or to a government?"

"No," was all she said with a cryptic smile.

Sean caught himself staring at her. The lightly tanned skin, the deep brown eyes, every physical feature was only enhanced by the fact that she was extremely learned and interested in ancient history.

"Got an extra cup of that coffee?" Emily's voice startled the two of them.

"Of course," Adriana said, momentarily caught off guard. She stood and walked back to the coffee maker and poured another cupful.

"Thank you so much," Emily said, taking the cup with a look of relief.

"How'd you sleep?" Sean piped up.

"Fine, thanks," she replied and took a seat on the opposite end of the couch from where their host had been sitting. She gazed out the gigantic windows. "What an amazing view."

"I love the enormity of it," Villa said.

"So, now that Em's up, I'll ask you a question that she and I are both probably thinking," Wyatt interrupted.

"Yes?" The chocolate eyes probed his face.

"How did you happen to know those guys were going to show up at the Venetian?"

She walked over by the window and gazed out at the sunrise over the far-away mountains as if considering her answer.

"A long time ago, my father told me a story, one that many have heard before. It was a legend really, a myth."

"Let me guess," Sean chimed in, "the seven cities of gold?"

Adriana nodded. "Yes. The stories of Quivira and Cibola reached one of my family's cousin's, a governor in Mexico. He spent his entire family fortune on expeditions into what is now the southwestern United States, searching for this supposed treasure."

"Wait a second. You're not talking about Francisco Coronado? Are you?" He seemed more interested now.

"Very quick to make the connection," She seemed impressed. "Yes, that is correct. He was a cousin of my ancestors. He frequently sent letters to my family back in Spain, mostly depicting the stories he'd been told about the magnificent cities and how when he discovered them our family would be the wealthiest on the planet. Sadly, he failed miserably and died a bankrupt man."

"So, you're trying to pick up where he left off," Emily threw in her two cents.

"No," Villa shook her head. "I have no grand delusions about seven cities of gold."

"Then what is it?" Sean looked sincere as he asked the question.

"When Francisco Coronado first came through the American southwest, he was led to believe there were magnificent golden cities that could be easily overtaken with a small army. He thought the gold could be plundered and taken back to Mexico and then Spain."

"You said, 'first came through.' What do you mean by that?" Sean questioned.

"When Coronado returned to his estate in Mexico, he realized there must have been some sort of flaw with the story. If there were truly seven cities of gold someone would have discovered them by then. Even rival tribes would have been tempted to overthrow the natives that had built them. Such a construction would have been nearly impossible to keep secret. "That's when he began to research the idea of the golden cities more deeply. None of the local natives from the Yucatan had ever heard of such a place, save for a few who had only a faint recollection of whisperings from the past."

"Are you saying the people who told Coronado about Cibola and Quivira were lying?" Emily wondered.

"You two already know the answer." She pointed to Sean, "Your friends Joe and Tommy figured it out rather easily, I might add."

The light went on in Sean's eyes. "Coronado figured out that it was something else. He must have come across some information that told him there weren't any golden cities but they were actually four golden chambers."

He wondered how she knew about his friends but decided to let it go for the time being.

"Exactly," she smiled at him. "But there was something else that Coronado learned of that is of far greater importance."

Starks and Wyatt looked on, intrigued by the exotic woman silhouetted by the sunlight now pouring into the great room.

"Your friends, McElroy and Schultz realized that there was something more to the chambers than just a treasure. They know that the rooms point to somewhere important for some of the ancient peoples of this hemisphere. What they didn't realize is what lies at the end."

"The end?" Emily moved to the edge of the couch, completely intrigued.

Their host turned to face them both. She sipped the last of her coffee and set it on an end table nearby as she stepped closer. "The end of the path."

Sean nodded. "That's what Joe called it, essentially. He said that the chambers were beacons, a trail to lead them home."

"Yes. He is mostly correct in saying that."

"Mostly?"

"There is something else that your friends don't know about."

The audience of two waited, anxious to hear the revelation. She leaned close to both of them, eyeing one then the other. "It is rumored the fourth and final chamber is the resting place of an ancient power, one that, if discovered, could change the course of human events forever."

Chapter 18
Atlanta, Georgia

Tommy hadn't slept well during the night. He didn't like sleeping in unfamiliar places. Other people always kept their home temperatures either too cold or too hot. Not to mention the fact that he liked to have a floor fan going to provide a little background noise.

Will's house had been a little cold but he'd had worse. His inability to get any rest had more to do with the events of the previous night than his sleeping environment. A friend murdered for the second time in the last month and the ensuing shootout had rattled him more than anything. Regret and anger mingled in his head as he sat overlooking downtown Atlanta from Will's mid-town condo. He scratched his messy hair and looked down at his phone.

No messages.

Tommy's thoughts went back to the events of the previous night. He'd been playing them over and over again in his mind. *Who was the killer? They had to be a pro.* The only trace of the mystery shooter the police found were bullet casings laying all over the floor of the hallway and near the lab entrance. There were probably more police stationed there since the occurrence. It was still odd they couldn't find anything. No fingerprints. No blood. Nothing.

He sat, thoughtful, for a few moments and then moved his hand across the glass-top coffee table to grab his cell phone. His fingers scrolled the touch screen until he found Sean's name and pressed it. The other line rang a few times until the familiar voice came over the other line.

The phone began to vibrate in his hand. Tommy looked down and saw it was Sean. "Hey, man," he said into the device.

"You doin' okay?" Sean's voice asked from the other end.

"I've been better," Tommy replied. "Got shot at last night over at Tech." He hesitated then added, "Terrance is dead." His response skipped all pleasantries and got straight to the point.

Tommy let the words sink in for a minute.

"What happened?" Sean asked after a moment of thought.

"Someone broke into his lab. They must have been looking for what we had him working on. I guess when Terrance wouldn't give it to them, they shot him."

"Does the family know yet?"

"His ex-wife has been notified. But his son is over in Iraq right now. Not sure if they told him yet or not."

"I don't mean to be insensitive but did the software work?" Sean asked, carefully.

"Yeah. We got the translation, though I haven't got a clue what it means yet. I've been trying to work it out most of the morning, but I think I'm gonna have Joe take a look at it." His voice trailed off.

"You ok, buddy?"

"Not really, man. I can't help but feel like it's my fault that Terrance and Frank are both dead."

There was a long silence. There was nothing Sean could say that would change how his friend felt. But he said it anyway. "There's no way we could have known this would happen. We were just doing what we always do." Tommy continued, "I'll be ok. I just wanted to touch base with you." He changed the subject in hopes that his mood would lighten. "How's Vegas?" A laugh came through the earpiece. "What's funny?" Tommy's face turned curious.

"Emily and I bumped into a hit squad last night. We barely got out thanks to some help from a new friend."

"Hit squad? Emily's there?" His tone changed drastically.

"Yeah. Apparently there's a group called the Order of the Golden Dawn that is interested in the same thing we're looking for. Ever heard of 'em?"

"The Order of the Golden Dawn? They haven't been around since the 1920s."

"Apparently not. A bunch of them tried to take out me and Em last night."

"What's she doing there?"

"Still trying to figure that out."

There was another moment of silence.

"I'm going to call Joe and see if he can help with this translation," Tommy said.

"You think his wife will let you talk to him?"

Tommy laughed. "I hope so. He knows more about this stuff than both of us."

"Good luck, buddy. You safe?"

"Yeah, I'm at Will's place right now. He was there when the shooter returned last night. I crashed at his place."

"Alright. Let me know what Joe says."

"Will do."

Chapter 19
Las Vegas, Nevada

Sean hung up the phone and slipped it back into his pocket. He'd gone upstairs to speak privately with Tommy and also to give the ladies a few minutes to get to know one another. He was still suspicious of the mysterious Spaniard who had miraculously come to their rescue. Maybe it was just part of his training and experience. In his mind, someone always wanted something. It was a rare thing to find a genuine Good Samaritan who was just out to step into the line of fire and help a stranger. Her story seemed legit, though. But he felt like he needed to more. A part of him wanted to know more. And for now, they were just going to have to trust her. He hoped she was one of the good guys.

He climbed back down the stairs and found the two women talking casually where he'd left them.

"How's Tommy?" Starks asked as she saw Sean appear at the base of the stairs.

"He's fine except that he got shot at last night."

Emily looked concerned. "Lot of that goin' around."

Adriana spoke up. "Your friend is in grave danger."

"He's ok," Sean answered. "He spent the night at a cop's house last night. That's where he is right now."

She shook her head. "You cannot trust anyone. Especially not the police. The order has their fingers in many pockets."

"Should we trust you?"

"Probably not," she squinted her eyes. "But if I wanted you dead you already would be. And unlike someone who would use you to find something I needed, I have brought you something."

"What do you mean?" Emily interjected.

"Come with me and I will show you."

Sean and Emily gave each other a "why not" glance and followed the Spaniard towards the rear of the house. She led them down a flight of stairs that headed towards the garage. When they entered, they saw the familiar surroundings from their arrival the night before.

"I still wanna take a ride on that duke," Sean commented coolly as they walked past the bright red sport bike.

Adriana cast him a playful glance. "You would look silly on the back, I think."

He snorted and the side of his mouth rose to a flirty grin.

"I like her," Emily poked quietly.

Their host stopped at a plain looking door at the other end of the garage where a key panel kept the portal locked. She punched in a random sequence of numbers and a moment later the mechanism opened with a click. "What I am about to show you has only been seen by two sets of eyes in over three thousand years," her tone was respectful and serious.

Sean and Emily looked at each other briefly with wide eyes. "Why are you showing us?" Sean asked.

Adriana eyed him sincerely. "Because you are not searching for the treasure for worldly gain."

She pulled open the heavy door and a small burst of air escaped from within. Inside, a series of florescent lights came on automatically leading into a staircase cut from the stone of the mountain. The three entered and followed their hostess down the stairs that led further and further into the man-made cavern.

After walking for a minute or so, the group entered a circular room. It had been carved smooth out of rock. The walls were decorated with odd-looking engravings. There were Petra glyphs from Assyria, Sumer, Babylon, Egypt, as well as others that seemed far more unique, possibly from farther back in history. A small safe sat atop an old wooden stand off to the side.

"How did you find this place?" Emily questioned as she turned around in circles, staring at the wondrous display of history surrounding her.

In the middle of the chamber, a pedestal stood alone rising up from the rock floor. An oddly shaped piece of gold lay on top of it. The object was designed to look like a leaf from a tree. It was decorated intricately with lines and cellular irregularities just as a real leaf would have. From one end to the other, the piece was probably eight inches long and four inches wide at its broadest point.

Sean stepped closer to get a better look at the strange plate.

"I discovered this room after years of searching," Adriana said. "It was actually luck that led me here. Initially, I was not even searching for anything related to the golden chambers."

"What were you looking for?" Sean asked.

She cast him a cryptic smile. "I was looking for a painting. It had been taken by the Nazis during the second World War."

"Searching for stolen World War II loot?" he grinned, cynically. "Lot of rumors about that kind of stuff. Hard to find, though. The Nazis were very meticulous about how and where they hid things. Who was the artist?"

"Van Gogh."

He was impressed and gave Emily a sideways glance showing it.

"How did a Van Gogh lead you to Nevada?" Sean inquired.

"It is a long story, Mr. Wyatt. Like I said, it was mostly luck that led me here. I also had a little help from some new friends as well as some old ones. The painting's maker has little to do with why I am here, though."

Sean doubted it was mere luck. Still, he didn't press the issue. "How long have you had this?"

"Not long. A little over a year," she said plainly. "I had the house built around it to keep it safe until I could figure out the next piece of the puzzle."

"Next piece?"

"Francisco Coronado's expedition was mostly a disaster. He lost money, resources, and years of his life in the pursuit of the cities of gold. However, it wasn't a total failure." Adriana pointed to the golden leaf. She continued, "Coronado had considered that the men who had told him the stories of Cibola and Quivira could have been delusional or simply liars. But he believed that there was probably an element of truth to what they'd said. So, he was careful to investigate every possibility. "He met a shaman from a local tribe in what is now New Mexico. The old man gave Coronado a riddle. He said that if the Spaniard was able to unravel that mystery he would find the treasure that he sought."

"Coronado figured out the riddle," Sean said quietly, running a finger along the unusual piece of gold.

She nodded. "Yes. He found it here in this cave. Even though the medicine man had underestimated Coronado, he still knew that the explorer would only uncover a piece of the greater riddle, one he could never hope to unravel. "So, he left the piece here in this chamber to return in secret. He soon after became ill and never returned to the mountain. However, he did leave clues in some of his writings as to how to get back here."

"Writings?" Emily asked.

"The Diary of Francisco Coronado."

Adriana stepped over to the safe that also featured a keypad like the door leading into the secret room. Her fingers entered a set of numbers and the little metal box opened with a click. Gently, she reached her hand inside and withdrew a small, leather bound book. The object was worn. Its original owner had probably carried it through a vast array of circumstances. Sean knew that rain, snow, dry desert, humidity all had different effects on the way artifacts were preserved. For as old as it was presumed to be, he was impressed with the book's excellent condition. She brought it close and held it out to Sean so he could have a closer look. He clutched it carefully in both hands as if simply touching it might break the thing.

"The dry air in here has helped preserve it. I was surprised it was in this good a condition considering where I found it," Adriana pointed out.

"Where did you say you found it?" Emily piped in.

"I didn't."

Starks puckered her lips in understanding, letting the topic go.

Sean stared at the nearly worn out letters in the faded brown cover. *La Journal de Francisco Coronado.*

Chapter 20
Atlanta, GA

Tommy paced around the cavernous apartment, deep in thought. *Terrance was dead. He could have been. And Sean had been shot at as well. It was difficult to make sense of it all. Now Sean was telling him that the Order of the Golden Dawn was possibly at the center of it all? He'd only learned a little bit about the secret society in passing. Maybe he had seen it in a presentation somewhere.* Tommy couldn't remember. But he did remember that they were an odd group, bent on ancient rituals and the idea that there was some sort of ancient power they could call upon.

The Order of the Golden Dawn had been historically insignificant, dwindling away in the early 1920s. Maybe that was their plan all along. He needed to talk to Mac. The new riddle he'd retrieved the night before had to be solved and he had a feeling that his friend would have an answer. *Of course, there was a problem. Joe had been shot during the adventure a few weeks ago. He was fine and his shoulder was healing nicely, though still in a sling. The real issue was his better half.*

Mrs. McElroy had been less than happy when her husband was nearly killed.

When she had arrived at the hospital, she didn't say anything to Tommy or Sean. But the look she gave said a million words.

He knew Sean felt guilty about involving their long-time friend with the pursuit of the golden chamber. Although, it wasn't like someone put a gun to his head. Well, none of the good guys anyway.

Tommy felt like he could get a pass from the wife simply because he had been kidnapped in the fiasco. Surely she held a little sympathy for that.

His thoughts were interrupted by the sound of the front door unlocking.

Will came through the opening with a bag from Panera Bread Company and a couple of coffees in a drink carrier.

"Breakfast?"

"Yeah, I'm starving."

"Coffee with milk, right?"

Tommy eyed him with a suspicious grin. "How'd you know that?"

Will raised his eyebrows. "Seems like you mentioned it a few weeks ago."

Smiling, Schultz seemed to accept the explanation and took the proffered beverage. He smelled the intoxicating and soothing aroma of the brew.

Good coffee was something Tommy loved. On one of his trips to Spain he'd learned of what they called *white coffee*. The smooth consistency of the milk was a great combination with the bitter earthiness of the coffee. He drew a big sip into his mouth, careful of how hot the drink was based on the warmth of the cup. "Ahhh," he exhaled. "Now that's good Joe."

"Glad you like it. Got an egg soufflé for you too," he added as he set the food out on the counter nearby.

"Thanks," he said and grabbed a fork from within one of the brown bags. "Oh, speaking of Joe, I need to see him as soon as possible."

Will looked dubious. "You sure that's a good idea?"

"She'll get over it," he said confidently, masking his uncertainty.

"You think Joe knows what that riddle means?"

Tommy shrugged. "It's worth a try. He probably has a better idea than I do. Joe's good at these sorts of things."

"Maybe you should call first."

"Yeah, probably," he laughed at the thought and took a bite of the soufflé.

Chapter 21
Nevada Desert

The morning had been less than hospitable to
Alexander. His conversation with Jennings did little to
reassure him. He knew that his mole in the justice
department would do anything he ordered. The
problem was whether or not he could follow through
without drawing more attention from the public eye.
Last night's shootout had been just as much of a fiasco
as the ordeal in Georgia a few weeks prior. That was
the sort of thing that got far too many people asking
questions. He sipped his coffee while sitting on a
balcony overlooking the desert to the west.

In the distance, The Grand Canyon wound it's way
through the landscape. Lindsey had gone there once as
a child. He recalled the experience as unpleasant. It
had been a particularly hot day. At the time he hadn't
cared for the desert climate. His father told him of how
sacred the land was. He believed that the veil between
God and man was thinner out there in the desolate
plains. Young Alex didn't fully understand at the time.
But as he grew older, his appreciation of spiritual
things became stronger. He spent hours each day
studying Biblical texts. Raised a devout Mormon, he
also spent a great deal of time researching the books of
the Latter Day Saints and believed strongly in their
ideals and teachings. He had been a zealous advocate
for the church. Until sixteen years ago.

Lindsey had been chosen to be one of the twelve
apostles, a group that was part of the council of the

church presidency. It was his father's dying wish that Alex become part of the presidency's cabinet and, because he was one of their primary benefactors, the church conceded to the old man's request. The other members of the group of apostles were receptive, at first, to the younger Lindsey's ideas and thoughts. He'd brought about new revenues and means of bringing in more converts through outreach programs and fundraising efforts. His influence grew stronger both within the church and outside of it. He had headed up subtle public relations campaigns that began erasing what had, for a long time, been a beleaguered opinion of Mormon beliefs. Then everything changed.

The church's President, Howard Hunter, passed away after serving only one year in the position. It was an unexpected event, and it forced the cabinet of advisors and apostles to prematurely gather together in prayer to elect their new leader.

It was no secret that Alexander wanted to be the next president, or prophet, as it was known. During the months leading up to Hunter's death, Lindsey had become noticeably more aggressive in his pursuit of the head position, something that was out of character for any apostle. Alexander had even mentioned publically how he would run things if he was in charge, something that left a foul taste in the mouths of the other council members. Apostles were pious men and were not expected to promote their own ends towards advancement since it was believed that God would choose the next leader through inspiration. When it came time to elect the new leader, he was not even among the final few nominated, a fact that had incited him to question the chamber's chairman.

The group elected Gordon Hinckley, effectively ensuring Lindsey's path to succession would never happen. Alexander was outraged. His family had contributed tens of millions of dollars to the church. The fundraising and outreach programs that he'd put together had helped double the church's revenue in just a few short years. Yet, he'd been told he was too young to be elected and that his brazen pursuit of the presidency belied a character not in keeping with the traditions of a prophet. They claimed that some of his ideas were too radical and would set a bad precedent. In the proceeding weeks he resigned from his post with the council and officially left the church, effectively wiping his name from their record books. He vowed then to make the old fools regret their mistakes. He never forgot that vow.

A warm breeze swept up the mountainside as he sipped his coffee. Caffeine was something the church had warned against. After his brisk exit he'd immediately revolted against most of their teachings, including many of the temperance beliefs.

His quiet reflections were interrupted by the ringing of a cell phone on the table next to him. He reached over and picked it up, hoping it wasn't more bad news.

"We have their location, sir," the voice came through the earpiece.

Weaver and Collack had done their jobs after all. "Where?"

"In the mountains outside of Las Vegas. We traced a call from Schulz's phone a little while ago. We are moving in now," the voice continued.

Lindsey wondered what Sean Wyatt was up to.

"Wait." He thought for a moment. "Fall back and watch. They may still be of some used to us. Perhaps they will lead us to the next clue."

"Yes sir."

Lindsey hung up the phone and peered out into the vast desert. *Let the pawns make their moves.*

Chapter 22
Cartersville, Georgia

The phone near the computer rang loudly. Joe McElroy was busy reading through the day's news on the monitor when he heard the ring.

His wife was outside working in the yard. Since he'd gotten home from the hospital, he'd not been able to do the kind of things he had before. One day last week he went by his office at the ranger station at the state park just to grab a few things but other than that Joe had been resigned to staying at home while his arm healed. It drove him crazy being cooped up like an animal. Even though the things that happened a few weeks ago were harrowing, he had not felt so alive in a long time. Adventure was something that he missed but he was content with his life. He had a good woman, a great job, and a beautiful cabin in the woods. But helping Sean had brought out something in him that he'd thought was long since dead.

Another ring snapped him back to the cabin. "Hello?"

"Joe!" the familiar voice said loudly from the other end. "How you feelin' buddy?"

"Tommy...," he shifted uneasily in his chair. "I'm doing much better, thanks." While he spoke he stood up and looked outside to make sure his wife was still blowing leaves. She was down the driveway a good hundred feet away accompanied by the distant sound of the machine attached to her back. "What's going on buddy?" he asked, satisfied she wouldn't know what he was doing.

"I need your help with something."

Joe eased back into the chair at his workstation, eagerly anticipating what Tommy had to say. His beady eyes gleamed and his smile raised the beard on his face slightly. "What ya got?"

"The translation for the second stone."

McElroy was already busy typing on the keyboard. He stopped suddenly. "Really? That was quick. How'd you pull that off?"

"A friend had some software that solved the riddle." Tommy paused. "Now that friend is dead." He paused a few seconds. "There are some odd lines in this one. It says, '*In desert mountains above the meadows' sand, the sunlight points the way. The lions watch the gate to the spider's lair. Though the distance is great, take guidance from the eagle's wings to the river between the great mountains in the southern land. Leaves of three unlock the door.*'"

Joe sat quietly thinking for a minute. The sound of the leaf blower still permeated the wall from outside confirming his wife was still busy. "Lions?" Joe sounded confused. "I don't remember hearing much about lions in Native culture. Although there is one place...." He began typing furiously on the computer's keypad again. After a few moments, he clicked the mouse on something that caught his eye on the screen. Bandelier National Monument. That's probably your best place to start lookin'."

"New Mexico?"

"That's what Google says."

"You're not looking at Wikipedia are you? Because —"

"No," Joe cut him off. "I'm looking at the government site. Bandelier had a Native settlement there a long time ago. They left behind some ruins and a couple of stone lions lying side by side on the ground." He read a few more lines on the screen before continuing. "Seems that no one really knows why the two lion sculptures are there."

"I'll take a look at it. Any idea about the rest of the riddle?"

Joe typed in some new words and phrases into the search engine, but, as he scanned through the content, nothing caught his eye. "I'll have to get back to you on the rest of it, buddy. Nothing is really popping out at the moment."

"Okay, Mac. I appreciate your help."

"No problem, Tommy. Sean still out in Vegas?"

"At the moment."

Suddenly, Joe heard the door leading into the garage start creaking open. He realized the sound of the leaf blower was painfully absent.

"Sorry partner, I gotta go. Talk soon." He didn't wait for Tommy to say goodbye and hung up the phone just as his wife entered through the door.

Chapter 23
Las Vegas, Nevada

Sean stared at the book in disbelief. He'd heard rumors that such a thing existed. But in his line of work he heard a lot of things. *Adriana was turning out to be a woman full of surprises.* "May I?" he asked, longing to see the pages within.

"Of course," she motioned for him to proceed. "Put these on." She produced a pair of white gloves from a pocket.

After he slipped them on, he cautiously opened the first page of the old book. Fortunately, he had learned enough Spanish over the years to be able to interpret most of what he saw. A lot of the contents were just gibberish, mentioning conditions, supplies, etc. There was a picture of the golden leaf drawn on one page, probably from the description the shaman had given. But what came after that was what interested Sean.

This morning, before the sun arose, I left our camp in secret and climbed high up into the mountains. So much of this rugged terrain looks the same. I feared that I would never discover the relic I sought. My suspicions were becoming greater that the medicine man who had led us to this place had either deceived me or believed that I was not clever enough to solve his riddle. When I had reached the peak of a nearby mountain, I sat in quiet prayer as the sun began to peek over the mountain range to the east. As I finished, I noticed a beam of sunlight shining through an odd hole located in a stone formation about one hundred feet away. The strange alignment of the rocks appeared to be manmade, the hole itself bored out through the center of a large, square stone. I turned to see where the light was shining and found that a tiny dot of sunlight rested on a rock about twenty feet away. Curious, I walked over to the spot and upon further inspection realized that the stone-- about the size of a man-- had been put there by humans. I checked behind it and noticed there was a narrow sliver of space. With renewed vigor, I climbed up onto a ledge behind the large stone and leveraged it with my feet, pushing with my back against the wall. The giant piece toppled over and I fell down and into the opening of a cave. Inside I found an ancient leaf of gold, which was illuminated by the ray of sunlight shining into a stone chamber.

I do not know who left this relic here but they went through much trouble to hide it. Standing before it, I realized that I could not remove it from this sacred resting place.

Perhaps the medicine man believed I could not remove it or perhaps would not. He told me only the worthy could take the leaf to re-unite it with the others. And the person who did so would have the power of the gods. I deserve no such power. The person who accomplishes this must be of a purer heart than mine. Still, I wonder where the other pieces are.

Sean finished reading the passage and turned the page. There were no other entries. He looked back at Adriana and handed her the book. "Others?" he asked, curious.

"The others Coronado refer to are known as the Sumar Plates. They are supposed to point the way to the second chamber."

Emily spoke up suddenly. "Second chamber? What if no one found the first one? Couldn't we just skip a few steps and get to the end?"

Their host turned to her as she spoke. "The path from one chamber to the next cannot be completed without the stone from the previous. Each stone, like the one discovered in Georgia, have unique qualities. The original stone does not point the way to the second chamber, only the first."

"The stone we found at the chamber looked exactly like the first one except for the message on one side and the picture on the other," Sean stated.

Adriana looked uncertain. "The message from each stone points the way to the next. It would be impossible to find the chambers out of order."

She took the diary back to the safe and laid it inside carefully. "Did you happen to notice anything usual about the stone's shape?"

Sean took a minute to think but nothing came to mind. A beeping noise suddenly sounded from her front jeans pocket. Adriana reached in and looked at her cell phone.

"What is it?" Emily asked.

"Looks like we need to be leaving," Adriana replied with a concerned look in her eyes. "I believe they found us."

Chapter 24
Las Vegas, Nevada

The two black Ford Explorers were parked behind a few abandoned campers on the plain at the foot of the mountain. The rotting remains of the trailers provided the only cover in the desert plains leading up to the mountains.

"How long are we going to sit here," Angela said into her microphone as she wiped a bead of sweat off of her forehead.

James responded from the other SUV. "As long as it takes."

"As long as it takes for what? Our engines to blow up?" He ignored her snide comment. "What if they decided to just hang out for a few days?" Frustration was evident in her voice.

"We were ordered to hold back and observe. I'm certain they will be on the move soon."

"What's the problem?" Emily asked as the three left the stone corridor and closed the heavy door behind them.

"I have a perimeter warning system here," Villa answered. "Someone is on the premises."

She led them back up into the house to a small room that was probably meant to be an office but instead looked like a small security center. Six computer screens displayed camera views of different places surrounding the property. She typed a few keys and the screen with a blinking red border zoomed in. Two black SUVs sat waiting by a couple of old RV campers down near the base of the mountain.

"Our friends from last night?" Sean asked.

"Probably," their host answered as she zoomed in on one of the trucks with a toggle.

"Looks like they're waiting to ambush us." Emily theorized.

"Maybe," he said. "More than likely they're waiting to see what we're going to do next. If they were going to keep trying to kill us they'd have already come up the mountain."

"What are we going to do next?"

Both women looked at him expectantly.

"Well, we can't just sit here all day. I say we make a run for it." He looked at Adriana. "You up for a little car chase?"

She smiled and twirled the keys on her index finger.

Villa guided the SUV carefully along the mountain road until they came to the last hidden turn near the bottom. She looked back at Sean who was strapped in and ready. Then she punched it, kicking up dirt and gravel behind them.

The black Audi roared across the desert plain back towards the city. Up ahead they could see the campers and just behind them, the two trucks of their pursuers.

Suddenly, Sean's phone started ringing in his left pocket. It was Joe. "Hey Mac. I'm not sure I got a lot of time to talk right now. What's up?"

"In more trouble?"

"You know me." Sean said as the Q7 sailed off of the dirt road and onto asphalt again. He turned and looked behind them, switching his cell phone to the other ear. In the dust cloud behind he could make out the two black vehicles pulling out and heading in their direction.

Joe chuckled. "Yeah. I do. Listen, Sean. I just got off the phone with Tommy a few minutes ago and then tried calling him back but he didn't answer so I thought I'd give you a shout. You still in Vegas?"

"Yeah, sorta."

Adriana veered the car into the outskirts of town. Their vehicle was much faster than the two chasing them. He just hoped they didn't see any police. With the crazy scene that was surely still going on over at the Venetian, he doubted many would be out giving speeding tickets.

"Good," Joe's deep southern accent brought his mind back to the phone call. "You need to go to the Grand Canyon."

"I've been there before. Not sure if I'm going to have time to do it again today, buddy."

"Not for sight seein'," McElroy corrected. "Tommy gave me the interpretation for the second stone. I believe that the first part of the clue leads to Bandelier National Monument in New Mexico. It talks about two lions guarding the way."

"So, why The Grand Canyon if the first place is Bandelier?"

"Tommy is already headed to Bandelier. The next part of the riddle talks about eagles wings guiding the way. I didn't really think about it while I was on the phone with him, but I did a little looking around after we hung up.

"There is a place called, 'Eagle Point' at the Grand Canyon. That's where I think another piece of the puzzle is."

"Are you sure? I mean, there could be a few dozen places named after eagles or other birds in this country. Why that spot?" Sean speculated.

"It's the only one that makes sense. If we go on what we know based on the first chamber, the people that left the clues did so in a general area. All the ones we found before were within a few hundred miles of each other. Stands to reason they wouldn't change that method now."

"Ok, ignoring the fact that these locations are much further apart, before one clue led to the next one. You're making it sound like there is no order to it this time."

"I thought about that too. This new riddle is different. Even though the location perimeter might be similar, the way to get there doesn't have to be. From what I can tell, you don't need to visit the spots in any order this time. Well, except the last one. Plus, you will need to find three items. They should look like leaves. We are still working on the third location. I'll let you know if we find it."

Sean smiled. He realized that Adriana had already found one piece of the puzzle. "We already found it, Mac."

"Really?" Joe sounded amazed. "How'd you do that?"

Sean looked into the back of the cargo area. A towel lay on the floor, bundled as if it was wrapped around something. "It's a long story. I'll explain when we get back."

"We?"

"I'll explain that too."

Adriana swerved onto a side street then another, trying to lose their followers.

"Thanks, Mac. I gotta go."

"No problem, Sean. I'll let you know if I can figure out any other part of this thing."

Wyatt hung up the phone as Adriana pulled the car into an alley between a pawn shop and a tattoo parlor.

"What are we doing?" He asked.

She glanced over at him. "Giving them a chance to lose us."

A few tense minutes went by as they waited to see if the people chasing them would appear. The only thing that cut the quiet in the air was the easy hum of the engine and the gentle blowing of the air conditioner.

Adriana turned to Sean. "Who was that on the phone?"

"My friend Joe. He's an expert in Native American history. Says we should go to The Grand Canyon." She looked uncertain. "He said he thinks that Eagle Point is where we can find another clue."

"Is he sure? That's a few hours from here," Emily asked.

"I wondered the same thing. Joe said he thinks that's it. I trust him." He paused. "You ever been to

The Grand Canyon?" Emily shook her head. "What about you?" he asked Adriana.

"No," Adriana answered bluntly.

"Oh," he smiled. "Now there are *two* reasons for us to go." A cute grin crept onto the side of her mouth as she eyed him.

She didn't say a thing as she stepped on the gas and steered the Audi back out onto the road towards the interstate.

Chapter 25
Santa Fe, New Mexico

Tommy and Will had taken the agency jet from Atlanta to the desert southwest a few hours before. Will had gotten clearance from the boss to provide police protection for Tommy, which meant he had to go wherever the archaeologist went. The pilot was not exactly happy about having to file a flight plan on such short notice but then again, he knew the deal when he signed up for the job. It was good pay and really very few hours. The only catch was that sometimes Schultz or Wyatt needed to fly somewhere on short notice. It was early in the afternoon when they had landed in the high desert. The sun beat down warmly on the tarmac as they'd exited the plane and hopped in the car that had been made ready by agency connections at the airport. Nothing fancy but it would do the job.

Tommy guided the gray Chevy Cruze down the highway leading out of Santa Fe towards Bandelier National Monument. He had been paranoid, constantly checking in the rear view mirror to see if they were being followed. There hadn't been anything out of the ordinary, though. The craggy desert mountains that had lingered in the distance were now surrounding them as the straight road became curvy, weaving in and out of the dry terrain. Cypress trees dotted the landscape along with some Schultz didn't recognize, their pale-green foliage splashed a contrast of color onto the natural canvas setting. The drive up had been somewhat silent. Both men were tired from the events of the night before and didn't feel much like talking. Tommy was okay with that. He didn't like forced conversation anyway.

"That the place?" Will broke the long silence.

Up ahead, the tourist and information center for Bandelier National Monument appeared in a clearing situated in the middle of a rocky canyon.

Tommy eased the car into an empty parking spot in front of the tourist information building. The air was cool and dry, fairly typical for the high desert during that time of year. In the winter, temperatures could reach zero at times while the summer sported highs in the 100s.

Will took a deep breath. "I love the air out here. Clears up my sinuses," he said with a big smile.

Tommy laughed. "Well, we do live in one of the worst places in the world for allergies."

"I think I remember reading about that."

The two men closed the car doors and made their way into the wooden structure and over to an information desk. There were only a few tourists milling around inside, probably belonging to the two other cars that were in the parking lot.

Behind the desk, a happy looking Native American woman stood next to a computer checking something on the screen. As they approached, she turned and greeted them with a robust and genuine smile. Her round face and long, black hair framed the squinting eyes and huge grin. She was fairly short, but stood proudly in her park ranger uniform. "Welcome to Bandelier. Can I help you, gentlemen?" She asked in a perky tone that surprised both men. Apparently, she liked her job.

Schultz returned the smile. "Yes, we are doing a little research on ceremonial artwork of Native Americans from this region, and we were wondering if you could show us where the stone lion sculptures were located."

"Actually, we have a replica of the sculpture right outside that door over there if you would like to see it. It was cast directly from the original." She pointed past some display cases to a door off to the side of the large room.

"I don't mean to be rude but would it be possible to see the originals? I'm kind of a history buff."

She opened up a drawer and pulled out a small piece of paper with a little map on it. "The original site is right here," she pointed to a spot on the map that had a drawing in the likeness of the sculpture. "Just take this trail to get there. It's only a short walk. "We do ask," she added, "that you treat the location with care. It is a sacred site for our people and should be treated with great respect." Her smile had been replaced by a solemn look.

"Understood," Tommy replied. "We will leave no evidence we were there. Thank you so much."

The two men walked out the door and found the prescribed trail.

"What was that all about?" Will asked. "Sacred site?"

"Ancient Native locations are all some of these tribes have left of their ancestors or their traditions. Most

131

Native Americans had everything taken from them in one form or another. The last few spots they can cling to must be respected by all since they are their only direct link to the past."

Will nodded silently, understanding the gravity and implication of Schultz's words.

The path was actually well maintained, evidence that the place they were going was still visited consistently. There weren't a lot of sounds along the desert path that wound through the canyon. An occasional bird would chirp for a minute or two in one of the scattered trees nearby. Tommy wondered if they might see any snakes. He and Sean both had a healthy fear of that particular reptile, venomous or not. In the area they were walking through, rattlesnakes were common. Even though they had their patented warning sound that resonated from their tails, rattlers didn't necessarily use them all the time.

The two men plodded their way through the warm air until they came around a small curve in the trail and found themselves entering a small clearing. The scent of sage filled their nostrils. It seemed the plant grew vigorously in the high desert. Then up ahead they noticed a circle of large stones. Each rock was laid on its end as if pointing to the sky and they were all packed in tightly next to each other. In the middle of the stone circle, two ancient pieces of what appeared to be boulders lay side by side. As the men drew closer they began to see clearer, the design of the ancient sculptors.

The stones were carved in the shapes of two mountain lions, both facing the same direction. It was unlike anything Tommy had ever seen before.

Even though history or archaeology wasn't necessarily Will's thing, he still had an odd sense of reverence about him as he observed the site. "What did they use it for?" He asked just barely above a whisper.

Tommy shook his head. "I'm not sure. I believe they currently use it mostly for ceremonies. Originally?" He shrugged. "I'm hoping that we're about to find out."

He stepped around the circle carefully, looking at every angle trying to see if he could notice anything out of the ordinary. Nothing jumped out at him, though.

"See anything?" Will was copying Schultz but was essentially useless. He had no idea what he was looking for.

Tommy appreciated his help, though. At least the cop was trying. "No. Not a thing." He put his hands on his hips and let out a deep sigh of frustration. Whatever was there had been hidden for thousands of years, so he doubted it would be easy to find, if it was even still there.

The possibility that ancient looters had taken whatever had been hidden was always something that endangered any artifact recovery mission. He'd seen it dozens of times in the years since IAA was founded.

One of the more noted instances of such a problem was the great pyramids in Egypt. Grave robbers had taken nearly all the treasures from them centuries ago.

"What was it Joe said about these lions?" Will wondered out loud as he stepped lightly around the big rocks.

Tommy set down the small backpack he'd brought on the trip and reached inside, pulling out a circular piece of stone. He palmed it reverently as he spoke. "The riddle says that the lions watch the gate."

"Is that the one from Georgia?"

Schultz nodded. "I thought it might come in handy," he said as he ran his fingers along the smooth stone with the spider engraved on one side, the ancient text on the other. He eyed the unique piece's carvings. His mind went back to the lions in front of him. It didn't make sense.

He stared at the time and weather-worn faces of the old sculptures and wondered. The only thing that lay beyond them was desert plains and cacti. "I can't figure out what it is they're guarding," he said finally. "According to the message on the stone, they are supposed to be guardians, but the only thing that lies in that direction is desert. We could walk for miles and still not see anything."

Will turned around and looked in the direction Tommy was pointing. Then he spun back around and pointed at a rock formation in the Canyon's edge behind where Schultz was standing. "What about back there?"

Tommy spun around and looked at the smooth rock face of the canyon with several large stones standing at its base. Random holes and mini-caves dotted the wall, probably worn out by time. Some were probably used by natives from the local tribes in ancient times, accessed by ladders in case of flooding or attack.

"The lions are supposed to be guarding the location," Tommy responded. "They would have the gate to their back if that's the case."

Will frowned, deep in thought. "But the clue said they 'watch the gate.' If that's the case, wouldn't they be looking at it?"

Tommy pursed his lips. Will was right.

He turned around and faced the reddish-tan stone of the canyon wall then looked back at the lions. Cautiously, he straddled the stone perimeter and stepped into the sand-filled circle where the lions rested silently. There was a narrow space between the two figures, so Tommy got down on the ground and wedged himself into it. He peered at the wall from the point of view of the sculptures. A fairly large, rounded piece of sandstone lay directly ahead abutted against the canyon wall about fifty yards away. "It's over there," he said confidently.

Will leaned over trying to see exactly the spot where Schultz was pointing.

"See it?"

"Yeah," Will nodded. "Let's check it out."

Tommy stood up and dusted off the sand from his jeans and flannel shirt and made his way out of the circle, grabbing his backpack off the ground.

Will joined him on the other side and the two started walking towards the area they'd just seen.

"It's interesting," Tommy spoke suddenly as they crested a small sandy hill and descended down the other beyond sage brush and some small cacti. "These little hills hide that spot unless you are looking at it from just the right angle. The dip in the terrain reveals the location. Otherwise, no one would think that big rock was anything out of the ordinary."

Will nodded in agreement.

Suddenly, the sound of a rattle began shaking nearby. Both men froze instantly.

Chapter 26
The Grand Canyon West

It had taken a little under two hours to make the drive from Las Vegas to Grand Canyon West. The occupants of the black Audi hadn't said much except for comments on how desolate the area was on the way.

Emily had asked a little about Adriana's past, where she'd gone to school, lived, worked, those kinds of things. The answers had been an intriguing hodgepodge of seemingly random locales and activities. Adriana had come from a town about thirty minutes from Madrid, as Sean had already learned. She left home, briefly to attend high school in Copenhagen, Denmark until she was seventeen years old. When her mother had become sick Villa returned to Spain. From there, she went to Boston College in the United States, majoring in History with a minor in Chemistry.

"That's an odd combination," Sean had commented.

Her reply was cryptic. "The chemistry has bailed me out of trouble more than once."

He hadn't followed up with the line of questioning.

After earning her undergraduate degree she had worked for one of her father's enterprises for a short time, establishing a global network of coffee growers and partners. They had coffee fields in Central and South America, as well as a few locations in Uganda, Kenya, and Ethiopia.

"One of the primary things I wanted to do with our company was improve the quality of life in countries where people were in need. We established *fair trade* coffee farms and helped the ones that already existed get better international distribution. "Because of the work of our company, more than 10,000 people have jobs with decent wages or own their own businesses. Infrastructure and education has improved in those places as have the lives of the populations."

"All from coffee." Sean said quietly, thoughtful.

"Mmhmm." She confirmed.

Shortly after the drive through the outpost town of Dolan Springs, the paved roads came to an end, and they found themselves cruising down a dirt and gravel road that led through the desert. Joshua trees and sage grew intermittently in the sandy, rocky earth. Huge stone formations jutted up into the sky and loomed ominously near the dusty road that wound its way through a ravine. Eventually, they ended up on a sort of plateau that ended at the Grand Canyon West visitor's center.

Helicopters buzzed around the area like bees in a hive. A few were flying high above the canyon giving their passengers an overall view before diving down into the colossal crevasse. Others were sitting with rotors turning slowly, either just returning from a flight or about to head out.

After parking the SUV, the three got out and headed towards a white-fabric domed building. The ceiling of the structure was held up by air pressure from the inside, a fact that was reiterated by the revolving doors at the entrance and exit.

Sean made his way over to one of the information desks while the women looked around the room at the various souvenirs and trinkets available for purchase. A cheerful looking Native American woman with long, black hair and a narrow face stood behind the desk, smiling as he approached.

"Good afternoon," she greeted him. "How can I help you today?"

He returned the smile while he answered, "I was wanting to take a look at Eagle Point, preferably as close as possible."

Her grin turned to confusion. "I don't understand."

"I'd like to get close look at the location called, *Eagle Point*. What's the best way to do to that?"

His new explanation didn't help her out much. "Sir, Eagle point is a rock formation in the middle of the canyon. You can't get close to it."

He thought for a minute, uncertain what to do.

"You could take a helicopter ride. That could get you pretty close to it." Her suggestion seemed like a possibility.

After a few moments of contemplation, he thought that doing a little recon work first might be the best course of action. "Can I just get three tickets to take the short tour around the area?"

"Sure. That will take about one hour to visit Eagle Point and Guano Point before returning here."

"Guano Point?" Sean snorted a small laugh. "Isn't Guano bat crap?"

"Yes, sir it is," she cut him off with a laugh of her own. "It's the best fertilizer in the world, and it has been harvested from a cave on site here for a long time.

"Would you like to add tickets to the sky walk?" She added while she rang up the tickets.

"Is that the glass walkway that goes out over the canyon?"

"Yep," she seemed proud.

He shook his head violently. "I'll pass. I have a thing with heights."

She puckered her lips and nodded in understanding then handed him three tickets.

"Just head out that door right over there and you will see the line forming to get on the next bus out to the point."

"Thanks," he said as he clutched the tickets and walked over to where Emily and Adriana were eyeing some Native American jewelry.

"You two ready to go?"

"What did you find out?" Emily asked.

"Apparently we have to take a tour bus over to Eagle Point, but we can't get close enough at the moment. I thought it would be a good idea to see what we're working with first before we do anything else."

Emily nodded in agreement. Sean's thoroughness was something she wished more of her agents had.

He handed them their tickets. "We get on the bus out there," he said as he pointed to the exit.

A few minutes later they were on the air-conditioned shuttle, a major contrast to the desert warmth outside. Even though the evenings and mornings could be cool that time of the year, the afternoons could still get fairly hot by southern standards.

The ride over to Eagle Point was only about ten minutes. After arriving, the tourists on board got out in an orderly fashion despite a few people wishing they could edge their way out a little faster.

Once outside, the magnitude of the location set in. The Grand Canyon spread out before them as far as their eyes could see. The red stone walls jutted down thousands of feet until they reached the Colorado River below.

"I cannot believe how enormous this is," Adriana said quietly. Sean had gotten the impression that she was not easily amazed so seeing her awe of the landscape surprised him.

Emily and Adriana stepped over to the edge to get a closer look of how far down it really was. Sean wasn't nearly as eager to get near the precipice. "Don't you want to take a look?" Adriana asked.

Sean simply shook his head slowly. "No. I'm good."

"He's deathly afraid of heights," Emily explained.

Adriana raised an eyebrow. "So, the great Sean Wyatt is afraid of something after all."

"We all have our things," he defended. *She didn't need to know beautiful women was another one.*

He made his way over towards an old railing that stood about ten feet from the edge. Even being that close to such a huge drop off was somewhat unnerving to him. He'd been afraid of heights since he was a child.

When he was young, Sean would play with his friends and cousins in the trees near his house. They built tree houses and seemed fearless with how high they would climb. Young Wyatt would regularly find himself at the top of an old cedar tree near their house. For some reason, climbing those trees never bothered him. But it never cured him of a fear of heights either. Being up in tall buildings or high cliffs always bothered him. He figured it always would.

Out across the giant gash in the earth, about five to six hundred feet away, a narrow rock formation rose up in the middle of the canyon. It had a thin ridge that ran parallel with the canyon walls. In one spot in the middle of the formation dropped down about fifty feet. It then ran another few hundred feet.

In the middle of where the break in the ridge was something that caught Sean's eye. A smaller rock formation popped up in the middle of the other and looked somewhat like a large bird with wings spread in both directions, the head of peering silently off to the east.

"Eagle point," he whispered to himself. He understood what the lady at the visitor center meant when she'd said they couldn't get close to it. The other realization that hit him was that a standard helicopter ride wouldn't get them close enough either. They were going to need another way.

Chapter 27
Bandelier National Monument, New Mexico

A thick diamondback rattlesnake sat coiled about seven feet from where Tommy and Will were about to walk. Its tail shook violently, so fast that the movement appeared blurred.

"Maybe we should go around it," Will said.

Tommy's eyes were wide with terror. The color had left his face a pale ashen color. He nodded silently, and the two men began to carefully step backwards at a snail's pace.

The pointed head of the snake pulled back slightly towards its body, as if readying for an attack. After backtracking a few steps the men turned and continued around the snake's location, careful to keep a good distance from the reptile. Upon reaching the rock wall, Schultz walked around to the other side and began investigating the area where the rock met the canyon wall, trying to see if he could detect anything behind it. Will did the same, running his finger along the back edge of the stone to see if he could feel an opening.

"There's no way we can move this thing," Will said.

Tommy knew he was right. The big rock had to be at least a few tons. It was oddly shaped, like a tall finger pointing up at the sky. Near the top of it, about ten feet high, a rut was carved into the stone, providing a groove that wrapped around the entire piece.

"Can you feel anything behind there on your side?" he asked Will after a minute of examination.

"Nah, man. I can't feel anything. You sure this is it?"

"Pretty sure."

Tommy stepped away from the pillar and rubbed the scruff on his face in silent contemplation. A few moments later, he sat his backpack down and pulled out some black rope.

"What are you thinking?" Will asked curiously.

Tommy's hands worked the nylon rope quickly, forming a loop at one end. "We can use that grove at the top to leverage the thing over," he answered as he walked back over to the stone and tossed the lasso towards the top.

The first throw didn't catch but the second one did, slipping down around the head of the stone and into the groove. A few moments later, Tommy had pulled the nylon tight and was stepping backwards with one end. Will grinned and grabbed another piece of the rope just above Tommy's hands. The rope went taught and both men pulled steadily. Their leverage on the top of the stone moved it almost immediately, and the gigantic piece of rock tipped over with a loud thud onto its side in a matter of seconds, sending rolling clouds of dust up into the air. They dropped the rope and walked over to the wall where the stone had been standing. Both men turned to look at each other for a second after what they had seen. A narrow portal entered into the canyon wall.

"That rock was a perfect fit, huh?"

"Yeah," Tommy agreed. The dust continued to settle while he grabbed a few flashlights out of his backpack.

"Are there gonna booby traps or anything like that in there?" Will sounded sarcastic yet a little uncertain.

"You never know." Tommy played with him.

"Really?"

"No. Well, not usually anyway. Most of the time the stuff that was designed to protect ancient treasures has long since gone into disrepair. Pretty sure we're not going to be getting chased out of here by a giant rolling stone."

Will laughed at the reference. "That was a cool movie, though."

Tommy smiled as he passed him a flashlight. The two men stepped over the foot of the big stone they'd just overturned and into the darkness of the entrance. The thin passage was only about six feet high and three feet wide. Its walls were smooth, cut with laser-precision from the ancient rock of the canyon. The shape of the corridor was wider at the bottom than the top, giving it the appearance of a kind of pyramidal hallway. A floor of solid stone lay under their feet.

Tommy ran his hand along wall as they proceeded slowly away from the light outside. "No one has been in here in a long time," he said reverently. There were a few dusty spider webs where the angles of the walls met the ceiling. Tommy brushed them away with his light as they moved further into the rock mountain. The passageway came to an abrupt halt a few feet ahead, turning a perfect ninety degrees to the left. Both men moved carefully, leery of what lay around the corner. Will pulled his gun out of its holster and held it at the ready. Tommy looked at him with a funny expression. "What are you gonna shoot in here?"

"I don't know," Will answered. "You can never be too careful."

Tommy shook his head mockingly then eased his way around the corner, shining the light down the next part of the passage. There was nothing ahead except what looked like another turn in the hall.

The two pressed on and discovered four additional sharp changes in the corridor. After ten minutes of working their way into the mountain Will was beginning to wonder where the path was leading. "I'm starting to feel like a rat in some kind of maze."

"I know what you mean," Tommy agreed but kept moving slowly ahead.

After one more right turn Tommy came to an abrupt halt. Will aimed his light in the direction Schultz was looking. The bright beams illuminated a large room that opened up out of the passageway. Some parts of the chamber were carved out of the mountain rock by human hands, while other bits of it looked somewhat natural. The dusty scent in the air had given way to the moist odor of a cavern. In the center of the room, about thirty feet away, a rectangular, stone pedestal rose from the floor.

On top of it rested something shiny and metallic.

Will started to take a step forward, but Tommy put his hand out and stopped him. "Careful."

The young cop appeared confused. "I thought you said there were no booby traps," he said sarcastically.

Tommy gave him a warning glare. "I said there were *probably* none." He made sure to emphasize his uncertainty as he scanned the floor with his flashlight.

"What are you looking for?" Will asked while he moved his light around the vaulted ceiling of the enormous room.

"Pressure points. I've heard of some places that had false floors. If you step on them, it triggers some kind of ancient security measures."

Will looked at him with wide eyes. "Take your time."

He looked around for another minute or so; satisfied that nothing appeared sinister, he stepped from the passage into the chamber.

A few moments later both men were standing at the pedestal, eyeing the odd piece of gold that rested on it's top. The stone altar had various forms of writing on it that had not used in millennia. Tommy was busy looking over some of it in an attempt to understand what it said. Will reached out his hand to feel the golden leaf. "Don't touch that," Tommy stopped him without looking up from his investigation of the altar.

"Let me guess, booby trap?"

"You never know."

Tommy set his backpack down and pulled out his digital camera from the front pouch. The flash of the camera seemed odd in the ancient room.

"Can you read that?" Will asked after a few moments.

"Some of it," he answered while moving to get some different angles. "Ancient languages are not my area of expertise. I'm better at identifying timeframes and cultures. Most of this language comes from a very long time ago. It's kind of a predecessor to ancient Hebrew.

"It says something about the eagles and where the rivers unite, which we got from the stone." Tommy pulled the small stone out of his backpack and held it up to examine the similarities of some of the writing. "It's very curious." He put the small stone back in his bag and began evaluating the gold piece. He'd never seen anything like it in all his years of archaeological work. The yellow metal was thin, almost delicate. It had been carved to an incredible level of detail to look almost exactly like a real leaf.

"What is it?" Will asked just above a whisper.

"I have no idea."

Hunter Carlson moved along the canyon path with his team. He was a strong man with short, dark blonde hair. He wore Ray Ban sunglasses, a rolled up sleeved-flannel shirt, hiking boots, and some khakis. Three other men followed him. All four of the men carried Glock nine millimeters in a ready position as they stepped quickly through the canyon. The long, box-type sound suppressors may have been a bulky and perhaps unnecessary precaution out in the wilderness but one never knew if there were curious tourists around. *Best not to attract too much attention.*

The three other men were dressed just as casually, wanting to look more like sightseers than a hit squad, save for the weapons.

They had gotten word that Schultz was heading to New Mexico to visit an area north of Santa Fe so they had made quick preparations, all taken care of by the Order. Carlson wondered who shot at him the other night at Georgia Tech. He had gone back to the lab to see what else he could find on the computer. His assumption that there would only be a few police officers at the scene had been correct. He hadn't anticipated Schultz and the other man showing up, though.

Up ahead, his point man was drawing nearer to a large, overturned stone that lay next to the cave entrance. They'd watched silently from a distance as Schultz and his companion had discovered the hidden opening in the canyon wall. After waiting a few minutes, Carlson was satisfied his team could safely advance without being seen. Suddenly, the man in front screamed out and dropped his weapon, clutching his right leg in pain. The other men froze momentarily, unsure of what had just happened. "Thompson, what's happening up there?" Hunter asked into the microphone strapped around his neck.

The man nearest the fallen member stepped close to see what the problem was. The man on the ground was writhing in pain, gripping his leg tightly. Then, the flank man who'd come to check on the issue turned quickly and fired off three rounds towards the ground. Hunter moved up quickly to see what had happened.

"It's a snakebite, sir," the man who'd just fired his weapon explained. He pointed to the large diamondback rattler that lay motionless with three bloody wounds in its scaly flesh, a prominent one in its head.

The injured mercenary tried to keep from moaning too loudly as the venom of the snake moved through his bloodstream. Terror filled the man's eyes.

Out in the middle of nowhere, they were at least forty-five minutes from the nearest hospital. That was about how long the poison from a rattlesnake took to kill a man, depending on the last time the snake had used its fangs.

Hunter recalled what a friend had told him once about receiving a snakebite. He'd said that the venom moving through the body felt like every inch of bone was being crushed as it progressed through the bloodstream.

"They should have a snakebite kit in the information center," one of the other team members declared.

Carlson looked down at the man who continued to writhe in agony. Hope welled up in the bitten man's eyes for a moment as he realized the tourist center would certainly have a kit. A typical snakebite kit could stabilize him long enough to get him to a hospital. It would also draw unwanted attention. Hunter raised his weapon and fired a single shot into Thompson's head. The body went limp on the sandy earth. Dead eyes on either side of a dark hole stared up into the desert sky.

The team leader looked at the remaining two men. "I would do the same to you and would expect both of you to do the same to me. Understood?"

Both men nodded immediately.

Following Hunter's lead, the other two helped drag the body over behind a large patch of sage and left it on the ground unceremoniously. He hadn't wanted to kill one of his assets, but the man had been careless. The three stepped towards the entrance to the canyon passage with renewed caution. They could ill afford any more surprises.

Tommy stared at the magnificent golden leaf. Its odd shape was like no artifact he'd ever seen before. He'd thrown down several glow sticks that he'd taken from his pack. The devices cast an eerie, pale light across the room. He squatted down to get a better view underneath the bottom of the yellow metal. Reaching up, he tipped part of the object up just slightly. Just as he suspected, there was a small stone column that the gold rested upon. "That's what I thought," he stated in frustration.

"What is it?" Will asked, curiously as he stepped around to the side Schultz was investigating.

"A weight spring," he said plainly. Will raised an eyebrow, obviously not sure what a weight spring was. Tommy explained, "Since they didn't have real springs back then, they had to improvise. So, they came up with a small weight and balance system, sort of like a teeter-totter. If you take the weight off of one side the other side will go down. They didn't use strings or metal for stuff like this because those materials would deteriorate over time."

"There's a contraption like that inside that pedestal?" Will looked amazed by the thought.

"Looks like it. If we take that piece of gold off I'm not sure what will happen."

"No booby traps, huh?" Will's voice was every bit as sarcastic as the look on his face.

Tommy didn't respond. Instead, he carefully lowered the edge of the piece back down and stood up scratching his head. "We need to get this thing out of here," he said after a moment of thought.

"Why don't you just replace the gold with something else that will keep the weight down?" Will interrupted his thoughts.

"That's the other problem. It could be designed for a particular weight. That would mean anything too heavy or too light would set off the mechanism. There's no way to know."

"So, what do we do?" Will asked.

"I wouldn't do anything if I were you." The new voice startled both men; they quickly turned their heads towards the dark passageway.

Three new beams of light entered the dimly lit chamber, each mounted on the top of a handgun. Will started to make a move for his own weapon but one of the figures emerging from the corridor flashed a light in his direction. "I wouldn't do that either," the same voice warned.

Tommy turned to Will but could see the cop wasn't sure what to do either. They were trapped.

Chapter 28
Salt Lake City, UT

Alexander Lindsey sat in a high-back leather chair at the end of a long, mahogany conference table, staring at the seven men occupying the rest of the seats. His face was stern and his eyes unfeeling as he peered at each and every one of them. "The answer is no," he said plainly.

An older man positioned near the middle of the table, to Lindsey's right, looked outraged. "You have some nerve, you ungrateful swine. After all we have done for you--"

"All you have done for me?" Lindsey interrupted. "Tell me, Wallace, what you-- any of you-- have ever done for me."

Another man, probably Alexander's age, spoke up across the table. His face was thin and his hair had obviously been receding for years. "We brought you in. Took you to places you'd never have gotten on your own. Then, you abandoned your faith, your church, and your honor."

"Honor? Don't speak to me about honor, Nicholas," he replied with disgust. "I did more for the church and the faith than anyone else. It was my programs, my ideas that created the vast revenue stream that you so enjoyed for such a long time. "The well has dried up and you have overextended yourselves. Now you come to me asking for a handout after turning your back on me sixteen years ago?" No one else at the table said a word. They were all obviously frustrated. He continued, "All I asked for was to be the next president of the church. I could have taken it to new heights. You would all be richer than anyone in the country and all of your precious little mission work would be better funded than if it had come from the Vatican. "But you wouldn't have it." His voice became bitter.

"You wanted control. Your motivations were not pure, Alex," the older man spoke up again. "We offered you a chance to stay with the cabinet, but you wanted it all. And you wanted it for your own glory, not the glory of God."

"How glorious is your God now that you're broke?" The dark cynicism of his voice resonated through the room.

"That is blasphemy, Alex. May God have mercy on you."

Lindsey grinned on one side of his mouth. "Mercy on me? I'm doing just fine. You're the ones who need my money."

"We know what you're up to," a younger man who'd sat silently at the other end of the table spoke eagerly, as if he'd been holding it in the whole hour. A hushed silence fell across the room. The man who looked mid-thirties appeared uncertain that he should have said anything.

"What, pray tell, am I up to?" Alexander narrowed his eyes, curious as to who this buck thought he was.

"My name is Rick Baker," he replied, trying to keep his voice steady, "and I know about the treasure you're trying to find."

"Is that so?"

The rest of the men at the table looked confused. One leaned in close to Rick and asked him silently, "What are you talking about?"

Baker ignored him. "I know what you are trying to find, and why you're trying to find it."

"I have many hobbies, one of which is archaeology, but that is no concern of yours or this little 'committee'." Lindsey said the last word with deep sarcasm.

"You won't find it," Baker continued with more confidence. "God won't allow it. He hasn't for four thousand years. He won't let it be discovered now, not by you."

Everyone at the table was completely lost by the exchange. Apparently, Baker was the only one at the table who knew anything about what Alexander Lindsey was really up to, which was good. He would only have to eliminate the one committee member. *It might do some good to kill off one of them anyway to put them in their place and keep them off his back.* He stood and brushed down his suit jacket and tie, clearly getting ready to leave. "I don't have time for these ridiculous children's games. And my answer is still no. If you are short on money ask for more tithes and offerings from your congregations. It's what you preachers do best."

With that last stab, he stepped over to the door and exited the conference room, making his way down a long office hallway toward the exit sign. While he walked, his fingers typed a text message. *Rick Baker. Clean.*

Chapter 29
Bandelier National Monument, New Mexico

With guns trained, the three men stared at Tommy and Will. They had nowhere to run and essentially no cover in the large open room.

The pedestal was the only hiding place and wasn't going to be much help. Or would it? Tommy wasn't sure.

"Step away from the gold," the man ordered.

"Who are you?" Tommy asked, trying to stall them for a moment. His eyes searched the ceiling for anything. Then he saw it, above the entrance to the passage, a huge rectangular stone seemed oddly out of place, jutting out of the vaulted ceiling just slightly. He noticed other similar pieces above and realized what they were.

"You don't need to worry about that," the leader of the group said. "Just put your hands up and get away from the gold, nice and slow."

Will began to back up cautiously, raising his hands while he moved. Tommy moved too, but when he raised his hands he pushed them out sideways, knocking the gold leaf off the pedestal with his left hand. The artifact clanked to the floor, and the three men with guns flinched as the pang echoed through the room. A deep rumble began to resonate through the chamber as if the whole mountain was shaking. The armed men looked around for a moment as dust began to break loose from the ceiling. The ground beneath their feet vibrated violently.

Suddenly, the large stone Tommy had noticed over the doorway fell to the floor, crushing the man who still stood closest to the corridor. The rock instantly buried him under its weight; he never had a chance to scream.

The other two men realized what happened and looked up to the ceiling. Another stone, a little farther away and to their right, dropped and crashed to the floor with a thud. The man to the leader's right just barely dove out of the way.

Tommy watched one of the men flattened by the heavy object. It gave him a brief second and while the other two were distracted, he took a chance and dove towards the gold leaf. He grabbed it and stood in one motion.

The remaining two armed men caught the movement near the altar and turned to fire.

Tommy darted back towards Will. The young cop reacted quickly and pulled his weapon out of its holster. He fired three quick shots at the newcomers who went sprawling across the stone floor in opposite directions.

Another large stone dislodged from the ceiling and landed near Will, missing him by a mere few feet.

Muffled shots popped from the other side of the room as the men returned fire from behind one of the big stones.

Will and Tommy ducked behind the one that had just fallen nearest them to take cover.

"Got any idea how we're going to get out of here?" Will asked as he peeked around the corner of the stone and squeezed off a shot.

Schultz looked around frantically. "Honestly, I hadn't thought that far ahead."

The opening to the passageway was blocked so there was no going back the way they came.

"Keep them pinned down over there," Tommy ordered suddenly. He crouched down and shuffled to the wall nearest to where they were hiding, looking closely for anything that would help them get out. Several more shots ricocheted around him making him flinch and sending sparks flashing off the stone. *There had to be another way out.*

The sound of Will's weapon was deafening in the cavernous room. Each volley was amplified by the stone. The air began to smell acrid from the gun smoke.

Tommy tucked in behind a large piece that had fallen and tried to stay out of sight. As he did, his flashlight caught the edge of something peculiar in the wall. A small, circular indention of a familiar size was nestled in the rock. Tommy leaned in for a closer look and noticed four notches protruding from the edge of the round impression towards its center. He ran his light along the smooth surface until he found an edge, then up until he found another. An ancient door. Hurriedly, he pulled out the stone from his backpack and slid it into place in the impression. It was a perfect match, but something was wrong. He pulled the piece away from the indention and looked at it closely. Then he looked at the small hole. There were little raised areas inside the hollowed out circle. A closer look at the stone revealed something he'd not noticed before.

There were little areas of discoloration that appeared to be the same size as the ridges in the wall's impression.

More muffled shots sent rounds off the floor nearby. A ricochet passed so close he could have sworn he felt the air move from the bullet. Will continued to hold them off but was being more conservative with his firing due to the fact that he didn't have that many bullets left. Tommy had noticed the cop had already switched to his reserve magazine of rounds. He looked back at Will who fired another shot at the two attackers.

Will squeezed the trigger. He'd been counting the rounds fired. Only four left. He held up four fingers so Tommy could see. *Time was running out.*

Chapter 30
Grand Canyon, Arizona

It had been a little over an hour since Emily had made the call. While waiting, they'd gotten back on one of the tour buses and visited Guano Point for a few minutes before heading back to the main information center. A black helicopter bearing a Justice Department seal was landing in a space near the parking lot just as they exited the shuttle. "That must be our ride," she said as she pointed over to the chopper.

Up ahead, the blades of the rotor began to slow slightly. A pilot wearing the stereotypical aviator-style sunglasses hopped out of the front. He also sported a light brown jacket and dark-brown pants. The man appeared to be in his upper forties with streaks of gray flicking through the thick, cocoa hair. Emily strode out in front and extended her hand, which the pilot took firmly. "Heard you needed a ride," he said casually, speaking loudly so his voice could be heard over the whine of the turbines.

"We appreciate you coming down on such short notice." She expressed their gratitude. There was an awkward pause for a moment while they shook hands a little longer than would be expected.

"This is Sean and Adriana." Emily pointed to the two onlookers.

"You two know each other?" Sean asked.

"Jim Caldwell," the pilot responded while offering his hand. "I've done some field work for Emily in the past. I've been doing some stuff out in Los Angeles for the past few years, but I happened to be in Vegas when the call came through."

"That's a happy coincidence--" Sean eyed her suspiciously.

Emily rolled her eyes at the insinuation.

"So, you guys need me to fly you somewhere? What's the story?"

"Actually," Emily answered, "We need you to fly us into the canyon."

Caldwell looked surprised and confused. "Why didn't you just get one of those tourist choppers to take you in there?"

Sean responded. "Because I don't think they would be willing to do what we need."

The pilot looked intrigued. "Sounds sketchy. Let's do it."

The group followed him over to the helicopter and climbed in, Emily taking the front seat while Sean and Adriana hopped in the back. A few minutes later they were rising slowly off the desert floor. Jim leaned the black machine forward and headed them around towards the western entrance of the canyon. "We have to take a certain flight path going in," he said into the headset. His voice was somewhat crackly, like most radio communication devices.

The helicopter cruised along for a few minutes, running parallel to the enormous gash in the earth. Then, Jim veered to the right and the ground dropped out from under them. Awestruck by the view, Sean and Adriana looked out their respective windows in the rear.   Villa was in wonder by the spectacular sight. Wyatt was a little more uneasy about the whole thing. They had gone out beyond Guano Point and were sailing past it, flying high over the Colorado River as it wound its way through the deep crevasse. Some of the tourists waved from the tour stop as they went by.

"Up ahead is Eagle Point," Emily said into the microphone. Jim simply nodded his understanding as they drew nearer to a large, forked rock formation in the river gorge. He slightly slowed the helicopter down to make sure he didn't pass the location. Emily pointed to the right. "Take us over there. Get us as close as you can." Again, the pilot nodded and obeyed, guiding the flying machine to the right side of the rock ridge that jutted up from the canyon floor.

Emily looked across through the pilot's window as the formation passed by on their left. It only took them a few minutes before they reached the spot they were looking for. "That's it," she said as she pointed at the enormous shape of the eagle that had been formed out of the ancient red stone. The wings of the creature stretched out in both directions of the river. The head though, was facing upstream.

Carefully, Jim inched the helicopter closer. Sean and Adriana were peeking through the cockpit windshield, trying to see if they could find a hint of anything unusual or out of place but nothing caught their eye. "What are we looking for?" Caldwell asked, turning his head slightly towards the middle of the cabin.

"We're not real sure," Sean replied over the hum of the cabin noise. "A cave, some Petra glyphs. Could be anything."

"What was it that your friend said was the clue for this location?" Adriana asked.

"Mac said that the Eagle's Wings would guide the way or something like that." Almost in sync, the four inside the cabin turned their head upstream in the direction of where the Eagle's head was pointing. "Can you get us over top of it?" Sean asked. "I'm talking like almost sitting on top of the head."

Jim nodded and steered the helicopter up and over top of the rock formation. Slowly and carefully, he lowered it down as close to the rock as he could. The stone eagle was situated in a dip in the ridge, so hovering right over top of it put them at almost eye level with the pinnacle. As the four looked down the ridge they noticed it sloped slightly at an angle, like a path. Where the path ended was extraordinary. Off in the distance, several thousand feet away, they noticed a black spot on the cliff wall. Even though the end of the ridge was separated from the canyon face by a large span, from the angle they had it looked as if the ridge path led straight to the spot.

"Is that a cave?" Emily asked.

"Only one way to find out," Sean replied.

Agents Angela Weaver and James Collack watched the black helicopter take off and circle around to the southwest towards the mouth of the canyon. Following their targets in a chopper of their own would have been foolish. Instead, they opted to be patient and see what they could observe from afar. A close listen by one of their operatives who'd been sent to the tourist center had apprised them that Wyatt and his little group had taken a shuttle out to Eagle Point. The man had done the same and got on the same bus without being compromised. He took note on Wyatt's special interest in the eagle-shaped rock formation when they arrived at the overlook. At the last stop, Guano Point, the group hadn't really spent any time at all looking around. Angela and James took that to mean that whatever Wyatt was looking for was around Eagle Point.

Their team had taken up a position off to the side of the tourist information center with special permission from the residing authorities. No one ever questioned high level government agents once they flashed the credentials. Access to so many restricted areas was easy.

They both held their binoculars tightly as they watched the black chopper cruise in from the southwest. "What are they doing?" James asked his partner, lowering his device for a moment.

She shook her head, still peering through her binoculars. "Not sure. But it looks like they are taking a keen interest in that area of the ridge."

He raised his binoculars back to his face and continued staring out. Three other agents stood guard behind them making sure no curious tourists came near. Angela and James watched as the helicopter maneuvered into a position hovering over the rocky ridge. After a minute or so the helicopter lifted up a little higher and headed northeast, flying upstream over the river below. At one point, the chopper flew past their position but since they were safely a few thousand feet away, being spotted by its passengers was highly unlikely.

"What do you think?" James broke the silence again. He seemed a little on edge.

She was tired of always having to make the decisions. Even though they were of equal rank, it seemed like she'd been playing mommy to him for a while now. Sometimes she wondered how he'd gotten to the level he was at with the ignorance he displayed on an almost daily basis. She'd made little effort to withhold her frustration with his inability to kill Wyatt when he had the chance at the Venetian. How he'd let some woman sneak up on his position was still something she considered inexcusable. And just who the mystery woman was still tugged at her.

James still looked at her awaiting a response. "I'm guessing they saw something off in that direction," she pointed towards where the helicopter had flown. "We wait to see where they land and what they're doing. Keep our distance and observe."

"What if they find what they're looking for?"

A breeze picked up and played with a few loose strands of her brown hair that had escaped the neat ponytail in the back. "Then we take it from them."

Jim lowered the aircraft down gently onto the hardened desert plateau about a hundred feet from the cliff's edge. "Did anyone bring climbing gear?" he asked the three passengers.

"I did," Adriana said matter-of-factly.

Sean raised both eyebrows, impressed with her preparedness.

"What made you think we would need that?" Emily prodded, as turbines above the cabin began to slow.

"Just call it a hunch," she replied with a smirk.

She grabbed the small backpack she'd brought along and hopped down onto the ground, walking low to avoid the blowing wind of the rotors overhead.

Emily looked a little stunned.

"I like her," Jim said as he flipped a few switches and knobs, bringing the chopper to a rest.

Sean's former partner rolled her eyes while he chuckled under his breath.

Jim stayed with the aircraft as they made their way over to where Adriana was unpacking some thin climbing rope, rigging, and a few harnesses. She'd already set up a long stretch of rope across the dusty ground. She reached out her hand to Sean with a harness dangling loosely from it. "I think I'm gonna pass on this one," Sean said as he put both hands in the air.

"I wasn't asking," she replied slyly and tossed him the harness.

He snatched it out of the air out of reflex but looked at the thing like he'd just caught a bag of snakes.

Emily grabbed the last harness from the Spaniard and began to slip one leg through the loops and then the other.

Wyatt reluctantly copied what the two women were doing. "What are we going to anchor the rope to?"

Ignoring him, Adriana removed a small bolt gun from her bag and walked purposefully over to the cliff's edge. She laid down on her stomach and stretched the tool out over the precipice and pressed it against the rock wall. A muffled shot sounded then repeated as she moved the bolt gun slightly to the left.

"Oh," Sean said, resigned to the fact that he would indeed be going over the edge of the cliff, whether he wanted to or not.

He struggled to slip the harness on over his khaki pants. "I've never done this before," he said confessed sheepishly.

Adriana smiled with a raised eyebrow. "Don't worry. I'll take care of you."

He wasn't sure how to take the comment, and it did little to suppress his apprehension. She stepped over to him and grabbed a loose part of the harness webbing and tugged it sharply, tightening the rigging.

Emily just shook her head slowly at the sight, having already finished up her harness adjustments. "Not a word out of you," he pointed at Emily as Adriana completed her work with his device, looking awkward the whole time.

"I wouldn't think of it."

The late afternoon sun gleamed off of Villa's creamy, dark skin. A light gust of wind rolled across the desert plains, flicking her dark hair back a little and causing it to dance around her ears and neck.

"We should hurry. The sun sets early this time of year and it gets cold very quickly."

Sean turned and gazed to the west. They probably still had a few hours, so time wasn't going to be a problem. If everything went according to plan.

Angela watched the group with her binoculars from behind a small rock formation. Her team was well hidden though, at one point she had noticed Wyatt pause and look in their direction. James was right behind her trying to peek over her shoulder. So much like a child. From the looks of it, the group she was observing appeared to be gearing up to repel down the side of the canyon.

What had they found? Angela kept the thought to herself. She wasn't sure but she knew what their orders were. *Observe only.*

The Prophet had been clear in his instructions, though she wasn't sure why he'd changed their course of action. Perhaps he was losing faith in them. Or maybe the man hadn't been unable to decipher the location of whatever it was he was looking for and these people were going to lead him to it. It was a plan that had worked before, she supposed. But Angela doubted it would work that way again. Sooner or later there was going to be another confrontation.

Sean had seen the glint of glass off in the distance. He'd assumed that the people who'd tried to kill him in Vegas the night before had decided to see what they were doing before moving in. Even out in the desert, there weren't a lot of places to hide from the curious eyes of the canyon tourists. The hit squat was probably hanging back, waiting until the moment was right.

There wouldn't be any mistakes this time. Not like last night. He didn't voice his concerns to the others.

The information center was still within view, though it was far away. And their presence on the cliff's edge was known by some of the local authorities, informed on the radio by Jim before they touched down. Still, it was disconcerting not knowing what move their pursuers would take next.

Sean watched as Adriana ran the rope through her harness clamps and casually stepped over the cliff's edge. She pushed out with her feet and disappeared into the canyon.

Emily stepped closer, far less afraid of the dangerous precipice and watched as the Spaniard repeated her repelling motion like a pro. About twenty feet down she stopped and leaned in towards the cliff face, peering at something. "What do you see?" Emily yelled down.

"It is a cave entrance." She swung herself down and into the opening. A few seconds later she poked her head back out. "There is a lot of writing on the wall. This must be the place!" Adriana yelled up.

"What did she say?" Sean asked as he stepped uneasily towards the edge. He crouched at the knees in a feeble attempt to maintain his stability.

Emily turned and raised both eyebrows at the site of Wyatt squatting near her. "She said this is the place. Said she found some markings in the cave opening."

"You sure you want me to go in there?"

The look she gave was answer enough but she said what he needed to hear anyway. "You're going to tell me that Sean Wyatt is going to pass up a chance to go into an ancient cave where there may be treasure that hasn't been seen in probably several thousand years just because he's afraid of heights? Maybe I was wrong about you."

He grabbed the rope from her and laced it through the braking contraption the way Adriana had showed him before. "You know what you are?" He asked as he eased unsteadily towards the lip of the canyon.

"A woman?"

Another slight gust picked up as he leaned out over the drop below. Chills went through his body as he made the mistake of looking down. They must have been a few thousand feet up and the drop made his vision blur for a moment. He clenched his teeth, gripping the braking device with all his might. "Manipulative. But same difference." With that, he released the brake and started inching his way down the rock wall.

Chapter 31
Bandelier National Monument, New Mexico

They were in a fix and Tommy knew it. He and Will had been cornered in a manmade cave at Bandelier National Monument. They'd gone there to look for clues but what they'd found was trouble. Will was running out of ammo and there was no way to tell how much ammunition the other guys had. Tommy figured it was more, though.

He struggled with the stone for a few more seconds trying to fit it into the round impression in the wall, but it wouldn't seat properly. Then it hit him. The oddly colored notches in the stone were additions. Frantically, he began searching his backpack. A few seconds later, he pulled a small pocketknife from it. With the butt-end of the tool, he started chipping away at the lighter-colored areas of the stone. As he suspected, the softer material broke away after only a few knocks. Quickly, he repeated the process on the other three marks.

Again, Tommy slid the stone into place inside the recessed wheel in the wall, matching the notches with the gaps he'd just created. This time, it fit perfectly flush against the back of the ancient mechanism. He gripped the stone tightly and began twisting counter-clockwise. To his surprise, the thing moved fairly easily. Deep within the walls, a new rumbling began. All of the pieces from the ceiling had fallen, creating an odd maze of huge stone pillars in the room. Some were taller than others. The ground shook more and more violently. Then he realized something was moving beneath him. In what could have only taken a few seconds, the floor shifted and then dropped away beneath him.

Will heard the noise and looked over to the corner where Tommy had been toiling furiously. He was gone.

It took Sean about five minutes to do what Adriana and Emily were able to do in less than thirty seconds. He had slowly eased his way down the face of the canyon wall, careful not to make any sudden movements. Once inside the lip of the cave, he pressed forward quickly but Adriana stopped him short, blocking his path.

"I wouldn't go too far in there if I were you." She pointed her light into the darkness and revealed a deep, circular hole that seemed to go down forever.

Sean simply crumpled down to the ground, shaking his head. "I can't believe I let you two talk me into this. Why couldn't this thing be down in an underwater cave or maybe in the plains somewhere?"

She simply shook her head at him.

A few moments later Emily had joined them and cast Sean a degrading glance, chastising him for being fearful. "Walk it off soldier," she shined her own light down into the deep pit. "Looks like we got more to do."

He simply returned Emily's jab by squinting his eyes at her, as if he was just fine sitting on the sandy stone floor.

"I've been trying to figure out how we get down there," Villa spoke up, returning from the edge of the cave. She'd been busily tidying up the ropes for the return trip back up to the helicopter. She pointed to some odd engravings on the wall just above Sean's head and he stood up carefully to look at it, still unsteady with his environment.

"Can you read it?" Emily asked.

He shook his head. "Only a little bit."

His finger traced the outline of the engraved stone symbols that were so common in North Africa but extremely out of place in the United States. He scanned the wall with his eyes, trying to fit all the pieces together.

Adriana stood behind him, watching as he tried to decipher the ancient text.

"Looks like it says something about an eye and the afterlife, I think."

"It says the eye of Akhanan can be the path to death or the stairway to life," Adriana interrupted him. "And that only the righteous may have eternal life."

Sean and Emily gazed at her, slightly amazed.

"I was getting to that," Sean stammered.

Starks raised both eyebrows. "Sure you were." She turned to Adriana and asked, "So what does it mean?"

Adriana stepped curiously over to the pit again and shone her light into the vast, deep darkness. The thing seemed to literally go on forever. An intense look on her face showed she was trying hard to work the riddle out in her head. As she spun back around, her flashlight passed over something at the corner of where the wall ended and the big hole began. She stepped over to get a closer look and realized what she was seeing. On the wall, a stone panel with twelve, slightly raised pieces were positioned around eye level. She gazed at it in wonder as she traced the outline of the ancient script with her index finger. The other two came near to see what had gotten her attention.

Sean kept one hand on the cool wall, bracing himself in case some unseen force pushed him towards the pit.

"What is it?" Emily wondered out loud.

Adriana answered by shining her light away from the panel and around the corner into the dark.

A narrow ledge came into view that seemed to wrap around the left side of the huge shaft. It was difficult to see the other side but as she followed it around the wall with her light, it came to an end at what looked like a doorway.

"So what do we do?" Emily asked.

"I think we go climb back up and get more rope, more gear, and come back down here tomorrow to see how far down we can get in this thing. In fact, maybe we could bring someone instead of myself to do that part of the search." Sean looked hopeful. Just as he finished his sentence with a childish grin, an odd sound came from outside the cave entrance.

They watched in horror as one rope and then the other whizzed by, falling downward into the depths of the cliff. Adriana made a break for it and dove out recklessly trying to grasp the second rope just as it slithered over the edge and into the canyon depths below.

She lay on the dusty stone floor, her arm still outstretched. Sean ran over quickly and reached down and grabbed her hand, helping her up as she dusted off her tight, black pants with the other hand. "What happened?" She asked.

Wyatt turned to Emily to see if she had an answer. Suddenly, a large object whooshed by the entrance and Sean stepped to the edge to see what it was. Their pilot's body tumbled through the air below. Sean turned away as it neared the rocky bottom below.

Emily had seen the body as it passed by the entryway and rushed over to look down. Sean grabbed her, but she wrestled him away in time to see Jim Caldwell hit the bottom. She shook violently. "No! No! No!" was all she could get out.

Sean pulled her away from the edge and put his arm around her. He'd worked with her a long time. Emily was a brilliant woman, but not cut out for fieldwork. She'd always been a more administrative type. She handled herself well enough in tough situations but having to keep on full alert all the time had worn her down. Just like it had him.

A solitary tear had formed in the corner of her right eye. Several minutes went by before Emily began to calm down. She took several deep breaths and tried to steel herself against her emotions. She hadn't been a field agent in a long time, but it wasn't the first time she'd lost an ally in the line of duty. *It probably wouldn't be the last.*

Sean broke the long silence. "Em, we need to go."
She nodded and the three trudged slowly back into the cave.

Will fired off one of his last three bullets then dashed over to the hole where Tommy had been sitting only moments before. He shone his light down into the darkness and saw that there was a rushing stream of water but no sign of Schultz. The drop down to the small river looked to be about fifteen feet. He looked back in the direction of the two enemies and decided he'd rather take his chance with the underground river. Something caught his eye in the wall just over the hole. Will realized it was the stone disc and carefully reached over and pulled it out of the indention in the wall.

Will gave one more quick glance back towards the assailants. One of the men had moved into the open and was rushing his way. He raised his weapon and squeezed off one quick shot. The bullet sunk into the target's mid-thigh, sending the man to the floor in a crumpled heap. His partner glanced around from a position behind one of the large columns that had fallen but stayed put. Satisfied he'd done what he could, Will jumped down into the cold, flowing water below.

Carlson watched from behind the large piece of fallen rock as his quarry disappeared into a large hole in the floor. The man had fired off one last shot, dropping his remaining agent. Quickly, he stuck the gun around the front edge of the column and stepped out, waving the weapon around methodically just in case. His man was lying on the ground, clenching his left leg about six inches above the knee. "Can you make it?" he asked, feigning concern.

The agent looked up and nodded, knowing what the other answer would result in. He'd already seen what his boss was capable of and wasn't in the mood to die in a desert cave.

Hunter reached down and offered him a hand to stand up. The agent hesitated momentarily, then reached up and accepted the assistance. "You gonna be able to walk?" Hunter asked.

He nodded again. "Yeah. The bullet's in the meat of the leg. I'll be fine."

"Let's go after them, then." Carlson said as he pointed to the hole in the floor.

The man gave a quick nod and started hobbling towards the other side of the room. He knelt down and shone his light down into the rushing water below and around the dark surroundings of the underground river. "Looks clear to me," he announced over the sound of the flowing water.

"Good," Hunter replied. Then he raised his gun to the back corner of the man's head and squeezed the trigger. Dark red fragments splattered the cavern wall and a moment later the body of the agent dropped into the gushing stream below. If anyone *was* down there, they would have made it known when the corpse dropped.

Hunter shone his light down into the subterranean tunnel and, satisfied that the coast was clear, jumped in.

The cold, mountain water had initially shocked Tommy, but it was carrying him away from trouble--or so he hoped. He had no idea where the underground river was taking him. It was shallow and almost moved him along like a lazy river at a water park. Fortunately, his light was waterproof so, he could see around the passageway. He'd been able to right himself as he floated along downstream so. There wasn't much to see, just carved out rock for the most part. It was hard to tell whether the place was natural or manmade.

The cavernous room they'd just left clearly had manmade components to it. He was amazed by the constructive ability of the ancients to build such elaborate and large-scale things. At the moment, though, he was more concerned about where he was going. As he peered through the darkness in front of him, something terrifying came into view ,or disappeared from view as it were.

The river seemed to drop over the edge of an underground waterfall. Swimming against the current would be impossible. The only thing Tommy could do was brace himself and hope the drop wasn't a big one. He neared the edge and pulled his legs and arms in tight, preparing for the fall. The sound of crashing water grew louder as he got closer. The moment he went over the lip of the river's end, he felt the air below him open up. Instinctively, he kicked his legs back and forth, wondering when the fall would end. It only lasted a few seconds before he hit the churning water below. He sunk deep into the black pool of liquid until he felt the bottom. Frantically, he pushed hard off the floor with his feet and shot towards the surface. His head emerged and he took a big, wet breath of air. Quickly, he searched around the area with his flashlight and spotted what looked like an underground beach where the water met land.

Tommy paddled hard and soon found himself staggering up onto the sandy earth. He hunched over with his hands on his knees, gasping for breath. Out of the corner of his eye he caught movement on the ceiling. Another flashlight was bobbing around. Someone was coming down the river.

Adriana walked back over to the corner of the short corridor and stretched out, wrapping her foot around to the ledge.

"I hope you know what you're doing" Sean said as he looked on with a concerned eye.

"So do I," she sighed. "That path leads to another corridor on the other side. It's our only way out, now."

He didn't like the sound of that. But there was no choice.

"What's that noise?" Emily asked as she stepped closer to the lip of the drop off.

"I hear it too," Adriana said, breaking her concentration for a moment as she brought her right foot next to the left on the ledge.

"It sounds like a lot of squeaking and flapping...oh crap," Emily backed away from the edge slowly, eyes wide with fear. "Bats!" she screamed loudly as she jumped back.

A gust of air blew up into the alcove where the three were standing and within seconds they were engulfed in the small, flying beasts. Hundreds of bats fluttered around them, squeaking incessantly. The three occupants of the ledge covered their faces and heads and crouched low to the ground in hopes that the creatures would ignore them. Emily screamed as one of the animals got stuck in her hair momentarily. She stood up, yelling, and swatted her hands wildly at the winged rodents like she had walked into a cobweb.

Adriana pressed herself hard up against the shaft wall and tried to remain calm.

After what seemed like several minutes, the horde of bats gradually disappeared.

Emily was still waving her hands around in the air as if the bats were still there. Sean smiled at her. "Hey, Em! They're gone." She stopped waving her hands and looked around, uncertain. "By the way," he added, "don't ever give me crap about being scared of heights again."

Tommy didn't know who was coming down the river. Even if Will had seen what happened and tried to make a break for the trap door he could have been shot by the remaining two pursuers. Hurriedly, he turned off his own light and crept into a recessed area of the cave. He watched as the person in the river above tumbled over the waterfall and into the pool. The man broke the surface and as his light floated near by, it illuminated his face just enough for Tommy to tell that it was Will.

"Will," Tommy yelled over the sound of the crashing water. He turned on his light as he emerged from the dark corner. "Over here!"

Will grabbed his light and shone it on the shore where Tommy was waving. "I took out one of them, but the other guy is still up there," he said after he climbed out of the water next to Schultz.

Tommy looked around, shining his light onto the drab walls of the cavern. In a corner about thirty feet away he noticed that the sandy floor seemed to continue around the cavern wall. "Over there," he said quietly.

The two men took off towards what appeared to be a path. They reached it a few moments later and Tommy looked back at the waterfall. Nothing. He and Will turned and darted into a narrow corridor, not seeing the dark figure of a body falling into the black pool.

In the pale light of their flashlights, Sean could see that the bats were making their way through the door across the abyss. Apparently, the alcove provided no means of escape for them either.

After a few minutes the obnoxious noise had grown quieter. He looked at Adriana who, for the first time since he'd met her, appeared to show a little uncertainty. He nodded reassuringly and stepped carefully over to where the ledge jutted out from the left side of the pit's wall. Then he turned with a feigned playful grin. "Ladies first?" he motioned with his hand to Emily, obviously not excited about traversing the deep crevasse over the narrow stone bridge.

Starks had apparently gotten over her moment of weakness and was back to being her confident self. She stepped out boldly, pressing her back up against the wall as she shuffled along the ledge right behind Villa.

Once the two women were on their way, Sean lingered momentarily at the edge. His former partner looked back at him and shined her flashlight on his face. "You realize this is the only way out, right?" She asked sarcastically. "Just don't look down and keep your body pressed to the wall like we're doing."

Adriana was already halfway to the other side of the pit when he finally forced himself to step over to the narrow walkway. He gripped his flashlight tightly and pressed his back to the wall as hard as he could. A slight draft of cold air drifted up from the abyss below. Wyatt felt a vein of fear tear through his abdomen as his nerves went on overload. A quick glance to his side told him that the two women had nearly reached the door already. So he shuffled his feet, inch by inch, trying hard not to look down into the empty blackness.

"Come on, you're doing great," he heard Emily encourage him loudly from the ledge about twenty feet away. "Just keep moving slow like that and you'll be fine."

He continued inching sideways, his intense focus was on the wall just behind him. But his peripheral vision couldn't help but register the chasm below. Momentarily, he wavered and had to stop to take a deep breath. After regaining his thoughts, he pushed himself onward.

When he reached the other side he hopped down and leaned against the wall just inside the door. Then he glanced down at his Relic watch.

"I can't believe that only took ten minutes. Seemed like I was out there forever." He just stared ahead at the other side of the passageway.

"You did great," Emily comforted. "Now can we please keep moving?"

He nodded and stood up straight. "Yeah. It's going to be getting dark soon, and we have no idea where this passage leads."

Adriana smiled at his resolve. He'd just faced one of his greatest fears and seemed ready to take on the next hurdle without reservation. She'd seen many men come and go in her life. But Sean Wyatt seemed different. He could take a punch and keep going. *What was it about him? Was it his sense of adventure, his determination, his vulnerability she'd just witnessed? Or was it something else?* She left the questions lingering in her head and came back to the moment. "I scouted up ahead. This corridor starts sloping down." Adriana took off, leading the way down the passage so Sean and Emily followed behind quickly.

"I'm getting real tired of being underground," he commented as they moved along the tunnel.

They found themselves in a narrow hall, carved out of the canyon rock. The jagged walls and ceiling of the corridor appeared to have been done in a hurry, chiseled for usefulness and not for aesthetic appeal. But the sheer volume of rock that had to be removed was simply staggering.

They walked for nearly twenty minutes, continuing downward into the mountain. The path had been a slight grade with a series of right hand turns, winding deeper and deeper into the earth. Sean wondered who had constructed the place and why they would go to such great lengths. The group marched on in silence for another ten minutes until finally, they reached a point where the floor leveled off. Up ahead, their lights shone into what appeared to be a room. As they drew near, their flashlight beams shone through the dust particles in the air, illuminating an enormous chamber. The ceiling was at least fifty feet high with walls separated by the same distance. All three of their flashlights searched randomly around the room until Sean's light came to rest on something in the center. A stone pillar sat conspicuously in the middle of the room. On top of it rested another piece of gold, similar to the one that had come from the mountain near Adriana's home outside of Las Vegas. In unison, they moved towards the pedestal. Sean aimed his light around on the floor to make sure they were stepping safely.

"It's just like the other one," Emily stated quietly. Even though her voice was just above a whisper, it echoed throughout the giant room.

Adriana had taken her focus off of the shiny object in the center of the room and was checking out the rest of their surroundings. There were four enormous columns in each corner, every single one engraved with a separate set of writing. And every language was one of the most ancient in the world: Egyptian hieroglyphics, Sanskrit, Cuneiform, and Old Hebrew. The inner corner of each pillar pointed towards the pedestal in the center. Then she noticed the design of the floor. When they walked in, all she had seen was a plain, stone floor. But from each of the corner columns, a line about one foot wide ran to the center where the small stand held the golden artifact. The wide lines were unmistakably bluish-green.

Sean noticed what had gotten her attention, and he too broke away from admiring the golden leaf in the center of the room to get a closer inspection of the distinctly colored lines. He looked up at the massive stone column that had Sanskrit on it. "Can you read it?" Emily asked from across the room, this time turning towards him and shining her light his way.

Sanskrit was one of the ancient languages Sean had learned almost fluently. It was the only language that was mathematically perfect. The writers of the Hindu Vedas had delivered their entire set of scriptures in Sanskrit, and it was believed by many to be the language of the gods. He'd been fascinated by it in college. And while his friends wondered why he would take classes to learn about a three thousand year-old dead language, he continued to attend. There had only been a few dozen students in the small lecture hall. Word had it that it was anybody's guess if the course would even have enough people enrolled to run it each semester. But it always did, probably due to several students waiting too long to get signed up for one of the other more contemporary languages. With no options left, they had to go with Sanskrit. At the moment, Sean was glad he'd taken it. "It's a little different from what I learned, probably an early pre-classical form of the language. But yeah, I can read it."

Emily had slowly made her way over to where Sean was gazing at the stone. "What does it say?"

"It's a story," he said, staring in wonder at the ancient script.

"What story?"

He turned his eyes from the pillar and looked at both women with a semi-shocked face. "If I'm reading it correctly, it looks a lot like the beginning of the Old Testament."

Chapter 32
Grand Canyon, AZ

Emily appeared to be confused. "You mean, like the Old Testament from the Bible?"

Sean looked back up at the sculpted stone. "That would be the one," he answered nodding. "It's the early parts of Genesis, talking about the Garden of Eden. These four bluish-green lines that lead to the center represent the four rivers that ran through the garden: Tigris, Euphrates, Pison, and Gihon. Supposedly they all four ran into one larger river that flowed under the tree of life."

Adriana glanced back at the small pedestal in the center of the room. It was a simple, rectangular cube carved from the same stone as the rest of the chamber. As she moved closer to the object she noticed that there was something distinct etched into the sides. It was a tree but it was unlike any she'd seen before. The trunks were separate at the bottom but joined about halfway up, then opened into intricately detailed branches, fruit, and foliage.

Sean had also abandoned the corner pillar and walked over to the middle where Adriana was studying the pedestal. "The tree of life," he whispered reverently.

Adriana nodded.

"But why is all this Biblical stuff here in the United States?" Emily wondered out loud. "Those stories took place on the other side of the world nearly 8,000 years ago."

Sean started drawing connections in his mind. At first, they seemed impossible. But the more he reflected on the events of the last few weeks and the evidence in stone right before his eyes, the more he began to believe the plausibility.

"What are you thinking?" His old partner asked, interrupting his intense thought.

He shook his head quickly as if snapping out of a dream. "This is going to sound crazy. But what if it is all connected?"

"What do you mean?" Emily asked.

"The Bible, the Native Americans, all of this stuff. Could it be that all of it is connected somehow?"

"I don't follow," Starks shook her head.

Villa stood silently, just listening.

"The Egyptian connection to the Native Americans that we found in Georgia, the different forms of writing, all of the evidence that we have discovered from the ancient world all points to one thing. It's essentially all telling the same story and leading back to one place." He stared at the leaf shaped piece of gold resting on top of the altar.

"To the Garden of Eden?" Emily asked, finally starting to see the connection.

"Not quite," Sean corrected her. "If such a place still existed it would have been found by now."

"The tree," Adriana broke her silence in a tone more to herself than the others.

"What?" Emily looked confused.

"It all makes sense now," Villa continued. "Francisco Coronado was not looking for a city of gold. He was looking for something far more valuable. The golden chambers only point the direction. The chambers themselves serve as either a beacon to the righteous or a distraction for the wicked."

"What do you mean, distraction?" Sean chimed in, his voice resonating off the walls.

"For those of pure heart, the golden chambers would not have mattered. It was the journey that was of importance. The greedy and misguided souls would see the glittering gold and forget all about the path. They would figure they had found the ultimate treasure when, in fact, all they had found was worldly riches. "Coronado must have known this. And he surely must have known that he was far to old to take on such a journey."

"So you are saying there is something even more valuable than four golden rooms worth billions of dollars?" Emily seemed dubious.

"Money isn't everything," Adriana replied. "In Coronado's book he quoted the Gospel of Mark from the Bible. I wondered for a while, why that particular verse was there. It comes from chapter eight. *For what doth it profit a man if he gains the whole world and loses his own soul?*"

"The treasure is something else..." Sean trailed of.

"Something far more powerful and potentially more dangerous," Adriana added. "Perhaps Coronado knew this as well, confirming his thought that it should be left alone, hidden to history and time."

Adriana stared at both of them with an intensity neither of them had ever seen before. Then she looked back at the golden leaf, sitting silently on the pedestal. She drew in a breath as she considered the implications.

"El Arbol de Vida," she said finally. "The tree of life."

Chapter 33
Washington DC

Cars hustled by on the dimly lit streets. The air was colder than usual, almost unseasonably so. There was always a chill that time of year, but, after the brutal summer, the weather seemed to have skipped autumn and gone straight to winter.

Eric Jennings checked back down the sidewalk he'd just come from and then looked in the other direction before pushing open the heavy wooden door to Bellamy's Irish Pub. Old habits were hard to break. He was of the mindset that one could never be too careful.

Inside, the warm air washed over him, a stark contrast to the bone-chilling cold of the sidewalk outside. He took off his black trench coat and hung it on a hook in the foyer then loosened his blue and white striped tie.

Despite the establishment's rousing reputation, the bar was quiet that evening. Irish folk music played on the speakers throughout the room, but absent were the large groups of drunken revelers that one might expect based on previous experience.

There were only a few people: a man and a woman, finishing off the last of their beers at the other end of the bar. They laughed and talked quietly, perhaps teasing about what the rest of the night would hold. The man's back was to Jennings so he couldn't see his face.

Jennings nodded to a short, fleshy bartender who returned the gesture. Eric had been a patron of the joint for years and Bobby had been bartending there since before then. The man's gray, thinning hair looked like it was pasted to his round head. He wore the typical white button up shirt and apron over black pants.

The dimly lit pub had a random collection of sports memorabilia from Boston and Washington: Capitals and Bruins jerseys, autographed baseball bats, an old Washington Senators jersey next to one from the Red Sox, and some Redskins pictures all gave the impression the place was some kind of sports bar. Of course, the Irish tri-colors were everywhere mingled with Guinness posters and placards.

Many famous people had stopped in to Bellamy's over the years but not because it was a trendy spot. It probably had more to do with the fact that one could remain anonymous in the dark, quietude of the pub, at least on weeknights anyway.

"Usual, Mr. Jennings?" The bartender yelled across the room as Eric slid into his favorite booth in a corner and unbuttoned the top button on his white dress shirt.

He nodded. "Thanks Bobby."

It had been a trying week. A beer and some good food would hit the spot. Bellamy's was famous for having better than average bar food. With a full compliment of soups and hearty sandwiches, it was one of the only bars in town that had to be open for lunch simply because of the popularity of the menu.

"No problem, Mr. J," Bobby replied. The barkeeper smiled and hurriedly finished wiping down a spot on the bar that he seemed to be perpetually cleaning then exited the room through a doorway into the kitchen.

It was hard to get service like that anymore. Most bars and restaurants had such a revolving door of turnover in staffing that a person hardly knew the faces they would see from week to week. *It was nice that there were a few spots still left that had people dedicated to good service.* Jennings smiled at the thought.

Bobby reappeared through the swinging, wooden door. "It'll be right up, Mr. J," the chubby man stated.

He passed by the other two customers who were obviously entranced with one another and grabbed a pint glass from behind the bar. Through a technique he'd probably done a hundred thousand times, Bobby filled up the glass with the familiar black stout from Ireland. After topping off the foamy head of the beer, the old barkeep rapidly stepped around the edge of the bar counter and brought it over to Jennings. "Here you go, Mr. J."

"I appreciate it. Business good today?" Jennings asked the question every week when he came in. Part of him actually did care. After all, a quiet pub with great service and food was hard to find.

The squat man crossed his arms and smiled. "Business is always good when you work for yourself," Bobby beamed as he said it. "But, yeah, it's good. Had a bunch of execs come in from a convention this afternoon. So that was solid." The bartender's accent was thick, clearly from the Boston area. He paused for a moment. "Your...um, friend is running a little late tonight."

Eric pursed his lips slightly and nodded. He didn't need to say anything else.

Jennings was a man of few vices. Most worldly activities didn't interest him. He'd never gotten in to drugs as a young man, didn't over indulge with alcohol. Smoking had never been his thing, save for an occasional cigar after a nice meal. Women, however, were his one weakness. Fortunately for him, Bobby was more than willing to accommodate him with a rotation of escorts that met his strict standards, something that Jennings compensated the barkeeper for handsomely. "No problem, Bobby." He smiled back at the man who winked, gave one nod, and headed back to the kitchen to check on the food. Eric grabbed the cool glass of Irish stout and took a long, slow sip from it, savoring the creamy, bitter flavor after a long day at work.

"Who you meeting here, Eric?"

Jennings was looking down at his cell phone when the new voice startled him, nearly causing him to spill some of his beverage. Setting it down, Jennings looked to his left and instantly recognized the young, narrow face. "I thought I recognized that slimy laugh when I walked in?" He cursed himself silently for not realizing who was with the woman at the bar.

Sam Townsend was the director of the CIA's newest division. They focused mostly on corruption within government agencies. It was like internal affairs but for the whole party, not just one particular agency. Townsend had been in the Justice Department for five or six years. Eric couldn't recall exactly. But he knew the young punk had risen quickly, too quickly in many veterans' opinion. Eric hadn't recognized him at the bar a few moments earlier. He stood a few feet away, hands in both pockets of his expensive Armani suit. His short, dark hair was slightly spiked off to the side and dark brown eyes were narrow, accompanied by a smug grin. He wasn't even thirty yet.

Jennings had thought creating the corruption branch of the CIA was a political move by the president--foolish and a waste of taxpayer dollars. There was no way that one group within a government agency could get much done in the way of shutting down internal corruption. The U.S. government had thousands of people all over the world. The manpower alone would cost tens of millions each year.

Townsend was a scumbag. Jennings found it extremely ironic that the man they put in charge of the corruption division was probably involved with more unethical behavior than nearly anyone else. The other irony was that Eric had been an honest agent for most of his career. But decades of a flat salary and too many headaches had gotten the better of him. He wanted to retire on an island somewhere and play golf or sip margaritas on the beach. *This "tool" could change all that if he got in the way.*

"What do you want, Sam?" He went straight to the point, irritation clear in his voice.

The young agent helped himself to the seat in the booth across from Jennings just as Bobby came back to the table.

"Your food will be out in a second, Mr. J." He lowered his eyebrows at the new companion who had just taken a seat. The bartender was obviously confused as to why the man had left the bar to come over. "You need anything else, friend?"

"No, Bobby. He'll just be a minute," Eric answered for him.

"I'm fine. Thanks," Sam added, never taking his eyes off of the man across from him.

Sensing something personal was going on, the old bartender slinked back to the kitchen.

Again Jennings asked, "What do you want, Sam?"

"Eric," his voice was condescending. "Relax. What makes you think I want something?"

The music changed on the speaker system from a slow, Irish ballad to something a little more upbeat with a wild Celtic fiddle driving the melody.

"Because you're always up to something," Eric responded coldly after taking another draught of his beer.

"Me? I don't think so. After all, that's what my department does. We figure out who in the government *is* up to something."

"Convenient for you. No one there to check your tracks, huh?"

Townsend laughed for a moment and looked over towards the woman at the bar. She was spying on both of them through the mirror behind the drink station.

He turned his attention back to Jennings. "What are you up to, Eric? We know you have agents out in Vegas right now and another team that just headed to New Mexico. What I want to know is, *why*? There haven't been any missions filed for that region recently. So, you're up to something. You haven't gone rogue on us have you?"

Jennings resented the implication, even though it was true. *Who was this little prick to think he could just waltz in there to his favorite pub and start throwing accusations around?*

One thing Sam said caught him off guard, though. *True, Jennings had people in Vegas. New Mexico on the other hand, he knew nothing about, which made him wonder who else may have been involved in the game. Townsend was thorough. If he knew about the agents out west he had been following their actions for a while. What Jennings didn't know was for how long. He'd tried to keep a more administrative role in the whole operation, but with a hands-off approach. The man who called himself The Prophet had asked for his top operatives and had paid handsomely. A professional mercenary, Will Hastings, had handled everything, even communications directly with the mysterious man himself. The trail was beginning to lead back to Washington, which meant Eric Jennings was going to have to take more control of the situation. At the moment, he decided to redirect.*

"I'm under strict orders not to reveal that information."

"Oh, come on," Sam said loudly. "You know good and well I have access to everything you do." He had a pleading look on his face that backed up what he was saying, as if it should be extremely obvious.

Although, the fact that Sam was aware of their southwest presence meant he could get his own team on the trail eventually. Eric guessed Sam would rather not do that if he didn't need to.

"Why are we having this conversation, Sam?" he said with a smirk.

It was a good point, one that obviously caught the younger agent off guard.

Since Townsend didn't respond, he continued, "Let me guess, Sam, you want less corruption or more opportunity to participate in it." The statement was lathered in cynicism.

Townsend's eyes narrowed. "Listen to me, Eric. I can pull the plug on every single operation you're running right now. The only person with more authority in this government than me right now is the president himself. And last I checked, he's signing off on my direct deposit."

He was right. Townsend could shut him down. Rather than rattle the hornet's nest, Eric decided to offer a carrot.

"What I'm about to tell you stays between you and me." Eric looked around, feigning paranoia. "I've been investigating the operations of a secret society. They were fairly inactive for a long time but then a few years ago they blipped back onto the radar. I think they're looking for something, something big."

Townsend leaned in closer, obviously interested in what he was hearing. "And what might that be?"

Jennings continued, "Did you hear about the golden chamber they found down in Georgia a few weeks ago?"

Sam nodded that he had. The discovery had made national news. It was like a real life *Indiana Jones* tale.

"This group was there. But they're not just interested in a golden chamber. Apparently, there's something else out there. Something much bigger."

"What would be bigger than that treasure? Its estimated value is thought to be in the hundreds of millions."

Jennings nodded in agreement. "Chump change compared to what they're going after."

Both men sat silent for a moment, Jennings letting the words sink in.

The kitchen door swung open, shattering the silence with a loud creak and accompanying sounds of dishes rattling.

Bobby brought the plate over and set it down in front of Jennings. The bartender smiled as he slinked away, apparently knowing he wasn't to take part in the conversation.

Jennings changed gears. "They have an excellent Ruben here," he said as he grabbed the thick sandwich and took a huge bite. He added while chewing, "They make it with pastrami instead of corned beef. Adds a little kick." He set the sandwich down on the plate, thick pieces of beef slathered in a creamy, yellowish dressing dangled out from between the slices of marbled rye bread.

"You really should try it," He continued as he offered Townsend a small piece of the concoction.

"I don't eat after seven," he said sternly, not amused that the conversation had turned to the topic of food.

Jennings shrugged. "Suit yourself." He stuffed another huge bite into his mouth then washed it down with another sip of beer.

"You obviously think me a fool, Eric," Sam placed his elbows on the table and leaned in closer. "I want to know what you're up to."

"And you want a piece of whatever it is. Don't you?" The snide remark was accompanied by a sarcastic grin.

Townsend ignored the jab. "If you are using justice department funding and personnel for some wild treasure hunt or to somehow jack a score from this so-called 'secret society' then you are going down for it. I'll personally make sure of it."

The menace in his voice was threatening. Eric Jennings wasn't a man to be easily bothered, but Townsend's implication sent a momentary chill up his spine.

"Do you understand me?" the younger man added. He stood up and took a business card and a pen out of his suit jacket pocket and quickly scribbled down a few words then tossed the card carelessly next to the plate of food. "I'll be in touch," Townsend said and walked out of the room.

The woman at the bar who'd been watching took that as her signal that the meeting was over and threw some dollar bills on the counter to take care of their tab. Then, she too stood and strode out of the building.

During all his years as a high-level government agent, Jennings only had to answer to a few people. *Who did Townsend think he was?*

Jennings snorted as he looked down at the small, government-issue business card Townsend had left. It contained only a three-word sentence in sloppy cursive. *I want in.*

Chapter 34
New Mexico

Tommy and Will were soaking wet, which was a bad thing considering darkness had settled in the desert. More stars than Tommy had ever seen sparkled in the dark blanket above. Nights could get very cold there so it was imperative that they get back to the car quickly. That, and the fact that someone was trying to kill them. The corridor that had led out of the cavern had opened up near a clearing surrounded by desert rocks and hills.

It took several minutes before they could get their bearings and find their way back to the information center where their car was parked. The building was empty and only a few lights glowed dimly within.

Both men noticed the black BMW SUV sitting quietly on far side of the parking lot. It must have been the shooter's vehicle.

"Start the car," Will said as he eyed the other car.

"What are you going to do?" Tommy looked confused.

"Slow them down."

Schultz understood and jumped into their rental car and revved up the engine. He looked out the window as Will fired his remaining two bullets into a front and rear tire of the SUV then sprinted back to the car. Tommy wheeled the vehicle out of the parking lot and down the dusty road.

"What's the plan now?" Will asked as he slid his weapon back into his jacket pocket.

Shultz thought for a moment before answering. Paranoid, he checked back in his rearview mirror even though he knew there would be no way their pursuer could be behind them.

"We head back to Atlanta. This thing needs to be analyzed," he held up the small golden leaf. "We need some answers. And I think I know who can help us find them."

Chapter 35
Grand Canyon

When Sean and his companions finally reached fresh air, night had settled in across the desert. The exit for the mysterious chamber had come out right next to the Colorado River. It was hidden by a large array of stones, keeping the cave completely hidden from view. With some effort, Sean had been able to leverage one of the giant rocks out of their way.

Fortunately, there was a rafting expedition spending the night in a clearing just downstream. The young, rough looking guide and his tour had been more than willing to let Sean and the two women to join them. They even had a few extra sleeping bags and some food to help settle their hunger. A quick explanation of how they'd been hiking and lost track of time had seemed acceptable to the scruffy river guide.

Sitting by the campfire brought old memories from a distant past back to Sean's mind. He remembered the days he'd spent as a boy with his parents out in the mountains of Tennessee and North Carolina. It seemed like they'd gone camping once a month. His current surroundings were much different than where he'd gone as a child. High desert canyons and no canopy of trees provided a severe contrast, but a beautiful one.

Adriana lay quietly nearby, staring up at the stars as they fought with the flickering glow of the fire at their feet.

The guide and his half-dozen whitewater tourists were already asleep in their tents or lying around in different places in the clearing. Emily had passed out a few feet away. She wasn't a field agent anymore and the events of the day had been a little more stressful and exhausting than she was used to. "You sure can see a lot of stars out here, huh?" Sean broke the silence.

Adriana smiled. "Yes. I love to stare at them." Her eyes just stared into the night sky. "What do you think about when you look at them?" She asked in a whisper.

No one had ever asked him that before. It made him feel something deep down that he had not felt in a long time. He thought for a moment before answering. "I think about what is out there and who is out there. I wonder what it would be like to be able to visit other planets. It makes me think about how small we are here on this earth and how vast and huge the universe really is." Then he asked, "What about you?"

She took a deep breath. "I wonder where God is and how he did all of it. How does his science work? How does he hold it all together? Or does he hold it all together? Does he just set it in a perfect mathematical motion that will maintain itself forever?"

"Wow. Those are some heavy thoughts," he said.

She smiled at him for a second then went back to gazing up into the darkness. "Are they? I just want to know how it all works, I guess."

"That's a pretty complex thing to try and understand," he paused. "But I like it."

He looked at her for a minute. She was beautiful in the dancing light of the campfire. Her brown hair had

205

been pulled back to one side behind her ear. He wondered if she could be trusted, if she had been completely honest with them. At the time, he didn't have a choice. Besides, she'd saved their hides in Vegas.

"What do we do next?" she interrupted his thoughts.

He diverted his gaze to the bright orange coals of the fire. "We head back to Atlanta and regroup with Tommy. He needs to see the piece," Sean said as he cradled the concealed piece of gold. "And I think there is someone else I know who might be able to help us figure this thing out."

She seemed satisfied with the plan and rolled over on her side, bracing her head on her arm as she closed her eyes. "Good, I'm coming with you."

Sean slid into his sleeping bag and closed his eyes, too. His mind ran wild as he tried to fall asleep. He'd been shot at several times in the last few weeks. After leaving the Justice Department, he believed those kinds of days had been left behind.

Now he wasn't so sure. And he felt like there was certainly more to come.

Part II

Chapter 36
Nevada

The phone rang in Alexander Lindsey's pocket. He looked at the number and answered immediately.

The voice on the other end spoke quickly, "We have a problem."

It seemed like that was all he was getting lately: problems. It was growing tiresome. He missed the days when things were simpler. When *he* rose to power, he solved problems for other people. It was straightforward for him.

Alexander had always been a thinker, a doer. He didn't understand nor have compassion for those who could not get things done on their own. It was an interesting irony that now, in his current status and with his endeavors, he had to rely on underlings to get things done for him. And he loathed it.

"What is the problem now, Eric?" he asked into the phone as he stood from his opulent desk and its accompanying high, leather-backed chair.

"There is a new player in the game. He has a lot of connections, security clearances, access to important information," Jennings said plainly. "He's watching us."

Alexander thought for a moment as he stepped over to the large window overlooking the Sierra Nevada Mountains. The rocky peaks jutted into the sky as far as the eye could see.

"I know who you are talking about. I figured he would come around eventually. You have too many resources at work under the table for someone like him not to notice."

"How would you like me to proceed?"

Lindsey took a deep breath. There it was again, solving another's problems. What was he paying them for if they couldn't provide solutions? Only now, their problems had become his. He wiped his forehead and tried to shake off his aggravation. If he was to succeed, he knew more hand holding would have to be done for a little while longer.

"Let him in on the deal. If Samuel is anything like I have heard, he's just as greedy as the people his department seeks to expose. I'm sure he probably told you he wanted a piece of whatever you're doing, yes?"

There was a momentary pause on the other end. Then, "Yes."

"Good," he replied. "We'll let him in and then cut him off when the time is right. For now, having an ally like him could prove useful. Better the devil you know."

"Understood."

Jennings was silent on the other end for a second before he spoke again. "Wyatt and the two women went into a cave at the Grand Canyon. We've had no visual or any other kind of contact since they entered. There is no way out except through us. When they find the next piece of the puzzle and exit the cave, we'll be waiting."

Lindsey thought for a few seconds. Uncertainty arose within him. But for now, he had to trust his lead asset. "What about the New Mexico situation?"

"I haven't heard back from them yet. But I am certain Hastings has it under control. Last he reported, they had rented a car and were heading toward Bandelier National Monument."

Alexander didn't like the fact that he had so many irons in the fire. Loose ends were easier to turn up that way. And since an additional branch of the government had become involved, that meant that others could come along sooner or later. Eventually, there would be a cowboy who would try to expose the whole thing. That was something he simply could not afford. There was too much at stake. "Let me know when you hear from him."

"Yes, sir."

Lindsey hung up the phone. A small, LED television glowed brightly on the wall nearby. A news headline ran across the bottom as a scene from a car accident appeared. A local businessman named Rick Baker had lost control of his automobile and run off the road. He was pronounced dead at the scene. One problem solved. If his operatives were successful and recovered the three golden leaves, they would only need one additional piece to the puzzle. The diary of Francisco Coronado.

Chapter 37
Atlanta, GA

The rafting guide had showed Sean an old mule trail up the canyon that would take him and his friends back to where they could find their way to the car. It had been a long hike, taking a few hours to wind their way to the top. Fortunately they had eaten a good breakfast, provided by the generous guide.

He'd been a friendly fellow, with narrow eyes and light blonde hair and beard.

The man had asked if they wanted to come aboard their enormous touring raft but taking the mule trail was a faster way to get back to the car and given the events of the last 48 hours, speed was of the essence.

When they'd finally reached the top, their legs burned and all three of the hikers were gasping for breath.

Where the trail had come out on the desert plateau, they were actually fairly close to the parking lot.

When they'd finally reached the top, their legs burned and all three of the hikers were gasping for breath.

After a two-hour drive and paying way too much for a plane ticket out of Las Vegas International, the group of three arrived in Atlanta's Hartsfield International Airport about eight hours later.

With the time change, the daylight was already waning when they arrived at IAA headquarters in downtown Atlanta.

Tommy received the group's entrance as he would have on any other day, casually and to the point. He laughed, "You guys look rough."

"Vacation was great. Thanks for asking," Sean said sarcastically as he plopped down in a standard-looking office chair with black leather upholstery.

The conference room had various maps from all over the world posted on the walls with pushpins and notes tacked in different places. The room itself had a warm feel to it. Lots of wood appointments, including ceiling lattices and beams, that made it feel more like an opulent home rather than a workplace. A burnt-red wall made the place seem cozy yet trendy.

"Well," Sean spoke before his long-time friend could get another word in, "it *was* fine until I got shot at. That kind of took the enjoyment out of it."

Schultz gave him a rough grin. "I know the feeling. Had some similar issues here and in New Mexico, too."

"Odd. Seems like I remember we got into this business to leave all that behind," Sean said reflectively. "Who was after you?"

"I have no idea." Changing the subject the subject, he said, "Hello Emily. Nice to see you again."

"Likewise, Thomas," there was an odd tone to the way she said his name.

His gaze lingered for an awkward extra second on Emily before turning his attention to the Spaniard. And none of his other friends called him by his formal first name. "And who is this?" he shifted his eyes to the other woman in the room.

"My name is Adriana Villa," she stated as she reached out her hand.

He extended his hand as well and got a polite but firm shake.

"She saved our butts in Vegas," Sean threw in.

"Maybe I should hire her to help keep you out of trouble," Tommy ribbed. Then, he sat back down. His long-time friend simply gave an amused shake of his head.

Tommy went on, "By the way, saw what happened at the poker tournament. Brutal beat, man."

"It happens," Sean replied as he set a small book bag on the table. "At least we came out of the desert with *something*."

Tommy pulled the bag closer to him and unzipped the main compartment. "What is it?" he asked as he pulled out one wrapped towel and then another.

"We're not sure. You and I have seen a lot of stuff all over the world. But this one has me stumped. They look like golden leaves."

Schultz stopped unwrapping the package momentarily.

"Leaves?"

"Yeah, like off a tree. But a little bigger."

Tommy's eyebrows came together, revealing he was perplexed about the new information. He reached into the bag and pulled out one of the objects, much like the one he and Will had recovered in New Mexico. Curious, he unwrapped the second piece and held both up, comparing them side-by-side. They were nearly identical. Their structure and detail matched almost perfectly.

"They're fairly light considering what they are made out of." Sean said while his friend examined the relics. "Whoever made them must have been an expert metal worker."

Tommy carefully laid both objects down and stepped over to a box that was sitting next to a window. He reached in and pulled out a piece that appeared exactly like the two he'd just been looking at. "They match the one we found in New Mexico," he said with a perplexed look as he set the third leaf next to the other two.

"So what I want to know is, how does all of this come together?" Sean asked.

"I think I may be able to lend a hand with that." A familiar voice, gruff and southern came from just outside in the hall. Joe McElroy appeared in the doorway. His hair was thick, flowing brown with some streaks of gray, just to the bottom of his ears. He was in jeans and a flannel jacket, one arm in a sling from the bullet wound he'd received a few weeks before. His face was shaved clean, making him look a lot younger than he was.

Sean grinned. "I thought I smelled something funny around here." He stood up and slapped his friend on the back as Joe entered the room.

"It's probably you three," he joked loudly. "Y'all look like you haven't had a shower in days."

"How'd you get away from the wife?" Sean jeered with a laugh.

"Actually," Emily interrupted, "we could really use a shower and a good night's rest. So could we move this along?"

"Hello, Emily," Joe greeted her. "Nice to see you, too. And, Ms. Villa, it's nice to meet you."

Adriana raised an eyebrow and spied the newcomer suspiciously. "How did you know my name?"

"That's for another time, I suppose. For now, I'll just tell you that I like to know things, lots of things. But at the moment, you all are lookin' for answers about these here golden leaves." He reached down and picked one up, eyeing it with a grin.

Joe collapsed into a chair as if he'd been standing all day. "Tommy, cue up the screen so I can show them what we've learned so far."

Tommy nodded and stepped over to a laptop that had been connected to an overhead projector that hung from the ceiling. The lights went dim and the shades closed to the subtle hum of an electric motor. After a few seconds, the projector came to life and the screen changed to an old man in priestly robes. His face appeared worn with the wrinkles of time and the thick, gray beard matched a thinning patch of hair on his head. There was something wild about the man's eyes, an intensity and determination that belied his years. He stood with a younger man, dressed in a white button up suit and some dark pants. From the look of the picture quality and the style of the clothes, Sean estimated the photograph to be from the 1970s.

"Have you ever seen this man before?" Joe asked the group.

"Which one?" Sean requested.

"The older one," Joe refined. "The younger guy is Stan Hall."

"Doesn't ring a bell."

Emily shook her head in agreement while Adriana said nothing.

"That there is Padre Carlos Crespi. He was a missionary to the town of Cuenca in Ecuador until 1982."

Tommy handed Joe a remote control, which he quickly used to change to the next slide. It was a photo of the old priest with three small children smiling next to him.

"This guy, Crespi, was a saint to the locals in Cuenca. Along with servin' as a priest at the church of Maria Auxiliadora, he ran an orphanage there and helped the people in any way he could. His life was dedicated to the ministry of true Christian service."

The next slide caused Sean to perk up in his seat. In it Father Crespi stood awkwardly, holding what appeared to be a metallic sheet. The thin, yellow material had been imprinted with symbols and a language that Sean recognized instantly. Sanskrit.

Joe continued, "The padre had a love for history and archaeology, a fact that most of the villagers knew. So, they started bringing him artifacts, like the one in this picture."

He changed to the next slide. This one was of a stone sculpture that looked just like it had come from Babylon itself. Another slide flashed onto the screen, one displaying relics that could have come right out of an ancient Egyptian tomb. Still more pictures appeared with objects from Assyria, Sumer, and Israel. Sean sat speechless, wondering how he'd never heard of this mysterious priest before, while Joe finished his presentation with a video showing the padre speaking with the man named Stan Hall they'd seen in the initial photograph.

The priest was speaking in a rush of Spanish, his voice loud and impatient. It was as if he was trying to get Hall to understand something important. Crespi opened a pair of large, wooden doors and led the way into a high-ceiling room with a single light bulb dangling from the top. The old man pulled on a string and the bulb instantly illuminated the room. Shelves that went all the way to the fifteen-foot high ceiling were packed with objects and relics from cultures nowhere remotely close to the location of Cuenca. Pieces of stone, bronze, and gold were scattered on the shelves and overflowed onto the floor. Enormous sheets of copper and gold were rolled up, leaning against the shelves or in the corners. Hall asked the priest where all of the objects came from to which the old man kept saying the same word, "las cuevas." The caves.

The video stopped running. Joe reached over and turned the lights in the room back on.

"I would love to see that collection." Sean said in a matter-of-fact tone.

"Me too," Tommy agreed. "Unfortunately, Father Crespi died in 1982."

Joe nodded. "When he passed away, it was discovered that his vault of ancient artifacts was empty. It had been completely cleaned out. No one is sure where all of the pieces went or who took them."

"Vanished into thin air," Tommy added quietly.

Joe went on. "People often asked Father Crespi who had brought him the items in his vault, to which he always responded, 'the people from the forests.' Only one man has come forward and claimed to know the location of the items that were taken from the cleric's vault. Mysteriously, that man was murdered soon after. He was found shot dead in his apartment."

"So no one has a clue where to look?" Emily asked after remaining silent for the previous few minutes.

"The 'caves' the old man was talkin' about are apparently near a river, though nobody has found them yet. A few people thought they did, but no one has ever produced any evidence. Neil Armstrong was even brought in as an investor and participant in one of the explorations, but all they found were empty caverns and a few skeletons."

"Neil Armstrong the Astronaut?" Sean seemed impressed.

"Yep," Joe confirmed then continued on. "In the riddle from the stone we found in Georgia, it mentioned some rivers. We think that the contents of the cleric's vault in Cuenca are part of the greater collection mentioned on the stone. If that is the case, it would make sense that the rivers they are referring to are not far from his church. Seems like Father Crespi's collection has been returned to one of the caves there along a nearby river, but there are several within a hundred miles of Cuenca. Of course, a lot of other people have gone looking for it, too."

Sean eyed his old friend suspiciously. "You think you know where it is, don't you?"

Mac's eyes grew narrow as he grinned. "Maybe. See, the problem with that area is that there are lots of caves and lots of rivers. Some of the caves are completely flooded now. So it is anybody's guess which cave is the right one. Obviously, Armstrong and Hall never found it."

"What makes you so confident?" Adriana asked cynically.

"Because I know something they didn't." He let the moment build up as he eyed them carefully. "I think the old priest left clues at his church that point the way."

Chapter 38
Nevada Desert

"Things," Lindsey began, "have been put back on track." He peered at Mornay and Carrol. He'd ordered them back to their meeting room late in the afternoon to update them on the fact that he'd effectively cleaned up their mess.

"What do you mean, back on track?" Mornay sounded dubious.

Mornay was such an irritation, Lindsey thought.

"Wyatt and his friends have found the next pieces. It is only a matter of time until they lead us to the second chamber."

"How long are you going to let them keep going? If you don't reel them in now, we may lose another treasure like we did with the last chamber."

Carrol shifted uneasily in his chair while Mornay spoke to the Imperator.

"We have to let them lead the way, Albert," he said the name with disdain. "They have no idea what they are really looking for. And with the fools from the IAA running the show, things will happen much faster."

"Yes but what happens when they figure it out? It's only a matter of time, Alex. If they're smart enough to figure out a way to solve the riddles then they will eventually learn the truth about the golden chambers."

Mornay was right, as much as it annoyed him. But it was true. Eventually, Wyatt and his friends would learn of the true nature of their search.

"I don't believe we have a choice," he paused, selling the line of thought. "We must let them lead us to the chamber. Then, we will kill them all." The serious tone of the statement left an ominous energy hanging in the room.

In the shadows of one of the room's alcoves, a figure stood in hidden in the dark, listening as he'd been instructed to do. Lindsey spoke as if the man wasn't there. The other two could not know of his presence or what he was about to do. They had to be led to believe that the only course of action was to allow the fools from IAA to lead them to the destination. The man in the shadows, though, was the ace up his sleeve. And the game was about to change.

"A map?" Sean was intrigued by what Joe was insinuating.

"Maybe. I'm not really sure what it is," Joe explained. "See, Crespi was extremely fond of Archaeology. As I mentioned, he spent a lot of hours reading and researching ancient civilizations and cultures. That was one of the reasons the people brought him so many of those pieces. And while he was grateful for the gifts, he longed to know exactly where they had come from. If I had to guess, I'd say that Padre Crespi recognized that most of the artifacts brought to him could not have been found in the western hemisphere. So, he searched for the location. And I believe he discovered it.

"The Vatican had been pestering him for years about the items in his vault. Not only was it financially valuable, the collection may have had some kind of historical significance. The priest knew the Vatican would like to get their hands on his relics for a number of reasons. That's why he arranged for every single piece to be returned to its origin. But he was a crafty fella'. He'd found the way to the secret caves by following an ancient set of clues. Crespi felt it only proper to leave the clues the way he found them but with one addition: his map."

"So, where is this map?" Sean asked, fearful he already knew the answer.

Joe and Tommy both smiled at him.

"Well, old buddy," Joe said, "where do you think? It's in Cuenca." He laughed as he said it.

"You couldn't bring it here first?" Sean asked sarcastically.

McElroy shook his head as he leaned over and smacked Wyatt on the back. "Nope. Heck, I don't even know what the thing looks like. You're going to have to go to Crespi's church to see for yourselves."

"The plane will be ready to head out to Ecuador tomorrow morning around ten," Tommy announced.

"I guess we better get some rest then," Sean stated. "I'll call Mauricio and let him know we're coming. That's his neck of the woods."

Emily stood, ready to leave. "You guys have fun. I have to get back to the office. While I'm there I'll try do see what else I can dig up about our new friends from Golden Dawn."

"That's probably a good idea. Dangerous bunch, those," Joe warned. "Secret groups the public knows about aren't the ones that scare me. It's the ones that are still a secret that I'm concerned about."

Adriana spoke up, "I'm coming with you, Sean."

He smiled. There was something about that woman that he liked. Maybe there were a lot of things. She was certainly beautiful, even after the events of the day and the night before, she had managed to look stunning. But there was something adventurous about her that kept his curiosity piqued.

"You can stay at my house," he said. Then added, "I have plenty of guest space."

"I'll see you two at the plane in the morning," Tommy interrupted. "Mac, I guess you won't be coming with us on this one."

"Sorry fellas. I gotta sit this one out. I'm still in the dog house back home and with my arm still in this contraption I'm pretty sure I'd be more hindrance than help." He raised the sling up slightly to emphasize his point. "I'm always here to help, though. All you gotta do is call." Mac gave a huge grin, which made his eyes squint.

"What's the story on the golden leaves?" Sean asked.

"I'm not sure," Tommy answered. Mac and I have a theory but it's pretty far fetched. We doubt it's a viable explanation at this point. Mac, you want to tell them?

Mac nodded. When he spoke, it was a different, more serious tone than he'd been using the last few minutes. "I don't think it's something we should even really consider at this point, but it is possible, given who seems to be chasing after the same prize."

Tommy accented Mac's thought. "There's a book written by a man named Adam Clark. He wrote it in the late 1700s. Clark was a very pious man and moved to the colonies to help start up a new religious order, one of purity and righteous values, much like many others did during that time. His book was meant to be a guide or concordance that could help church followers through the Bible in a way they could understand.

"He tells the story of how Adam and Eve were cast out of the Garden of Eden and that God put an angel with a flaming sword at the gates of the garden so that humans could not enter it. Specifically, the angel was put there to guard the way to the tree of life so that man could not eat of it and live perpetually in sin."

Joe nodded and continued for Shultz, "Clark's book then, oddly, warns anyone reading the book not to search for the Tree of Life for it could not be found and had been hidden by God Himself. He goes on to say that eternal life can only come through the grace of Jesus Christ."

Sean was intrigued. "So you're saying that these Golden Dawn guys are looking for the tree of life?"

"Yeah," Mac confirmed, "but like we said, probably not viable."

Sean unwrapped one of the objects and picked it up. He looked over it reverently. When he spoke, it was mostly to himself. The Tree of life. Now that's a very interesting theory."

Chapter 39
Atlanta, GA

"What happened in the lab?" The man's voice sounded oblivious.

"What do you mean? The part where you didn't show up ore the part where someone started shooting at me? I'm assuming that wasn't you." Will was irritated

"I couldn't find anything, so I got out of there."

"You obviously didn't look hard enough," Will walked down the hall that led to his apartment. He lowered his voice out of habit.

Will was playing a very dangerous game. He'd hired the man on the phone without Lindsey's consent. At first, it had seemed like a good idea. Having an extra pair of eyes and ears could always help. But the guy had been sloppy. He was supposed to have taken care of the Georgia Tech professor and retrieved the information. Instead, he'd fouled up, which required that Will take Tommy to the scene.

Alexander Lindsey was paying Will a great deal of money to make sure Tommy Schultz discovered the four golden chambers. The archaeologist was not to be harmed until the final chamber had been discovered. At which point, he was to be disposed. The Prophet had promised an enormous reward for the completion of the mission, more than half of the treasure. And after seeing the first golden chamber in Georgia, Will was convinced. He just had to make sure that nothing else got in his way.

"Jennings has been asking questions," the voice said through the earpiece. "Something's got him nervous."

Will was afraid that would happen. Jennings had been careless, a real liability looming over the mission. Still, the man wasn't completely stupid, but he had too many loose ends.

"What do you want me to do?" The voice on the other end startled Will from his thoughts.

The man he'd hired to retrieve the solution to the code from the Georgia Tech professor had simply made a mess of everything. "Meet me in one hour in Piedmont Park. Same place we met before."

"Sounds good. I'll see you there."

Centennial Olympic Park was lit up brightly with Christmas lights. A large tent on the south lawn of the park housed a temporary ice skating rink. Apparently, the city wanted to put the Christmas decorations up a little early. The park was empty, for the most part. Most of the patrons were likely at home getting ready for bed

Hunter Carlson had found his way out of the cavern in New Mexico. He was frustrated that the men he followed had escaped. He knew where they would end up, though. So, he decided to lay low and see if he could find out what they would do next.

He listened in to Will's phone conversation from inside his black Mercedes, trying to look inconspicuous. Thanks to the darkly tinted windows, no one would really take notice of him.

Will Hastings seemed to have several irons in the fire. Carlson heard him mention Jennings. If he was working for Eric Jennings, that could present new issues. Will had also told one of his assets to meet him in Piedmont Park on the other side of town. It would be a surprise if a body didn't turn up the next morning in that area. That was one thing assets were generally stupid about. They just followed the money trail, doing as they were told, often times right up to the end of a gun barrel.

Carlson thought briefly about his own team. He'd executed a few of them without regard. They were easily replaceable, which was a good thing in his line of work. He'd considered the idea of going it alone. However, Hastings had proven to be more difficult than he'd anticipated, as had the archaeologist.

His wiretaps at IAA headquarters were working perfectly. Just half an hour ago, he'd been listening to the conversation regarding Wyatt and Schultz's next destination. Apparently, there was a map somewhere in Cuenca. *Good thing he never went without a passport on him. That was where he would make his next move.* He had a team in South America he'd worked with on a few other missions that would be easy to put together on short notice, but something told him this one needed to be played a little closer to the chest.

A delivery truck rumbled up next to him for a moment and paused as if deciding whether or not they should back in to the loading dock behind them or just double park on the street. After a few moments, the awkward looking vehicle backed in to the building next to where Hunter was parked. The annoying beep that trucks signaled for backing up faded off as they entered the tunnel of the building.

The phone in his pocket suddenly began ringing. He eyed it for a moment then answered. "Hello."

"We've been waiting for you to call." The voice on the other line said.

The two men who'd hired him were annoying. One was a sniveling subservient, the other overly domineering, probably to mask a great deal of insecurity and lack of intelligence. It had been easy to see which one was pulling the strings and why.

"I'm sure you have. But I wanted to have more information before I contacted you."

There was a pause. "Well, what do you have?" The voice continued, irritating and pushy.

Carlson let out a sigh. When this was all over, he'd have to consider taking out his two contractors as well, just for the pleasure of it. He decided to just tell the man everything he knew for the time being. "They are heading to Ecuador, Cuenca to be exact. There is a map that an old priest left there that supposedly leads to a cave where they think the treasure is. Sounds like they are going to head out tomorrow."

"What are you going to do?"

"I'll let them lead the way to the map then intercept it when they're done. A few missing tourists won't be a big deal in South America. It happens all the time. Once they are out of the way I'll forward you the location."

"Good. See to it that you do. We have taken a great risk in this venture, one that could cost us everything."

"Look, your boss bought the whole Las Vegas fiasco, didn't he? He thinks that was your only move. I guarantee you no one knows who I am or who I'm working for. So relax. I have it under control."

The voice on the other end went silent, apparently contemplating what had been said. "Fair enough, Mr. Carlson," he finally replied and ended the call.

Hunter looked quizzically at the touch screen of his smart phone. "Thank you, Mr. Mornay," he said to himself as he stuffed the device into his pocket.

Chapter 40
Atlanta, GA

Sean and Adriana stepped out of the gray Maxima after he'd eased it in the long, six-car garage.

Her eyes grew wide with the sight of the collection of motorcycles. She instantly recognized several that she'd dreamed of having but never really pursued. Norton, Royal Enfield, Ducati, Triumph, Harley Davidson, and several Japanese makes occupied the space within the confines of the hall-like garage. There were even some that she'd never heard of before. She reverently walked over to the small fleet and eyed each machine carefully. "They are beautiful," she said respectfully. "When can we go for a ride?"

He smiled as he watched her. "I guess as soon as we get back from South America and we get a warm day."

"You don't ride when it's cold?"

"No. I can't stand it. Once the temperature drops below sixty-five, it's too cool for me."

She nodded. "I can see that. It gets a little chilly in the desert once winter hits. Takes the joy out of it when you are shivering the entire time."

"Indeed."

She walked slowly back towards him, her eyes probing his deeply.

Caught a little off guard, he stammered while he spoke. "I...I...should show you to your room. Gonna be a long day tomorrow and we need to get some sleep."

She pulled close to him. Her eyes locked with his as she gazed up at him for a long moment. The cold night air seemed to hold them in place.

Sean broke it off suddenly and turned to open the door to the short flight of stairs that led up into the kitchen. "This way to the house," he said awkwardly.

Her expression was clearly that of disappointment and confusion. Nevertheless, she smiled at him. "Lead the way, Senor Wyatt."

After showing Adriana to her room, Sean retired to his own. There were a million thoughts running through his head at the moment, most of which concerned the beautiful Spaniard down the hall. She must have thought him odd. Men surely threw themselves at her on a daily basis. *Yet here he was turning her down, running away.* He wanted her. So what was he doing? Things with Allison had ended abruptly. Actually, nothing ever really got started. It would have been too complicated with her being off on assignments and various missions all the time for Axis. He'd lived that life. He knew exactly what the demands of the job were. But Adriana Villa...*what was holding him back? Fear?* He didn't know but for tonight, he wasn't going to do anything about it. They had a late morning flight to catch the next day and he needed to sleep. As he lay in his bed, his mind drifted to memories from years before. They lingered on a face, a young woman calling his name before fading into darkness.

Chapter 41
Atlanta, GA

Will sat quietly on a bench under a growth of oak trees. The man he was there to meet was running a few minutes late, something for which he had little tolerance. It didn't cost anything to arrive a few minutes early. But tardiness seemed to be the culture of the younger generation. They felt like it was completely acceptable to show up late and simply apologize it away.

The sound of traffic was light at that time of night. Big cities always had at least some street activity during all hours. The area around Piedmont Park was no different. Some local bars and music venues were still busily serving their patrons while an erratic stream of cars hustled by.

He tried to clear his thoughts of the annoyance by taking in a deep breath of the cool evening air. Late fall in Atlanta brought a vast array of temperatures. Sometimes it could be as cold as the teens during the holiday months while at others, temperatures could reach into the low seventies. That night was somewhere in-between, probably in the upper forties. The nearly barren branches rustled above in a slight breeze, causing him to pull his coat a little tighter.

Piedmont Park was home to a number of city activities throughout the year. From concerts to parades and even cooking festivals, it was often the center of activity. Around late November, though, it seemed temporarily forgotten, which was why Will had chosen the location for the evening's meeting.

"Sorry I'm late," a man's voice slightly startled him from behind.

Will's irritation resurfaced with the artificial apology. He peered at his paid help with disdain. The brown haired man was probably in his mid-twenties, dressed like he just jumped right out of an Abercrombie canoe with a striped, cotton polo, a black pea coat, and some artificially torn jeans. Cocky and careless didn't last long in their line of work. A lesson he would soon learn. "You should never keep an employer waiting," he replied.

"I know. I got caught up in traffic." The young man was sheepish but obviously lying.

As bad as Atlanta traffic could be, there wasn't enough to slow anyone down at that time of night.

Will decided to let it go. It wouldn't be an issue anymore anyway.

"We have a new assignment. And it's more money this time." He began walking towards the center of the park and the younger man fell in beside him. The two crested a small rise and then descended down the other side, out of the view of the streets surrounding the park.

"What's the gig?"

Will stopped in the shadows, just far enough away from the reach of one of the streetlights that dotted the sidewalk. He put his hand into a coat pocket and pulled out an envelope. "It's a lot of money this time. Fifty grand up front and fifty more when we finish the job. That's a hundred grand a piece." He handed the manila package to his subordinate who started unwinding the twine.

"Hundred grand a piece? Who we going after? Someone political?" From within the envelope, he pulled out an 8x11 black and white photograph. His eyebrows lowered and confusion filled his face. The picture he held was of him. "Is this some kind of joke?"

He barely got the sentence out before the face on the photo erupted to the pop of a silenced gun. His legs wavered and he staggered backwards a few steps, only then seeing the black gun that Will had pulled out from the other side of his jacket. The bullet hole in his chest was already leaking a great deal of blood through the yellow shirt. He dropped to his knees, confusion and terror filling his eyes. Will stepped closer, holding the weapon at his side. "Your generation just doesn't get it, do you? You think it's ok to cut corners, show up late for appointments, and just by saying you're sorry it makes everything ok." He raised the gun, aiming it at the stunned victim's head. "Well it's not." The barrel popped again sending a second bullet into the man's forehead. Will looked around casually as the body slumped over sideways onto the sidewalk. There was no one in sight, just as he'd planned.

Placing the gun back into his inner coat pocket, Will strolled back out to his car on the street. There were a few drunken revelers walking down the road, but they were walking the other way. No one had seen a thing.

Chapter 42
Washington, D.C.

Emily yawned as she walked down one of the many corridors in Axis headquarters. She'd taken an early flight out of Atlanta, sacrificing a good night's rest. Still, she felt better than she had the previous night. A good shower and at least a few hours of sleep had done wonders. The office was quiet, as it always was. One of the nice things about Axis was size. A smaller agency provided a less crowded working environment. Serenity was something Emily needed. There were several questions that needed answering, and she wouldn't really be able to rest until she found some kind of resolution. She would have to call Jim Caldwell's boss and explain to him that he'd been killed. It was a call she didn't look forward to.

As she approached her office she fumbled with her keys for a second before she realized her door was slightly ajar. Cautiously, she pushed the glass entrance open. In her chair behind the desk, sat a familiar and unwelcomed face. Sam Townsend.

"Good morning, Emily," he said dryly.

"Your little 'all-access pass' doesn't include my chair, Samuel," she returned with resentment.

"My mistake," his tone was lathered in insincerity.

He stood and slipped around the edge of the desk and into one of the guest seats. She never took her eyes off of him as he moved. Emily knew everything about Townsend, probably more than he knew about her. His unusually fast rise to power, the people he'd run over to get there, and even his favorite flavor ice cream were no secret to her. She'd made it her policy to keep an eye on potential enemies both foreign and domestic.

"What do you want, Sam?" She asked as she placed her laptop case on the dark, cherry wood desk.

He pulled out his cell phone and gave a quick glance at its face then slipped the device back in his pants pocket. "What were you doing out in Las Vegas, Emily?"

His voice was genuinely curious.

"I was out there on vacation. I had some days to use and what better place than Vegas? Plus, I wanted to check up on an old friend who was playing in a big poker tournament."

His tone became wry. "Yes, Sean Wyatt. How is he these days? Shame he didn't stay on with the Justice Department longer. He was a good field agent."

"He's doing fine," she replied as she sorted a few papers on her desk and placed a few things from her bag into the top drawer. And he's happy working for IAA. Pretty sure he's never looked back. So why don't you spare me the bs and tell me why you're in my office, Sam?"

"Fair enough," he said with a smile. "I need your help with something." He shifted slightly and loosened his red and white striped tie.

"My help?" She appeared dubious. "I doubt that. You have pretty much every single agency at your disposal. What could my little operation do that they can't?"

He crossed his legs and leaned back, folding his hands together in his lap. His face looked thoughtful as he considered how to word his next sentence. "Eric Jennings has gone rogue. I need someone to find out what he is up to."

The statement was brazen and to the point. Emily stopped what she was doing and stared at him for several seconds, considering what he'd just said. Even the few, quiet sounds of the office outside seemed to pause with the information. "What do you mean? Eric is the director of a very respectable, very powerful agency. It's not like he's just some field agent or an asset."

She wasn't buying it.

"All true," Sam waved a finger at her, "but a desk job and a government salary don't do a lot for the more ambitious souls of the industry."

"Eric's made plenty of money," she argued. "He has to make at least in the low six figures with his years of experience."

"A couple hundred grand won't buy what it used to. Jennings has some expensive tastes and habits."

As he finished the last sentence, Townsend pulled out some photos and slid them across the desk. Emily picked them up warily. They were photos of Jennings with various women. Some were on a sidewalk, outside of hotels, and in other random locations. "Looks like you already have someone watching him," she dropped the pictures on the desk. "He can't be spending all his money on women."

"Not all of it. But he has other vices too. Eric has never managed his money well. And that also spills over into his professional life as. You don't have to look very far to see that his agency is almost always over budget, recklessly spending in areas where agencies like yours and others always come in under."

She still wasn't convinced. The gears in her mind were turning. Emily knew Townsend was a slime ball. *He wasn't a man to be trusted, but he wasn't a man to meddle with either.*

"Again. It looks like you already have someone on him. So why do you need me, Sam?"

He smiled like a kid who knew a secret that everyone else wanted to know. "It's not just why I need you, Emily. I think whatever he's up to will interest you as well."

Will awoke to the sound of his cell phone ringing and vibrating violently on the nightstand next to his bed. Groggily, he reached over and picked it up. His partner, Trent Morris was on the line. That could mean only one thing. Someone had been murdered. Technically he was still on vacation for three more days but he'd learned that when his partner called, it was important.

"Where?" He already knew the answer. He was somewhat surprised it had taken that long for the call to come in.

"Piedmont Park. Happened last night. Double tap, chest and head."

"On my way," he said and ended the call.

"What do you mean it will 'interest' me?" Emily sat down in her plush leather chair and peered at her counterpart.

"Jennings was the one who tried to take you out in Vegas. Not only that but as of late he has taken a keen interest in your friends with the IAA."

That got her attention. She pressed him. "So, you were observing them, but you didn't have your team try to stop them? Thanks a lot."

He laughed. "Who am I going to use? I didn't have a team I could call at that point. My division is primarily used for observing and collecting information. I only had one guy on it." That part was true. Townsend's portion of the CIA had been dubbed a paper tiger of sorts. They could bring down just about anyone without ever firing a weapon. She figured that most of his agents were capable of lending assistance in the field. If there were only a few on the assignment, though, it really would have taken a lot time to get members of another agency's team into the area in time to help.

"So what were you doing in Vegas?" she asked after a few moments of reflection.

"Like I said, we were observing." He knew what her next question would be so he went ahead and answered it. "Specifically, we were watching Jennings' agents."

Emily appeared incredulous. She had a hard time believing that so many government agents could be recruited and operating outside the boundaries of their organizations without being noticed.

"Are you trying to tell me that all of those operatives in Vegas work for the Justice Department and you were there to see what they were up to?"

He shook his head, uncrossed his legs then leaned forward slightly. Apparently, he understood her problem with that idea.

"No. We don't think any of them do. We believe they're all mercenaries, probably international contractors. They were recruited by Jennings."

"Who are they?" she asked, her interest piqued just slightly. "There was a man and a woman. What do you know about those two?"

He placed a manila folder on the desk and slid it over to her. Emily eyed the packet then opened it up, revealing two photographs. One was a young man and the other a young woman. Their appearance was neat and professional looking. Both were attractive, probably in their mid-twenties. There was a coldness to their faces that seemed to emanate from their eyes.

"James Collack and Angela Weaver," Sam said as he leaned back. "I want to know who they are working for."

"Couldn't find that out on your own?" she asked in a snide tone.

He ignored the barb. "We believe that they may be working for a secret organization known as 'Golden Dawn.' However, it appears that this secret society has a reach into our government, of which we had previously been unaware."

"So you think they are connected with someone? Who? White House? Senate? Supreme Court?"

He shrugged. "Maybe all of those. Maybe none of them. There is one particular part of government, though, that we know Golden Dawn has infiltrated." Townsend let the thought hang for a moment, building the suspense before he continued. "How much do you know about Eric Jennings' agency?"

Emily's eyes widened slightly. "The Hoover Directive?" He nodded. "Not much, really. It's a branch of the FBI that J. Edgar Hoover put together as a sort of 'black cell' operation to work outside the bounds of the laws the bureau has to obey. No one outside of their little group really knows what they've been involved with, although we usually have a pretty good idea. "Surely your operation knows more than I do."

Her placating tone bounced off of him like a rubber ball. Nothing fazed him. "We know a great deal about their operations. However, most of what we know has to do with financial information and use of resources. My team does not usually get involved with much of the actual engagement."

Then it hit her. *That was why Townsend needed Axis. It was all starting to make sense.* "So you need someone to do the grunt work?"

He smiled. "In a manner of speaking, yes. But more than that, I need someone I can trust." The irony was not lost on him. He knew people didn't necessarily trust him. Nor did he care. "I realize," he added, "that you don't trust me and that is fine. But your reputation and career have been exemplary. I know that if I ask you for assistance you will do everything in your power to make sure that justice is done."

"Justice?" She asked warily.

"Yes." He waited for her reply without adding anything else. His expression was serious and anxious.

She considered what he was asking. All of her agents were in the field at the moment. Her best one had left a week ago to head to Uganda on a special assignment. He was the last one available for the foreseeable future.

"I suppose I can look into it," she said finally. "But I can't make any promises. And I'll have to use some external resources."

He held out his hands. "That's all I'm asking for." Then he stood and headed for the door. He stopped and turned around and said, "Thanks Emily. I owe you one." With that, he closed the door and disappeared into the hall.

She looked down again at the photographs. The faces definitely belonged to the two attackers from Vegas. She'd recognized them immediately. Now Sam Townsend wanted to know who they worked for. Something didn't quite make sense. If he believed they worked for Eric Jennings and the Hoover Directive, what else was there to know? Plus, he'd already made the connection to Golden Dawn. It seemed like he already had it all figured out. Townsend must have believed the story went deeper but couldn't figure it out, something that also didn't add up. Sam had just as many resources as she did.

Emily laid the photos back on the desk and plopped down into her chair to think for a few moments. Doing the favor for Townsend was a bi-product. She'd been planning on looking into Golden Dawn and its "prophet" anyway. Now she could kill two birds with one stone. Never the less, *something still didn't feel right.*

Chapter 43
Atlanta, GA

Detective Hastings held up his badge as he walked through the police line and past the onlookers and flashing cameras. It was too early in the morning to have to deal with this.

Growing up in an orphanage had made him tough. Will had been at the top of his class in everything he'd ever done all the way back to first grade. He'd applied to a special program in the Justice Department right out of college and had breezed through the rigorous physical, psychological, and mental trials that had been the downfall of many others.

Upon completion of the training course, he had received an odd letter requesting a meeting in a specific location. All the letter had said was that he would be provided the opportunity of a lifetime and would never have to worry about money again.

Later that night, at the appointed time, Will had gone to the meeting place specified in the correspondence. He'd been curious and the place was public enough, just outside a coffee shop in downtown Washington.

A black Yukon had pulled up and the rear door opened. Inside, an old man sat smiling at him. "Looks like rain. Need a lift?" he'd asked insistently.

Will nodded and stepped into the vehicle.

His life had changed dramatically since that day. The Prophet had told him about the mission of Golden Dawn and how it would make the world a better place.

He explained that soon, they would have the power to wipe out all of the useless and evil people in the world and start the human race over again.

Will had developed a keen hatred of criminals and other people who bled the government dry every month. He hadn't really bought into the religious mumbo jumbo that The Prophet had been spouting. For him, it was enough that he wanted to cleanse the earth of the riff-raff. Extreme? Maybe. Or was it more extreme that criminals were housed in prisons all over the country at the expense of billions in taxpayer dollars. And what of all the useless people who'd been on welfare for years, doing nothing but sucking money out of the system. To Will, the Prophet's proposal appealed to him on that level.

When an archaeologist in Atlanta had discovered clues the old man believed would lead to an ancient stone somewhere in North Georgia, Will had moved to Atlanta to work with the city's Police Department. The paperwork had been put together quickly and no one had thought anything about the transfer. Even fewer bothered to ask questions. The Prophet was well-connected, indeed.

The only downside to having a cover as a police officer was actually having to do police work. Small price to pay for the benefits he was receiving. The Prophet had been very generous.

Will walked through a few more ranks of officers and CSIs before arriving at the motionless heap on the ground.

The body was on its side, lifeless eyes staring off into the hill to the east. A hole in the forehead signaled the likely cause of death, a thin line of dried blood tracing from it to the point where it had dripped onto the ground.

Hastings had no problem looking at the man he'd killed the night before. The man had served his purpose. The man had been Will's surveillance puppet, ordered to watch Tommy Schultz from the moment he'd announced his initial discovery. The man had followed his orders, for the most part. In the end, though, he had to die.

"How was your vacation?" The familiar voice of his partner Trent Morris came from behind him.

Will turned and saw the tall, stately figure holding two cups of coffee. His tan trench coat was a contrast to his dark brown skin. Trent had grown up in a tough neighborhood on the east side of Atlanta. He'd decided early in life he would choose the right path, something that had gotten him in a few tight spots as a youth. As he'd grown older, though, his reputation commanded respect from all.

"One of those for me?" Will asked with a grin, his breath coming out of his mouth like fog in the cold air.

Trent held out one of the steaming cups. "It's the least I could do."

Morris had been a police officer for a few decades and was extremely popular within the department. He always took good care of the people around him and treated everyone with respect yet was unafraid to use his authority when needed. He was a true leader.

Will hoped he wouldn't have to kill Trent at some point. He liked the man. Personal ties, however, had to be severed sometimes.

"I suppose I don't really need you here but I just want to make sure your involved as much as possible whenever something comes up. The more you get hands on the better." There was a hint at something in the tall, black man's voice but Will couldn't place what it was. He went on. "Obviously, two gun shot wounds. One to the head. One in the chest. Looks to be close range."

Will knelt down and examined the body more closely, examining his handiwork. "Forty caliber," he said in a hushed tone.

"Mmmhmm," Trent agreed. "Ballistics should confirm that."

Hastings stood again and took a gulp of the hot coffee. "Who is he?"

Trent looked distant for a moment then said, "Walk with me."

Confused, Will obeyed and followed as his partner began walking away from the crime scene towards a little patch of bushes and trees just out of earshot of the other people working in the area.

"What is it?"

Morris looked around in all directions as if making sure no one could hear. "Officially, we don't have a positive ID. When the report comes out, it's going to be listed as a drug deal gone bad. It has all the makings of an execution so that's what we're going to call it."

246

"So we're going to do a cover up? Why?" Will appeared dubious.

Trent pulled closer and when he spoke it was barely above a whisper being extra careful that no one could hear. "Because the victim is a federal agent."

Chapter 44
Atlanta, Georgia

The morning had been busy. Sean and Adriana had gone to some shops in Buckhead that he knew would be open in the morning hours. His Spanish companion had needed some clothes due to their hasty escape from the desert. So they'd spent thirty minutes grabbing some things she would need for the next few days. Hardly the way either one of them would have prepared for a trip to another continent but under the circumstances, it would suffice.

Satisfied they had all their required supplies, they drove in contemplative silence to the airport. Sean pulled his sedan up to the outside of a private hangar on the outskirts of Hartsfield International. Enormous black letters designated that the gray-metal facility belonged to the IAA.

After they'd removed their bags from the trunk, he and Adriana walked around the front corner of the building and through the huge opening. Inside, a white G5 jet with the same black lettering stood silently in the cavernous recesses of the hangar.

Tommy was busily checking some paperwork off to the side where his car sat near the interior wall. A few mechanics and maintenance workers were going through their routine check sheets to make sure the plane was going to operate as it should.

"That's quite a jet you have there," Adriana commented as they approached.

Sean grinned. "Thanks. Having your own company plane certainly has its advantages."

"I can imagine," she said, her mind drifting off as she spied the sleek vehicle.

Tommy noticed them as they drew near and handed the clipboard to his driver who acknowledged him with a nod and retreated to the black car forty feet away. He reached out and offered to take one of the bag's Sean was carrying. "I'll get that for you," he said with a smile. "Did you guys get some sleep last night?" There was a playful tone in his voice.

"Yes, it was nice to get some proper sleep," Villa commented as they followed Schultz up the steps into the cabin of the jet.

Apparently, he was either going to get no details or there were none to get.

At the entrance to the plane, the passengers were greeted with a luxurious aroma of leather and rich wood. The plane's interior opened up into a lavish space decorated in cream-colored floors and walls, accented by dark wood panels and furniture.

Several rows of tanned, Napa-leather seats faced each other with plenty of space in-between each. A wall jutted out towards the aft of the cabin and was separated with a doorway.

"This is our main travel quarters and meeting room," Tommy said, extending his hand.

"All of these seats recline but in the back," he pointed to the door, "we have some sleeping rooms as well for the longer trips.

"Impressive," Adriana said as she stepped over to a window and leaned over, taking a look outside.

Tommy took the baggage and stowed it in an overhead bin near the exit. "If you will excuse me, I've got to take care of a few other things before we head out."

Sean plopped down in a comfortable leather seat and leaned back while Adriana took a seat opposite of him. He cast her a casual smile, which she returned in kind.

"Thank you for being a gentleman last night," she said after a brief moment of silence.

The grin eased over to one side of his mouth. "Don't give me more credit than I deserve. I was just tired, that's all."

She wasn't buying it but decided not to press the issue. What she hadn't determined was whether or not he was holding back because of choice or because of some deeply seeded pain from his past. Maybe it was a touch of both. He seemed genuinely attracted to her. Men usually were.

Villa had had her share of suitors through the years, none of whom captured her interest. As a younger woman, boys had shown little interest in her. They had always paid more attention to her school friends than her. As a result, she'd spent much of her time in high school and college doing things like rock climbing, traveling, and studying.

The ugly duckling, though, had grown up. Now men threw themselves at her on a regular basis. She was glad she had the experiences of her youth because she had learned a lot about human nature. Most men didn't seem to look beyond the exterior of a woman. For the last few years she'd blown off several different men and she rarely associated with women. Adriana was comfortable being a loner.

Her thoughts were interrupted when Tommy re-entered the plane. "Look who we just picked up."

Will stepped through the entrance with a duffle bag in hand.

"Hope you don't mind if I crash this little party," he said with a grin.

Sean returned the smile. "We'll take all the help we can get."

The young detective sat down in a seat next to Adriana, across from Sean. She had an uncomfortable look on her face but said nothing.

"So," he began, "this morning I got a call for a homicide in Piedmont Park."

"Aren't you on vacation?" Sean interrupted.

Will lifted his hands, "When the boss calls you gotta go."

Wyatt nodded in understanding.

"Turns out it was a government agent. Former FBI guy."

At this news, Sean leaned forward. "Who?'

"Jack Turner."

Sean thought for a moment, staring off to the vacant side of the plane. Then shook his head. "Doesn't ring a bell."

Tommy stood quietly listening to the conversation. He apparently didn't know the victim either.

Will went on, "It shouldn't ring a bell. He's with the Hoover Directive." He let the news settle on his audience.

Adriana clearly didn't understand. Sean gave her a quick version, "It's a top level government agency. They operate outside the bounds of most of the other parts of the justice department. To the general public, they don't exist. Very secretive."

Will assumed she understood and continued, "Looks like he was executed last night in the park. We still don't have any leads. Just a few bullet casings and the body. No witnesses. No suspects."

"So Trent didn't want you on the case?" Tommy spoke up.

"He called me early this morning but by the time I got there, feds were already taking over." A serious look came across his face. "I can tell you this much, that little story is not going to reach any of the media outlets. They're calling it a drug-related shooting."

Sean was pensive. "What do *you* think it was?"

Will leaned back in his chair. "I don't know. Our connections are limited. But Trent was able to get the guy's name, which is probably more than the Directive would have liked. They prefer to remain anonymous. Real anonymous."

"You look tired," Sean commented casually.

For a brief second, Will looked uncomfortable but then resumed his casual demeanor.

"I just need some sleep." Then he changed the subject. "Since Atlanta PD was taken off of the case, I went back on vacation and called Tommy to see if you guys wanted me to tag along. Never been to South America."

Tommy beamed. "We can always use another gun."

Sean nodded in agreement. "Hopefully we won't need them." He looked out the window, thoughtful again. "But my guess is this Golden Dawn group is not going to go away easily."

Chapter 45
Washington, D.C.

The streets of Washington always seemed busy. Traffic lights were too short and it seemed one could get stuck at a crowded intersection for hours. Congested city streets, however, were not at the forefront of Sam's thoughts at the moment. After he'd left Starks' office at Axis headquarters, he had intended to head back to his own building a few blocks away and get back to his normal routine, if there were such a thing. Instead, his thoughts were focused on the dark-haired man in the cliché-black trench coat following him about thirty feet behind. The tail was a younger guy, probably early twenties. Sam didn't recognize him, which immediately placed him in the ranks of some foreign contractor or agency, probably eastern European. That and the fact that his gray business slacks were slim and slightly shorter at the ankle than they should have been were two major giveaways.

Given his career choice, Sam was accustomed to being observed but it was always a little disconcerting to have a tail. He could wonder who the stranger was or who had sent him but at this point, he really didn't feel like playing any games or worrying with all of that. So he took a different approach and turned, walking straight towards the man.

Townsend's sudden move and change of direction threw off the pursuer. It was probably what the kid had least suspected would happen. The moment of confusion was all Sam needed. He stepped quickly towards the target, deftly dodging the people busily walking the other direction. At the same time, he withdrew a small knife he kept in his jacket pocket and unsheathed the weapon. The tail never saw the blade in Townsend's hand as he reached within his own jacket to pull out what Sam assumed to be a gun. Whatever it was never made the light of day as he deftly dropped down to one knee and ran the sharp edge of the knife across the back of the younger man's heel. The Achilles tendon snapped up into the back of the man's leg, causing him to scream out loudly. Sam was already heading back in the direction from which he'd come. None of the confused passersby knew what was wrong with the man on the sidewalk, clutching his leg.

Townsend didn't turn to see the tail collapse to the ground in excruciating pain. He assumed he'd severed the tendon, rendering the man completely incapable of pursuit. Someone had made a play at him. Perfect. One more thing he would have to think about. His other appointments were going to have to wait.

He neared his government-issue sedan and glanced at it suspiciously. He turned his head and noticed a homeless man sitting in an adjacent alley close by, trying to stay out of the cold, late morning breeze. "Hey," Sam got his attention. "Can you do me a favor?"

The scraggly fellow looked around for a moment then replied, "If you got a dollar."

Townsend smiled wickedly. "I've got ten for you." He handed the vagrant a crisp ten-dollar bill and the keys to his car.

The man was obviously confused so he explained, "I need to run up to my office for a minute and you look cold. Would you care to warm up my car for me? You can sit inside while I'm there and when I come back there will be another ten bucks in it for you."

"What's the catch?" the old, white man peered suspiciously at him from underneath a wool cap. His face was dirty and he reeked of the streets.

"No catch. You won't steal my car. It has a tracking system on it so that would be pointless. I just want you to warm it up for me." Sam began to walk away. "I'll be back in twenty minutes or so." Sam dropped the keys and money in the man's hand and rounded the corner, disappearing from sight.

The homeless man stood up, checking both ways to see if there really was something suspicious going on. He couldn't believe a total stranger had just left him with the keys to his car and paid him to do it. Feeling like it was his lucky day, he quickly opened the car door and inserted the keys into the ignition. At first, the engine didn't turn over and just clicked once. The clueless man tried again.

Sam heard the explosion as he casually walked down the street and stopped next to a boutique cupcake shop. The earth shook violently beneath his feet for a second. His eyes scanned everyone suspiciously to see if he could find the other tail he was sure was hiding in the crowd. Hundreds of panicked pedestrians hurried in the opposite direction of the blast. Cautiously, Sam moved back towards the corner of the busy intersection, staying against the wall both to stay out of sight and out of the way of the rushing mob. It only took him a moment before he found his man. Black trench coat. Sharp jaw and nose. And running *towards* the burning car up the street. He was the only one going in that direction. Satisfied he'd dodged the hit, Sam blended into the terrified mob and disappeared into the chaos.

Chapter 46
Cuenca, Ecuador

The flight had taken the private jet just over five hours before landing in the picturesque city of Cuenca. Spanish-tiled roofs dotted the landscape in the city sprawled out across the high valley and up into the foothills of the Andes.

Will had been sleeping for the last few hours, apparently still exhausted from the trip back from the southwestern United States. He snapped awake as the plane landed with a sudden jolt. He rubbed his eyes and stretched out his arms.

"Have a good nap?" Sean asked from across the aisle while he massaged his face for a moment. He stared at Will, a slight grin barely visible at the corner of his mouth.

"Yeah. I was exhausted. How long was I out?"

"About three hours," Tommy jumped into the conversation from the other side of the plane.

"Wow. Guess I was tired." He looked out the window as the city landscape passed by. The mountains in the distance loomed enormous over the colorful town.

"Well, I hope you're rested. I just got off the phone with my contact down here, and he is taking us to Crespi's church first thing after we check in to our hotel." Tommy had always been one to get right to work on everything he ever did. There was no beating around the bush. It was a trait he'd carried since high school. Procrastination was a word that didn't exist in his vocabulary.

Adriana spoke up for the first time in a while. "There is somewhere I need to go when we arrive at the hotel. I can find my way to the church and meet up with you there. Would that be alright with you?"

The men were a little thrown off by the sudden request, but Sean and Tommy both shrugged and nodded.

"Sure. We can work it out. You want me to come with you?" Sean asked sincerely.

She smiled at his offer. "I will be fine. Just need to see an old friend for a few minutes. Shouldn't take long."

The conversation ended as the plane slowed to a stop on the far end of the tarmac where a small group of private hangars sat against the backdrop of the dramatic Andes.

Two black SUVs were waiting just outside one of the empty hangars.

After a few more minutes, the occupants were descending a set of stairs onto the tarmac. A gusty breeze blew across the surface. The temperature seemed fairly mild compared to where they'd been just a few hours ago. Being closer to the equator certainly warmed things up, but Cuenca was a city of high elevation. At nearly 8400 feet, the mercury never really reached the higher temperatures. Off in the distance, dark-gray clouds rolled towards the city. Rain, evidently, was a pretty regular occurrence that time of year.

One of the doors opened to the SUV in the front. A short, squat man stepped out wearing a pair of aviator sunglasses and a black suit and matching tie. Apparently, he didn't care that the sky was fairly overcast. Sean and Tommy had known Mauricio Delgado for nearly a decade.

A big grin crossed Tommy's face as the man approached. Schultz set down his bags and opened up his arms to embrace the squat Latino. "Buenas tardes, Mauricio!" Tommy embraced the shorter man and gave him a huge clap on the back.

Mauricio pulled away and returned the slap with one on Tommy's shoulder. His round face beamed. "It's good to see you again, my friend. It's been too long," he said with a thick accent. With no hesitation, he turned to the other three and extended his hand towards Sean. "You seem to be in better health than the last time I saw you, Senor Wyatt."

Sean shook his hand firmly. "I still owe you one, amigo."

Delgado wagged the index finger on his free hand. "No, amigo. No one ever owes me anything. I was just glad I could help. We were fortunate we found you before," he paused for a moment. "Before anything worse happened."

"Whatever, man. I'm grateful," Wyatt smiled widely.

"You're welcome. Although," the man paused, "it's a shame we never found your partner. It's as if he disappeared into thin air." Mauricio scratched his head while he and Sean shared a silent moment, both men pondering what could have happened to Nick.

"We'll probably never know," Sean said. "Although, some part of me still thinks he might be alive. I can't say why. Just a gut feeling."

"Perhaps, my friend," a wide grin crossed Mauricio's tanned face. His dark brown eyes brimmed. "Let's hope so." Then he changed the subject and stepped towards the others. "Who are your companions?"

"This here is Will Hastings," Sean answered as Will put out his hand. Delgado shook it heartily. "He is a police officer in Atlanta."

Mauricio raised his eyebrows and pursed his lips. "Excellent. We will make sure that local law enforcement has our full cooperation. But it is always good to have another gun, just in case. No?"

Will nodded. "Never hurts."

The four men shared a quick laugh before Mauricio turned his attention to their female companion. "And who is this?" he asked as he stopped in front of Adriana.

"My name is Adriana Villa," she answered for herself and offered her hand. He began to shake it gently but she squeezed his hand just as firmly as Will had. "Pleasure to meet you."

His look of surprise turned to one of respect. "The pleasure is all mine. Bienvenidos a Cuenca."

"Gracias," she replied.

"De donde eres?" he continued.

This time she answered in English so the others would understand. "My family is from central Spain. But I have lived in many places."

"Intriguing." There was a brief moment of awkward silence before he got back to business. "We will head to the hotel where you can check in and get refreshed. After that we will have a light dinner. I understand you want to visit the church as soon as possible?"

Everyone nodded.

"Good," he said, lifting his hands. "We will take a look around this evening. I've made arrangements with the head priest. He said we can have a few hours tonight after their evening prayers."

Chapter 47
Washington D.C.

Eric Jennings had played the game a long time. He'd worked hard for the government and done more for the protection of the nation than most people in his line of work. In his mind, the things he'd done were justified.

Protecting his retirement and the well being of his finances was worth a few sacrifices. For what the Prophet was paying him, it was worth a few more.

The dead man on his living room floor had been an asset he'd used a few times, a mercenary with no family or known acquaintances. It had been easy to lure him there under the guise that another well-paying job was waiting.

Upon entry, Eric had invited the man in towards the direction of the kitchen. Jennings' had his back turned so there was no way the unsuspecting asset could see the gun in hand. When the man was a mere few feet away, Eric spun around and fired three bullets into the chest of the visitor. The weapon couldn't have been audible outside of the apartment. With the curtains drawn, the gun's flash couldn't have been visible either. To people watching the news, it would look like a burglar had gotten his just desserts, a simple cover up to an otherwise intricate plan. After the execution, Jennings wrecked the place, destroying mirrors, picture frames, vases, and even crushing the coffee table. It had to appear as if a struggle had occurred and as a result, he'd killed the intruder.

The next step would be trickier. His target from earlier in the day had somehow managed to escape the car explosion, though he wasn't sure how. Witnesses had said they saw a homeless man climb into Townsend's car. It didn't matter. The arrogant prick had only postponed the inevitable.

Sam Townsend had made dozens, maybe hundreds of enemies in his brief career with the Justice Department. Whenever anyone had a sudden rise to power there always seemed to be resentment from legions of others who thought they'd have been better suited for promotion. As someone who was tasked with upholding the law, he'd seen his fair share of bad guys but never actually arrested anyone. Faces ran through his mind while he sipped on a glass of vodka and cranberry juice. His nerves had settled down for the most part. Yet, while he sat in a low-back, leather chair, his Glock .40 rested nearby on an end table. There was only one light on in his Georgetown townhome, giving the impression that no one was there. He had spent the rest of the day double backing through the streets and metro stations of D.C., making sure that no one else was following him. But whoever had arranged the attack would surely know where he lived.

What had occurred previously in the day had been sloppy. He doubted those who would attempt to clean up the mess would be so careless. Then he thought of the charred body of the homeless man to whom he'd given his car key. That would help cover his tracks for a short time. It could be weeks before dental records revealed the man's identity. Plenty of time for him to disappear and figure some things out. Still, something told him he wasn't out of the woods just yet.

The waning glow of twilight had given way to evening and the yellowish tinge of streetlights radiated outside his parlor window. He took another sip from the pinkish-red liquid and placed the glass back on the end table. A sudden knock on the door startled him. Sam grabbed his gun and stood quietly. Visitors were something he never had. But if someone was going to kill him, he doubted they would knock. He stalked quietly over to the door and took a look out the peephole. It was Eric Jennings.

"Sam, open up. It's Jennings," the voice echoed the visual confirmation.

Townsend lowered his weapon and unlocked the deadbolt and main lock to the door. He opened it cautiously and looked around outside.

"Were you followed?" Sam asked suspiciously.

Eric shook his head. "No, I wasn't followed."

"Are you sure?"

"Yes I'm sure. Now open the friggin' door and let me in." Jennings' coastal Maryland accent was thicker than usual.

Townsend obeyed and Jennings crossed the threshold into the younger man's home. Inside was fairly plain. The bare walls were colored with a neutral beige. No photos or artwork adorned a single inch. The only thing that stood out was a simple clock on the wall with black numbers and hands. There were a few leather chairs and a leather couch that faced towards a high definition television along with a simple glass coffee table. It was as if he'd just moved in and hadn't unpacked all his things yet.

"So, what happened?" Jennings asked as Sam locked the door again and took another peek outside. Eric walked casually into the living room and helped himself to the seat in which Sam had previously been sitting.

The surprised host didn't push the issue; relieved to see someone he believed to be an ally, albeit a scumbag. Townsend grabbed his glass walked casually over to a small wet bar near one of the opposite windows where he refilled his nearly empty rocks glass. "What have you heard?" He asked Jennings as he raised an empty glass, offering his unexpected guest a drink.

"Not much. Just that someone blew up your car today. They found a body in there. No ID on it yet. That will probably take a few weeks."

"The cops have already been by here. I told them my car must have been stolen. When you're connected they will believe anything."

Eric nodded. "So who was the corpse?"

Sam took a big sip of the brown liquid and swallowed hard. "I don't know. Some homeless guy. A goon came after me so I took him out. When I ran back to my car, something told me whoever was after me would have taken precautions. Jennings laughed loudly. "Well, well, well. I never figured you for much of a field agent. That was good thinking."

After another long sip, Townsend sat down across from Jennings and set the glass on the table.

"What do you want Eric? Why are you here?"

Eric put his hands out as if proclaiming his innocence. "I'm here to check on you. When I heard what happened I headed here immediately to see if you were ok."

Sam was unconvinced, eyeing his guest suspiciously.

"What's your next move?" he continued.

"I'm leaving the country tonight. Gonna lay low for a while until I can figure out what is going on."

Jennings nodded. "Probably a good idea. You can never be too careful. Do you have any idea who came after you?"

Townsend sat pensive, searching through the database of his mind. "Could be anyone. The nature of my commission pisses off a lot of knowledgeable, well-connected people. Some top-level personnel have lost everything because of me. And that's a pretty long list."

"Anyone recently?"

He shook his head. "Not that I can think of."

"Who was the last person you spoke with today or this week about anything?"

Sam's reluctance was obvious as he paused before answering. "I spoke with Emily Starks. Saw her this morning."

Eric seemed surprised at this new revelation. "Axis? Why?"

"We are doing an audit of their agency in the coming months, and I just wanted to extend the courtesy to her for her help in the past. I simply made her aware that we were going to need to see some documents and reports. Nothing major."

"Ahh."

Jennings seemed to accept the lie.

Silence pervaded the room for a minute. A timer went off in the kitchen, startling both men.

"I put a pizza in the oven earlier. You hungry?"

Jennings shook his head. "No thanks."

Sam stood up and disappeared through a doorway that led into the kitchen. The sounds of the oven opening and other items rattling echoed into the empty living room.

Townsend hurriedly slid the pizza onto a pan on the counter and closed the oven. As he turned around to leave the kitchen, his face turned ashen as he stared down the barrel of a sound suppressed Glock. Eric Jennings stood in the doorway with a stern look on his face.

"What are you doing?" Townsend asked, frozen in place.

"Isn't it obvious, Sam? You come to me and threaten me about my operations. You say that I'm up to something and that you want a piece of the pie." He shook his head and took a step forward, extending the gun further towards his target.

"What? That's what this is all about?"

"You have no idea the people I work for, Sam. You think you're so special with your little 'all-access pass' the government gave you. The people I work for own the government! And they don't like it when outsiders start snooping around."

Fear flooded the younger man's eyes. "Look, Eric. I didn't talk to anyone. I didn't tell anyone anything. You have to believe me."

The older man shook his head. "You said you talked to Emily earlier."

"About audits! Nothing else. She doesn't know anything about your little operation! I swear!"

"Ok," Eric said. For a second, it seemed like he believed the story and lowered the gun temporarily.

Then he raised the weapon again suddenly. "But you are a loose end."

"No. Please. I'll do anything. Just please don't shoot me."

Jennings thought it funny how men with extensive power could be lowered to the same level of a beggar, pleading for any scrap they could get. Sam Townsend had become one of the most powerful men in the government. He'd been reduced to nothing more than sniveling rat willing to do anything for an extension of life. "You're pathetic," Eric remarked. "All that power and here you are begging for your life. I'm doing the government a favor by killing you."

The long barrel quickly puffed twice, sending two rounds into Townsend's ribcage. He collapsed backwards onto the floor as dark crimson began to bloom around the two blackish holes in his white shirt. Shock covered Sam's face as he clutched his chest. A thin red line began to trickle out of the corner of his lips. Violent, gurgled coughs ensued as blood began to fill the lungs. "You," he managed to get out between fits of coughing but couldn't get out anything else.

Jennings took another step forward and without saying a word, lowered his gun and fired one more round into Townsend's head. The man's body stopped shaking as the blood pooled around it on the tiled floor. After pocketing the weapon back into his jacket, he took another look back at the lifeless body. Satisfied with his work, Eric stalked back to the front door and drew back a nearby curtain to give a quick check outside.

No one would even remember seeing him exit the townhouse. He headed down the steps and veered onto the sidewalk towards his car. Only one more stop to make before heading home for the night.

Emily had already slipped into some pajama pants and a t-shirt and slumped down in a comfortable spot on the couch to watch her favorite show. A glass of dark cabernet waited beside her on the nightstand nearby as she turned on the television with a flick of the remote. About ten minutes into the show, a knock came from the front door. Puzzled at who would be coming by at that hour, she set her drink back down and pulled on a robe over her t-shirt and pajama pants. When she arrived at the entryway, she gave a quick look through the peephole. Eric Jennings stood appearing frantic outside her door. His face was panicked and he kept looking around in both directions. Curious, she opened the door. "Eric? What's the matter with you?"

"I need to get off the street. Can I come in?"

His words were rushed, unnerved. She'd never seen him that way.

"Sure, Eric. Come in. What happened to you?" She held the door wide open for him as he passed by. She noticed a cut on his arm that was bleeding through the white long-sleeved shirt he wore. His face had a small, similar wound and his hair was completely disheveled. His forehead was also dotted with beads of sweat.

"Close the door. Quickly, please," he begged.

"Ok. Ok. Just relax," she said in response. A quick glance outside yielded nothing suspicious. She closed the door and stepped into the living room where he'd helped himself to a seat on the couch.

He sat nervously on the edge. "They came after me, Emily. They sent someone to my house to kill me."

"Whoa! Slow down a second there. Who sent someone to kill you?"

"Golden Dawn. Those pieces of crap sent someone to kill me. I think they found out I was investigating them. Maybe I got too close. I don't know for sure," his words came out in a gush.

"Just take it easy. Sit down and tell me everything." She gave another quick glance outside to make sure no one was there before returning to the sitting area.

Emily had known Jennings' main experience with the Justice Department had been as an office guy. Unlike her, he wasn't accustomed to being shot at or put into harrowing situations.

"I was at the house," he began still panting a little, "cooking some supper, when some guy came in. It's all a blur, but I guess I turned the corner from my kitchen into the living room and bumped into him before he was ready to shoot. In his surprise I was able to knock the gun away and fight him off." He paused for a moment before finishing. "I shot him. I killed the son of a ..." his voice trailed off in deep thought.

"Have you called the police?"

He shook his head, lost in his own mind.

"So the body is still there at your house?"

A slow nod gave confirmation.

"Eric. I need you to focus," she tried to regain his attention. "You said something about Golden Dawn. How do you know it was them that sent this guy?"

"I've been investigating them for some time. I've always known they were working with someone on the inside, but I was never certain who. Now I think I know."

She waited for the answer.

"Sam Townsend."

The words hit her like a lead weight but her expression never changed.

"You don't seemed surprised," he said.

She decided that Eric didn't need to know that she had met with Sam earlier that day. "I am and I'm not," she said flatly. "I always had my suspicions about him. He gained so much authority so quickly. And I am always wary of those internal affairs types. You never know whose best interest they have in mind." Her response seemed to settle Jennings down momentarily.

He nodded. "I know. I'm just shaken up from the whole thing."

She relaxed a little too. "It's going to be fine. You're safe here."

"Thanks Emily. I really appreciate it," he forced a slight smile.

"Would you like something to drink? Seems like you're a scotch guy, right?"

"That would be great, Emily. My nerves are shot." He seemed grateful.

She stood up and headed into the kitchen. Quietly, he rose from his chair and followed her. His movements made no sound with the background noise of the television peppering the silence.

In the kitchen, she pulled a rocks glass from the cupboard and filled it with ice from the freezer side of a stainless steel unit. The ice clinked in the glass as she set it down on the counter. The golden liquid caused the cubes to crackle as it poured over them. She stopped when the glass was half-full and swirled it around for a second.

Jennings stood at the edge of the kitchen, watching her closely. Slowly, he reached his hand into his jacket, feeling for something within. He watched as she finished making his drink. Just as she turned to head back to the living room, he pulled his hand out of his coat.

Chapter 48
Nevada

On the outside, The Prophet seemed as stoic as always. "What do you mean they've left the country?" he said calmly.

"Wyatt and a few others went to Ecuador. They just landed in the city of Cuenca about an hour ago." The voice on the phone was quick and concise.

"Do we know why they are there?

"Yes, sir. We believe they may have found information regarding an old priest who once lived there. Apparently, he had a fairly significant stash of ancient relics."

Realization slightly changed the old man's demeanor. "They must be looking for the missing artifacts from Carlos Crespi's vault. But why?"

A silent moment passed before the voice on the other end answered. "We aren't sure why, sir. But we think they are after some kind of map and that there is a connection between the priest's collection and what we are after."

Lindsey's eyes grew wide. *Of course! All the signs were there. How could he have missed it before? The old priest's cache of ancient pieces represented a wide number of cultures from the other side of the globe. They had no business in the western hemisphere.* He silently cursed himself for not thinking of it sooner.

"Is your team in place?" he resumed the conversation quickly.

"They will be within the hour. We know where they are staying and where they are headed."

"Really?" he was pleasantly surprised.

"Yes, sir. We believe they are going to inspect one of the Cathedrals in the city."

"Do you know what they are looking for, other than the priest's treasure?"

"Not yet. But we will."

"Watch them closely. When they find whatever it is they are looking for, take Schultz alive. We may need him to put the final pieces in place. Execute the others."

His voice was cold as he gave the order. The sentence came out as easily as if he'd told a dog to roll over. He didn't wait for a reply from the other line and simply hung up the phone. A curiosity lingered in his mind, though. *What was Wyatt up to?*

Chapter 49
Cuenca, Ecuador

The Hotel del Vista Magnifico rested halfway up a nearby mountain that overlooked the twinkling city. It was a popular tourist attraction because of the breathtaking views of the town, as well as the natural beauty of the area. Originally, in the late 1800s, the hotel had been a coffee factory. Ecuador's coffee exports were unique in that they were the only country in the world to export all varieties of coffee. The plantation had suffered through a series of poor harvests and bad processing practices. The building sat vacant for a decade until a young Spanish entrepreneur purchased the old facility for an extremely small fee. He spent two years remodeling the facility and turned it into one of the grandest hotels in Cuenca, even in the country.

The high ceilings of the original building had been left intact for the main entrance and hallways. The walkways on the upper floor were surrounded by wrought iron railings and wall sconces. Sandstone tile covered the floors giving a rustic yet glamorous feel to the facility. Enormous, black Spanish-style chandeliers hung both in the entryway and down each hall. Originally, they probably held candles but were now illuminated with fake, candle-shaped electric bulbs. The black, iron wall sconces still used real candles, though. Their little yellowish flames reminding patrons of years long gone. Just below the second floor balcony was a rectangular pool surrounded by more sandstone tile. The coping on the edge of the pool, though, was black marble, an absolutely exquisite accent to the lighter colored flooring.

An attendant in a vintage bellhop outfit had showed Sean, Adriana, and Tommy to their rooms, all on the front side of the hotel that overlooked the city. After dropping off their gear in their respective rooms, the group met up with Mauricio back in the main lobby.

Mauricio spoke like a man who was used to being in charge. "I've made arrangements to eat at here if that is alright with you. They have an excellent menu of local fare that I'm sure you will all enjoy. I know it is a little late for dinner, but I assume everyone is hungry from the journey. After that, we will go to the church. Good?"

Everyone nodded their approval and Mauricio motioned for them to follow him.

He led the way down the hall to a place where the rooms ended and the corridor opened up into a larger space. There were wooden bistro tables dotting the area and a bar at one end. Huge glass windows opened up to a courtyard outside and yet another view of the city below. An older couple sat at the bar having a few drinks but other than that the room was empty. A few tables had been pushed together to accommodate the large group. Four plates with a variety of appetizers of fresh chips and salsa, potato cakes, tamales, and a green salad were spread out before them.

"It looks awesome, Mauricio," Tommy said as he sat down.

Their host pulled a chair out for Adriana, an act of chivalry she accepted with a slight smile. A waiter brought out two pitchers of fresh juice with large chunks of yellow, pink, and white fruit in it and poured a glass for each person.

"Dig in everyone," Mauricio said with a huge smile.

While the group ate, the waiter continued to bring out more dishes for them to share: Spanish rice, avocado halves filled with tomato, onions, and chopped tuna.

"How long have you been with the police in Atlanta, Will?" Mauricio asked.

Will finished swallowing his food before answering. "I've only been with the force in Atlanta for a short time." After he spoke, he grabbed a glass of juice to chase the spicy salsa and salty potatoes.

Mauricio pressed on, "So what made you decide to become a police officer?"

Will coughed slightly and set down his drink. He looked extremely uncomfortable as if all eyes at the table were on him.

"Well, I don't now. I guess it made the most sense to me." He wiped his mouth with a napkin before continuing. "Bad pay. Long hours. Jackass bosses. Seemed like a fun choice at the time."

Everyone at the table burst into laughter and continued eating. He took a deep breath, satisfied that everyone seemed to accept his answer.

The conversations continued in a random fashion for another twenty minutes or so until the waiter returned; light from the chandeliers shone off of his bald head.

"Will your party have dessert tonight, Senor?" He asked politely in a slight accent.

Maurcio shook his head. "No, gracias. We must be going. Just the bill, please."

The food had been so delicious, everyone felt a little disappointed that they wouldn't get the chance to see what dessert would be like. There was a sense of hurry, though; they couldn't get to the church soon enough.

Sean doubted they would find anything tonight. They would probably have more luck in the daylight. From his experience, those sorts of things could take weeks or months to uncover. Ancient secrets didn't remain secrets because they were easy to find or decode.

After a few minutes, the waiter returned with the bill, which Tommy called for. Mauricio seemed indignant. "Please, my friend, allow me."

Tommy shook his head and smiled. "Tell you what, I'll get this, you get the cervezas later." The stout Ecuadorian seemed satisfied with the accord and allowed Tommy to pay the tab.

The group stepped out into the cool, fresh air. A little rain had come through while they were eating, coating the cobblestone sidewalk and road. They got back into their vehicles and, few minutes later, were weaving their way back down the mountain towards the town.

"Have you ever been to Cuenca?" Mauricio directed the question towards Adrianna.

"Yes. But it has been a long time," she responded, looking out the window at the shops and colorful buildings as they passed in the streetlight.

"Sean tells me you have some friends here in the city you want to see. Perhaps I can take you where you need to go while they investigate the church."

"That won't be necessary," she said quickly. "I can get there myself."

"Fair enough," he ended the conversation, sensing she didn't care to keep it going any further.

Sean smiled. She was a confident, strong woman. But there was something so mysterious about her. He had realized that whatever she was doing in Cuenca was her business and interfering or asking too many questions might upset the apple cart. He was glad to have her along, though. She'd proven herself more than useful in the short time he'd known her. And though he hoped they wouldn't need that usefulness again, he doubted they would be that lucky.

He'd seen organizations like Golden Dawn before. Men who were bent on something didn't give up easily, especially when they had lots of money. Kill two henchmen, four more pop up in their place. It was part of the reason he'd quit working for the government. In two short years, he'd lost track of all the men he'd killed. While some people had problems dreaming about victims or some sort of post-traumatic stress, Sean had never experienced those things. And that fact bothered him. To him, killing the men who were trying to kill him was justified. They were bad people trying to bad things. What got to Sean in the end was the fear of never knowing when someone would get the drop on him. With every mission he'd completed during his short career, the paranoia grew a little stronger.

The more he traveled, the more he realized how many things he wanted to do in his life, how much he wanted to see, how much he wanted to learn. He could sense these things slipping away as his life went deeper and deeper into government work. A life of international intrigue was definitely exciting, but he began to realize that the life he could have outside of it was worth living. Sean had forged few, lasting relationships throughout the years. While living a typical, suburban life wasn't ideal, it certainly had some benefits: friends, stability, not getting shot at, maybe even a wife and family.

Sean thought about the day he'd quit the agency. *When he approached Emily about retiring, she'd scoffed. "This is who you are, Wyatt. You're a machine. You're the best Axis has."*

"You're the best agent Axis has, Em," he'd replied. The comment had made her blush.

"I appreciate that but you know it isn't true," she paused. "We need you. The government needs you. Your country needs you, Sean."

"I've heard that speech before, Em. I've done my time. And that time has done me. I can't sleep at night. I'm tired every day. I'm slipping. I know it. If I keep going at this rate, I won't last long."

She knew he was right. She had seen it in his eyes. "What will you do?" she asked.

"I don't know yet. Something else."

"Here we are," Mauricio announced as he opened his passenger door. "Iglesia de Carlos Crespi."

The small caravan of vehicles had come to a stop just outside an enormous church. The enormous stone structure was breathtaking. Lights had been positioned pointing upward to accentuate rounded columns at various points of the church. Great wooden doorways presented three entrances into the building near where they had parked. The group exited the car and stared at the building. Standing on the side street, they could see the glorious domes at the other end of the cathedral.

Adriana touched Sean's shoulder. "I'll be back in an hour," she said quietly. He just smiled and nodded. She took off at a jog and disappeared around the corner of the street.

"Where's she going?" Tommy asked.

"I don't know but she can take care of herself."

Mauricio never saw her run off. He got out of his car and stepped close to the three visitors and gave an odd tip of the head to his two drivers. They immediately got in their cars and drove away. "There is something you should know," he said quietly, just above a whisper. "This is not the church you came to see."

Chapter 50
Washington, DC

Emily turned around with a glass of scotch. Jennings was standing in the doorway of her kitchen pulling something out of his jacket pocket. For a second, she wasn't sure what he was doing.

"Please excuse me," he said as he withdrew a handkerchief from the folds of his coat. "Coming in out of the cold and all the stress has made me sweat a bit." He dabbed at his forehead as she brought the drink over to where he was standing. "Thank you," he said gratefully.

"If you aren't going to call the police, you need to lay low for a bit," she spoke suddenly and walked by him back into the living room.

"I have an extra room upstairs you can sleep in tonight and for the next few nights if you need to."

"Emily," he cut her off. "I can't impose like that. I don't want to put you in any kind of danger."

"I'll be fine," she responded quickly. We have no social or personal connections so there is no reason for anyone to think you came here."

He followed her back into the living room and sat down with a sigh. "You're sure I'm not imposing?"

She shook her head. "Don't be ridiculous. I'll get the guest bed ready for you. Tomorrow we can figure out what is going on."

He nodded and took a drink. It seemed like he was beginning to settle down.

Emily headed up the stairs, satisfied that her guest was going to be ok for a while. In the back of her mind, though, something didn't quite add up.

Chapter 51
Cuenca, Ecuador

"We are in position and have the targets in sight."

Agents Weaver and Collack heard the transmission as they sped down the bumpy road leading into Cuenca. "Good," Collack answered. "Let them find whatever it is they're looking for. Then take them out. But leave Schultz alive. The rest are expendable. We are en route. ETA is ten minutes."

"Roger that," the voice responded.

Sean's face filled with confusion. Mauricio shook his head slowly and pulled a black gun from within his black blazer. His two other men who had stayed behind with the group did the same, keeping their weapons trained on Wyatt and his companions.

"What is this, Maury," Tommy asked. "Playing for the other side now?" Schultz's face washed over with disappointment and betrayal.

"Not the other side, my friend. The treasure of Carlos Crespi is only the tip of the iceberg. There is more to be found, once his lost relics are discovered. And you are going to show me the way."

"Where is the woman?" Delgado finally realized she wasn't with them anymore.

"She's gone," Wyatt answered. "Ran off to see a friend or something. She wouldn't tell me where. You don't need her anyway. She isn't important."

Mauricio considered the statement for a moment then said, "I'll have one of my drivers track her down once we're inside the building."

"I guess I was wrong about you," Sean said.

"Quisas, amigo. Perhaps."

"Sir?" the voice came over the radio again in Weaver' and Collack's earpieces.

"Go ahead," he responded.

"We have a situation here." The voice didn't wait for the question. "The men with Wyatt and Shultz are holding them at gunpoint now."

This was an unexpected development. Angela and James both looked at each other somewhat bewildered. "Can you hear what they're saying?" she asked after a few seconds of thought.

"Not really. Something about a treasure."

"Delgado must be making a play. Stay close but don't make a move. We will be on site in six minutes."

"Roger that."

The two looked at each other again as they sped along the old road into the city. "This changes things a bit," James said flatly.

"Not really. They were all hostiles anyway. Let's sit back and see what they do next. My guess is Delgado is wanting the same thing we want. We let them force Wyatt and Schultz to get it for them; then we take it."

Will stared hard at the man nearest him but said nothing.

Mauricio noticed the unspoken interaction. "Don't try anything, policeman. He will cut you down if he has to." Then he motioned towards the entrance of the cathedral. "Now, quickly. Everyone inside. If you try anything, I will shoot you."

Sean shook his head but said nothing as the three men moved slowly towards the huge stone structure. Once inside its wooden doors, the familiar musty smell old churches always seemed to have filled their nostrils. The vast expanse opened up into a high arched ceiling. Longer than it appeared from the outside, the building stretched at least two-hundred feet to the other end where it opened up into a wider worship area.

The group moved a little further into the foyer, and the giant wooden door closed behind them. Once it had shut, Mauricio's demeanor changed completely. Suddenly, he and his assistants lowered their weapons. The two men accompanying him kept their weapons in hand and moved quickly down the center of the church towards the presbytery. "Sorry for that little ruse, my friend," he began as he holstered his weapon. "But we are being watched."

"What is going on?" Tommy exclaimed. "Watched? By who?"

"We must move quickly. Hurry, follow them," was all he would offer.

Sean and Tommy were completely lost. Will simply did as he was told and hustled behind the two, armed men.

"I'll explain everything soon," Mauricio urged as he turned and started jogging down the aisle.

Sean hesitated. "What about Adriana?"

Delgado stopped, "We must hurry. We will find her later."

Unsure, Sean glanced at his friend as if looking for an answer he knew wasn't there. It seemed they didn't had a choice at the moment.

Shame they were in such a hurry, Tommy thought as he ran past stone columns that supported dramatic domed arches and side porticos. Up ahead, the presbytery was ornately highlighted with a crown-like altar, topped by a crucifix and centered underneath another cross. The ornate construction was held up by four, spiraled columns of white stone.

The group reached the end of the aisle and veered left towards a side door. Just through it, a narrow corridor extended in both directions. They turned right and headed through the dark hallway, moving towards the back of the church.

Hunter Carlson observed the scene from a bar on the other side of the plaza. He casually sipped a golden beer and, to everyone else, appeared to be just another tourist.

His eyes, though, were trained on the hit squad he'd been watching for the last half hour. He'd noticed them when they arrived, dressed in utility service clothing and maintenance uniforms. It was a good enough disguise. They'd set up cones and taped off an area as if they were working on something in one of the sewage drains.

But to him, the two vans stuck out like sore thumb. It would surprise him if they had gone unnoticed by Wyatt and his group. Still, he decided to sit back and see how things played out. The winner in a Mexican standoff was always the guy who showed up last. Let everyone else shoot each other then scoop up the loot.

Across from where the hired guns were positioned, a black sedan pulled into a parking space on a side street with its headlights off. A new player had just entered the game.

James and Angela were careful to make sure they didn't attract a lot of attention and cut off the lights to their car before stopping in an alley near the square. They immediately recognized their team positioned directly across from the cathedral. Quietly, they slipped out of the car and James touched his earpiece. "We are here. What's the situation?" he asked in a whisper.

"They just went into the church. What would you like us to do?" the voice responded.

"Hold here. We will set up just outside the entrance. When they come out, we grab them. No shots fired here in the open. We don't want the locals getting involved. Keep it quiet and quick. We can take them outside the city and finish them there."

"Roger that."

Towards the end of the hall, Mauricio's men had stopped and were holding open an interior wall door.

Sean and the rest stopped and looked through the opening. Inside were candelabras, robes, sashes, an old desk, a bookshelf with a sparse collection of books, and a few goblets that looked like something out of the middle ages.

"A storage room?" Will asked. "Why don't we just go out the back?"

"Just trust me," Mauricio answered.

Will shrugged and looked at Sean who extended an arm as if to say "you first."

Mauricio's assistant held the door until everyone was inside. Once the door was closed, Delgado's other man stepped over to an old, iron wall sconce and pulled it down slowly. The ancient lever creaked as it moved. Clearly, it hadn't been used frequently. Just like something out of a movie, the bookshelf started sliding out away from the wall. Old-looking light bulbs flickered on in a stone, spiral staircase on the other side.

"Seriously?" Sean asked in a sarcastic tone. "A secret tunnel?"

"The priests had it installed long ago because they were afraid of looting during a period of unrest with the government. It leads under the city streets to a place where my drivers are waiting to pick us up." The robust Latino man smiled with pride. Tommy patted him on the shoulder in approval and headed down the spiral, stone staircase. The rest followed into the dimly lit corridor.

The staircase ended in a stone, arched hallway, dotted every twenty feet with small lights hung on candle sconces. "So what's going on?" Sean asked as they strode quickly down the stairs into the bowels of the city.

"My connections go deep, my friend," he looked back and smiled as he walked along, panting slightly from the activity. "After you told me what happened, I suspected that whoever was after you in the States would follow you here. Since they want what you want but don't have a clue where to find it or perhaps even what they were looking for, we let them have a little false information to buy us some time."

"You told them we were coming here?" Tommy looked befuddled.

"In a manner of speaking," Delgado continued. "This is not the church of Carlos Crespi. This is Iglesia de San Blas. It is much older and fit the part of our little act perfectly. It looks like an ancient building where secrets would be kept. I doubt the men who are after you have researched it at all."

"Nice work, amigo," Sean said with a grin as they rounded a curve. Up ahead, faint lights could be seen through a metal grate at the end of the passageway. Fresh air began to mingle with the musty air of the tunnel.

"So," Tommy interrupted, "they think we are inside that church trying to find clues to Crespi's vault, but that isn't Crespi's church. Now where are we going?"

"The Church of Maria Auxiliadora."

Hunter Carlson was growing restless. The group had been in the church for around thirty minutes. What was taking them so long? The team of assets watching the church seemed content to wait. He knew they had all the exits covered since he'd observed them setting up a perimeter around the building previously. Still, he'd had enough waiting. Pulling a hat down low over his head and bunching up his green, canvas jacket so that the collars covered part of his face, he set off across the plaza's cobblestone streets towards the entrance of the building.

"Sir?" The voice came through the earpiece again.

"We see him," James Collack answered before his team leader could finish asking the question."

Angela looked over at him, puzzled. "Who is it?" she asked.

They'd been sitting behind a dumpster, out of clear line-of-site for almost an hour. The stranger walking from the bar to the front of the church was the first movement they'd seen in a while, save for the occasional cab that would pull up and take away another of the bar's patrons.

"Sit tight," James ordered the team leader.

They watched as the man strolled casually to the large doorway and disappeared inside.

"Must need a late night confession," Angela joked.

Still, James wasn't so sure. What was taking Wyatt's group so long? And who were the men that had driven them there and then pulled guns on them?

"We're giving it fifteen more minutes and then we're going in," he said finally.

Angela nodded, though in her mind she was becoming more and more tired of her partner's weakness.

Hunter lowered his jacket slightly once he was inside the building. Iglesia de San Blas was one of the religious crowned jewels of Ecuador and beholding it in person was extremely impressive even for someone with no historical background. It wasn't as dramatic or elegant as some of the European cathedrals he's seen in his travels but for South America, it was definitely spectacular. The musty smell of old stone and religion filled his nostrils, like so many of the old churches he'd visited in the past. Something, though, was missing. The group of men who'd come in previously were nowhere to be found.

He walked quickly to the confessionals that were located off to the side near the center of the building but a quick check revealed them to be empty. Looking in the presbytery in the front, as well as a few side rooms, also proved futile. Finally, he made his way over to a doorway to the left of the pulpit area and opened it. The door revealed a narrow hallway that extended down the length of the building, which most likely contained the priest's quarters, church offices, and maintenance rooms. He decided to go to the right first since that direction was closer to the end of the facility. If there was nothing there he would make his way back to the front and hope he could figure out where they'd gone.

A few doors on the left, one marked "Prayer Chamber" and another "Treasury Office," were locked. The lone door on the right, though, was unlocked. Upon opening it, Hunter noticed that it was essentially just a big storage closet. He flicked a light on and took a quick inventory of the room. A candelabra sat nearby, an old desk, and a bookshelf with a sparse collection of books. Satisfied there was nothing of note in the room, he began to turn off the light switch when he noticed something out of the corner of his eye. On the smooth, stone floor in front of the bookcase, there was a slightly discolored line. It wasn't so distinct that many people would notice but he was different than most people. Keen observation of settings had been a trait that had saved his hide on more than one occasion. He stepped back into the room and eased the door shut, creeping over to the heavy-looking bookcase. As he neared it, he knelt down onto one knee and ran a finger over the thin, curving line. The realization hit him. Something had scraped the stone.

Outside the church, The Prophet's team was getting anxious, especially it's two leaders.

"I say we go in," Angela stared hard at James while she spoke.

"We were told to sit and wait," he replied sternly, with a glare that was equally as steadfast.

"We've waited long enough," she stated as she stood from her hiding place.

Before he could stop her, she was already talking into the microphone. "Team, we are moving in. Units two and three cover the rear entrance. Unit's one and four, take the front with us. We will meet in the middle." Within seconds, the square was flooded with agents, all sprinting hard towards the building from four different angles.

Upon reaching the front door, Weaver and Collack placed their backs against the cool stone pillars next to the center door. The other assets assumed similar positions near the other doors. Angela took the lead and opened the center door first, leading with her weapon, checking left and right and up above. "Clear," she announced.

The other units followed into the cavernous building. They were greeted with a cool, damp air. The cathedral, however, was empty. The group hustled down the aisles, checking in corners and between pews as they moved. A few moments later, the units that had come from the rear of the building appeared at the Presbytery.

"Nothing up here, boss," a familiar voice said through the earpiece.

Confused, the agents continued to look around. One man in the center, lowered his weapon held out his hands as if their targets had just vanished. When he spoke, it was the voice from the radio communication.

"Where'd they go?"

"Nothing in the back of the church?" Angela was furious.

"Nothin, boss," he answered.

"And you were covering the rear of the cathedral the whole time?"

"The whole time," he didn't like her tone. "If anyone had left out the back of this old building, we would have noticed. Plus, the back door was locked. We had to smash it to get in."

James looked at his partner, confused. He was used to things being easy. During their time together, they'd completed many missions, killed many people, and always done it in a timely and simple fashion. The whole affair was starting to get under his skin. "They couldn't have just vanished!" he yelled. "Teams one and two, search every room and office in the rear of the building. Teams three and four, check all the confessionals and chambers in the front."

"But sir, some of the priests live in a few of those rooms," a young man said to James' left.

Angela looked over at him with disdain and raised her weapon. She squeezed the trigger and fired one bullet into the man's forehead. The muffled pop echoed off of the stone walls and arches. Smoke lingered in the still air of the church. The body collapsed to the stone floor between some pews. "Anyone else have a problem?" She asked, angrily. No one said anything.

"Good, if the priests give you a hard time, tell them you are with the police and are looking for a fugitive that killed one of our agents. Understood?" Everyone in the room nodded and began dispersing to their assigned areas.

A pool of blood had started forming around the head of the man Angela had just killed. James' eyes were wide. She was getting out of control.

Chapter 52
Cuenca, Ecuador

Sean stared at the unspectacular structure, half amazed, half disappointed. "It's not what you expected, eh?" Mauricio chuckled and slapped his friend on the back.

The entrance was beneath a dramatic, triangle of large beams, founded in stone at the base. Stretching out to each side, most of the building looked flat and boxlike. It was painted a dull yellow. The main sanctuary rose up behind the entrance from a point that extended out in both directions like the shape of an eye. A statue of The Virgin Mary stood guard over top of the center doorway, set into a corner shaped pillar.

Mauricio noticed their confusion and decided to explain the scene before them. "The original church was destroyed by an act of arson in 1962. Up until that point, the church housed a spectacular museum of artifacts from many corners of the world. Padre Crespi had been collecting them for many years. Sadly, most of the relics were destroyed. "Some believe that a group of radical locals thought the museum was an abomination and therefore wanted to destroy it."

"Why would a bunch of old trinkets be an abomination?" Will asked.

Mauricio turned to him and continued, "Many of the artifacts in the collection are believed to show that the ancient civilizations of this planet had far greater technologies than we first believed. After learning about Crespi's museum, Erich Von Daniken wrote a book about the collection in which he postulates that the gods of ancient times were actually aliens and that those aliens gave us technologies to help us in the beginning of time. It was because of a fear of theories like Von Daniken's that caused some people to feel like the museum should be destroyed, lest it be considered blasphemous." He paused for a moment. "There were other theories as well. Some of them followed along the same lines, though the source of the crime was a little more sinister."

"What do you mean, more sinister?" Sean wondered aloud.

"It could never be proven but one rumor is that the Vatican itself ordered the church be destroyed. Again, they were concerned with the idea that God was some kind of alien and that he gave ancient people technologies that were completely unexplainable by modern science or religion. They felt it would fly in the face of doctrine and would lead many people to question their legitimacy."

Tommy raised an eyebrow. "What do you think it was?"

"Me?" Delgado laughed as he started walking towards the entrance of the large facility. "I don't really look too much into such things." He stopped and turned around to face the group, his men stayed behind with the cars. "But if I had to guess, I'd say it's a combination of both."

Adriana had run for nearly a mile through the city streets of Cuenca and the man following her was still keeping up. She knew he was trying to stay hidden in the shadows but a few times he had bumped into something near a building that made enough of a noise for her to know someone was behind her.

Apparently, he was in pretty good shape. She assumed that the team watching Mauricio's caravan would send someone after her, so she wasn't exactly surprised that someone was following her. Still, she had to lose him.

Up ahead, the street opened into a small intersection with a fountain at the center of a roundabout. *Almost there*, she thought. As soon as she reached the corner at the edge of the plaza, she darted right, sprinting hard down the narrow street lined with dark shops and small businesses. Without even thinking, she turned right again into a shadowy alleyway. Up ahead was her destination. She prayed the door was open like it was supposed to be. She reached the threshold and in one motion twisted the doorknob and pushed.

*****

"There's no one in here except the head priest," a man in a black, skin-tight outfit informed Agent Collack.

The team had been searching the church for fifteen minutes, giving it a thorough investigation. But it had yielded nothing.

"They couldn't have just up and vanished," Angela was infuriated.

Clearly, the man reporting the bad news was becoming less and less comfortable. One angry boss was bad enough.

"We'll keep searching, sir," he said and began to slink away.

"No," Angela halted the agent and extended her hand. "Bring the priest to me."

*****

The door opened easily as Adriana pushed into it. With one motion she tucked in behind it and eased it shut as quickly and quietly as possible. She locked it as it went flush against the frame. She squatted down on one knee, waiting for her pursuer to attempt to enter at any given moment. A few harrowing minutes went by like hours. Finally, satisfied that whoever was following her had lost her trail, she stood slowly and took a deep breath.

The room she was in was lit only by the moonlight shining in through draped windows. Shelves lined the walls, filled with books. A leather sofa sat behind where she stood. Towards the front of the shop, a large window was covered with dark, drawn curtains, protecting the place from the view of the street. An unlit floor lamp stood nearby. The smell of old paper and dust filled the cool air. Just like she remembered.

A gruff, Spanish accent broke the silence of her hiding place. "Were you followed?"

She was hardly startled, only barely turning her head around to see where it had come from. "Yes, but I lost him."

"Are you sure," An orange glow illuminated a black-bearded face with dark, stern eyes then died away as the pipe was lowered.

"If I hadn't, he would be breaking down the door right now."

The man seemed satisfied with the answer. "It is good to see you again," he said, a puff of gray smoke encircled the shadowed figure as he exhaled.

She turned around to fully face him.

"It has been too long," he continued.

"I know," she paused thoughtfully. "I wasn't sure it was safe to come."

The man stepped across the room, walking with a slight limp. He wore a large fedora accompanied by a brown leather jacket and a pair of green trousers. The heavy boots on his feet were anything but quiet on the ancient planks of the wooden floor. Each step caused it to creak slightly under his weight. "It is always safe for you to come, Ija."

Adriana smiled as a tear formed in a corner of one eye and she stepped towards the older man. The two embraced in a firm hug, squeezing tight. "Gracias, Pappa."

Chapter 53
Cuenca, Ecuador

The interior of the Church of Maria Auxiliadora was just as unremarkable as the exterior. Compared to the dramatic architecture and design of San Blas, the church Carlos Crespi called home was humble by comparison. That was, a fact Sean and Tommy both believed to be by design the more they looked around.

The little group walked around in the main sanctuary for a few minutes but found nothing of interest. The bland interior décor left nothing to the imagination and certainly represented no clues as to the whereabouts of Crespi's map.

It was getting late in the evening and Sean was starting to wonder if Adriana knew how to find her way to where they were. He'd thought about it before. Did she know about Mauricio's little plan? If so, she would know where to meet them. But his friend had said nothing about her. However, being familiar with Cuenca, she must have known they were not at the right place before. For now, he'd have to believe that she knew what was going on.

The group scoured the building for anything that might give them a hint as to where Crespi may have left a map or anything that could point in the right direction. After almost a half-hour of searching, though, they'd come up empty.

Sean had discovered classrooms and several prayer alcoves. Mauricio had also shown them the dormitory where Crespi had lived. However, there had been nothing of note in the barren chamber. The sanctuary, too, had proven fruitless.

They arrived back in the foyer of the church as the cathedral bells rang out the hour.

"Is there somewhere we may have missed?" Tommy asked Mauricio. "I looked all over this place and didn't see anything remotely interesting. "

"I can only provide the location, my friend. I'm afraid that when it comes to finding lost things, I am fairly useless." He smiled as he made the confession.

Sean wandered over to a window he'd passed a few minutes before. Light from the evening moon poured in through the clear glass panes. Beyond, a vast courtyard opened up in the shape of a rectangle, surrounded by the walls of the church compound. He gazed out at small benches, prayer coves, stone paths, and small trees. "What's that out there?" he asked as he pointed at the window.

"That's the courtyard," Mauricio answered. "We can go have a look if you want. Out there is the last place where Crespi's collection was seen, in a storage room on the other side of the space."

Sean raised an eyebrow at his friends. "We may as well go have a look then."

It had taken Hunter a few minutes to navigate his way through the hidden passageway beneath the church that led to the streets of Cuenca. He had reached an exit point where a gate of iron bars had been left open. It was fortunate for him since he didn't much feel like going back out through the church. At some point, he figured that team of assassins would get tired of waiting and make their move into the building. He found a bicycle nearby, locked to a streetlight. It only took him a few seconds to pick the lock. He decided to play a hunch and head towards another church he'd seen earlier in the evening on his way to the bar.

As he weaved his way through the sleeping city streets, doubts filled his mind momentarily causing him to wonder if he was indeed going to the right place. He would have to chance it. Without any other leads to go on, it was time to take a gamble. If Wyatt's group found the map and left, Carlson could miss his window of opportunity. The thought pushed him to pedal faster. He could be at the other church in ten or fifteen minutes if he went hard.

"I didn't want to come. There are dangerous men following us," Adriana looked into her father's eyes.

The old man laughed and stepped back. He removed his hat and set it on the table. "I've dealt with dangerous people before, my dear. You of all people know that."

She tried to force a smile. "These people are well-trained. They will not let anyone get in their way."

Before she could say anything else, he held up his hand and interrupted. "You needn't worry about a thing. I know exactly who is following you and what they are looking for." She sat in stunned silence for a moment. He raised both eyebrows and his face squinted in a big smile. "What, your old papa can't hear things?" He laughed again as he said it, though she still looked confused. Seeing she still wasn't convinced, he stepped close and put his hand around her shoulder. "Come, my daughter, let's go downstairs and have a tequila. Perhaps that will settle your nerves a bit." She nodded as he led her around the corner out of the front room and down a darkly lit staircase.

The courtyard presented an eerie silence as the men made their way through a pair of large wooden doors and into the open space. It was like a small park built right into the center of the church complex. Off to the side, the huge structure of the sanctuary formed a high wall while the orphanage and school encompassed the rest of the area. The cool air filled their lungs as they walked reverently past statues and potted plants, trees and flowerbeds. A gentle breeze rustled a few leaves on a tree near Tommy as he passed by.

"They say that Padre Crespi planted most of the plants here and even designed a great deal of the layout for this place," Maurcio broke the silence. "He had a great love of architecture and design. I was told that he wanted a place for the people of this church to be able to escape from their busy lives and get back to the basics of prayer and meditation."

"Sounds like an interesting guy," Sean added.

Delgado nodded his agreement. "Honorable men like that only come along so often."

Mauricio's two men remained at the door to keep watch while the group continued moving through the courtyard. Several doors dotted the space along the perimeter wall. Most of them were of simple design, made of wood. Some had a single window in the center-top. Others did not. "Which one of those doors housed the collection?" Tommy asked just above a whisper. He spoke as though his voice would disturb the peace of the place.

"I believe it was that one over there," Mauricio answered. "Of course, we cannot go in there," he continued. "It has been locked since the time of the Padre's death, never to be opened again. However, I assure you the vault is completely empty."

Tommy was clearly disappointed he couldn't have a look inside the room, despite it being empty. To be in a place where such an amazing collection was housed would be worth it.

Sean snapped him back to the moment. "I'm going to go take a look over here. I suggest we spread out and see if there is anything out of the ordinary." The others nodded and each went in separate directions towards the four corners of the great courtyard. When he reached the corner he had chosen to investigate, Sean left the stone pathway and began checking around on the dusty ground for anything that might give a clue as to where Crespi's map could be. He noticed the other men doing something similar. After a few more fruitless minutes of searching, he started to head back to the path when his eye caught an old wooden ladder leaning up against the wall about twenty feet away. That gave him an idea.

Carlson pulled up to a darkened bakery at the corner of the square across from the Church of Maria Auxiliadora. He leaned the bicycle against the wall of the building and crept to the edge to get a better view of the scene. Two black SUVs sat quietly out front of the cathedral's entrance. From his vantage point, it appeared that two men dressed in black suits were waiting next to the vehicles. One smoked a cigarette while the other seemed to be passing the time by doing something on his phone. *If the two men were supposed to be keeping a lookout, they were doing a less than adequate job.* Hunter shook his head at the thought.

From within his jacket, Hunter pulled a small, black handgun. Quickly, he reached into another pocket and withdrew a sound suppression barrel. In less than thirty seconds, he'd attached the barrel to the gun and was leaving his position at the corner. He tried to space out his movements to keep as far away from each streetlight as possible as he crept hurriedly towards the two parked cars. Half-way across the plaza, he ducked down to hide behind a park bench that rested near the grass median separating him and his targets. There was one giant tree planted in the center of the green space with a few other bushes planted near by. If he used the tree for cover, he could take out one guard and then the other without causing a ruckus. Of course, even with the suppression barrel on his weapon, there would still be a muffled pop. The noise would only be loud enough for the other guard to hear and before he knew what was happening, he would be dead too.

Adriana couldn't believe what was before her eyes. Her father's basement looked like a war room for a small government's military. Several computer monitors sat in a cluster in one corner of the room, each screen displaying something different. One was showing a live broadcast of CNN. Another one was a direct feed to the BBC and the others.... She wasn't sure what those were doing. They looked like some kind of surveillance feeds. "Where are those coming from?" she asked as she stepped slowly over to the array of LCD screens.

Her father had made his way over to a counter where he kept a small supply of liquor. A cigar box made from reddish wood sat at one end of the little bar. He was busy pouring two short glasses of tequila when she raised the question. So he turned and looked in her direction as he finished pouring the drinks. "Depends," he stated flatly.

"On what?" she asked as she leaned over and tried to get a closer look at what she was seeing on the screen.

He picked up the glasses and took one over to Adriana and offered it with an extended hand. "It depends on which monitor you're talking about," he smiled as she grasped the drink from him, a little uncertain. "Salud," he said as he raised the glass to her. "It is good to see you again, daughter."

She raised her glass as well and said nothing. They both finished their drink in a few quick gulps. He took the empty glass away from her and set it on a nearby bookshelf.

"You see," he said as he pointed to some of the screens, "I'm getting surveillance from several different places. Some of them are here, in Cuenca. Others are coming in from all over the place. The United States, Russia, Brazil. China is a little tougher to get, but I've got a few there, too."

Adriana stared hard at all of the technology in the room. A rack of servers sat humming quietly in a small closet nearby. A few laptops lay on a table. Cords and wires ran all over the place, behind the workstations and along the wall. "Why?" she asked after a few moments of awed silence. "I thought you quit doing all of this a long time ago. Who are you working for now?"

He looked at her with a sincere expression. A thick cigar hung between his fingers.

"My sweetheart, I'm not working for anyone anymore," he ignited a butane lighter and held the end of the cigar near the flame, rotating it slowly until the entire tip had turned bright orange. He brought it to his mouth and took a few quick puffs sending bluish-gray smoke drifting slowly toward a vent on the side of the room.

She looked more confused than before. "What do you mean you're not working for anyone? What is all this?" Her hand stretched out, pointing to all the gizmos and gadgets.

"It's complicated." The answer didn't appease her and she crossed her arms, clearly not pleased with the response. He took the cigar out of his mouth and walked back over to the mini-bar. He opened the bottle of tequila and refilled his drink then held up the bottle, offering her another as well.

She shook her head. "No thank you. I have to get going soon."

He nodded. "I know. I had a feeling you wouldn't be here long." With glass and cigar in hand, he made his way over to a smooth, brown-leather seat and sat down. He rested the drink on a wooden side table made from dark oak. "That tequila," he said pointing at the glass, "is the smoothest I have ever found. And I have certainly tried my fair share on this planet." He laughed momentarily. "It's made from pure blue agave. Very rare. Usually very expensive."

"I don't care about the tequila, Father. What are you doing with all this stuff?"

Her directness failed to dishevel the old man. "I work for myself," he said as he took another puff off the cigar, chasing it with a sip of the golden tequila.

"What do you mean?" she stepped forward and turned a desk chair around, sitting in it backwards while she interrogated him with an unwavering glare.

He stared at the end of the cigar for a moment, watching the smoke flow smoothly from the tip and flitter into the air. "There are many bad people in this world, Adriana. Too many for governments or police to find." He paused for a moment and took another drink. "I find them."

Chapter 54
Cuenca, Ecuador

The priest looked up into James' eyes, kneeling on the stone floor of the Iglesia de San Blas. There was no fear in the old man's eyes. His wrinkled face was stern, clearly casting rebuke upon those who disturbed the sanctity of his church.

James held a gun in one hand, giving an unspoken threat that would demand answers. "Where did they go?" he asked plainly.

"I don't know what you're talking about," the priest answered bitterly.

This caused James to raise his voice. "The people who were in here earlier! Where did they go?" He shouted the last part.

Resolve filled the face of the priest. His white hair and beard were a stark contrast to the black robe he wore. "Most of our patrons are gone after the evening prayers," he spoke honestly but in a firm voice.

"These were not patrons, old man! There was a group of men who came in here an hour ago. Where are they?" This time, James held up the gun to the priest's head.

"Ah," he said after a moment of thought. "You must be talking about the group who searching for the map of Padre Crespi." He left the sentence hanging.

"Yes. Where did they go?"

"I'm not sure," he said with a sinister sounding chuckle. "But I can tell you for certain, this is not Carlos Crespi's church."

"What do you mean?" Angela struck the old man across the face with the butt of her gun.

The blow shocked the old man momentarily. A thin cut opened high on his cheek and began oozing blood down his face. James just stared as did all the other men in the group. The priest looked down at the ground for a few seconds before looking up into the woman's eyes. "I do not know where the people are whom you seek. But if they were in here, perhaps they got out through the secret tunnel below the building."

"Secret tunnel?" she asked impatiently.

"Yes. There are old passageways that lead out of the church. It is possible that they left through one of those if they knew where to find the entrance."

"Where does the passage end?"

"A few thousand meters due west of the church," he answered calmly. His breathing had intensified, though. Obviously, the old man wasn't used to any sort of physical punishment.

James glanced at his partner. The old man was being honest. But he still hadn't answered the original question so James decided to take a different approach.

"Where is Crespi's church, Padre? The people who we are looking for represent a great evil. If they find what they are looking for, the world will be in great peril. Many souls will perish." He stared hard at the priest while he spoke. The voice carried conviction. "We are doing the will of the Lord, Father."

The priest glared at him. "Does the will of the Lord mean spilling blood in his house?" he asked as his hand motioned to the dead body a few rows over.

"We carry the sword," James replied referring to a verse in the Bible. "Sometimes those who get in God's way must be sacrificed." Collack stood back and let the priest think for a moment.

The old man could not lie. It was against what he believed in. He only hoped that he had delayed the murderers long enough for Wyatt and his team to escape.

"The church you are looking for is the Iglesia de Maria Auxiliadora. That is probably where they have gone." He lowered his head, knowing that with the information, his execution would be next.

Angela gave a signal with her hand like a circle in the air and the entire team started moving quickly out of the building. She then stepped back over to the still kneeling priest and pointed her gun at the top of the old man's head. James had turned away but saw her movement out of the corner of his eye. He lunged towards her and kicked up with his right leg just as she squeezed the trigger.

Her arm jerked up into the air, the silent pop of the gun sending a round into the ceiling above. Rage filled her face but he had already grabbed her by the throat and had his own weapon pointed at the base of her skull. "What are you doing?" she asked through clenched teeth.

"We do not kill men of God," James said with a stern voice. His grip on her neck got tighter. The rest of the team in the room stared in shocked silence.

"He's a loose end," Angela replied. "We leave no loose ends." She struggled for air while she spoke.

"We do not kill men of God," he repeated. "Do you understand?" James gave one last squeeze of her throat and shoved her away.

She staggered for a moment and bent over, trying to catch her breath. James turned and started heading for the front of the church. Angela straightened up, rage filling her face. Strands of her dark hair had come out of the ponytail she always wore and dangled around her cheeks. Then, the same muffled pop echoed through the cathedral. James stopped in his tracks. All of the other men had already left the building, not sure they wanted to see the conflict. He turned to look over his shoulder in time to see the priest fall over on his side, a thin trail of smoke tracing off the top of his bleeding skull. Angela stood defiantly, still aiming the gun at where she had fired it, a look of indignation on her face. "No!" he yelled and raised his own weapon from his side. His movement was too slow, though. Her gun was already trained on him. Two quick puffs exploded from the end of her barrel sending rounds of metal into his chest. The impact of the bullets sent him stumbling backwards. Shock filled his eyes. He could taste a sickening flavor of iron in his mouth. As he tried to regain his balance, again Collack attempted to aim his weapon but another shot puffed from her gun, this one hitting him right below the neck. This time, he collapsed on the cold stone floor. Blood spurted out of the third wound. He tried to pressure it with his hands but it was no use.

Angela walked casually over to the man who had been her partner for such a long time. She looked down at him with mock pity. "When did you become so weak?" she asked him. There was no answer as he continued to struggle with the leaking hole in his neck. He gasped for air but blood filled his lungs. He gurgled loudly as he tossed on the floor. "We made a good team," she continued. Weaver squatted down low, watching him almost curiously. His vision began to blur as he struggled not to lose consciousness. "I was tired of you holding me back, anyway. It is so much harder to get things done when you have to check with someone else first. I always hated having to get your opinion on how to do things. I guess now I won't have to worry about that anymore." She stood back up and started walking away.

James Collack's hands were sticky with blood, his neck and face were covered in it. His movements began to slow and his hands dropped down to his side. "Tell your priest I said hello if he happens to be in hell with you," she said without looking back as she walked towards the entrance. The sound of her shoes clicked against the hard floor and echoed throughout the silence of the church. She didn't hear the last few gurgled breaths of her partner as she passed through the giant doorway and out into the plaza.

Sean looked down from the rickety ladder. His eyes scanned the immense courtyard, unsure of what he was even searching for. From the high point of view, he could now see the pattern of the walkway that wound its way through the open space. Four stone paths began in separate corners, twisting and turning until they reached the center of the courtyard. There, the four pathways merged beneath an odd stone sculpture of a tree with two trunks. A single path led away from the sculpture towards a pair of doors on the side of the sanctuary. "Hey Tommy!" he shouted from his perch. "What's that sculpture in the middle of the garden?"

Schultz had been investigating some of the Latin words that were inscribed, somewhat randomly, along the walls of the area. Most of the inscriptions were Bible verses talking about service to others and spreading the Gospel of Christ. "Gimme a sec," he yelled back and started making his way through the flowers and landscaping towards the center of the commons. Wyatt watched while his friend looked over the sculpture. "Sean, I think we may have something," Tommy finally said. "Come take a look at this."

He descended the ladder and jogged over to the odd piece of artwork. He'd never seen anything like it. Two stone pieces, shaped like tree trunks, rose up from the ground as if they were rooted in it. The trunks were each about three feet in diameter at the base and narrowed as they twisted upward. As the trees got higher, they arched inward until eventually they joined in the middle and became one, rising still higher until the single trunk opened up with intricately detailed branches. The entire piece was impressive, standing about ten feet high.

"Notice anything odd about this tree?" Schultz asked as the other two men joined them in the center of the courtyard.

"Other than the fact that there are two trunks?" Sean replied cynically.

Tommy pointed. "There are no leaves. The tree is dead. With one little exception."

The others followed his finger to what he was pointing at. A single piece of fruit carved from stone dangled from one of the middle branches.

"What is it?" Will spoke up.

"You don't know what this is?" Tommy asked, a little surprised.

Will shook his head.

"El arbol de vida," he whispered reverently. "It's a sculpture of the tree of life."

Chapter 55
Cuenca, Ecuador

Angela Weaver strutted out to the SUV that was sitting in front of the church. The three others waited behind it. She climbed into the driver's seat and closed the door.

"Where is Agent Collack," one of her mercenaries asked.

"He is staying here," she answered coldly. The man didn't say anything else. She added, "I'm in charge now. We need to get over to the other church, and we need to be there five minutes ago." Her face was contorted in frustration.

She stepped on the gas and pulled away from the scene. The other SUVs with her followed suit, their drivers unaware of where they were headed.

"What about the woman who left the group earlier?" she asked as the vehicle sped along.

"Our tail lost her but we know the area she's in," he wasn't happy to report the bad news.

Angela looked thoughtful. "Do we know where she was going?"

"No. Nor why." The driver watched for her reaction out of the corner of his eye.

"Send unit three over to help out. We need to find her. She could become a useful bargaining chip at some point."

The driver touched his earpiece and gave the order into the microphone. Immediately, the third SUV in line turned off down a side street.

Hunter Carlson waited patiently, crouched behind a large tree just outside Iglesia de Maria Auxiliadora. He'd made his way to the church on a hunch. Even though the cathedral he'd visited earlier was much more prominent, it had been the wrong place. Fortunately, he'd been asking around earlier in the day and knew where another church was nearby. It was the only one that made sense. Now, it appeared that Sean Wyatt had left a few guys to watch the cars while he explored the church. One of the men had slipped into an SUV and had been there for several minutes. For the attack to work, Hunter needed both guards out in the open.

If he went after the man in the car, any noise at all would alert him and give him a chance to let the other guard know something was wrong. He decided his original plan was best and continued to wait. The annoying laugh of the other man on the cell phone boomed through the square as he continued to carry on a conversation in Spanish that was apparently quite humorous. It was mind numbing to Carlson how men like these two were considered to be worth anything more than minimum wage. He knew, however, bodyguards were usually well paid in many circumstances. He quickly banished the thoughts so he could concentrate on the task at hand. The sound of the door slamming to the sport utility signaled that his mark was back on the street, in the open.

The four men stared at the odd, stone tree for a few silent moments.

"So what does it mean?" Will asked, breaking the silence.

Tommy scratched his head before responding. "I'm not entirely sure."

Sean noticed something above where the two trunks came together. Carved into the stone bark was *Revelation 22:14.*

"Do you know what that verse says?" he asked his friend while he pointed to the engraving.

"Not off the top of my head, no," Tommy shook his head.

Sean pulled out his smart phone and quickly typed in a few words into his Google app. A light breeze passed through the area again, carrying with it the scent of the city mixed with the familiar smell of rain. The wind picked up slightly and was joined by a few raindrops. A few seconds later, he was reading an information page about the verse written in the stone tree. "It says, 'Blessed are those who wash their robes, that they may have the right to the tree of life and go through the gates of the city." A few more raindrops began to spatter the ground and the sculpture. The breeze whipped up again, stronger than before. "What do you think it means, Schultzie?"

"May I suggest we figure this out inside?" Mauricio interrupted.

The others nodded and jogged across the courtyard to the doors they'd come through a few minutes before. Once they were inside the shelter of the church, the rain started pouring in earnest almost instantly. The men brushed the water off their arms as they looked around, once again in the entryway of the church.

"Wash their robes," Tommy muttered under his breath, still trying to figure out the meaning of the text. He put his hand to his mouth, focusing on the thinly carpeted floor.

"What robes?" Mauricio asked. "Priest's robes? Where do they keep priest's robes?"

"Those would be in an office somewhere in the building," Sean answered. The expression on his face showed that the gears in his mind had started turning.

Tommy shook his head slowly. "I don't think we're looking for robes," he contradicted the thought.

"No?" Mauricio questioned.

"No. The verse said that those who wash their robes will have the right to enter the gates. There are two parts to the riddle there, but the robes are not one of them. The verse is referring to common people. So the robes are a figure of speech. It could be any clothes a common person would wear. It wouldn't even have to be clothes. The act of washing is the important part."

"So what are we looking for, then?" Sean asked.

Tommy stared beyond where his friend was standing, towards the entrance of the sanctuary. Beneath the arched doorway and to the left, a large baptismal font made of stone sat on the floor just in front of the threshold. Strange engravings surrounded the outside of the container's lip. Beneath the odd symbols, pictures of people were carved into the stone. They were in a line as if they were waiting for something. Tommy walked past his comrades to get a better view of the front of the object. As he got closer, his suspicions were confirmed. The others watched him as he went over to the large bowl and got down on one knee. He traced a shape with his finger. The men joined him, looking at the engraving from behind where he knelt. "Baptism," he whispered. "All the people here," he pointed to the line of patrons on the stone, "they are waiting for baptism. Baptism makes the sinner clean. And gives them the right to," he pointed to another, familiar shape in the stone, "The Tree of Life."

The gun's sights followed the first guard. Hunter's finger tightened slightly on the trigger. He would have only a second to take out the other guard as soon as he dropped the first.

Raindrops started pattering the leaves in the tree overhead. A large gust of wind rolled through the plaza. Carlson could see the guard on the other side of the SUV through the tinted windows. The man was about to clear the back end of it and would be in the open. The other guy on his cell phone would only hear a muffled pop from the sound suppressor and in his confusion would be an easy target.

Suddenly, the rain picked up as if a faucet in the sky had been turned on. The guard he was targeting stopped moving and looked up. Then, he turned back around and got in the front passenger side of the truck.

The other man did the same, effectively ruining Hunter's plans. He didn't have a clear shot. But maybe the storm would be to his advantage. He could take out one man in the rear vehicle; then take out the other. With the noise of the pouring rain falling on trucks, they wouldn't hear anything. Plus the guard in the front SUV was still on his cell phone. Hunter decided to make the best of the situation and scurried quickly over to the rear of the second SUV, careful to stay low as he moved.

Tommy's theory made sense, Sean thought as he ran his finger along the rim of the baptismal font. He still had a question, though. "What do these symbols mean?" he asked.

His friend stood from his kneeling position.

"I have no idea. They look similar to some of the things we saw from the pictures of Crespi's collection." He took out his smart phone and started taking pictures of the object.

"What are you doing?" Will wondered.

"We may need to investigate this further at some point." Schultz took a few more pictures then placed the phone back in his front pocket.

"Now what do we do?" Mauricio asked.

The rain was coming down hard outside, evidenced by the deep sound of it impacting the roof overhead. The low droll echoed through the hallway and throughout the sanctuary.

This time, Sean got down on one knee and started looking at the floor surrounding the font. He didn't notice anything out of the ordinary. "It isn't bolted down or anything," he stated after a minute of investigation.

"You think we need to move it?" Will asked.

Sean tilted his head and shrugged. "I mean, yeah. We'll move it back." He smiled as he said it.

Mauricio was already on task, stepping over to one side of the container and rolling up his sleeves. The other three joined in, with Sean and Will on the opposite side of Mauricio and Tommy, pulling it while the other two pushed. All four men strained against the weight of the object. The stone font turned out to be much heavier than at first suspected. Mauricio leaned on the container, pushing hard with his shoulder against the edge.

"I suppose," Sean strained to talk through clenched teeth as he pulled, "it would be out of the question to take the holy water out?"

"Probably," Tommy answered sarcastically as he continued to push with all his strength. The heavy stone basin started to move slightly, sliding on the smooth carpet surface.

"Keep pushing guys, we almost have it," Sean announced.

A deep rumble echoed through the floor beneath them as they moved the object.

After a few more seconds of heaving, Tommy looked down and saw an opening where the base of the container had been. It was a small, round hole about six inches in diameter. He and the others stopped heaving as they all noticed the same strange cavity in the floor.

Tommy got down on his hands and knees and tried to peer into the dark space.

"See anything?" Sean asked as he and the others crowded around the little area.

Schultz said nothing. Instead, he reached his hand into the opening. The others silently watched, mesmerized by the moment, the sound of the rain the only noise filling the facility. Tommy's arm was into the hole up to his elbow and he was feeling around for something.

"Is there anything in there?" Will asked, eagerly.

This time Schultz nodded. A second later he pulled his hand out. Firmly gripped within it was a simple wooden cylinder, about six inches long and two inches in diameter. The surface of the caramel colored, round container was smooth; there appeared to be a cap on one end. Tommy inspected the piece thoroughly before looking again at what had first caught his eye on the lid of the cylinder. Some numbers and letters had been burned into the top reading, "II Kings 5:10."

Sean was already on it, looking up the information on his phone.

Mauricio had decided to wander over to the window to take a look outside and check on his men. It was hard to see through the downpour. Both guards had apparently taken shelter in the black SUVs. Then, across the other side of the plaza, headlights from three vehicles came into view. They looked like they were in a hurry. No doubt it was the team of agents that had been watching them before. "Gentlemen," he announced in a serious tone. "We have company."

Hunter was about to make his move towards the first guard when he saw the beams from the headlights coming from behind. He figured it would only be a matter of time until the group of assassins caught up, though he thought it would take them a little longer. Now he was caught in the middle with nowhere to run. The trucks whipped into the square and were coming around the corner. He had to act fast. So he did the only thing he could think of. He dove underneath the nearest vehicle. Since he was already soaking wet from the monsoon-like rain, he didn't care that he was lying in a puddle. He just hoped that between the rain, the curb, and the SUV, no one would see him under there. The first vehicle in line pulled up about thirty feet behind just after he scuffled underneath.

"Stop right here," Angela commanded. The driver obeyed, halting the SUV immediately. Two black trucks were parked directly in front of them. She couldn't believe their luck. Somehow they'd managed to catch up.

It looked that the vehicle closest to them had someone inside, the faintly dark silhouette was somewhat distinct, even with the blurring of the falling rain. She quickly surveyed the building's exterior.

Without any prior planning, they wouldn't be able to cover all of the exits. The church facility was too large and there were too many possibilities. Splitting up and searching the building was their best move. "We'll have to split up and search the place," she said to the driver who was obviously awaiting instructions. She touched her earpiece and spoke into her microphone. "Team, this is Agent Weaver. I am in charge now. Our plan of attack is to go in through the front and split up by vehicle. My group will go forward and search the sanctuary and anything else straight ahead. We need Schultz alive. Kill the others." She divided up the remaining men into two groups. Group one, she ordered to search the left part of the building. The other half were to go left.

"Don't we have one of our own with them?" the driver asked.

"Not anymore," she said coldly.

Will noticed the headlight beams flash on the walls and stepped over to the window. A quick look through revealed the three vehicles pulling in behind their own. He'd wondered how long it would take Angela and James to catch up. He watched as the group in the last vehicle opened their doors and stepped out into the rainy night.

Mauricio pulled his gun from inside his jacket. He touched an earpiece and said something quickly in Spanish, then cracked open the front door.

"We need to hurry, gentlemen," he stated the obvious.

"Got any more of those secret passages?" Sean asked, only a little hopeful.

His big friend turned around for a second, smiling at the sarcastic remark. "Not this time, amigo."

Sean stepped quickly to the door and looked out at the scene in the street. Without warning, Mauricio's guard in the second SUV opened his door and fired his weapon toward the new vehicles. A round caught one of the men in the stomach, sending him to his knees. The man behind the fallen assailant froze momentarily before lurching behind the second truck in their caravan. Mauricio's guard in the front vehicle poked out of the driver's side of his car and squeezed off four shots. One of the bullets caught a target's shoulder and the man fell backwards behind the cover of his SUV.

Maurico had an excellent vantage point in the doorway of the church. Calmly, he raised his weapon and aimed.

All hell had broken loose and there wasn't a thing that Hunter Carlson could do about it. He had his gun in hand, ready to fire in any direction. Bullet casings fell near him onto the wet pavement as the guard in the car above continued to lay down a consistent barrage towards the newcomers. He watched as one man took a bullet in the stomach and collapsed to the ground, writhing in agony. Then, he saw three others jump behind one of the other trucks behind his position. He could see their legs and feet but not much else. A different sounding gun fired from the direction of the church. Hunter looked back and saw one of the attackers who'd taken cover behind the second car had fallen to the pavement. The man wasn't moving. A shot rang out again and another of the men fell backwards but managed to scramble to the other side of the car. Unfortunately for him, more rounds were coming from the driver's side of the SUV in front of his position and he was cut down almost instantly.

Angela felt a wave of panic for the first time in a long while. She ducked down just before a bullet pierced the windshield directly in front of her and thudded into her seat's headrest, rupturing the black leather. Everything had turned to chaos in just a few seconds. *Why weren't her men in the other trucks firing back?* As if hearing her silent question, the doors in the second truck opened and a barrage of rounds were unleashed at the two guards.

The men in the second truck were more careful than the other group, making sure they used their car doors as shields from onslaught. One man fired shots towards the church, shattering one of the windows. Then the men in the back seat of Weaver's vehicle opened up their doors and started firing. The two guards had maximized the element of surprise but now they were out-gunned and out-numbered. What had been a precise pre-emptive attack had turned into firing blindly from the cover of their vehicles in an attempt to keep the attackers at bay.

Angela sat back up cautiously, her own weapon in hand. She opened up her door slightly to assume a safe attack position. "Finish them," she ordered. She raised her weapon and found the front passenger's seat of the car directly ahead of her in her sights.

A bullet shattered the window next to where Mauricio was standing, sending shards of glass across the thin carpet. He shut the door and jumped back. "We're going to have to find another way out of here," he said to the others.

Tommy clutched the wooden cylinder in one hand, a small .22 caliber Walther in the other. Sean also held his Ruger .40.

"There are probably exits on the other side of the building. That would be our best bet," Sean said. "Can you get our rides over there?"

Mauricio nodded and said something in Spanish into his microphone again. "I told them to meet us on the other side of the building. We must hurry."

Agent Weaver squeezed the trigger sending a bullet through the back window of the SUV in front of her. A few seconds later the guard dropped to the pavement next to the vehicle. A bullet hole at the base of his right ear oozed blood. The first SUVs engine revved and spun its tires on the wet street. The volley of bullets continued to pound into the metal of the rear door and a spider web of cracked glass stretched across the back window. Weaver's group continued shooting as the truck whirled around the corner and out of the plaza, narrowly making an escape. She jumped out of her position and ran forward to the guard she'd just shot. He lay face down on the wet street, his head turned sideways. Her shot had gone through at the base of his skull and out the front left of his face, leaving nothing but a bloody crater of bone and tissue. The rain carried away a thin river of blood towards the curb. She had seen some gruesome things but that site was disturbing even for her. The rest of her team had joined her position and were awaiting orders. "Split up once we are in the church. Remember, Schultz alive. Execute the others. Find them!"

For the moment, Hunter Carlson was glad he'd hidden under the second SUV. Problem, was, he was still trapped in the wet and, now bloody street underneath the truck. He'd seen the guard fall to the ground, shot from behind in the back of the head, the ugly visual just a few feet from his hiding place. He watched the feet come close to the body. Fortunately, no one bent down. Apparently, they were satisfied that the man was dead. The rain continued to pour, sending a stream of blood and water just past his head. Over the sound of the deluge, he could hear the woman barking out orders. They were going into the church to find Wyatt and his group. He knew they would most likely be heading towards an exit on the other side of the building. The team of killers ran off towards the entrance of the building. If he was lucky, he could head off Wyatt at the back.

Slowly, cautiously, he pulled himself along the undercarriage of the SUV and over to the curb. He grabbed a rail step and pulled himself out from underneath, careful not to draw the attention of any stragglers. He peered through the driver's side window and saw the armed group entering the church. With his left hand, he pulled on the wet door handle. As soon as he did, the vehicle started dinging, signaling the keys were in the ignition. Quickly, he eased the door shut and ducked down, fearful the annoying alarm had caught the attention of the enemy. Another peek through the windows revealed that everyone had already entered the church.

Carlson let out a long breath of relief and opened the door again. He slid into the driver's seat and started up the engine. Odds were, the other driver went to pick up Wyatt's group from behind the church. If they hadn't seen the guard get shot, they might be expecting both trucks. Perhaps, he finally had an advantage.

Sean and the others ran down the corridor between classrooms and offices. The hit squad would no doubt be coming in at any moment. They turned right down another hallway that looked the same as the one before and kept pressing on. The floor panels in the hallways were hardwood and were significantly loud underfoot as they made their way, clacking and creaking with every shoe's impact. Light flooded into the dim hall up ahead. An exit.

The men came to a halt at a pair of metal doors with a bar handle. Through the wire enforced glass they could see the two bullet-riddle SUVs in the street. "Sean," Tommy said quickly, "you and Maury take the first vehicle. Will and I will take the second. Meet back at the hotel." Wyatt nodded.

Mauricio opened the door slightly to give a quick glance down the street in both directions.

Empty. The sounds of running footsteps echoed down the corridor. Their pursuers were right on their heels.

"Gotta make a run for it boys," Sean said. He opened the door and held up his gun to cover the others. "Go!" he ordered.

The other three men took off across the street towards the two SUVs. Once they were clear of the building, Sean darted towards the first vehicle. He and Mauricio jumped in quickly on the same side.

"Get us back to the hotel," Delgado ordered the driver. The guard didn't hesitate and stepped on the gas.

Tommy arrived at the front passenger's door and flung it open as Will opened the back.

They were greeted by a pale, damp face and a gun extended across the center console.

"Get in right now or I will shoot you both." Tommy glanced to his right as the other SUV sped off. He started to get in but Will stood still.

"Leave your guns on the ground," the stranger's voice added.

His eyes were cold, full of resolve.

Tommy obeyed and dropped his weapon. Will hesitated for a second then dropped the gun he'd been given earlier by Maurcio. The black metal clanked against the wet street.

Both men slowly got in the car. Will peered angrily at the driver of the vehicle.

"If you get any ideas back there," the stranger spoke firmly, "I will kill your friend here and then you."

He kept the gun trained on Tommy as he closed the door

"Who are you?" Tommy asked.

"Don't concern yourself with the inconsequential," the man replied. Then he noticed the wooden cylinder in Schultz's hand. "Now what is that thing?" he asked.

"We aren't sure," Tommy responded angrily.

The man put his clammy hand out in a silent request for the item. Tommy shook his head, clearly not wanting to give up the map. "I can just shoot you and take the thing if you want."

"Yeah. You could. But what if you can't read what's inside?" Schultz played the only hand he had.

"Ah," he said with sudden realization. "So that *is* the map. "Very well, then. Hand it over and I won't shoot you in the leg." This time, he lowered the weapon and pulled the hammer back on his weapon.

Tommy held his breath for a moment and then, handed over the wooden object.

The man only glanced at the top with the verse from the Bible burned into it before he set it down in the cup holder next to him. He stepped on the accelerator and turned the SUV down a side street in the opposite direction that Wyatt had taken. Things were finally going Hunter Carlson's way.

Chapter 56
Cuenca, Ecuador

Adriana gazed at her father with a mix of anger, confusion, and curiosity. The cigar smoke lingered in the room, filling her nose with the sweet, earthy smell.

He seemed to read her thoughts. "What, my dear? You think me too old for things like this?"

She didn't know what to say at first. Her father had been in the intelligence game for a long time. On the outside, the family had many thriving businesses. They operated in such a transparent manner that no one would ever question anything that may have happened behind the scenes. It was from beyond that veil, though, that her father had helped western agencies bring down terrorists and criminals all over the world. Diego Villa's resources helped cripple communism in the late 1980s. He'd been influential in helping find Saddam Hussein during the American war with Iraq. But Adriana thought he had retired.

Once he moved from their native Spain to Ecuador, he was supposed to be spending his time in cafes and bookshops, relaxing for the rest of his life. Apparently, the old saying was true. You can't teach an old dog new tricks. "But why, father?" she asked finally. "It's not like you need the money. All those years of looking over your shoulder, wondering if someone was coming for you, this was your chance to leave all that behind."

He smiled tiredly at her. "I know, dear. I know. But sometimes we have to do things that don't make sense. There are still a lot of bad people in this world. And there aren't enough of the good guys to go around. I have to keep going until someone else can take my place."

She sighed heavily.

It was an argument she knew she could not win. Her father was a stubborn man, very set in his ways. Perhaps it stemmed a little from when her mother had died or maybe he was like that before. He'd watched the cancer eat away at his wife for eight long months with the same steel resolve he'd always possessed. When she finally passed, only a solitary tear found its way to the corner of his eye. How someone could be so unmoved by such a tragic event boggled her mind. Adriana might never know the real answer. And, while she didn't hold it against him, she always wondered why he wasn't more upset by her mother's passing. Maybe she just wished she was a little stronger.

"So what do you do? Call the CIA or Interpol every time you find something unusual?" she asked after a moment of thinking about where his reconnaissance would lead.

"Something like that," he grinned as he took another draw on the cigar. "Although, my role now is more direct than it used to be."

She didn't like the sound of that. "What do you mean, more direct?"

"I'll tell you more later, dear. Are you hungry? Thirsty? How long can you stay?"

She shook her head. "Don't try to change the subject, papa. I want to know what you're up to."

Suddenly, her cell phone started ringing.

Her father looked surprised by the interruption.

It was Sean. She held up a finger suggesting that their conversation would continue after she got off the phone. "Hello?"

"Adriana, it's Sean. Where are you?"

"I'm in the city at a friend's house," she decided to keep things secretive about her father. "Why? Is everything ok?"

"I don't know. We just got back to the hotel but there's no sign of Tommy. He and Will were right behind us."

Concern washed over the young woman's face.

"How soon can you get back here?" Sean asked.

"I'm on my way now," she said and ended the call.

It was her father's turn to look worried.

"What's going on?"

She faced him as he stood. "I have to go. Do you still have the old motorcycle?"

"Si. Of course. The keys are hanging in the garage," he answered, still confused.

"I will explain later, Papa. And I have not forgotten our little conversation. You have some more explaining to do when I return."

He forced a smile. "Okay, Ija."

She gave him a quick but firm hug then stalked quickly back up the stairs. Adriana didn't see the sad expression on his face as she rounded the corner at the top and disappeared from sight.

A few moments later, she opened the old door into the garage. The fluorescent lights flickered on, illuminating a simple workshop with tools hanging around on the walls, a workbench, and the bottom of a motorcycle. The top half was covered by a canvas tarp so that only the wheels and the lower part of the motor were visible. Quickly, she yanked off the cover revealing the work of art she hadn't seen in so long. The Vincent Motorcycle company stopped production in 1955. There were literally only a few hundred bikes still left in the world. The 1948 Black Shadow was part of the company's series "c" line and an extremely rare item. Vincent bikes were far ahead of their time in performance, capable of speeds that other stock motorcycles could only dream of. It was one of the first motorcycles she'd ever ridden as a young girl. She didn't have time for nostalgia at the moment, though, and grabbed the keys off the ring by the door. After flinging open the garage door, she hopped on the two-wheeler and hoped her father had kept it properly maintained. One push down on the kick-starter told her he had as the old machine rumbled to life. She shifted into gear and twisted the throttle, bursting from the garage and into the dark, rain-soaked street.

The team inside the SUV saw the motorcycle emerge from a garage a few hundred feet away. They'd been sitting, waiting for the woman to leave. The man who'd chased her earlier wasn't sure exactly which building she'd gone into but he knew the general area so when the rest of his team had shown up it had been a matter of just being patient. The driver didn't turn his lights on immediately since he did not wish to alert the target to their presence. Instead, he just turned on the ignition and pulled out of their parking place between a few three story buildings. She was driving fast making it difficult to keep up, especially in the tight streets of Cuenca. They couldn't lose her again.

Angela was standing in the street on the backside of the Iglesia de Maria Auxiliadora. She was soaking wet from the rain and frustration was beginning to take over. The best assets she knew of were at her disposal yet they had been unable to make any progress. She wondered how had Wyatt been able to escape again? Their vehicles must have gone around and met them in the back. A terrible feeling began to creep up inside of her. The Prophet was a man not to be meddled with. As fearless as she was, Angela knew just how far his reach really could go. If she failed him, there would be no mercy. And there wasn't a place on earth she could hide where he couldn't find her.

"Agent Weaver," a familiar voice came through Angela's earpiece, interrupting her thoughts. "We are following her now. Looks like she is heading towards the mountains. Will let you know once we get an exact destination."

Angela considered the information. *There was a chance after all. Perhaps the Spaniard would lead them to Wyatt and his friends. They could eliminate him and the others, leaving Schultz to lead them to the treasure.*

Eric Jennings eased open the door to Emily's bedroom as slowly as possible, fearful that it might creak and alert her to his presence. A mixture of pale white and orange lights seeped through her window curtains from the street outside. In the dull illumination, Jennings could make out the outline of Emily Starks' body in the bed underneath a pile of down comforters and blankets. She was the last loose end, the only one left who knew about the Prophet's involvement. Of course, he was assuming that the others had been taken care of in South America. And why would he think otherwise. He had his top agents on it. He stepped carefully across the threshold of the bedroom, hoping the old wooden floors did not give away his presence. In a gloved, right hand, Eric held his gun equipped with a narrow sound-suppressor. In the other hand, he held a pillow he'd been given by Emily earlier in the evening.

Jennings crept closer, inching his way over to the sleeping woman. It was dark in the room but, he could see her long, brown hair poking out from under one of the blankets where she'd tucked her face. He stared at her momentarily as he stood over her. The only noise in the room was a small floor fan that was humming loudly in the opposite corner.

No one would find her for a day or so. He would help lead the investigation, vowing that the crime would face justice. Of course, he would find someone to pin it on. One of his lower assets would do. It would be easy to arrange a meeting that ended in a tragic shootout. Evidence would be planted. Emily would be given a hero's funeral. There would be political giants in attendance, perhaps even The President himself. And the whole problem would go away.

He banished the thoughts as he leaned closer to the side of the bed. He could have his way with her if he wanted. She had always been an attractive woman, strong of will and of body. The thought lingered for a moment. *Murderer, yes. But he was no rapist. His stable of prostitutes satisfied all of his carnal urges. Tonight he just had to finish this job. Maybe tomorrow night he would call up his escort connection. An evening of fun might be exactly what he needed after all the stress he'd experienced lately.*

Very slowly, he held out the pillow and gently placed it on the outline of Emily's head. He pressed the long barrel to the fabric and pulled the trigger three times. Feathers erupted from the pillow with the popping of the gun. He left the mangled cushion on the body and walked casually out of the room, never even glancing back. And all of his loose ends were tied up.

He felt good about himself as he descended the stairs. The air was brisk outside, chilly from a cold front that had come through, typical of that time of year.

The streets were empty save for a few cars several hundred yards away. They wouldn't even notice him as he slipped into his own car around the corner and drove off.

The Prophet would be extremely pleased with his work. No doubt he would be well rewarded. He smiled at the thought of the things he could buy with the money he would receive. It would be significant which meant no more government salary. No more scraping by, dealing with the bureaucratic bull. He could retire to somewhere in the Caribbean, sipping Mai Thais and playing golf for the rest of his days.

I deserve it, he thought to himself as he got in his car and started the engine. Finally, Eric Jennings was going to get what he had coming to him.

Chapter 58
Southeastern Ecuador

Hunter had driven to a spot about thirty minutes outside of the city. There, he'd turned off the main road in favor of an old dirt one that led through a field to a grove of trees at the foot of a hill.

Once he reached the patchwork forest he stopped and ordered both of his passengers to get out of the car slowly. He still held the gun firmly in his hand making sure the two men were aware that he had not wavered since exiting the city.

The rain had subsided on the drive out and now a cool breeze rolled across the meadow and through the treetops nearby.

After he made his way around the front of the vehicle, Hunter held out the wooden cylinder towards Schultz. "Open it," he ordered, pointing the gun at Tommy's chest.

He hesitated for a moment then reached out and took the object. Instead of obeying, he scanned the outside for a moment, again taking a look at the inscription that had been burned into the cap. Then, carefully, he raised the tube to his ear and tilted it back and forth slowly.

"What are you doing?" Hunter asked, shaking the weapon in Tommy's direction.

Schultz gave him an indignant expression. "You don't do a lot of this sort of thing, do you?" he asked, sarcasm lathering the question. "Sometimes these have a separate glass filament on the inside. Within that inner cylinder is acid and if opened incorrectly would destroy any paper contents immediately."

Hunter frowned at this new information and lowered his weapon slightly.

"Fortunately," Tommy continued as he lowered the container back to his waist, "this isn't one of those."

"How do you know?" Carlson looked skeptical.

Schultz sighed, obviously annoyed. "Because if it were one of those, I could hear the liquid sloshing around on the inside. And typically, those types of cylinders have a sort of combination lock to them. They're called codices. This one," he held up the container, "has nothing like that." Satisfied he'd convinced Hunter it would be alright to proceed, Tommy squeezed the cap of the wooden object and started pulling and twisting.

Hunter tensed up for a second, not sure what was going to happen.

The lid popped off, sealed by a cork on the underside. Tommy peered in as Will watched with high interest.

Carlson observed carefully as Tommy turned the container upside down and a small scroll slid out. "What is it?" Carlson asked, impatiently.

Tommy was already unrolling the tiny scroll very slowly. "It's vellum," he said as he continued to work with the old piece. "Made from an animal skin. Whoever created this piece knew that it would stand a better chance against the elements and time than ordinary paper." He turned towards the car and laid the scroll out flat on the hood. It had been dry for fifteen so minutes so he doubted it would hurt.

Carlson stepped close to get a better look and held up a small, key ring flashlight. The LED bulb illuminated the old writing surface, revealing a dull shine. What they saw was a very simple, crude drawing. There was a squiggly line that went from the top right of the writing surface to a point where it forked into two similar lines. At the point of the fork was a darkened circle. "What is that?" Hunter asked and pointed at the dot.

Tommy shook his head. "I don't know. There's no other information." He picked up the map and turned it over, hoping to find another clue as to where they were supposed to go but there was nothing. Not even a hint as to who had drawn up the old piece.

Carlson stepped away from the vehicle. "Is this some kind of joke? There has to be more to it than just this."

Tommy stared at the stranger. He had a tired and frustrated look in his eyes.

It was late and they were all tired. Maybe Tommy could use that to buy some time. "Look, it's late. We're exhausted. Let's hole up somewhere and get some rest and maybe we can figure this out in the morning." He tried not to sound like he was begging, but he had the feeling the man with the gun wasn't buying it.

"You think I'm stupid?" Carlson answered. "Yeah, let's all just take a nap and when I wake up you two will still be here."

Will interrupted. "There's rope in the back of the truck. Tie us up if you want."

Tommy nodded in agreement. "Tomorrow morning we can drive to the next town and ask around about this drawing, see if it turns up any leads."

To Hunter, their idea was starting to make a little sense. He was tired and they weren't going to make any progress at that late an hour. He could tie them to a tree in the grove nearby and in the morning maybe he could find someone who could tell him the location of the circle on the map. "Ok," he said after a few more moments of thought. "Get the rope out of the back. I don't have to remind you of what will happen if you try anything. And I am a very light sleeper." Part of him considered killing Will and dumping him on the side of the road. No one would know and he only needed Tommy. Hunter had learned, though, one could never have too much insurance. At the moment, he felt like he had all the poker chips at the table.

Adriana ran into the hotel after parking her motorcycle at the side of the building. She flashed by the concierge and up to the second floor room where she knew Sean would be.

Catching her breath for a second, she knocked on the door. She heard Sean tell her to come in from the other side so she obeyed.

Sean looked up as she entered the room. Her dark hair was tousled. In the black leather jacket and tight, black pants she was quite the vision. His mind, though, could only think about his friend. The bond he and Tommy had was brotherly. They'd known each other a long time. And they took care of each other. Tommy had offered Sean a way out of the Justice Department. And he'd had always tried to protect his friend from unsavory characters. In the last three weeks he'd failed twice.

Adriana put a gentle hand on his shoulder and stood next to him, not saying a word. Her thoughts were understood. She didn't need to ask how he was feeling. And he appreciated that. "What are you looking at?" She looked at the computer screen as she spoke.

He turned the laptop slightly so she could see a little better. "It's a text from the Bible," he answered. "Second Kings five, verse ten."

She leaned over and read what was on the monitor silently. *"Go and wash seven times in the Jordan River, and your flesh will be restored and you will be cleansed.* "What does it mean?" she asked.

He turned the computer back to where it had been then quickly typed in a few more commands.

She was impressed with how fast he could type. Obviously, he had some kind of computer training. The realization caused her to think back to her father and for a second, she glanced out the window and down at the city. Somewhere down there, he was up to his old tricks. Worry started to creep into her mind again, but she had to push that away for now. Her father could handle himself, at least a little while longer.

Sean turned the screen back towards her again. It displayed a map of Ecuador and all the main rivers. He was particularly interested in the region around Cuenca. "We found the Bible text engraved on a wooden cylinder last night at Crespi's church. It was hidden under the baptismal font."

She raised an eyebrow. "What was inside it?"

He shrugged. "The map, we think. We don't know for sure. Before we could open it all hell broke loose. There was a bunch of shooting. We barely got out the back of the church alive. When we did get out, Maury came with me. Tommy and Will got in the second truck."

His face washed over with regret. "That was the last I saw them."

"What happened to the other truck?"

He tipped his head towards Mauricio who was still on the phone. "We don't know. But Mauricio is trying to find out. He's talking to the local cops. My gut tells me the car was hijacked during the shootout. So whoever was following us has Tommy and Will now."

She looked at him sadly. "I should have been there. Perhaps I could have helped. I am so sorry."

He shook his head. "It's okay. I'm glad you weren't. You might have been in trouble now too. "Did you get to do what you needed?" He changed the subject for the moment.

She just nodded and offered a forced smile, which he returned.

Delgado hung up the phone and joined in the conversation next to the desk. "The local police haven't found the vehicle yet, and no one has seen or heard anything. Whoever took them left town immediately and didn't say a word to anyone. They found my driver's body outside the church, along with a few other unknowns."

The news was what Sean had expected. That still didn't make it easy to hear. "We have to assume that whoever has them wanted whatever was in that cylinder," he said. "Without knowing what is on the map, it makes it a little harder to figure out exactly where they might be going. "I tried calling Tommy's phone but he didn't answer. Whoever jacked the car probably took whatever they had, including their phones."

Her mind was racing as she took in all the new information. "So, you think that the Bible text from the inscription is meant to refer to one of these rivers?" she pointed at the screen again while she spoke.

Sean nodded. "Problem is, there are several rivers within a hundred miles of here. And even if we can figure out which one is the right one, you're potentially talking about hundreds of miles of shoreline on both sides we would need to cover." It was a big problem and Sean knew it. "We have to assume that the map pinpoints the location on a specific river," he added.

"Do you have any idea what we are looking for?" Mauricio asked.

"Not really. It could be a cave or maybe a big rock that marks the location. We really have no idea what we're looking for." Sean sighed in frustration and closed his laptop. His fingers rubbed tired eyes.

"You need to get some rest," she spoke firmly.

He shook his head. "I won't be able to sleep."

"There is nothing you can do right now. It's late. In the morning maybe we can go into town and see if there is anyone who can help us."

He knew she was right. They could stay up all night trying to figure out where Tommy and Will were or the location the clue eluded to, but they would most likely be unsuccessful with both. He doubted he would sleep much, but even a few minutes of rest would be welcome.

"Okay," he nodded finally. "We'll get up early and see what we can find out."

Mauricio agreed. "I'll check around first thing in the morning. Perhaps I can find a clue as to what happened or where they headed."

She patted Wyatt on the shoulder as if confirming his decision was a good one. "We will find them."

He wished he had her confidence.

Chapter 59
Utah, United States

Alexander Lindsey stood silently overlooking the
mountain range from the third floor office in his
mansion. It was early in the morning. The sun was
just beginning to slip above the horizon to the east. He
wore his usual morning robe, featuring a burgundy silk
with a dark green collar and belt. It looked more like a
smoking jacket. The coffee in his hand was still
steaming, a stark contrast to the cold outside. Snow
covered the mountains as far as he could see, a possible
look into the season to come. Cold winters were
something he'd grown accustomed to over the years.
There was something about the cold that afforded him
a great deal of privacy. The harsher the winter, the
fewer people bothered him. However, soon the
comfort of privacy had been unable to soothe his
nerves for the last few days, though. He'd tossed and
turned each night for nearly a week and his eyes had
big bags under them as a result. The deprivation of
sleep was something he loathed. He usually needed a
full eight hours to be completely functional.

Agent Weaver had called him late in the night to
report that her team was staked out at a hotel in
Ecuador, observing Wyatt's group.

In her report, she had informed him that Agent
Collack had been killed in a gunfight at the church, as
had three more of her men. Weaver had tried to assure
him that things were under control but shootouts in
the streets of Cuenca were hardly easy to cover up. A

quick search on the web confirmed her story. Local news outlets all over Ecuador were covering the odd killings outside the Iglesia de Maria Auxiliadora.

He'd spent a tremendous amount of time and money making sure that the policing agencies of the world had no way to track his operatives. When a mercenary signed up to take a mission for him, they were completely removed from the grid, untraceable except by him. Still, it was unsettling that Collack had been killed. James Collack was one of the best assets to have ever worked for the Order. How many missions he'd completed was for Lindsey to remember.

Another issue on his mind was the lack of communication between he and his other agent in play. Will had not reported in for nearly two days, which was very untypical for him. Lindsey understood Will's plan. He was no doubt in the midst of the enemy at this point and most likely couldn't get time for a phone call. It was still unnerving, though.

Alexander liked to be in total control. He liked to have all the strings attached to his fingers so that everything went according to plan. Clearly, the people they were dealing with were dangerous. He had to press on, though. Finding the last chamber of Akhanan was all that mattered. Once he found that, nothing could stop him.

Perhaps it was time to cultivate a new relationship within the Justice Department. Then there was the little clandestine problem. Emily Starks had been an irritation, as had Sam Townsend. So when Eric Jennings came up with the plan to eliminate both,

Lindsey had been more than willing to provide him with a sacrificial lamb, an operative that had gone rogue a few times and had a problem with drinking. The problem being that when he drank, he talked too much.

Jennings' call about twenty minutes after Weaver's had been somewhat of a consolation. Starks and Townsend were both dead, effectively eliminating government interference from Axis or internal investigations. He smiled at the thought and sipped a cup of the hot coffee, trying to remind himself that everything was going according to plan. It was God's plan, after all.

Chapter 60
Southeastern Ecuador

It had been a long night for Tommy and Will. They had been unable to sleep save for a few minutes of dozing off here and there. Each time their heads lowered in sleep, they woke to the tightening of the rope around their chests as their body weight pressed against it. The man who'd taken them had also slept lightly, if any. It seemed every time Tommy looked over at him, his cold, alert eyes were staring at he and Will. Tommy wondered if their captor slept with his eyes open.

The early morning dew had been an annoyance, virtually soaking their clothes as they sat on the ground, tied to a small tree. It was doubtful the stranger had that problem since he slept in the back of the SUV with the rear door open so he could watch his two prisoners throughout the night.

Schultz saw the man rouse from his vague slumber and walk over to where he sat upright on the ground. He carried his gun in hand for both men to see.

"Time to go," he stated simply.

"Where are we going?" Tommy asked, unable to move against the tight ropes.

"There's a village not far from here. We'll drive there and ask the locals about the place on this map."

"I've been thinking about those lines," he offered. "My guess is that either they are trails or rivers. I doubt they're roads. If they are rivers, one of the locals might be able to point us in the exact direction we need to go."

Their captor seemed happy with the notion for a moment. Then, his face took on a sinister look. "You, I need," he said to Tommy. "But him," he paused, "I don't." Carlson raised his weapon and pointed it at Will.

Hastings just stared up at him, not an ounce of fear anywhere on his face. Anger was there though. A rage filled his eyes like a hurricane.

"Wait!" Tommy pleaded. "If you need me then you have to take both of us. You kill him and I won't tell you anything else."

"Maybe I don't need either of you," the stranger said coldly.

Schultz stared through him. "You know that isn't true. Even if you find the location on this map you won't be able to find the treasure without the information I have."

"What information?" Carlson asked, skeptical.

"You'll just have to wait and see," Tommy narrowed his eyes.

The stranger lowered his gun. "I'm pretty sure you're bluffing. But I'd rather be safe than sorry." He waved the gun towards the car. "I'm going to untie you both but once you're free, tie him up again in the back of the car."

Tommy nodded while Will just continued to stare.

Ten minutes later, they were back on the road heading southeast. Tommy had tied Will in the back as he was told. He had his cell phone in his pocket but wasn't sure if the battery still had any power left in it or not.

Schultz hadn't been bluffing when he told the stranger that there was something he knew. The problem was, Tommy didn't have access to what he needed either. The golden leaves they'd found before were certainly a necessary part of the puzzle. Even if they found the location of the next chamber, he doubted they would be able to get to it. At the moment, he wasn't sure if that was a good thing or a bad thing. It was anybody's guess how this wildcard would react to a situation like that.

Adriana was already awake when the sun peeked over the mountains to the east. She'd been up for a while, wrestling with a problem in her mind. After some consideration, she'd picked up the phone and made a call. The conversation had been brief but maybe it helped their situation.

She made her way over to Wyatt's room and found the door propped open with the little locking bar near the top. After politely knocking, she heard Sean tell her to come in. Apparently, she wasn't the only one up early. She figured that everyone probably had the same anxiety she had, if not more. She noticed that he looked as if he hadn't slept all night, his weary eyes scanned the computer screen, looking for something. Mauricio was on the phone again, busily talking to someone in Spanish. She observed that Mauricio was on the phone, saying something about a stolen vehicle.

"How did you sleep?" Sean asked her while he typed on the computer. He didn't even look up.

She forced a smile. "I slept okay. Maybe a few hours."

He didn't respond. His exhausted eyes just continued scanning the screen.

"Did you find anything?" she continued.

Finally, he looked up. A serious look covered his face. "Unfortunately, no. But we are still checking some resources."

"What are you looking at?" she asked as she stepped around the corner of the desk and tilted her head to see what he was doing.

He pointed at the screen. "Just this Bible text again. I'm trying to figure out what it means."

She read the text on the monitor silently. When she was finished, she thought for a moment. "What is so special about the Jordan River?" she wondered out loud.

"In ancient Israel, it was a very important river to the Hebrews. Almost sacred. In this particular story, a general for a foreign army is stricken with leprosy and is desperate so he goes to see one of Israel's prophets, Elisha. The prophet doesn't even come out to greet him but instead sends his assistant who tells the general to go wash in the Jordan River seven times and he will be healed.

Adriana looked skeptical. "So why that river?"

Sean grinned out of the corner of his mouth. "That's exactly what the general said. He was furious that Elisha wouldn't meet with him personally and also at the fact that he'd told him to go wash in a dirty river. The general wondered why he couldn't just go back to his homeland and wash in one of their own rivers."

Realization washed over Adriana's face. "Wait a minute," she thought for a second before continuing. "Dirty river! That must be it!"

Sean looked confused. "What do you mean?"

"I think I know which way they were headed," she blurted out.

Mauricio stopped his conversation on the phone, excusing himself and telling whomever he was talking to that he'd call back.

She continued. "I spoke with a friend a little earlier today. Let's just say they are in the surveillance business. They told me that he had video of your truck heading east last night at the same time that we were coming here."

A flicker of hope came into Sean's eyes along with skepticism. "Can you trust them?"

She ignored his query and went on. "At first, that didn't mean much to me. Really, that car could have been headed anywhere. Adriana had a renewed energy. She pulled the laptop around and stroked a few keys. Google appeared and then she typed in a few more. A second later, a listing of Ecuadorian maps appeared, all featuring prominent rivers.

She scanned the screen with her finger and then found what she was looking for and tapped the screen with her nail. "The Zamora River," she said. "Mauricio, is that a dirty river? I've never been in that area before."

He nodded. "Hmm. Yes, it is. Lots of dirt and silt from the mountains wash into it. It's over towards the border with Peru. The original settlers in that area called it *Father River*."

Sean raised an eyebrow. "Ok, but that river has got to be pretty long, right? The odds of us finding the location or Tommy are both slim to none. Plus, we don't know for sure they went that way."

Her face grew stern. "It's the only lead we have, Sean. Right now, we don't have any other choice."

She was leaning close to him. He could smell a sweet, simple perfume that she must have put on earlier in the morning after her shower. The scent lingered for a second, distracting him from the job at hand. Quickly, he regained his senses.

"What about the washing seven times?" Mauricio interrupted his thoughts. "That must have something to do with the solution to the riddle."

Sean and Adriana looked at him.

"You're right," Sean said. He typed in a few more words and pulled up several different images of the river from tourist blogs and a number of other resources. Then something caught his eye. "Does the Zamora have any waterfalls?" he asked.

Mauricio nodded. "Not too many dramatic ones but yes, it has several waterfalls. Why?"

"Because if you go over water falls you will go under the river, right? Just like in the Bible story where he was told to go under seven times. Maybe the clue in the text is that the location of the entrance to the chamber is at the seventh waterfall."

The stout Latino man nodded slowly. Then he pointed at the map on the monitor. "Up here is where the river begins."

His finger moved slightly to the line of another river. "Notice this other river begins here. The two will join at this point." He traced the line to where it and the Zamora became one. "There is a waterfall right here." He tapped the screen to emphasize his point.

"I'm guessing there are six others, three in each river, before you get to that spot," Sean said.

"Probably," Delgado agreed. "It's worth a shot."

Sean became silent. His mind raced. Then he said, "Maury, remember the Priest's garden? The pathways became one under the tree. These two rivers," he looked at the screen again, "they become one here too."

"It would appear we are headed east," Adriana said with a smile.

Wyatt's face filled with determination. "Yes, it would."

Angela watched as the three exited the hotel. She sat perfectly still as they got in their cars and drove down the road leading back towards the city. She spoke to a middle-aged man standing next to her, telling him to get everyone rolling. He had a different appearance than the rest of her group, sporting a thick, brown beard with a few strands of gray. The beard matched the man's hair in thickness and in color. Most of the team were young, probably in their mid to late twenties. This man, though, looked to be in his upper forties. Mercenary work was not something that usually had a long career span. So either this guy was good at what he did or he was some kind of action junkie. Either way, she was glad he was on her side. He'd joined up with her team in the middle of the night, a special guest she'd heard of and called upon after the fiasco at the church.

She'd heard everything Wyatt and his friends had said thanks to a listening device positioned right outside their room. The little group was heading east to a location near some river. She'd never liked puzzles or riddles. It wasn't that she wasn't smart enough to solve them. She felt it was just a waste of time. It was much easier to be a parasite and just follow along, letting their host do the hard work. Then her unit could make the grab when the time was right. That was what she knew. Killing was as simple as pulling a trigger. Stealing was just reaching out at the right moment and taking it. Her team's vehicles had been parked back on the other side of the building so as to go unseen by Wyatt and his friends. She'd left drivers with them for the ability to get moving quickly when needed. As Angela expected, the SUVs pulled around a few moments later and her team loaded up.

The winding drive down the mountain was scenic, something she'd been unable to notice the night before. The expanse of the city spread out in the basin below, edging upward into mountains far away. She was not a nostalgic person, nor one who carried a great deal of sentiment. Most of the pleasures she enjoyed in life were not what others would consider "normal." But she didn't care. Her religious beliefs differed from most people. She and James had been tutored directly by The Prophet right out of college. He'd told them the truth about the Christian religion they'd grown up with and how it was a bunch of myths and grand tales built to control the masses with fear and promises of a fantastic afterlife. Instead, he'd shown them a different path. She never really latched onto his religious zeal. To her, life presented too many delights to pass up on the off chance there might be a judgment. On the other hand, Angela figured it was okay to hedge her bets just in case.

She smiled as the sun's rays splashed onto her face through the windshield. The convoy continued down the road, nearing the outlying buildings of the city. She was proud of herself for being able to push beyond mere human emotions and do the job she knew she had to do. And at last, she was close to her reward.

Chapter 61
Washington, D.C.

Eric Jennings sat casually in his desk chair, shuffling through some paperwork. He felt like nothing could touch him. Even the menial tasks of reviewing reports and checking up on other assignments couldn't bring him down. He'd managed to eliminate his two biggest loose ends, his only loose ends. Perhaps killing Emily Starks wasn't necessary. After all, she didn't know anything yet. But it was only a matter of time until she asked too many questions. Just like Sam Townsend had.

He felt no remorse for the murders. It was just a means to an end. Jennings had given the best years of his life for the Department of Justice and for what, some measly retirement account that would barely cover his monthly expenses? Well, *barely* as far as his needs were concerned.

His mind drifted to some of those needs. One of the escorts would do nicely for the evening. He deserved a treat, after all. Maybe he would get the tall red head. Since the police were still investigating the death of the intruder in his home, he was staying at a hotel a few blocks up from his office, which was perfect since he preferred the women not know where he lived. He became eager at the thought of the fun he would have and after a few more minutes of sorting out the last of the paperwork, picked up his cell phone. A key to his hotel room would be left at the front desk for his female companion. She could make herself comfortable and expect him around six in the evening.

Satisfied with his decision, Jennings hung up the phone and grabbed a television remote that was sitting on his desk nearby. He pressed a few buttons and came across the news report he'd been waiting for. A slender, African-American woman with creamy, cocoa skin was reporting that Sam Townsend had been found, shot dead in his home earlier that morning. Apparently, his maid found the body. The hysterical Russian woman was sobbing uncontrollably as they interviewed her briefly. It was hard to understand what she was saying because of her heavy accent. Jennings assumed she was saying something about finding the body on the floor with blood all over the place.

"Police still have no leads as far as suspects are concerned and have been, as yet, unable to find the murder weapon."

Jennings knew they would not find a murder weapon.

Eventually, they would make the connection between the dead man from Jennings's home and Townsend's murder, with a little suggestive assistance from him of course. The case would be open and shut before the end of the week.

The reporter was going on about Townsend's career and his meteoric climb through the ranks until his appointment to the new agency in charge of corruption. It was mostly stuff that news teams always reported when someone important or famous died. A quick bio and then on to sports.

He wondered why they hadn't mentioned Starks' murder yet but figured he'd either missed it or no one had discovered the body. It had surprised him a little that Townsend's corpse had been discovered so soon but that was the way things went sometimes.

Soon enough, he would get a call asking if he'd heard about Emily's untimely death and how weird it was that her and Sam were killed on the same night. He would play sad and confused for a few days and then move on. No one would know a thing.

Chapter 62
Ecuador

The SUV bumped and rolled its way along an old path that cut through the forest. Any signs of a road had long since been left behind. There wasn't much to tell that a road or a trail had ever even been there except the odd lack of trees and plants.

Hunter had stopped just outside a small village about twenty minutes before and asked for help from a few of the townspeople. He showed them the map and pointed at the dot where the two lines merged. Most of the people had turned their heads away and went back inside their buildings. It had been an odd thing, like they knew where it was but weren't going to tell him. That or they thought they'd seen the devil himself. Every single person he'd come in contact with had been full of smiles and very friendly until he showed them the map. Finally, he found a boy who looked to be about twelve, playing with a makeshift soccer ball in the street. When Hunter Carlson showed him the map and asked in Spanish if he knew where it was, the boy nodded happily. For a young one, the kid was extremely detailed about the directions. He'd basically walked them to the location in his mind. Carlson figured that he'd been there before, though he couldn't figure out why. Surely it wasn't for the same reason they were headed there.

Tommy had remained silent in the passenger's side the entire journey. Will was in the back, tied up so he couldn't cause any problems. It was, no doubt, an uncomfortable position probably made infinitely worse by the bumpy road trail that jostled everything in the vehicle.

"Who are you?" Tommy said, breaking the silence for the first time since they'd left the village.

Carlson smiled out of the corner of his mouth. He'd not felt like making small talk with someone he was going to end up killing. He learned a long time ago not to get to know your victims. It wasn't that it made things much harder when it came time to pull the trigger. But it certainly did make it easier if you knew the person had a cat at home. It was just simpler to not know personal stuff. "I'm just a guy," Carlson said plainly.

"Who do you work for?" Tommy persisted. He watched the driver with every bit of focus he could muster.

"Ah," Carlson raised a finger. "Now that is a fascinating question. You see, I don't really know who I'm working for. I just know these two guys needed me to do this job for them. They said there's a bunch of treasure and that I'll get a healthy cut of whatever I find. Plus, they gave me money up front. Hard to turn that down."

"Do you even know what you're looking for?" Tommy asked in a condescending tone.

"Some kind of ancient vault. Gold, I'm assuming."

Hunter stopped the truck at the end of the trail under the shade of a large, leafy tree and turned off the engine. He opened his door and motioned for Tommy to do the same. "Looks like the end of the line for driving. Guess we have to hike our way in from here."

Schultz said nothing but obeyed and exited the vehicle.

Carlson motioned towards the thick growth of trees. In the direction he was pointing, Tommy could make out a thin trail. It was barely visible but he could tell at least some kind of animals had used it in the past. "Let's get moving," Carlson said.

"What do you mean?" Tommy protested. "What about Will? You're not just going to leave him there in the back of the truck."

"I cracked a window," he replied as he pointed at a small sliver of space at the top of the window. "Besides, it's not hot out here. He'll be fine. For now." The last two words carried a sinister threat.

"Now move."

Tommy knew there was nothing he could do to change the man's mind. He refrained from arguing and started trudging off into the woods. Carlson followed close behind, holding the gun tight and aiming it right at the small of Tommy's back.

Sean stopped the vehicle in a small village about forty minutes outside of Cuenca. He had left Mauricio behind in the city to deal with the situation that had escalated the night before. He'd wanted to go with Sean but if he didn't stay and take care of things, matters could get out of hand. Sean understood. His stout friend may not have been of any help on their search anyway. He hoped that Delgado wouldn't find himself in any legal trouble, though he doubted that would be an issue. Mauricio had many friends in many important places.

Adriana had noted that Mauricio never revealed much about himself during the time she'd seen the man. She had asked Sean about Mauricio, but he offered no information, merely stating that "He's a man of many resources."

A few chickens ran here and there on the dirt street. The place seemed like somewhere time had forgotten. There were a few electrical lines that ran along the road but it was doubtful the area had many other amenities.

An old woman was walking along the street and looked at them with a peculiar stare.

"Buenos Dias, senora," Sean greeted the woman.

She was mumbling something to him that he couldn't quite pick up. However, Adriana was on the driver's side of the truck and was able to hear the conversation.

"The woman is saying how odd it is to see the same car twice in an hour with different people driving it."

Sean's eyes grew big. "They came through here?" he asked in Spanish.

Instead of giving an answer, she just walked away, seemingly angry at something.

Wyatt was confused.

"What did I say?" he looked at Adriana for an answer. She shrugged and said nothing.

Sean noticed a young boy in the street ahead, carrying a soccer ball. "Let's ask him."

The homing device was working perfectly. Angela
had it planted on Wyatt's vehicle during the night,
making it easy to follow her prey without the risk of
being noticed. Effectively, she could stay right on his
heels yet out of sight.

When the dot on her tracking screen came to a stop,
they pulled off to the side of the road just after entering
the small village. The little town was dirty, third
worldly.

She just couldn't believe that some people were still
essentially, savages, living like animals in some places.

The blinking dot on the screen started moving again
and Angela was about to tell the driver to get going too
but it stopped suddenly.

"What are they doing?" she asked, almost to herself.

"Traffic?" the driver half-joked.

"Only if it's a donkey and a bunch of chickens
blocking the road," she remarked harshly.

She tried to see down into the small, three-street
town to find out what was going on, but from their
vantage point on a small hill, she couldn't see anything
except some rickety buildings. Another anxious
minute passed. Angela wondered if Wyatt or one of his
companions noticed they were being followed. There
was no way for her to know. She shrugged off the
irrational paranoia and sat back in her seat. After
another minute the little red dot on the screen started
moving again. Angela nodded at her driver and the

man stepped on the gas and eased the truck back out onto the road.

Will had overheard the man's conversation with Tommy just before they headed into the woods. He had seen the man before. In fact, he knew who the guy was. Hunter Carlson. Will made sure to know who most of the top assets were in his field. And since his field was somewhat of a shallow pond, it was pretty easy to figure out who was who. Carlson was good. Very good. From what Will had heard, the man was ruthless, clever, and had a very short memory when it came to killing. He reminded him of himself, which made Will hate the man even more.

Carlson also carried himself with a casual nature. It was probably one of the reasons he'd been so successful. Will knew someone like that could lure in the most suspicious of marks before they even knew what happened.

The ropes were tight on his wrists, irritating the skin from the rubbing and jostling of the last hour. Will was angry that he'd let Carlson get the drop on him. He'd told himself it could have happened to anyone. That was probably true. The rope around his ankles wasn't as tight. Maybe that was all the wiggle room he needed. When Carlson had checked to make sure Will wouldn't be able to get free, he'd paid more attention to the bindings on his hands instead of his feet. It made sense. Hands seemed much more likely a tool of escape than feet. That was something that he was extremely glad for at the moment.

He twisted his body around and managed to get onto his back despite his hands being bound from behind. The thought had crossed his mind to try and kick the rear window out, but he figured the sound it would make would be too loud.

Instead, he decided to try to open the back door. His shoe was just small enough that he could hook his big toe under the latch. Just as he thought, the toe of the shoe slipped beneath the shiny metal and he pulled back on it. Nothing happened. His hope turned into distress instantly. The door was locked.

"That's Mauricio's other truck up ahead," Sean declared as they bumped and rolled along the old road towards the forest. He let off on the gas slightly and approached the other vehicle with cautious reservation. About twenty feet short of it, he stopped the car all together. Wyatt and Villa peered through the windshield to see if there was anyone in the other truck. Through the tinted back windows they could see all the way through the front of it. "Looks empty," Sean said and opened his door slowly. He gripped his Ruger .40 in his right hand just to be safe.

Suddenly, they heard a loud thud and instinctively both of them dropped to the high grass.

"What was that?" Sean whispered loudly.

She shrugged. "I have no idea. It came from the back of the truck."

Sean started to get up off the ground when the thud sounded again. It was definitely coming from the back of the SUV. This time, he stayed crouching low and made his way over to the rear door of the truck. The thud resounded again. Someone was in the back of the truck. Wyatt stepped back and around to the side of the vehicle, making sure to check up ahead in the trees of the forest to make sure it wasn't some kind of ambush. He pointed his gun around to different positions for a moment. Satisfied they weren't being watched, he risked a quick glanced into one of the back windows of the truck. Inside, he saw Will tied up and about to try to kick the rear window out. Sean tapped casually on the glass with the tip of his gun. Will heard the tapping and looked up to see Sean standing outside the truck. "It's Will," Sean said to Adriana as he quickly stepped back around to the rear of the truck and tried to open the back.

"It's locked," Will informed him from inside the vehicle.

A quick pull on the latch confirmed what he said. "Maybe Mauricio has a key to each vehicle on the key ring," Sean said as he fished out a set of keys from his pocket. He pressed one of the buttons; the lights flicked accompanied by a sound of the doors unlocking.

Adriana pulled a small knife out of a cargo pocket and made quick work of the ropes around Will's feet and hands.

Sean handed him a gun. "Glad you're okay," he said.

"Thanks," Will replied and took the proffered weapon.

"Where's Tommy?" Sean asked. "What happened to you guys?"

"We have a new player to deal with."

The sound of the rushing river was all Tommy could hear, the noises of the forest had faded away to millions of gallons of moving water. Ahead of them, the trees opened into the shore of the Rio Zamora. The river was smaller than Schultz had expected but was still of considerable size. Off to the right, about a hundred yards away, it dropped over a waterfall. The mist of the churning water plumed up into the air a good sixty to eighty feet above the drop point.

Hunter tipped his head towards the falls in a motion to head that way. Tommy reluctantly obeyed and started trudging along the water's edge. They only walked a few minutes before the bank of the river came to a sudden halt, falling away about fifty feet to the bottom.

Tommy noticed that leading down to the bottom of the precipice was an old path of stone stairs winding its way along the rock face of the cliff. It was wet from the constant barrage of mist and would no doubt be slippery. Still, it appeared to be their only way down. "We'll have to go down that old path there," Tommy yelled above the crashing of the waterfall. Hunter nodded and motioned with his gun. As they proceeded to wind their way down the ancient staircase, Tommy could see on the other side of the gorge was another waterfall, where two rivers poured into one.

Will had explained how he and Tommy had stepped right into the stranger's trap.

Sean was relieved to hear that Tommy was still alive, but he knew there wasn't much time.

"Do you have any idea who this guy is?" Sean asked as they marched along the jungle path.

Will shook his head as he ducked under a low hanging branch. "No. I didn't recognize him." He decided the most prudent course was to lie about knowing who Hunter Carlson was. Keeping up the illusion that he was just a cop was still necessary, right up until the point he executed everyone. Will figured the less they knew that he knew, the better.

Inside, though, Will was furious.. In his mind, the battle already raged. He hoped he got another chance to meet Carlson.

Sean interrupted his thoughts. "We'll just have to assume he's another hired gun with Golden Dawn. If you get a chance, take him out."

Adriana raised an eyebrow at the comment. She realized the sound of rushing water was starting to overwhelm the calm of the forest. "The river is just up ahead," She announced and looked back at the others. "Sounds like the waterfall isn't far from here."

Angela's convoy stopped behind the two parked SUVs at the edge of the forest. She exited her own truck and held her gun casually at her side, brazenly walking up to the first vehicle and then the other. Her team watched for a moment and then followed, satisfied that the coast was clear. She knelt down on one knee and inspected the dirt near one of the wheels. "They went into the woods," she stated. Her head turned as she gazed into the forest. "Probably down that little path there." She stood up and flicked her head sideways. "Let's move."

Angela's middle-aged driver stood next to her. He was an imposing figure with broad shoulders and a strong chest. Perhaps she would have some fun with him once they'd retrieved the next clue. "Who is in the other truck?" he interrupted her train of carnal thoughts. "There was just one earlier."

"I'm not sure," she said. "Looks like the other truck from last night. If so, that means there are more than just two of them. We still have numbers on our side. Just stay alert." The team locked and loaded their weapons and started to head down the trail.

Tommy stopped at the bottom of the path and looked up at the waterfall. At the base of the falls, a narrow path ran along the face of the rock. It appeared to lead behind the mist and falling water. Carlson noticed it too and motioned with his gun towards the ledge. Tommy obeyed and stepped up onto the rock.

Tommy had to concentrate hard and pressed his back against the wall of rock just to keep his balance. The little ledge was probably less than a foot wide and even though the drop to the pool below was only about ten feet or so, the rocks beneath were fully capable of breaking bones or fracturing a skull.

Both men inched their way along, shuffling carefully until they were underneath an overhang of the waterfall. It was wet and slippery from the constant lathering of the billowing mist. Once behind the curtain of the falls, the ledge opened up as the rock face receded into the earth. The path widened to where they could walk normally across it for a short distance until it came to a dead end with a flat wall. They were standing on a large, circular piece of earth that jutted out from the stone. Tommy stared into a door-sized opening in the wall. It must have been a cave but it looked manmade. The precision of the angles and edges was nearly perfect. Above the top edge of the doorway, a strange symbol had been engraved into the stone. It was almost identical to the image he'd seen on the stone they discovered in Georgia: a spider.

Chapter 63
Ecuador

"You recognize that symbol?" Carlson asked as he stared up at the engraving.

Tommy nodded. "Yeah. I've seen it once before."

"So this is the right place?"

"Seems to be."

"Then get moving," Carlson poked him in the back with the tip of his gun, prodding him to move forward. He handed Schultz a small flashlight as the two men moved into the darkness of the cave. Apparently, he'd grabbed a few out of the truck before they left.

They had entered a small, circular room with three new, stone doorways. Each one had a different symbol over it, etched into the rock. The smooth walls were completely barren except for what was above the doors. Beyond the thresholds of each doorway, the interior was completely pitch black.

"Which one do we take?" Hunter asked, confused.

Tommy didn't answer. Instead, he stepped closer to the door on the left, above it was a symbol that looked like a circle with a line through it.

"What is that?" Carlson pressed. "What does it mean?"

"It looks like Theta," he answered. "The Greek symbol for death."

"Death?" Carlson wondered as he stared at the symbol. "So I guess not that way then, huh?"

For the first time since his capture, Tommy noticed a bit of uncertainty in the man who had taken him

captive. He'd been stoic up until that point. It was
something Schultz had seen before. In awe of the
ancient and mysterious, men's minds filled themselves
with wild evils that lurked in the dark.

"No," Tommy answered flatly. "We won't want to go
that way." Then, he stepped to the center door and
examined the symbol above it. It had a circle with a
diamond in the lower part. Beneath the diamond was a
small cross. To the left and right of the circle were four
lines that looked like legs with claws at each end.

"What's that one?" Carlson asked impatiently.

"It's Egyptian. It's called Aten."

"What does it mean?"

Tommy sighed, "It can have two meanings." He
pointed to the circle. "The disk represents the sun,
giver of life," he pointed at the cross-like object. "This
is an ankh, the symbol of life. The eight legs originally
represented a time frame. There were four years of
famine and four years of plenty. The symbol was
basically brought about by a Pharaoh named,
Akhenaten. He changed the theology of the country
and brought them under this banner of one, all
powerful god."

"I don't need a history lesson. Do we go this way or
not?" Hunter was becoming anxious.

"I don't know," Tommy said. "The symbol also
represents the bringer of death. So it could be meant
as a warning." He stepped quickly over to the last door
and scanned the image above. It was a side view of an
oddly shaped head with an elongated mouth and large
eye. Next to it was a disk that had two curved lines

within it, forming a kind of broken "s." Above both symbols was something that looked like a snake. "This one is also confusing," Tommy started before Hunter could annoy him further. "The head is an ancient symbol of death in Aztec legends. The disk, however, is the symbol of life." He stopped for a moment and considered the image. "The serpent was one of their gods. But I don't think that's what it is here."

"What do you mean?" Carlson looked around, nervously. "I say we take the door in the middle."

Tommy shook his head. "No, I don't think so. You see, this is a cross referenced set of symbols here. This one isn't the snake from Aztec lore. This one is different. I think it's referring to something else."

"Like what?"

"It's referring to a choice that was given and a choice that had to be made: life or death. The serpent represented the choice."

Tommy stared thoughtfully at the symbol above the third door. It had to be the right one. The story was starting to make sense. He remembered the first chamber of gold they found in the United States and the clues that led to it. They all came together under several different ancient cultures. He began to think about the cultures that were missing: Asian, Nordic, European. *Why hadn't there been anything from those places mingled in?* Everything seemed to center around places that were predominant in the Bible.

As a child, Tommy had studied the Bible, as he did many other ancient scriptures, to learn about different beliefs and chronologies of old. But he'd not taken them to be entirely literal. His parents were not deeply religious. So he had not become entrenched into any religion.

As he stood before the darkened doorway, he began to make a connection. The Biblical references in Georgia and Tennessee, the clues left behind by Padre Crespi, and all of the symbols they'd seen so far were all places that were part of the ancient Biblical landscape. He wondered why. He felt the barrel of the gun pressing into the middle of his back again, cutting off his train of thought.

"Is this the door or not?"

The stranger was starting to get on his nerves but as long as he had the gun Tommy had to play ball. "I think so," he answered, somewhat certain.

"Fine. You go first," Carlson ordered.

Schultz did as he was told and started into the door. As he did, his foot tripped and he fell forward onto the stone floor.

Carlson stepped back, cautiously watching his prisoner's sudden, random fall.

"Sorry," Tommy said as he pushed himself back up off the ground. "I can be a little clumsy sometimes."

"Just keep moving," Hunter said, looking around, paranoid.

Tommy hoped he'd chosen correctly. One way or the other, they'd find out soon enough.

Adriana noticed the pathway leading down to the base of the waterfall and stepped onto the old, stone staircase casually. "Looks like this takes us down to the bottom."

The three moved as fast as they could, carefully navigating the slippery stone steps down to the base of the waterfall.

Sean's eyes fell upon the wall near the waterfalls. He noticed a small ledge leading around the rock face and behind the deluge. "There," he said as he pointed. "They must have gone that way." Sean stepped quickly up onto the narrow edge, careful not to slip, and started shuffling to the left towards the falling water. The others followed and copied his movement.

It was tricky going for Sean since he wore a small backpack. He wanted to press further into the rock to keep his balance but doing so was impossible. Finally, as he reached a point behind the waterfall, the path began to open up into a sort of platform. He turned and faced the rock wall and a dark door that had been carved into it. The others arrived at the same spot a few moments later and followed his gaze at the emblem above the entrance.

"You have seen this symbol before?" she asked Wyatt.

He nodded. "It was on the stone we found in Georgia. I guess that means we're in the right place." Without warning, he started moving toward the entrance.

"You sure about this?" Will asked, halting him in his tracks momentarily.

Sean tossed him a small flashlight and switched on his own. Wyatt turned and faced him. "No. But Tommy's in there. So that's where I'm going."

Angela's team had arrived at the river but saw no sign of the group they were following. After searching the riverbank they found several different footprints leading to a ledge near a waterfall. Further inspection led them to a stone stepping path that worked its way down to the bottom where the falls poured into a foamy pool. There was still no sign of their targets so they had proceeded down the only way that made sense. One of her men had nearly fallen over the precipice but had been saved by the team leader who had grabbed his shoulder just before he had completely lost his balance. Once they had reached the bottom, the trail went cold. On the rocks there were no footprints to track.

She ordered a few of the men to go over to the riverbank to see if they had left the rocky area and continued on downstream, but there was no sign of any movement beyond the point where they were standing.

The team leader walked over to the rock face and noticed the stone ledge. "They could have gone this way," he stated.

Weaver had been looking downriver when he spoke. She walked over to the spot and ran her hand along the narrow pathway.

"Careful not to fall into the water," he said to her as she climbed up onto the ledge. "That water looks harmless enough but there could be an undertow." His words carried and ominous tone.

Fortunately, she was thin and well balanced. She leaned back easily against the rock and started moving towards the falling water.

Sean stared at the three doorways, each with an odd symbol above it. Which one should we take," Sean asked.

Adriana was lost too. "I know a lot about these things but I'm not sure." She pointed at the Greek symbol of Theta. "I know we don't want to go that way."

"Why not?" Will questioned as he stepped over and dared to look closer into the portal.

"Because that is the Greek symbol for death."

He nodded his understanding and slinked away from the doorway.

"The other two are confusing, though," Sean added.

She agreed. "Yes, they both have conflicting messages."

Will looked confused. "What do you mean, conflicting?"

Sean pointed at the Egyptian symbols over the middle door. "This symbol was used mostly during the reign of a Pharaoh named, Akhenaten. He replaced some of the other religious symbols with this one. It represents the sun god, the giver of life."

Adriana continued his thought. "But the king introduced the idea that there was only one great god.

So the deity this symbol represents can also be the bringer of death."

"And that one?" Will asked, pointing to the door on the far right.

"It's a similar issue," Adriana answered. The two Aztec symbols on the bottom represent life and death. The snake, though, seems oddly out of place. It could mean that particular deity held sway over life and death as well, but, typically, that was not the case with the serpent god."

"So, how do we know which way to go?"

Neither answered. They turned back to the symbols and stared at them. Their expressions were of deep concentration, as if they could somehow will the answer out of the ancient rock.

Will stepped back over to the main entrance and peeked around the corner. He saw Weaver heading towards the cave entrance on the narrow ledge, followed by several agents. He looked back into the room and saw the two flashlights pointing back and forth at the symbols. Satisfied the other two were busy, he waved his hand at Angela, trying to get her attention.

Angela saw Will peeking out from a corner about forty feet away. It looked like he was attempting to communicate. His hand signaled her to stop moving. She'd been playing second fiddle long enough to Will Hastings. He had always been The Prophet's little pet. There was no way he was going to get the glory for this.

She pulled her left hand off the rock face and waved back at him, then with her right hand quickly raised her gun and squeezed off three shots.

Will had seen Angela going for her gun. Fortunately, he had only slightly revealed himself from the cover of the cave entrance. He ducked back as she fired her weapon, sending rounds pinging off the stone near where he was looking out. He didn't understand why she was shooting at him? She and James were supposed to be working with him. He risked sticking his own weapon around the corner. More shots resumed from her position, keeping him pinned down.

Suddenly, more bursts ensued from other positions. Her team had opened fire. Bullets sent sparks and stone fragments flying around him. And there was no way for him to fire back. Resigned, he hurried back inside the room.

Will looked grave. "We have company. Probably ten agents or so. We need to go now."

Adriana and Sean looked at each other. They were both standing in front of the middle doorway.

"We think it might be this one," Adriana said.

Will moved across the room but suddenly stumbled and fell to the floor in front of the door on the right. A few feet away from his hand was something shiny. He turned the beam of his flashlight on the object and realized what it was. "I think you might be going the wrong way," he said as he lifted up a shiny quarter.

Sean stepped over to see what he was holding. "Tommy must have dropped it for us so we would know which way to go," Sean said as he took the coin from Will.

"Looks like we're going through door number three," Will raised an eyebrow.

The others silently agreed and followed him into the passage. Sean stopped at the threshold and thought for a moment. Then he took the quarter and flipped it over to the far left doorway.

Chapter 64
Ecuador

Angela Weaver stood with her back to the wall, next to the entrance of the cave. The last man on her team was about to reach the flat area near the entrance when an insect flew near his face. He swatted at the bug with one hand causing him to lose his footing on the wet ledge. His feet slipped out from under him and he fell into the churning water below. Only a short scream could be let out since the drop was only twelve or so feet. Weaver and her team stared through the spray into the foaming pool. The unfortunate agent never resurfaced.

She noticed the men had gathered around her and were waiting to see what she would do. "We keep moving," she said, coldly. The others nodded. She clipped a small light to the bottom of her gun barrel and switched it on then spun around and led the way into the cave, shining her light around on the smooth rock walls as she moved ahead.

The cave was actually a passageway, carved out of the rock underneath the river. It was no natural occurrence by any stretch of the imagination. Human hands had created it a very long time ago. The corridor ran straight back for about thirty feet or so before opening up into a fairly large room with three doors that proceeded further underground.

Angela stepped over to the door on the right and examined the symbol at the top. Then, quickly, she did the same with the other two. She turned to her team leader. "This must be a test of some kind. Which way do you think they went?"

He moved to the door on the right and examined the floor and hard edges to the doorway. Then he repeated the process with the middle door and then the one on the left. He reached down and picked something up off the floor near the last door with a Greek symbol over it. "A quarter," he said. "Looks like they went this way," he stood up and tossed the coin over to her.

Weaver wasn't convinced but it was their only lead. She couldn't interpret the meanings of the symbols so she had to take the chance. However, she could minimize her personal risk.

"You two," she pointed at two of her remaining six men. "Lead the way."

The two mercenaries looked at each other skeptically but obeyed. They'd already seen what she was capable of in the church. Slowly, they stepped across the threshold of the doorway and into the passage. Angela and the others followed closely behind. The air in the corridor was cold, noticeably more so than the room they'd just left. A draft brushed passed their faces as they continued to move along. Just like the room before, the walls were smoothly carved from the rock beneath the river. There were no signs or pictures, only perfectly smooth stone walls and floors. The two men in the lead came to a point where the direction of the passageway came to a halt and made a sharp right. Cautiously, they leaned around the corner and shone their beams into the empty, stone hall. Simultaneously, they moved ahead around the corner, one on each side of the path. Suddenly, the floor shifted and tilted down where they stood. They lost their balance as the contraption lowered like an ancient teeter-totter. Both men yelled for a moment before dropping out of sight.

Angela and the team leader had jumped back at the sight but they moved forward again and risked a look down into the space where the men had fallen. On their side, the floor had raised and they could see down into a chamber. Their flashlights revealed a pit of what looked like hundreds of stone spikes protruding up from the floor. A few skeletons with very old looking armor were scattered among the stone spears. Like the decayed bodies of the skeletons, the two men who fell had been impaled.

One of them was already dead, a particularly large spike jutting through his chest in a bloody, mangled mess. His eyes stared up to the ceiling, lifeless. The other man was writhing in agony, a stone barb piercing through his abdomen and right leg. "Help...me," he managed to gasp.

"Leave him," Angela ordered. "We go back and take a different passage."

The man below reached up his right hand, begging for help when a deep rumble resonated through the cave. The floor began lowering back down again and the dying mercenary disappeared in the darkness below.

"Turn around," She ordered. "Let's move."

Tommy was amazed at how deep the passage went into the earth. It seemed like they'd been walking for thirty minutes. Maybe it had only been ten, but, either way, the task of carving out that much stone seemed an incredible one. Finally, he could see an opening up ahead. "Looks like something at the end of this corridor," he said to Carlson.

A few moments later the hallway opened up into an enormous room. The ceilings rose like the inside of a pyramid, coming to one point in the top where a small hole appeared to be bored into the stone. The smooth walls were about eight feet high, meeting the ceiling and amplifying the effect of the sloping angles. On the opposing three walls were three symbols, a leaf carved into the middle of each.

Tommy recognized them immediately. In the center of the room, a cube shaped pedestal rose up from the ground about four feet. The scene reminded him of the chamber he'd found in Georgia. With that one, they'd needed to place the stone on the little altar to gain access to the golden room. This pedestal, however, was different. Engraved on the side of it was a picture of a tree whose branches wrapped around, spiraling upward until they reached the top. On the surface were three imprints of leaves matching the ones on the walls. Within each imprint were dozens of little stone pegs.

"What is this?" Carlson asked as he whirled around in confusion. "Where is all the gold?"

"You know," Tommy answered in a snobby tone, "that is exactly what the last guy wondered when I found one of these things."

Carlson's anger spiked; he smacked Tommy across the face with the back of his hand.

Tommy fell backwards a few steps but stood tall once he regained his balance. "Yeah, about that. We probably need the three golden leaves to get into the real chamber," he said defiantly.

"What are you talking about," Hunter raised his gun and pointed it at Tommy's face. "What golden leaves?"

"You mean these," a new voice came from behind Carlson in the direction of the doorway.

Carlson turned around to see Wyatt open his backpack and reveal a shimmering, yellow object; he also noticed that Will and Adriana had guns trained on him.

Hunter cursed himself. Had he kept his gun on Tommy, he could have at least retained his hostage. Now he was in a tight spot. However, he still had the weapon aimed in Adriana's direction.

"Drop those guns or I kill her right now," Carlson made sure his barrel was pointing straight at her heart.

Tommy started to move towards him from behind, but Hunter saw the movement and halted him. "You move another inch and she dies! Understood?"

Schultz froze in his steps.

"Squeeze that trigger and you die next," Sean said in a steel voice.

Chapter 65
Southeastern Ecuador

Angela stood between the two remaining doorways, trying to decide what to do. Telling any other men on her team to lead the way down a dark passage would be futile after seeing what happened to the last two. She would have to take a risk.

"You two," she pointed at a red-haired man with a matching beard who was standing next to another mercenary with a shaved head and a goatee. "Take the middle passage. We'll go down the right. If you get into trouble, radio for help. And if you find anything, let me know."

They knew she had no intention of helping them, as just evidenced with the men who she'd left to die but by offering to take the same chance they were taking, their minds seemed to be a little more at ease. They nodded, full of new courage and watched as she led the way into the far right corridor. The team leader and another, younger mercenary followed her in. Convinced they had as good a chance to survive as the others, they moved ahead and disappeared into the center portal.

Angela moved carefully along the passage, staying close to the wall. Her light shone into the long hallway ahead. It seemed so far, she couldn't see the end of it. Suddenly, she heard two screams in her radio. They'd only been in the tunnel a minute.

Quickly, she and the other two rushed back to the room they'd just left. Both of the men she'd sent into the middle passage were laying on the floor. Their bodies had multiple puncture wounds throughout the torso and limbs. The red head had received one through the left eye. A pool of blood surrounded the bodies and was draining towards the main entrance to the room, slowly.

She'd been lucky. Whatever it was that killed them hit them with enough force to knock them out of the tunnel. "They're gone," she said two the last two as she pointed to the third doorway. "This must be the way."

Hunter Carlson considered the situation for a moment. There was no way he could take them all out. His only hope was to negotiate. He'd done his research on Schultz and Wyatt, though he had no idea who the others were. "The people I work for only want gold," he said after deliberating. "While you, Mr. Wyatt and your friend over here care more about the historical side of things. You want to make sure antiquities are preserved. The money is of no consequence, right?"

"What are you getting at?" Tommy asked from behind.

Carlson's gun moved a little to the right as he moved his head slightly at the question. That was all Will needed. His weapon fired, sending a painful echo around the room. The bullet was true though, and found its mark squarely on the gunman's wrist. The impact of the round caused Carlson to instantly drop his weapon to the floor, grasping his arm with the other hand.

Tommy grabbed the gun and held it at his side. Hunter's face contorted in mixture anger and agony.

"You ok?" Sean asked her. She nodded.

"Glad you could catch up," Tommy said, calming down a tense moment. He smiled at his friend.

Sean grinned, "Next time, make sure you check who's driving before you hop in a car."

Angela and the remaining two men on her team heard the gun shot echo through the passageway. They froze in place, wondering if the shot was directed at them. There was no bullet ricochet. Still, the sound meant that they weren't far away. "Keep your lights low on the ground in front of us," she ordered. "We don't want to announce our arrival."

Tommy smiled. "Glad you brought those," he said pointing at the backpack containing the golden leaves. "It looks like they go on that pedestal over there." He walked over and knelt down on the hard stone. Carefully, he lifted the frail looking objects out of Sean's backpack and admired them for a moment; the intricate craftsmanship was stunning. "There must be a counter balance system here like the one we found in Georgia."

"Not more ancient elevators, I hope," Sean joked.

"Only one way to find out." Tommy stood up and walked over to the stone altar. He gently laid the first leaf into place where it matched the design.

Will paid no attention. He just kept staring at Carlson with his gun pointed at the man's head. Carlson was returning the gaze but wasn't sure what was going through Will's mind. He clutched his bloody wrist with the other hand but gave no indication of pain. The gears of Will's mind were turning. He needed to find out who Carlson worked for. Then he would kill him.

Tommy had already laid the second leaf into place and was now setting the third one down. He cautiously let the object settle into its seat. A clicking sound came from within the pedestal and the center wall. It was then joined by a deep rumble that shook the entire room. Suddenly, the center wall then began to move, revealing a seam along the top and sides. A huge doorway was opening from the middle of the wall.

"A hidden door," Adriana marveled at the sight.

The enormous piece of stone continued downward, shaking ancient dust from its surface as it moved. Sean and Tommy pointed their flashlights through the opening as it continued to widen. Through the darkness, they could see the reflection of their beams on the other side.

Adriana stepped next to Sean. She could see a glimmer of something metallic just through the short passage between the rooms.

"You all go on ahead," Will said loudly. "I'll stay here with this piece of crap."

The others nodded and stepped slowly into the tunnel as the large door finished its descent with a loud thud. Sean reached into his pack and pulled out a handful a large, white glow sticks. He bent one until the bright light illuminated and he dropped it on the floor. The stick cast an eerie white light on the walls and ceilings of the stone. Then he took a few more, activated them and tossed them ahead into the next room. As the sticks began to glow, their eyes were filled with an unbelievable site. Statues, gold panels, scrolls, medallions, plates, ancient armor were all placed neatly around the room.

Sean glanced at Tommy. His friend's face beamed with excitement. Before he could say anything, Schultz was on the other side of the chamber looking at a stone placard with a Babylonian engraving on it. Then he moved quickly to another piece, a thin golden scroll with ancient Hebrew imprinted on it. He traced his fingers along the writing for a few seconds before going to the next object.

The room was gigantic, running around seventy feet long and probably just as wide. Each wall was decorated with precious objects from an ancient civilization. In the center of the room, a triangular stone pedestal sat alone. Sean walked over to it and noted the designs that covered the sides of it. On each side was a pyramid of varying sizes, shapes that were eerily familiar. At the top of the pedestal, a small, round stone sat silently. It was the third stone.

Adriana could not help but admire the work that represented so many ancient cultures. She wondered, "Why are all of these things here? They're from civilizations on the other side of the world." Something in her voice told Sean she had already come up with the answer.

"We've been trying to figure that out," Tommy answered.

"Think about it," she continued. "These relics represent nearly every major society from antiquity. There are even some here that the history books never mention. How did they get here?"

"There are theories that maybe there was an ancient trade route that people from the old world took long before Columbus came to the new world," Tommy responded as he kept examining the cache.

"Perhaps," she said. "But what if it was something else?"

Tommy stopped where he was and looked over at her. Sean did the same. "What are you getting at?"

"I have been investigating the lost chambers for some time now. When you two found the first one in Georgia, I knew that there were many symbols and signs pointing to ancient civilizations. But most of what you found was just words and gold. "Now that I see these relics with my own eyes. I am convinced of the truth."

"What truth?" Sean asked, suspiciously.

"The people who brought these things here were not traders. They left their home out of necessity. And they brought as much as they could from their history to preserve it." She looked at them both before continuing. "A collection like this could only have come from one place. The Library of Alexandria."

Will watched the others out of the corner of his eye. When he thought they were too far away to hear him he sneered at Carlson.

"Now here is what's going to happen. You're going to tell me who you work for; then I'll make sure that you die quickly."

Carlson's eyes flashed in surprise. "What are you talking about?"

Will held the gun lower, pointing it at the man's right knee. "Have you ever been shot in the knee, Hunter?"

"How do you know my name?" he asked, ignoring the question.

"Because I'm better at my job than you."

"Who are you?"

"Just answer the question, Hunter. Who do you work for?"

Realization came across Carlson's face. He let a smile creep to the side of his mouth. "Oh, I see. You're the one working for The Prophet, aren't you? I've heard about you but they work very hard to keep your identity a secret, don't they?"

Will raised the weapon back up to the man's chest. "You'd better start giving me names now or so help me..."

"You'll what?" Hunter interrupted. "You'll shoot me? They won't let you." He waved his hand towards the passageway.

"Maybe I'll kill them, too. You don't know my orders."

The last statement struck home with Carlson. He didn't know what this man was supposed to do. He'd heard about him and knew that The Prophet had sent his best to oversee the operation. But that was all the information he'd obtained.

"I can make it hurt real bad, Hunter. Or it can be over quickly. Either way, you aren't walking out of here."

The man looked into the other room at the other three who were examining the now illuminated room. "Ok," he said finally. "Let's just say that you're not the only one working for The Order." He raised an eyebrow as he spoke.

Will looked confused for a second. "I already know about the other team. They're right behind us. They are supposed to be working with me."

"I'm not talking about them. And they work for The Prophet, too. I work for the others."

Then the realization hit Will. Carlson was working for other members of the council. He'd met some of them once, primarily the two men directly beneath The Prophet. The impression he had received was of two men who could not be trusted. "Mornay and Carroll," he said quietly, more as a statement than a question.

"You should know that I'm not the only one working for...."

A gun fired from near the long passageway. The look on Will's face turned to a grimace and he dropped to his knees. A hole in the center of his small backpack smoked from the bullet's entry. Will fell to his knees and Angela Weaver came into view behind him. A thin trail of smoke drifted up from the barrel of her weapon.

"Boy am I glad to see you," Carlson said as he stood and started to move towards Angela and her men. She fired two shots into his chest, interrupting his statement and him reeling backwards. Shock washed over his face. Two red carnations started spreading from black holes on his gray t-shirt. The look in Carlson's eyes begged to know why. "We are on the same team," he stammered, trying to stay standing.

She lowered her weapon to her side as she spoke to him in a harsh tone. "A secret you obviously could not keep."

He fell down to his knees and over on his side.

The first gunshot had startled Sean and the others. They looked through the portal in horror as Will collapsed to the floor, shot in the back. Then the shooter executed the man that had taken Tommy, firing two rounds into his chest. It looked like she was saying something to him, but they were too far away to hear.

Adriana and Tommy looked at Wyatt. Sean's old reflexes kicked in. "Find cover," he ordered.

As soon as the words left his mouth, the woman with the gun and her two men turned and started firing in their direction. Adriana deftly dove out of range and behind the wall next to the door. Tommy was somewhat less elegant as he dove, looking more like an out-of-shape baseball player diving into second base. Sean moved to the edge of the door opposite of Adriana and held his gun up at the ready.

Angela and her two men unleashed a torrent of rounds at the little group in the next room. Bullet casings dropped to the stone floor around their feet with a clinking sound. Their targets all moved to the side of the door and out of range. She and her two men did the same on their end and simultaneously reloaded a fresh magazine of rounds. They each had several to spare, a luxury she doubted her targets could afford.

Angela poked her head around the corner and saw the silhouette of a gun near the left corner. She lowered her weapon and squeezed of two shots. The bullets sparked off of the edge of the hallway, just missing.

Sean pulled his hand back just in time before two rounds ricocheted off the wall near his head. He looked quickly over at the others who'd taken up a position opposite of him, staying close to the wall.

"How many," Adriana whispered just loud enough for him to hear.

"Three or four, I think," he answered.

Another three shots popped from the end of the passage and panged off the corner next to Adriana, causing her and Tommy to both take another step back.

Then, the woman's voice came from the other end of the corridor. "You might as well surrender and come out now, Mr. Wyatt. There's no other way out of this place."

"I don't know," Sean yelled back down the tunnel. "I think we might stick it out here for a while until you all get sleepy."

Tommy smiled at the humor. Even in extremely tense situations, Sean was still a wise guy.

"I assure you that will not happen," the voice returned. "You are outnumbered and outgunned. The only way out of this cave is back the way you came."

Tommy's face lit up. "Sean," he gasped across the opening. "That's it. Another way out."

Sean looked confused. "What are you talking about?"

"The stone," he pointed at the triangular pedestal. "They must have built in a backdoor to get out of this place. The stone might be our ticket out of here. Remember how the one in Georgia worked?"

Sean recalled the scenario.

"It's worth a shot. I'll cover you."

Will's back stung. He'd been shot before but this felt different. Something in his backpack must have stopped the bullet. As soon as the shot had been fired he knew what had happened. He fell over knowing his only way to get out would be to feign death. Fortunately, Weaver hadn't finished the job with a headshot. Apparently, she felt the need to execute Carlson immediately and her attention had shifted.

He wondered what had Carlson meant when he said he wasn't the only one working for the adepts? At the moment, Will didn't have time to think about such things. He just had to get out of there and live to fight another day. One of the mercenaries had taken his gun leaving him unarmed. Their attention, though, was on the people in the other room. He pulled himself over to the base of the pedestal that held the golden leaves, moving slowly so as not to draw attention. The stone altar had given him an idea. One he could only hope would work. Peeking around the corner of the stone object, he saw Sean suddenly emerge at the end of the hall and start firing his gun. Will ducked down as bullets smacked around on the stone, bouncing dangerously close to where he was crouched. He thought that he'd seen Tommy running behind Sean but couldn't be sure. As soon as the barrage ceased, Weaver and her men started returning fire, adding to the acrid smoke that was already filling the room. That was his moment.

Will reached up and grabbed the leaf on the right of the pedestal and lifted it off. The familiar clicking started again and immediately, he jumped up and darted into the cave entrance just before a giant stone began to lower over the opening.

Angela stopped firing her weapon and turned to see what was happening. The entrance to the chamber was closing from above while a huge piece of stone was rising up to the ceiling right next to their position, effectively closing off the passageway into where Wyatt was holed up. She wasn't sure what to do. The doorway they'd come through before closed quickly. Both passageways would be sealed off in moments. She looked at both of the men wondering what to do. The younger man started to climb over the rising wall but was greeted by a volley of shots from the other end of the hall, one of which struck him in the shoulder and sent him reeling back to cover. Blood trickled down his arm onto the floor as the moving wall reached its destination with a loud thud. They were trapped like rats in a box.

Then another rumble began overhead. "Another way out?" the middle-aged man wondered out loud. A trickle of water began to flow from the hole in the center of the ceiling. The three looked up in horror. That's when they heard a sound the chilled them all to the core. The sound of rushing water.

Sean wasn't sure but as he laid down cover fire for Tommy, he thought he saw Will pulling himself over to the pedestal in the other room. It was so dark he couldn't tell. He'd emptied his clip and ducked back behind the wall just as the three villains started returning fire. Through the haze of powder smoke, he could see that Tommy had reached the triangle pedestal and was tucked behind it as a hail of metal rounds blanketed the room. Then suddenly, their enemies had stopped firing and the room was filled with the sound of a deep grinding. Some of the metal objects on the floor were rattling as the earth shook beneath them. A golden statue with a doglike head fell over on its face, clanking loudly on the hard floor.

Adriana yelled over the sound. "What's happening?"

Sean risked a look around the corner. The wall where they'd entered was rising. One of the men appeared at the top, trying to climb over. Wyatt fired off a few rounds and sent the man scurrying back to the other side. "The door's closing!" he yelled. "They must have taken off one of the leaves!"

Nearly as quickly as it had begun, the rumbling came to a halt and the room became deathly quiet. "So we're trapped?"

"Maybe not," Tommy answered and stood up from his hiding place. He fingered the stone on the altar for a moment, unsure of what was going to happen. His eyes scanned the room of ancient relics, thinking he'd come so far to only behold them for a few brief minutes. Then he picked up the small disc. Where it had rested, four small pegs of stone were revealed. From deep within the pedestal came four loud clicks. Sean and Adriana looked at Tommy, wondering what was going to happen. Suddenly, the floor opened up underneath Schultz's feet and he disappeared from view.

Sean and Adriana ran over to the hole that surrounded the pedestal on all three sides. The floor panels had dropped away like a trap door, revealing an underground duct underneath with water rushing through it. There was no sign of Tommy.

"The water must have carried him that way," Sean said.

"You think that's our way out?"

Sean shrugged. "Looks like it's the only way."

"What about the treasure? Father Crespi's collection?" She looked around at all the ancient artifacts and precious relics.

Sean looked at her with a grin. "Sometimes you gotta leave the treasure behind," he said without resignation. "Maybe this is where it belongs." He took her hand and looked down at the gushing water. She nodded and the two of them jumped into the opening.

Angela never panicked. It was one of the reasons she was so good at what she did. But as the water flooded through the opening and gathered around their feet, fear began to creep into her mind. The two men sloshed over to where the original entrance to the room had been. They frantically tried to pull up on the heavy stone but couldn't find a seam to grip. Angela just stood in the middle of the room while they leaned on the wall in an effort to get the thing to budge. The water level continued to rise quickly and was already up to her waist. She waded to the pedestal and lifted a golden leaf off of the top in hopes that would stop the room from flooding. Nothing happened. There was no way out.

The men looked at her for an answer but she had none. She banged on the top of the pedestal with the leaf but again nothing happened. The water had covered it now and was nearly up to her chest. The younger of the two men had a terrified look on his face. He glanced at the older man and then back at Angela. His head shook violently as the water reached their shoulders. Suddenly, his hand emerged from the water with his weapon and he put it to his head. He pulled the trigger sending a splash of crimson into the water. The body went limp and floated face down on the surface while the bullet wound turned the water an eerie reddish color in the pale illumination of their flashlights.

Angela and her team's leader were treading water. As the level rose, they grew closer and closer to the ceiling. They looked at each other but said nothing. They were both killers, murderers. There was no comfort to be had. And none was sought.

Their heads bumped against the angled ceiling as the deluge carried them higher. She tried to keep her mouth near the top where there was still air. She watched out of the corner of her eye as the middle-aged man ceased his struggle and let himself sink into the water. A few moments later his body, too, was floating. His flashlight had sunk to the bottom of the room, illuminating the floor far below. She was angry. She had never failed at anything. And she was furious that someone had gotten the better of her. As the water covered her head her thoughts drifted to the events of the last few days: killing her partner, the shootout at the church, the dry desert air.

She needed air. Angela ceased fighting the reflex urge. She opened her mouth and inhaled.

Chapter 66
Southeaster Ecuador

Sean and Adriana flew through the underground flume. Thousands of years of water flow had smoothed out the stone underneath them so it felt like being in a dark waterslide. The light from their flashlights bounced around on the roof of the tunnel as they tumbled and slid along. After their initial clumsy ride, they both righted themselves and were gliding along in the gushing water. A quick drop sent them airborne momentarily with a sudden thud but the fall had only been a few feet. The tube continued to twist and turn its way through the old rock until finally, they could see a light up ahead.

"Looks like the end of the road," Sean yelled at Adriana who was sliding along behind him. "Brace yourself!"

The light grew brighter and brighter until suddenly, there was nothing beneath them.

Tommy swam hard through the huge pool that had collected at the base of the waterfall. From the looks of it, he'd come out near where they had entered the cave. The chute he'd gone through had dumped him out into an area where the water was surrounded by a half-circle of rocks. As he pulled himself up onto a large rock, he looked back up at the hole that had just spit him out. He hadn't expected the floor to drop out from under him when he lifted the stone medallion off of the pedestal. The sudden fall had jarred him slightly but nothing he couldn't shake off. Then he heard a yell from above just before he saw Sean and Adriana fly out of the chute and into the pool below. Both of them disappeared for a second before re-emerging at the surface, spitting out water.

"Wooo!" Sean gave a yell. "Now that was awesome! Did you see that?"

"I did it," Tommy answered from the stone embankment with a huge smile. "What happened to your fear of heights?"

Sean shrugged and looked back up at the hole in the cave. "It was only twenty feet or so."

Adriana seemed less thrilled about the water sports and swam quickly to the edge then pulled herself onto dry land.

The three of them sat for a moment and stared up at the water that was pouring out of the hole in the side of the rock face. Each one of them contemplated something in silence. After a few minutes of rest, they clumsily made their way over the rocks and across a narrow stone walkway that led back over to the shore. As if on cue, the beating sound of a helicopter could be heard in the distance.

"Mauricio?" Tommy looked hopeful.

"If it isn't then we might be in some trouble," Sean answered.

As the helicopter drew closer they could see through one of the windows that their friend was indeed inside. He waved to them from one of the seats in the rear cabin. A few minutes later, the aircraft had landed in a nearby meadow. Delgado beamed at them as they

413

approached from the river bank. "Tommy! I'm glad you're okay! We were worried sick about you."

Tommy smiled. "I'm fine," he said and held out a small stone disc. On the top of it were three pyramids of varying sizes.

Delgado flipped it over and saw another set of symbols. There was a small figure bowing down to a bird carved into the stone. His eyebrows lowered. "You found the treasure of Carlos Crespi?"

Schultz nodded. "It will be quite a task to get back to it, but I think we have the resources."

"What does it mean?" Delgado asked with intense curiosity. His eyes still stared at the disc.

Sean patted him on the back. "I think it means we're going to Egypt."

Chapter 67
Washington D.C.

Eric Jennings made his way down the opulent hallway of The Fairfax, one of the more prestigious hotels in The District. He'd decided to indulge a little, seeing how he felt like he'd been under considerable stress over the last week. He still hadn't received any news about Starks' death. Perhaps she wasn't going to be missed by anyone after all. It wasn't his concern anymore, though. There had been a slight hesitation when he was considering the booking. The Fairfax was extremely close to Embassy Row, but he figured he didn't really associate with many of the people in that part of town so the likelihood of being noticed would be negligible.

The halls of The Fairfax were decorated elegantly with gold painted molding and classic architecture. It was certainly far nicer than what he was used to getting with one of his women.

He arrived at his room and slid the electronic key into the slot. A moment later the green light beeped and the door unlocked.

When he opened it, he was greeted with an intoxicating scent of a woman's perfume. The room was dark, save for a small lamp that was lit from behind a curtain giving the chamber a soft, eerie illumination.

He removed his trench coat and loosened the tie around his neck then stepped towards the corner of the suite where a bed and sitting area were located.

In the pale light, he could make out the silhouette of a woman sitting in one of the chairs near the window. The outline of her body was lithe and firm. The creamy white skin of her legs was accented by tight, black lingerie. Her breasts were pushed up slightly by a matching black bra. Her face, though, was hidden by a dark shadow that began at the base of her neck. Jennings smiled as he stared at the woman. His old friend had outdone himself again.

"Hello," he said casually. "What's your name?"

"My name doesn't matter," the voice emanated from the shadows.

He shrugged. "I suppose not." He took off his belt and set his gun down on the counter next to the flat screen television. The television was on but the screen was blank. He pointed at it with his thumb. "Anything good on?"

"Actually," she replied in a slow, sexy tone, "there is. Someone has been a very bad boy."

She uncrossed her legs then re-crossed them while she spoke.

"Oh, have I?" He played along. "I guess I'm going to have to be punished."

"Indeed."

"Was that sarcasm in her voice?" he thought to himself. He liked this one. She had a little attitude. Maybe not as young as he would have liked but that could be made up for in other ways. He undid his pants and dropped them to the floor revealing gray, pinstripe boxers. As he was unbuttoning his tie, she lifted a hand with a remote in it and pressed a button.

At first, the vision on the screen was a little dark and blurry but when it came into focus, Jennings' eyes grew wide with realization.

It was surveillance footage of him entering Emily Starks' bedroom the night before. He watched in horror as the man on the screen walked over and fired bullets into the head of the sleeping woman then left quickly. His face was unmistakable in the footage.

He turned his head back to the woman in the corner. "Where did you get this?" he demanded.

Then she leaned forward, revealing her face. It was Emily Starks.

Jennings staggered backwards a few steps, placing his hand on the corner of the wall to regain his balance. He shook his head. "No. That's impossible!"

"What's the matter, Eric? You look like you've seen a ghost." She smiled as she stood up with her hands behind her back. Her long, brown hair dropped teasingly over one shoulder.

"I killed you!" he yelled.

"No." She stopped, keeping her distance from him. "You killed a dummy. I watched from the closet as you snuck into my room and pulled the trigger."

He kept shaking his head. He'd been so certain, so careful.

She continued, "I knew you couldn't be trusted, Eric. So I played it safe. Now, there are twenty agents waiting outside to take you away as soon as we walk out that door."

He stood silent for a moment. All his years of hard work, his pension, retirement, everything passed before his eyes. It was all gone now. The only luxury resort he would see would be Leavenworth, Kansas.

His eyes darted quickly over to the weapon on the counter.

She saw what he was thinking. "Don't do that, Eric. There's no way out of here." Jennings had information she needed. Emily needed him alive. "Who are you working for, Eric?"

His face was full of despair like a child who had been caught breaking a window. He said nothing at first, just staring at her.

"Eric," she urged, "who are you working for? Make it easy on yourself. I need a name."

Jennings's lips quivered. "I worked my way up," he finally said. "I did everything by the book." He laughed at the last sentence. If he was expecting some kind of pity from Starks, he was going to be disappointed. Her face remained stoic, hardened by the fact that he'd tried to kill her in her sleep. "They offered me a way out, promised me more money than I'd see in twenty years working for the government." He paused and looked down as he thought about the money he'd received from Golden Dawn. Then his eyes moved back to her for a second as if considering her words. *Make it easy on yourself,* she'd said. Then he lunged for the gun. Grasping it in his left hand, he was about to raise it when he saw that Emily already had her own weapon trained on him.

"Put the gun down, Eric. It doesn't have to end like this, but if you don't put the weapon down I will shoot you."

Her voice carried more than a threat. It was a fact. Starks may have been a desk worker in the Justice Department, but she hadn't gotten there by being soft. He knew her record, knew how many confirmed kills she'd had in the field. She meant every word.

"Eric. Who is running Golden Dawn, and what are they up to?"

He raised the gun slowly over his head as he turned to face her.

Visions of the beach and luxurious golf courses, women, gourmet food, and a life of luxury entered his mind. He would have none of that now. Then slowly, he began to lower the gun towards the temple of his head, just above the ear.

"Eric. Stop. Don't move, Eric! Don't do it!"

As soon as the barrel was pressed against his skin, he squeezed the trigger.

The loud pop was accompanied by burst of blood that splattered across the bed and wall. Starks turned her head at the sight.

Jennings's eyes stared ahead for a moment, his body wavering. Then he toppled over backwards.

Immediately, the door burst open and special agents wearing bulletproof vests entered the room with guns drawn. When they saw the body on the floor, they lowered their weapons.

Emily just stared down at the corpse for what seemed like an hour before being interrupted by one of the men from her team. "Orders, ma'am?" The young agent had stepped over the body and handed her a robe from the closet. She'd forgotten that she was still basically naked. She snapped out of her daze and returned to being the director she was. "Thank you," she smiled at him briefly. "We will take care of this quietly. The news report will be that we discovered the body. He had financial problems, and they had become too overwhelming for him to bear."

The young agent nodded. His loose, blonde hair shook when he did. "Yes ma'am." He immediately pressed a button on his earpiece and started sending out the orders as he turned and left the room.

Emily tucked the robe around her waist and sat down on the edge of the chair she'd previously occupied. A sickening stench of gun smoke and blood remained in the air.

She'd hoped to take Jennings alive. Now whatever information he had about his employer was gone.

Chapter 68
Southwestern United States

Alexander Lindsey made his way down a darkly lit hallway. Four large bodyguards accompanied him, following close behind. The corridor was lit with old candle sconces made from wrought iron. Unlike most sconces in the present day, the building's purveyors used fresh, real candles every day. Lindsey liked that about the establishment. It gave the place a serene, almost haunted feel.

The building they were visiting was called The Galleon, an elitist club that was named as tribute to the mighty ships of the Spanish Armada. Though its name hinted at an overall Spanish theme, the club actually paid honor to many different types of sailing vessels from years gone by. Near each sconce was an oil panting of a famous ocean going vessel. Some belonged to great captains from history. Others were associated with less reputable seafarers.

The Galleon was an oddity given that it was located in Salt Lake City, nowhere near an ocean. The founder had, no doubt, had a love of the sea and history so when he opened his club for Utah's elite, he combined the two to create a unified theme.

Lindsey had been there a few times for business meetings that would be better left out of the public eye. That was probably the greatest service that the establishment provided.

On the outside, it seemed just like any other private club, a place where businessmen could have a drink or a cigar and unwind after their daily toils. The inside, though, was a facility full of secrets.

Aside from the main lounge, there were ten smaller rooms, each featuring leather couches and chairs, mini-bars, restrooms, fireplaces, and even small tables for eating. It was rumored that hundreds of under-the-table deals had been made in the facility. Even two former presidents were members and had been said to visit the place when meeting with foreign heads of state or with high level business officials. The floor was made from dark, worn oak planks that had been said to come from two old merchant vessels the owner had purchased for scrap. A narrow strip of dark, red carpet ran along the center of the hall between each of the ten rooms.

Lindsey and his escorts arrived at a door marked with the name, *Sir Francis Drake*. He looked left to right at his bodyguards and then pulled the door handle.

As the door eased open, Mornay and Carroll looked over from their seats near the fireplace. Their conversation had come to an abrupt halt.

Alexander eyed both of them suspiciously. "Don't let me interrupt you, gentlemen. It sounded like you were talking about something." His tone was lathered in a condescending tone.

The two men's faces were awash with a combination of guilt and fear. The fire in the hearth crackled dramatically in the silence.

"Alexander," Carroll said with a stutter, "please, come join us." He stood, cautiously. "Would you like a brandy?" he offered, nearly stumbling over the coffee table as he headed towards the bar.

"Sit down, Jonathan." The harsh order startled the already unsettled man, and he felt his way into a seat near where he was standing. Mornay was less eager to acquiesce to the request and stood up defiantly. "You too, Albert," Alexander said with a tone that carried a warning.

The narrow, sharp face of Mornay clenched angrily. "I think I'll stand, Alexander. What are you doing here? It is against club policy to interrupt a room with closed doors."

Lindsey gave a quick nod to his escorts who walked over to where Mornay was standing and forced him to sit down, splashing the whiskey he was holding all over the floor and his pants.

"I said sit down," Lindsey replied coldly. "And the club makes certain allowances for its more generous patrons." He grinned slightly as he made his way across the room to where the two men were seated. The remaining bodyguards closed the door behind him and stood, staring lifelessly towards the fireplace.

Mornay's anger only heightened at the fact that two men pushed him into sitting in the deep leather couch. He hated being treated like a child. "What is this about?" he asked, incredulous.

Carroll tried a different approach. Perhaps thinking that being a little proactive would change the emotions of the room a bit. "How are things progressing with our project?" he asked sheepishly.

Lindsey turned to the fleshy man whose three piece suit protruded awkwardly around his rotund figure. "Ah. Our little project. Yes, Jonathan, it's interesting that you should ask about that. Very interesting indeed."

"What are you talking about?" Mornay interrupted.

"Things are progressing quite well, it seems. In fact, our lead operative has made an extremely valuable discovery."

"Another clue?" Carroll offered in vain hope.

Lindsey snorted. "I guess you could call it that." The old man stepped around the couch and eased into a leather chair facing both men.

"You see, Agent Hastings ran into an interesting situation while in South America." He paused momentarily and let the drama build along with the fear in his subordinates' minds. Neither man dared look at the other, still clinging to hope that their treachery hadn't been discovered. "It seems there was another player involved that I was previously unaware of."

"So," Mornay said defiantly. "Did our operative handle the situation?"

The old man let out a low chuckle and raised a finger towards Mornay. "Which operative are you talking about, Albert?" His tone had become almost playful, dangling his victims over the possibility of escape or doom.

"Hastings. Did he get rid of the problem?"

Even now Mornay was still obstinate. Lindsey knew he would never bow, never be trustworthy. To complete the mission at hand, Lindsey would need men he could depend on, those who would do anything he said without question. The two men before him had not only proven themselves unreliable but had actually gone behind his back and tried to sabotage the mission. Had they succeeded, Lindsey feared everything would have been lost. They would have, no doubt, simply taken the treasure and quit there, happy to fill their coffers with more loot. Men like that only cared about money.

Lindsey's thoughts still lingered on the two betrayers. *Mornay, especially, was infatuated with superficial power. He believed that money could buy power. Money could buy people and votes and material possessions, but a twenty-five-cent bullet could take all of that away in a second. Disease could destroy an entire life's work and cut short everything a person had worked for. An idiot texting on the interstate could swerve over and crash your car along with theirs, killing you without notice. No, money was not power. A greater power existed. And the two morons two whom The Prophet spoke had put the acquisition of that power at great risk. Their greed and foolish ambition could have ruined everything he had worked so diligently to attain.*

"He got rid of that part of the problem, yes." Lindsey looked thoughtful for a moment. Mornay and Carroll gave each other a cautious sideways glance. They may have actually believed they would get away with it.

"Good," Carroll chimed in. "So things will continue to move forward?"

He looked at Carroll then Mornay. "Come, Gentlemen. I have convened a meeting of the Order and need you both to attend. We must leave at once."

The sudden request caught the other two off guard. They both looked at each other with a combined expression of confusion and relief. "Lead the way," Carroll said as he stood simultaneously with Mornay.

"You will ride with these men here," Lindsey said flatly.

"What about our cars?" Mornay protested.

Alexander waved a dismissive hand. "We will take care of them." With that, he led the way back out the door and down the hall, followed closely by the two men. The bodyguards formed around the two as they exited the room.

Carroll looked around nervously. There were no other people in sight. As they rounded the corner towards the lounge, they noticed that it too was completely vacant. He said nothing but became immediately concerned about the odd lack of patronage. That time of day was usually fairly busy for the club. The group made their way out a side door where many of The Galleon's members entered and exited. It was another way the club provided anonymity to its valued clientele.

Darkness had fallen on the city and a cold chill burst through the doorway. Once through the heavy, metal doors the group was greeted by three black, GMC Yukons. The first two vehicles had guard standing next to them. The back passenger doors of the SUVs were open, awaiting their passengers.

As the group neared the parked convoy Lindsey suddenly stopped and turned around, facing his two vice-presidents. He said nothing for a few seconds and the two men stood, wondering what the awkward moment was for. They never saw the guards come up from behind and yank the hoods down over their heads. Each man was grabbed by two guards and their hands were bound quickly behind their backs. Before the unwitting adepts could even force a scream of protest they had been thrown into the backseats of the two vehicles.

Lindsey nodded to the drivers and as soon as a guard had closed the back door the trucks took off and disappeared around the corner at the other end of the alley.

Ten men sat silently in the small auditorium. The room was designed like a half circle, made from mountain stone. Walls were lit with weathered brass candle sconces. Most of the light, however, emanated from an iron chandelier that hung from the domed ceiling. Unlike the candles on the walls, it was powered by electricity. The seating area was much like a surgical observation deck, about seven or eight feet above the sand covered floor below. All of the faces were as blank as the stone that surrounded them.

Their leader, Alexander Lindsey appeared in a doorway on the floor level and walked across the sand to the center of the room. He stood next to something that would seem odd in any facility save for the New

York Stock exchange. A large, bronze bull standing about six feet high and eight feet long was in the middle of the small auditorium. Underneath it, a pit of logs had been built reaching just short of the figure's belly.

Lindsey looked around the room before he spoke. "Today," he began, "we must do something that has not been done in a long time. It has been many decades since one of our own has betrayed us. Yet today I present to you two who have directly opposed our leadership and our mission."

As he finished the sentence, two guards in black hoods brought out the two prisoners.

Their hands and feet had been shackled with chains and their clothes had been stripped down to their underwear. Hoods covered the men's heads, shielding their faces from view but all those in attendance knew who they were. Carroll and Mornay were the two highest ranking officials in the Order right beneath the Imperator himself. As adepts, they were charged with carrying out any directives the leader imposed. What they had done was treason and everyone present knew the consequences. As Imperator, only Lindsey had the power to execute another member of the Order. In a savvy maneuver, he'd actually allowed the subject to be put to a vote to the other members of the council. The evidence had been compelling. The vote had been unanimous.

Both subjects were positioned directly in front of the brass bull and their hoods removed.

Carroll's desperate eyes searched the small audience for some hint of mercy. "Please!" he begged. "You can't do this! This is murder! Murder!" The faces in the observation area were unmoved. One of the guards jammed an elbow into the sobbing man's kidneys, dropping him to his knees and ending the pleading.

Lindsey stared at them. "You knew the consequences of your actions," he said.

For the first time, Mornay's face was filled with terror. He dropped to his knees in front of Lindsey. "We made a mistake. But you don't have to do this. I'll do anything you say, Alex. Anything."

Desperation was in the man's voice. As was his act of falling to his knees. Unmoved, Alexander turned and raised a hand, waving it dramatically to the council. "The council has spoken unanimously." He paused for a moment. "So let it be done."

"No. No!" Carroll screamed as one of the executioners opened the door on the side of the bull and pulled out a mask attached to a metal tube. His screams became muffled momentarily as the mask was slipped over the squirming man's face and the harness tightened around the back of his head. Carroll was then shoved through the door of the beast onto a metal rack. His screams now transformed into an eerie, haunting sound coming from the mouth of the bull.

Mornay shook his head violently as the other executioner pushed him towards the device. The hooded man grabbed him by the neck and forced his head to stop moving as he slipped the mask over Albert's nose and mouth. Satisfied that the harness was tight enough, he began to shove Mornay into the belly of the bull.

Lindsey held up his hand, stopping the executioner momentarily. He stepped close to his former adept and stared into the man's wide, horror-filled eyes. "I told you not to call me Alex," he whispered and then stepped back. A slow nod told the executioner what to do.

Mornay's screams soon joined Carroll's as they filtered through the pipes and out of the bull's mouth.

The guards closed the side door and locked it tight, concealing the victims inside the device.

Within, the men could be heard wiggling around as their chains clanked against the inner walls. The guards then stepped to opposite sides of the fire pit and got down on one knee. Simultaneously, they reached down and picked up a long lighter from the ground and pressed the button, igniting the flame. A few seconds later, the kindling at the bottom of the pit had begun to flicker. As the logs began to catch fire, the screams became louder from the mouth of the bull until the eerie sounds echoed around the chamber.

The inside of the brazen bull had not really even begun to heat up yet. The victims were placed on a sort of shelf on the inside so that the hot sides and bottom wouldn't burn them immediately. It was more devious to prevent such searing. The dying men's screams would become louder as the hours progressed. Only near the end, would their voices cease. It was an excruciating way to die.

Lindsey watched for a few minutes with a disturbing grin on his face. Satisfied that the job was done, he turned to the council and nodded. Then he exited through the dark door where he had entered. The others proceeded to file out of the above exits as well, leaving the executioners alone to tend the fire.

Chapter 69
Atlanta, Georgia

Sean sat at a table with Emily Starks in a secluded corner of the Buckhead Coffee House. She'd come to Atlanta to help Sean tie up some of the loose ends from the events of the previous week. The shop was a nice change from some of the busier coffee places in the area. They did good business, but it never seemed like it was a corporate gathering hole for wannabe freelancers and consultants. Outside, people walked by, looking in the windows occasionally but usually continuing on to one of the boutiques that surrounded the café. The décor of the place was clever. It felt more like a log cabin than anything else. There were wood appointments and tables that went perfectly with the wood paneled walls. Sean likened it to a Cracker Barrel that specialized in coffee and tea. Typical noises of a coffee shop filled the air and mingled with the scents of espresso, house blends, and foamy lattes. His eyes scanned the scene as he sipped his mocha. Returning his focus to Emily, he set the cup down.

"So Jennings was working for the Order?" Sean asked as he lowered his cup coffee.

She nodded. "Apparently. And all this time I thought Townsend was the dirty one. Turns out Jennings murdered him and tried to frame some other guy, though we aren't sure why just yet. We are assuming it is because Townsend was getting too close to discovering Jennings's dealings."

"Any leads?"

"No," she shook her head. "Nothing that we can use. This man that is running Golden Dawn remains a mystery, at least for now."

"He'll turn up, eventually," Sean stated as he took another sip of his coffee.

She changed the subject. "I know you had a question for me before, about a woman who called herself Allison Webster."

"Yeah," Sean's facial expression remained stoic as he lowered the cup.

"She isn't one of mine," Emily said flatly.

His demeanor still didn't change. "Then who is she?"

"We think some rogue working out of London. She hasn't done anything to threaten us, so, right now, we are leaving her alone."

Sean smiled at the information but stared down at his coffee. "She's a treasure hunter," he said finally, more to himself than to Emily. "A thief, to be more precise."

Emily seemed puzzled. "What do you mean?"

Sean's mind reflected back to the week that Allison had left for her next "assignment." A few pieces they'd found at the chamber in Georgia had gone missing.

The majority of the collection was in tact and the historical loss of the items was negligible; however, they would fetch a high price on the underground antiquities market. "A few things disappeared about the time she left. She must have stolen them. That was her plan from the beginning," he lifted his eyes to meet hers.

"You want me to contact Interpol, put out a net?" Emily showed genuine concern.

"No," he said quickly. "The things she took won't be missed. In an odd way, I think she knew that." He sat quietly for a minute.

"There's something else you need to know," she interrupted his thoughts.

At this, his expression changed. "A surprise?"

"Sort of," she said and passed a cream-colored folder across the table to him.

"What's this?" he lifted the document and opened it.

"Will Hastings wasn't who he said he was either."

The words hit him hard.

"He was an asset, Sean. We are fairly certain he was working for Golden Dawn."

Sean looked through the dossier for a minute or two. When he finished reading the file, he flipped it back across the table to Starks.

"Impressive. He had me fooled. Apparently, that is getting easier to do these days," he sounded irritated then. He washed it away with another sip of coffee.

"Don't be hard on yourself, Sean. I just thought you'd like to know."

"They never found his body," he said, looking out a window at the other end of the coffee shop. "And I'm not being hard on myself. It's good that I got out of Axis when I did. I'm obviously getting rusty."

Beneath the window, a young woman with dark hair sat, reading a book.

"You know that isn't true, Sean. In fact, I'd love to have you back..."

He stood up and grabbed his cup. "Thanks, Em. I appreciate the offer. Still not interested," he started to walk away then turned back to his old friend.

Emily stared at him with a smile.

"I'll be in touch soon. You take care of yourself," he said and then strolled over to the woman at the window table. "Whatcha reading?" he asked playfully.

Adriana looked up from her book. She had on dark rimmed glasses that accentuated her strong facial features. "Just catching up on my Egyptian history," she answered him as he slid into the seat across from her. "From the details on the inscription we found, I believe we are looking for a specific temple, probably a Hathor temple."

Emily walked by and gave him one more quick wave of the hand as she exited through the glass door behind Adriana.

"Planning on going there soon?" he asked with a grin.

She set the book down.

"I think you need my help, Mr. Wyatt."

"Oh really?

She nodded.

"Maybe I do," he resigned. He sat silent for a few seconds before he spoke again. "When will you see your father again?"

The question caught her off guard and seemed to make her instantly uncomfortable. "What do you mean?"

He gave her a comforting smile. "I know you went to see your father when we were in Ecuador." Before she could refute his claim he spoke up again.

The confession surprised her she narrowed her eyes. "How did you know?" she asked.

"Men who work in the field your father works in can be good men to know. Emily has used his expertise on several occasions."

She absorbed what Sean was saying. Then finally, she smiled. "Somehow, I thought you knew."

"What other secrets do you have, Sean Wyatt?" she said in a seductive tone.

"I guess you'll just have to see."

He looked down at the book she was studying and picked it up. "First, though, tell me about Egypt."

Find out what happens next in <u>The Last Chamber</u>, the third book in the series. Click the link to grab it now.

GET MY BEST SELLING NOVEL, TWO NOVELLAS, AND EXCLUSIVE VIP ERNEST DEMPSEY MATERIAL ALL FOR FREE!

The best thing about writing is building relationships with people all over the world. Because of the stories I tell, I have met thousands of great folks I would have never met otherwise. I've had new experiences, heard great new stories, and shared some laughs with my readers. They also give me feedback on my books and blogposts that are beyond valuable, for which I am eternally grateful.

I occasionally send out an email when I publish a thoughtful blog post, or when I have a special offer for some of my content.

If you become a VIP reader and sign up for my no-spam email list, I'll send you the following free stuff:

1. A copy of my best-selling novel, The Secret of the Stones. It's the Sean Wyatt story that got it all started and has hooked readers on the saga for the last few years.

2. A copy of Red Gold, a novella I wrote specifically for my VIP readers as an exclusive giveaway. It's a short Sean Wyatt adventure that I'm sure you'll love.

3. A copy of The Lost Canvas, an action/adventure novella that introduces Adriana Villa and her particular set of skills.

You can get the novel, the novellas, and all the other exclusive content by becoming a VIP.

Just visit ernestdempsey.net/vip-swag/ to get it all FREE.

Other books by Ernest Dempsey
Looking for more? Check these out:

Sean Wyatt Series
The Secret of the Stones
The Last Chamber
Red Gold
The Lost Canvas (Side story to *The Cleric's Vault*)
The Grecian Manifesto
The Norse Directive (winter 2015)
Game of Shadows (winter 2015)
The Jerusalem Code (spring, 2015)

Science Fiction Series
The Dream Rider
The Dream Rider 2: Retribution

Personal Development
Chasing Comets
Dominate Your Anxiety
Dominate Your Day

About the Author

Ernest Dempsey lives in Chattanooga, Tennessee in the southern United States. He has a Bachelor's Degree in Psychology and a Master's in School Counseling. He loves to learn about history, especially the unconventional side of it. He is also an avid sports fan.

Be sure to sign up for the newsletter at ernestdempsey.net to receive exclusive updates on upcoming projects and events. And also check out the other books he has written: The Secret of the Stones (paperback or Kindle) and The Lost Canvas (available exclusively on Kindle.)

ernestdempsey.net

Author's Notes

There are lots of interesting facts and places in this story that are worth noting. The two stone lions in New Mexico are real as are the ruins of a nearby ancient settlement. The details about the Grand Canyon are correct, though the cave was my creation.

Part of the story about Coronado was my concoction while much of it was fact.

The Rosicrucians were a real group and some speculate they still exist today. The Order of the Golden Dawn was also real. They too seemed to disappear in the early 20th century. It is unknown if there are any active members at present.

The most interesting part of the story, to me, revolves around Father Carlos Crespi. Not only was he an intriguing personality, the mysteries he concealed in his vault are still unsolved to this day.

The cave in Ecuador is from my imagination, but there are many rivers in the region that intersect the way I described.

I highly recommend visiting all of the places in the story. Each one has a unique flavor and appeal that nearly any traveler will enjoy.

Made in the USA
San Bernardino, CA
21 December 2018